PRAISE FOR THE

CW01496435

"I am now officially in love with the Alexander family."
--*Smitten by Reading (Grade: A-) on One More Day*

"Malone has a winner with The Alexanders series! Please keep them coming!"
--*Joyfully Reviewed on One More Day*

"Malone does an exceptional job ... showcasing how two very different people can fall in love."
--- *4 stars, RT Book Reviews on The Things I Do for You*

"Nicholas is perfect leading man material..."
-- *4 stars, Romance Junkies on The Things I Do for You*

Ms. Malone does an excellent job of taking an unconventional way of coming together and developed it into a true love story. The sexual chemistry between the hero and heroine was off the charts
--*BookKraze Reviews on The Things I Do for You*

"Malone gives her reader a story full of smart dialogue, compelling characters, and a strong story-line. The Alexanders and their friends will draw you in and keep you coming back for more."
-- *4 stars, Romantic Reads on He's the Man*

all
I need
is you

M. MALONE

CRUSHSTAR ROMANCE

CS
★

CrushStar Romance
An Imprint of CrushStar Multimedia LLC

ISBN-10: 1-938789-15-6
ISBN-13: 978-1-938789-15-1

PRINTED IN THE UNITED STATES OF AMERICA

Book 3.5

christmas
with the
alexanders

1

Book 4

all I need is you

54

christmas
with
the
alexanders

NEW YORK TIMES Bestselling Author
M. MALONE

Kaylee Wilhelm knows what she wants for Christmas—for Elliott Alexander to notice her. Unfortunately, he doesn't like her much, so she's spending the holidays with her disapproving parents.

When Kay's car skids out of control on Christmas Eve, she's forced to reach out to the only man she trusts to save her.

Chapter One

ELLIOTT ALEXANDER CONSIDERED himself a pretty good sport. He wasn't overly sensitive and could take a joke as well as the next guy. But he was on the verge of knocking his younger brother upside the head if he didn't *shut up*.

"So, you opened the door and she was just standing there?" Nick glanced at him, a twinkle in his eye. "She wasn't peering in the windows like a stalker, was she?"

Their friend Matt Simmons was telling them about his final week at Eli's house last summer while he was in physical therapy. Now he was happily coupled up with his therapist, Penny, and living in New Haven again.

Matt shrugged and Penny laughed along with them. "All I know is I'd been doing some yard work and cleaning because I didn't want to leave the place a mess. On my way out, I opened the door and there she was, standing on the porch. Judging by the way she was dressed, it wasn't me she was expecting to open the door."

Eli gritted his teeth as their howls of laughter continued. His youngest brother, Jackson, clamped a hand on his shoulder in solidarity. Either that or he was trying to hold him back so he wouldn't strangle one of them.

"How did we get on this topic again?" Eli shot Matt a disgruntled look, but his friend didn't seem daunted at all. He'd lost his intimidation factor it seemed because they were all having a hell of a time making fun of him.

"Wait, *by the way she was dressed*? What exactly was she wearing? Or *not* wearing?" Nick added.

His sister-in-law, Raina, walked up and pinched Nick's arm hard enough to make his brother jump. "What did you just say?"

Eli watched in amusement as Nick's whole demeanor changed. His normally smooth younger brother turned into a total wuss when his gorgeous wife was around. Raina had a successful career as a model and he could see why. She was far too thin for his taste, but her light brown skin and wild curly hair gave her an exotic look. Best of all, she was something of a ballbuster. It was always a joy to watch her handle his brother.

Nick held up his hands. "Oh, hey, baby. Matt was telling us about his last week staying in Eli's house and all the women knocking on the door."

He had hoped Raina would corral his brother's antics, but that hope died when her eyes lit up. "Eli? I never knew you were such a ladies' man," she teased.

Elliott squashed the urge to growl. Half of his brother's fun in teasing him was watching him get more and more pissed off. "First of all, it was one woman. *One*. Second of all, I have no idea who he's even talking about."

Matt covered his laugh by taking a sip of the beer he held. "Sorry, man. I didn't mean to rat you out, but I couldn't keep that to myself. She looked pretty devastated when I opened the door. I guess I wasn't up to her standards."

The group dissolved into laughter again. Eli was the darkest skinned of all his brothers and, to his chagrin, the shortest. With his brown hair and tanned skin, Matt was about as far from Eli's looks as you could get.

"I don't even need to ask what she looked like. Let me guess, petite and curvy?" Nick smirked at Matt's nod. "There's never been a busty woman near Eli that was safe. That's been his type since high school. He had a crush on Janet Reed in the ninth grade because she developed a set of double Ds over the summer."

Even Eli had to smile at that one. He could still remember how obsessed he'd been that school year. His poor teenage hormones hadn't stood a chance against Janet's suddenly full figure.

"Okay, I think we've had enough fun at my expense. And I really don't think you want me to start sharing some of my high school memories of *you*."

Nick immediately stopped laughing. Raina looked at him with interest. "Oh really? Maybe I do need to hear this."

"Is that the baby crying? I'd better go check." Nick sauntered off, leaving his wife shaking her head as she followed.

Eli walked over to the window and shoved the curtains to the side. A profusion of snowflakes turned the landscape into an endless wall of white. Snowstorms were the norm at his house in Northern Virginia but not in New Haven. He couldn't remember the last time he'd been home while it was snowing.

"She's just fine where she is. Go on now!"

Eli turned at the sound of his mother's voice. His earlier annoyance vanished as he watched Nick try unsuccessfully to take his baby girl back from their mother, Julia. Eli could have told him that wasn't going to happen. Their mother was beyond excited about having a granddaughter, and she was probably going to have a grip on the baby all night. Finally Nick settled for pulling his wife into his arms instead. He nuzzled her neck and whispered something that made her smile. Eli looked over to where Jackson was similarly cozied up with his wife, Ridley.

It was a good thing to see his little brothers so settled and happy. He'd left New Haven years ago, sure he'd never return to live there again. But time had a way of putting things into perspective. A way of distilling life to what was important and what was window dressing. He was tired of casual encounters and empty nights. Strangely enough, he wanted everything he'd always had growing up. Family, friends, and the certainty that they weren't going anywhere.

When he finally came out of his thoughts, he was startled to see his mother, Julia, standing right in front of him. Instinctively he stood straighter. His mom had a way of looking at him as if she'd caught him doing something he shouldn't have been even when he was doing nothing at all.

"Mom. Are you okay?"

She smiled up at him and ran a hand affectionately over his bald head. "I just want to spend a little time with my handsome son. Now, what's this I hear about a girlfriend at your house? Why don't you ever bring anyone home to meet me?"

His brother Bennett was walking up behind his mother, his mouth open as if he was about to say something. When he heard her words, he clamped his lips shut and backed away slowly, sending Eli a sympathetic look.

"Welcome home," he mouthed before turning around and going the other direction.

Eli grunted and took another swig of his beer. "Yeah, yeah. No place like it."

And despite knowing that he was in for at least an hour of well-intentioned prying from his mother, he meant every word.

* * * * *

KAYLEE WILHELM WATCHED as her mom held her granddaughter in the crook of her arm and bounced her on her hip. Her mom made kissy-faces and talked in a singsong voice as she danced the baby back and forth.

The two of them formed quite a picture silhouetted against the darkening sky. Kay loved watching them like this when her mom didn't know she was looking. It was the only time she saw glimpses of how her mom used to be.

Before she'd disappointed her.

She shook off the dark thoughts and went back to what she'd been doing, folding the purple baby blanket she held into a neat square. It went into the diaper bag along with Hope's favorite plastic unicorn teething ring. She'd forgotten it the last time they visited and Hope had cried for hours without it that night.

"Are you getting ready to head out, baby girl?" Her father, Leeland Wilhelm, handed her a stack of baby wipes that she'd left on the coffee table.

"Yeah, I need to go over some things tonight. I have to practice the new songs Jackson sent me. We're supposed to record them right after the New Year."

Her father's face fell and she immediately wished she hadn't brought it up. He hated that she'd quit her job to pursue a singing career. Especially since she was singing "the devil's music" now.

"It's the holidays, pumpkin. You should be here for Christmas. I don't like thinking of you in that apartment all alone."

"I'm not alone." She glanced over to Hope. When she caught sight of her, the baby gurgled and tried to throw her little body sideways out of her grandmother's arms.

"You know what I meant." He handed her the diaper bag and followed as she walked over to her mom.

"Okay, Mom, we need to get going. I heard the snow is going to get worse tonight so I need to be home before then."

"You should just stay here. The ham is almost done and you can help me make the bread for dinner tomorrow."

Kay suppressed a sigh. "I'll be back tomorrow morning, Mom. I just have some stuff that I need to do at home."

Her mom clutched Hope closer. "You can always leave Hope here. It's foolish to drag her out in this weather when you don't have to. She has everything she needs here, anyway."

Kay gritted her teeth. Her mom had been doing this more and more lately, leaving not-so-subtle hints that Hope would be better off staying with them full time. Her mom thought she was helping out, but all Kaylee heard was *your daughter is better off without you* or *you're not a good mother.* Whenever she said anything about it, her mom brushed off her concerns as Kaylee being too sensitive.

"We're going home now. We'll see you tomorrow." Kay leaned over and gathered Hope in her arms, settling her on her hip. It was hard not to be rude sometimes, but she'd learned the hard way that she needed to be forceful with her mom or they'd be going back and forth all evening.

"I don't see what the rush is—"

"Just let the girl be, Henrietta. They'll be back tomorrow."

Kay sent her father a grateful look. He wasn't happy with some of the choices she'd made in the last year, but at least he tried to help her out.

"I'll see you guys tomorrow morning." She kissed her mother on the cheek and then stood still so her father could kiss her forehead.

"Don't forget her blankie," her mom said. She followed directly behind them, wringing her hands as Kaylee walked to the door.

"I've got it, Mom."

"And what about her teething ring? You forgot it last time, you know."

"Yes, I know. It's in the diaper bag."

Kay tried to block out the rest of her mom's warnings as she pulled the diaper bag higher on her shoulder. If she responded, it would just prolong the lecture. It was easier to let her mom get it all out of her system while she did the hard work of wrestling Hope into her fluffy winter coat and fastening her in her car seat. Finally, she stood and lifted the car seat with her right hand. It no longer felt like it weighed a ton since she was so used to lugging it around.

Her parents stood in the doorway, watching as she carefully navigated the walk from the front door to where her car was parked in their driveway. She leaned into the back seat of her sedan, her back protesting the whole way, to latch the car seat into its base. When she was done, she waved gaily at her parents before getting into the driver's seat and securing her own seat belt. At the sight of them standing in the doorway, a small pang of guilt made her hesitate, her hand pausing on the key in the ignition.

It was Christmas Eve.

It was the holidays and she was leaving her parents alone so she could practice. Yes, they were a little overbearing at times but they were still her parents.

Then she thought of what was sure to happen if she stayed. Her mother would start in on her usual lecture about everything Kaylee was doing wrong, from her career choices to her parenting. They'd end up having another argument and then they'd all sit in tense silence for the rest of the night. Good intentions or not, she just couldn't take it.

Not tonight.

"I'll be back tomorrow," she muttered, not sure who she was trying to reassure. It was her daughter's first Christmas. She had every right to want it to be filled with happy memories.

She grinned at Hope in the rearview mirror before backing out carefully. "Time to go home, baby girl."

*   *   *   *   *

"WHO ARE YOU texting? I'm starting to get a little jealous." Penny poked Matt in the ribs, though it was obvious she was just joking by the way she snuggled up against Matt's back and wrapped her arms around his waist.

"I'm not texting." Matt covered the hand she'd rested against his belly with one of his.

Elliott believed in love; it was hard to be a part of his family and not believe in fate, but he'd been a little skeptical that it could happen to guys like him. Rough, blunt guys who didn't have a Hollywood-perfect face and a lot of smooth lines.

But Matt was a rugged, ex-military man. Eli had a lot more in common with him than he did his brothers. If love could happen for him, then maybe there really was hope for the rest of them.

"Kaylee missed her check-in. She was supposed to e-mail when she arrived at her parents' house. The GPS on her car places her there but I didn't get a confirmation from her."

Eli snapped to attention. "Is she okay? Does she need anything?"

"She's on her way home now. It's just not like her to miss a check-in. She knows if she doesn't keep us updated, she'll go back to having a constant shadow. As much as we've enjoyed hanging with her these past months, I think she was glad to get back to normal."

More than anything, she was probably happy to get some time away from Eli. He sighed. There were a lot of thing he regretted about his summer and the way he'd treated Kay was at the top of the list. It wasn't her fault she rubbed him the wrong way, but there was just *something* about her.

He gritted his teeth. There was something about her all right. She was the epitome of his "type" except for one small detail.

The fact that she was frickin' jailbait.

When he'd been protecting her, fate had taken every opportunity to test his control, from her never-ending collection of snug sweaters to his sister-in-law Ridley *accidentally* booking them into the same hotel room on a trip. He'd offered her the bed that night and camped out on a small cot the harried concierge had brought them. But it had been a special brand of torture lying there all night, listening to the rustle of sheets as she moved. Imagining the fabric sliding over her skin.

Torture.

And enough to make him want to give his libido a scalding-hot bath. She wasn't actually underage, but from his perspective, she might as well be. He was disgusted with himself for even thinking about her that way. She was just a kid and he was now officially a dirty old man. There was easily a decade between their ages. And even if they could get past the age difference, how could she accept his past? He sighed and pushed the idea out of his head.

"I'm just glad we caught the bastard sending those threatening letters," Eli grumbled.

Over the past summer, they'd been working around the

clock trying to uncover the identity of the person sending Kaylee threatening letters. She'd had a near-constant security detail, which had been a challenge for her and for him. Elliott had finally traced the paper used in one of the envelopes to a local store and had been able to find the guy who'd bought it, an old classmate of Kay's.

His motive appeared to have been simple jealousy. When he'd seen how well she was doing as part of the new pop group, Divine, he'd asked her for a loan and she'd turned him down. So he'd decided to send her the letters as payback.

At least that was the story they assumed was true. The guy had claimed that he had no idea what was in the letters he was mailing. That someone had left him money in exchange for sending them.

Which was ridiculous.

Either way, Eli had spent quite a bit of time guarding Kaylee over the summer. Time when he'd had to constantly remind himself that he was thirty years old and she was barely out of her teens. That she was sweet and softhearted and he was more like a surly bear.

Most importantly that, despite having a baby, she was sheltered and innocent when it came to male-female interactions. He was... *not*.

He almost choked on his drink as he imagined her reaction to the things in his room at home. He kept a fully kitted closet with everything from blindfolds and bindings to clamps and floggers. He would never bring her there, of course. As soon as she walked in and saw the mirrors over the bed she'd probably faint.

They'd spent most of their time at Kaylee's apartment. Her *tiny* apartment. Then when Matt had come to work for him, he'd assigned Matt to her security detail because he trusted him.

Also because you can't deal with being that close to her all the time.

Eli realized that Matt and Penny were both watching him closely so purposely made his voice casual when he asked, "Is she coming over later?"

His attempt at nonchalance didn't appear to have worked because Matt gave him a knowing look. "No, she's not coming. Yes, I invited her. I even offered to pick her up. I think she was planning to spend the evening with her family."

"Good. That's good." Eli ignored Penny's smile and turned gratefully when he heard someone calling his name. He didn't even mind when he saw his mother waving him over. He'd rather deal with more of her pointed questions about his love life than think about all the reasons he needed to stay away from Kaylee Wilhelm.

Chapter Two

IT ONLY TOOK Kay a few minutes to drive to the new apartment complex she'd moved into six months ago. It was always a thrill to drive up and realize she lived here. It wasn't the flashiest or most expensive place, but it was *hers*.

One of the only things she'd accomplished completely on her own.

The temperature felt like it had dropped another ten degrees in the time it had taken her to drive home. Kay shivered and pulled the zipper of her coat all the way up to the top of her throat. She covered Hope with another baby blanket to keep her warm and out of the wind and hustled into the building, walking up the two flights of stairs as fast as she could. Her fingers struggled to turn the key in the lock, they were so cold.

"What I wouldn't give for a hot bath right now." She finally got the door open and then dropped the diaper bag as soon as she made it inside. Hope jumped at the loud sound.

"I'm sorry. Mommy's not doing such a good job today, huh?"

She uncovered her daughter and tickled her chubby little belly as she unfastened the buckles holding her into the car seat. Once she was free, Hope kicked and squirmed happily. She cooed nonsense words as they walked down the hall to her bedroom. Kay grabbed the bright blue bouncy chair sitting next to her bed and pulled it into the bathroom.

"I need you to be a good girl so I can shower. Hmm? Can you do that for Mama?"

Hope gurgled and gnawed on the end of her fist while watching Kay with her big bright eyes. With her perfectly smooth brown skin and curly pigtails, she looked like a little doll. Kay blew gently on the baby's face until she let out a belly laugh. Her heart flipped over the way it did every time. The sound of her daughter's laughter still had the power to stun her. It was the most beautiful sound in the world.

After carefully strapping Hope into the bouncy seat and giving her the plastic unicorn to bite on, Kay stripped quickly and stepped into the shower. Experience had taught her that she had about three minutes before Hope got antsy.

She soaped her body quickly and then scrubbed her hands over her face. At the sound of the first soft whimper, Kay stuck her head around the shower curtain and blew a loud kiss. Hope grinned and swung her legs vigorously, bouncing herself up and down in the seat.

After rinsing off, Kay grabbed her towel and wrapped it around her body, shivering slightly as the cool air hit her skin.

"Oh, my sweet baby girl. I remember the days when I could take a bubble bath for an hour and had time to do my hair and makeup. Now I consider it a good day if I remember to brush my teeth and put on matching shoes."

Kay smiled down at the baby as she corralled her long black hair and twisted it into a low ponytail. Hope smiled back, then grimaced. A few seconds later, Kay knew it was time for a diaper change.

"You just had to wait until after I showered, huh?" She laughed softly as Hope just continued to regard her with a sour look.

Kay changed into a soft, nubby pink sweater and jeans and pulled on thick socks. Then she went back up front to retrieve the diaper bag.

"Okay, let's get you clean and then you can play with your blocks." Kay strapped Hope on the changing table in her room and then reached underneath for the wipes and a clean diaper. When her hand hit empty space, she remembered that she'd put the last of everything in the diaper bag. She'd been planning to go to the store before the snow started. But she had enough to last them through the night.

She grabbed the diaper bag and pulled out the box of wipes. Then a change of clothes. A board book. She started pulling things out frantically. Hope's favorite blankie. A pacifier.

"I *couldn't* have left all the diapers at Mom's house." She let out a soft groan when she got to the bottom of the diaper bag.

Kay sat on the floor right where she stood and let her head fall forward into her hands. Her heart raced as the stress of the last few weeks finally caught up with her.

She'd never claimed to be a superwoman. Doing it all wasn't a statement of girl power but of necessity. She could take care of Hope, record another album, and work full time because she hadn't seen any other choices. Sure, she could have given up on recording and it would make her life a lot easier in the short run. No more late-night sessions or appearances. She could spend more time with her family and actually get some sleep for once.

Even though it would make her life easier right now, she couldn't do it. It would mean turning her back on an amazing opportunity. It would mean giving up on her dreams. If she didn't reach for her dreams, what kind of role model would she be for her child? Her own mother had given up on her career as a singer when she got pregnant with Kaylee. She was determined not to make that same mistake.

There were times when her mom looked like she was a million miles away that Kay knew she was thinking about the old days. Her mom thought she was selfish not to give it all up for Hope, but she couldn't. Did that make her a bad mom?

Maybe Hope is better off with them.

After a long, wretched moment, Kay shook her head. There had been many days she'd wondered what her mother would be like if she'd kept her career. If she'd be kinder. Happier. If she'd have a little more love in her heart for her daughter instead of criticism. Kay was determined that Hope would never have to think about that.

"Hope has the most important thing. A mother who loves her. She's happy." It was the only thing Kay cared about, giving her baby girl a happy childhood. Hope would never have a reason to question if she was loved or if she was a disappointment to her mom.

Kay brushed her hair back from her face and stood. She had a decision to make. Go back to her parents' house and pick up the diapers or go to the store and buy more. Her parents were closer and she wouldn't have to stand in line.

But at the store you won't get a lecture, she thought.

Quickly, Kay retrieved the spare diaper she always kept tucked in the inner pocket of her handbag. It had seemed like overkill to place an extra one there, but she was glad she'd done it now. A few minutes later, she had the baby cleaned up and redressed.

Hope squirmed under her hand, desperate to escape the changing table and get down to the floor to play.

"Okay, little miss. I guess we need to run to the store. Let's go!"

*   *   *   *   *

ELI PUT HIS beer down on the table next to the window. His mom stood next to him, looking out at the worsening storm. Every so often, she'd glance down at the watch on her wrist and then go back to frowning at the glass.

"What's wrong, Mom? Are we expecting someone else?" Eli looked out the window, but he couldn't see much beyond the flurry of snowflakes and the crystalline patterns the ice formed on the pane.

"I overheard Matt talking about Kaylee. He said she had to go back out, but then she never called to let him know she got back home safely."

Eli waved Matt over. When Matt joined them he asked "Did Kay call yet?"

Matt shook his head slowly. "Not yet. She's still not at home according to this, but she's not answering her phone." He showed Eli the blip moving on his cell phone screen. "She shouldn't be out in this storm. I don't know what the hell she's doing. It shouldn't have taken her this long to run to the store." He spoke lightly, but there was a thread of worry underneath.

Matt had been guarding Kay for months, and they'd become friends. He knew her usual habits, where she went and when. If he was worried, then there was reason to be.

Eli pulled up the GPS application on his own phone. It was useful at times to keep tabs on lower-risk clients, although technically he should have taken Kay's tracking ID out of his system since he wasn't guarding her anymore. He pulled up her identification number. A second later, there was a small red blip on his screen. She was definitely not home.

"Maybe she stopped somewhere else?"

"But then why wouldn't she answer her phone? What if something happened?" Julia twisted her hands, the fine bones showing prominently beneath the skin. "I hate the thought of her and that sweet baby out there in the cold somewhere."

His mom considered everyone in their town extended family, but she'd taken an immediate liking to Kaylee and her little girl.

By now the rest of the family had gathered closer. Everyone seemed to pick up on Julia's agitation. Raina hugged her daughter closer, rubbing the baby's back to calm her whimpers.

"I'm not getting a good feeling about this. She's usually really good about checking in and letting me know where she's going." Matt glanced down at his phone again. "I don't want to call her parents and alarm them, but this storm is getting worse by the hour."

A second later, the room was plunged into darkness. Julia let out a small gasp and grabbed Eli's arm.

"What was that?" someone whispered.

Eli's heart slowed slightly. "The power's gone out. Just hold on, everyone, the generators will kick in any minute now."

As if on cue, the lights came back on and there was a gentle hum as all the electronics in the room powered back on and reset themselves. His parents had done an extensive upgrade, which included generators, to the main house years ago, but he doubted if Kaylee's apartment building was similarly equipped. Even if she got home safely from the storm, she'd be stuck in the dark with the baby. In the cold.

Alone.

"I have to go." He disentangled himself from his mother's arm and grabbed his coat from the hall closet. After zipping it up all the way, he grabbed insulated gloves and pulled on a knit cap to cover his recently shaved head. There were several thick blankets on the top shelf of the closet, so he grabbed those, too. Just in case.

"Where are you going?" His mother appeared at his elbow, her brown eyes filled with worry. Everyone else crowded behind her.

"Are you going out in the storm? It's coming down pretty hard," Jackson added.

"You guys are forgetting something." He pointed at the slightly dimmed lights. "Not everyone has generators the way we do. The rest of the city is under a blackout. Even if Kay's at home safe, she won't have any power. And if something has happened and she's out there alone, it could be a while before anyone else comes along."

Julia pulled him into a quick hug. "Be careful out there." She tugged the ends of the hat down over his ears. He smiled at the familiar gesture. She'd done the same thing when sending him out to school in the winter as a kid.

"You know I will be." He hated to leave her looking so worried. "Don't worry. I put chains on my tires this morning.

I'll be fine." He kissed her on the brow and pulled the front door open.

The blast of frigid air that hit him in the face only strengthened his resolve to check on Kaylee. What if something had happened? It was below freezing already, and since most Virginians weren't used to this kind of weather, it was unlikely she'd be prepared for the cold if she'd gotten stalled somewhere. The image of Kay out there somewhere alone and cold without any emergency supplies quickened his step.

Luckily he'd been one of the last to arrive, so his truck was parked at the end of his parents' driveway.

Eli loved his truck. It was hardly a flashy sports car, but it was dependable and built for a man his size. Flashy wasn't his style and it wouldn't have suited him anyway. He wasn't classically handsome like his younger brothers. He looked more like a guard dog, and considering his line of work, that was more than fine with him.

Guard dogs were protectors. If there was even a chance Kay was in trouble, a protector was exactly what she needed.

*　*　*　*　*

GOING OUT TO get diapers should have been a fifteen-minute journey. Of course, getting her daughter into her coat and car seat had easily eaten up five of those minutes from the start.

Kay watched with mounting impatience as the woman in front of her loaded the checkout conveyer belt with what looked like half the store. All she wanted was to buy her diapers and get back to her car before Hope started crying again. Now it was just her luck that she'd gotten stuck in line behind someone stocking up for the apocalypse.

People are so ridiculous, she thought.

The shelves in the store had been swept clean of all the staple items such as bread, eggs, and milk. She'd figured she could run in and out since she only needed one thing, but instead she'd had to fight to get down the aisles since there were so many people in the store.

After she finally got through the line, she tucked the package of diapers into her huge purse with one hand and picked up Hope's car seat with the other. The outside of the store was just as chaotic as the inside. The parking lot was packed and there were abandoned shopping carts everywhere.

She looked up at the sky in trepidation after she'd hooked Hope's car seat back into the base. It was so much worse than when she'd left the apartment. It would have been smarter to just ask her dad to bring the diapers than risk getting stuck out in this storm.

Finally she was able to pull out of the crowded parking lot and back onto the main road. There was a long line of cars waiting to get to the light, so at the last minute she turned the opposite direction and headed for one of the back roads that would lead her to her apartment building.

Maybe she should have taken Matt up on his invitation to come with him to the Alexanders'. His four-wheel-drive SUV would have navigated the icy streets better. Then she could have seen Eli.

That's the last thing you need.

Although, she probably should have accepted the ride. She patted the steering wheel of her used sedan. It got her from place to place, but it was temperamental and no match for icy, wet conditions. At the moment though, it was all she could afford.

Jackson had told her the real money in music came from owning the rights to the music itself. Most artists who weren't songwriters made their money from touring and appearances. When he'd first signed her as part of the singing group Divine, she'd wanted to tell him she wrote songs, but she'd been too shy to show him anything she'd written.

Not that it mattered since Divine had never really caught on. They only had moderate success, so Jackson had disbanded the group and offered her a solo contract. She'd finally worked up the nerve to mention her songwriting and he'd offered to take a look at her work. Sadly, even though she'd promised to send him something, she still hadn't followed through.

Instead she was scrimping and saving, trying to make the

advance money he'd given her last a bit longer.

Her thoughts were jerked back to the present when she turned the corner onto a side street, and for a moment, it felt like the car was weightless.

"Oh my god!"

As the car slid across a patch of black ice, Kay instinctively jerked the steering wheel to the left. The sudden motion sent them sailing straight toward the side of the road. The car fishtailed and then hit the ditch with a terrifying screech of metal, which was then followed by absolute silence.

Kay had never known that quiet could be so horrifying. Then the sound of her breathing became loud in her own ears and she struggled to turn her head.

"Hope?"

It was quiet, but then she heard a soft giggle. Kay let out a relieved breath. If her daughter was giggling then she hadn't been hurt. Actually, she wasn't even hurt. She held up her hands in front of her face and gave her head a little shake. It must have been the front end of her car on the passenger side that had made contact. With what, she was a little scared to find out.

She sat up and reached for her seat belt. The car shifted and swayed. Her stomach lurched. "Whoa! What was that?"

Her windows were too foggy for her to see much but it had felt like she'd run into something. Had she hit the ditch on the side of the road?

"Mommy's gotten us into some trouble this time, baby girl."

Her handbag was on the seat next to her, gaping open. When her eyes lit on her cell phone, she leaned forward to grab it.

A horrible creaking groan from the front of the car halted her in her tracks. The car tipped forward slightly and Kay grabbed the steering wheel. "Okay, I won't be doing that again."

It felt like she was on the edge of the ditch. If she moved around too much there was the chance they'd slide in completely. She glanced back at Hope who gave her a gummy grin, exposing the two tiny teeth on the bottom row.

She couldn't take any risks that they'd slide into the ditch because they'd land on Hope's side of the car. She could be pinned or even crushed.

A hysterical sob bubbled up from her throat. She clamped a hand over her mouth to keep from making a sound. It wouldn't help anything for Hope to pick up on her distress. Right now the baby didn't seem to realize anything was wrong.

Kay pulled a hairpin out of her bun and straightened it. Leaning carefully, she poked the bottom button on her phone. There were two beeps and then she said, "Call Elliott."

"I do not understand," the automated voice responded.

Kay hung her head. Her movement must have shifted the car again because there was another creak and she sucked in a terrified breath. If she couldn't get the phone to work, she'd have to reach for it. If she reached for it, the car could tip over.

She took a deep breath, poked the button with the hair pin again, and then yelled, "CALL ELLIOTT!"

*   *   *   *   *

ELI PEERED THROUGH the windshield, scanning the side of the road and looking for Kay's car. There weren't that many people out driving since the local news had predicted that the storm would bring a heavy snowfall. Most New Haven residents were probably tucked into their homes safe and sound.

It had occurred to him that perhaps the GPS tracker on her car was malfunctioning. He'd had an image of her at home, completely unaware that they thought she was missing. So he'd driven by her apartment building. Her car wasn't in the parking lot.

She was somewhere out in the storm.

He couldn't even imagine what had possessed Kay to go out in this kind of weather. She was a practical, down-to-earth kind of girl. There must have been a good reason for her to drive in this weather, especially when she was supposed to be spending the holidays with her parents.

His cell phone rang, vibrating through the puffy layers of his coat. At the next available opportunity, he pulled over. The previous day's snow had hardened overnight to form nearly invisible patches of ice on the roads. He'd passed several accidents already. It was hard enough to drive carefully in all this mess, he wasn't going to attempt to do it while on the phone.

A car whizzed by, sending a spray of snow and ice onto the side of his truck. If people didn't slow down and drive more carefully, there would be even more accidents.

When he pulled out his cell phone, his heartbeat quickened when he saw Kay's picture on the screen.

"Kay, where are you?" He answered without preamble.

"Hello? Can you hear me?" Her voice sounded small. There were several shuffling sounds then he didn't hear anything else.

"Kay! What's happening?"

It was quiet, then he heard, "Eli, can you hear me?" A second later, she gasped and said, "Oh my god!"

"Kay, where are you?" he yelled. His hands clenched around his phone. If she was in trouble, he had to find out where she was. What if he couldn't get to her in time?

"I'm on Magnolia Avenue. I'm in a ditch. I'm not sure how far I was before we started sliding."

"Okay, Kay, I need you to listen to me. Are you hurt? What about the baby?"

The moments she was silent were some of the longest of Eli's life. He was on the verge of yelling into the phone again when she finally answered with "We're both okay. I don't think she knows anything happened."

Relief surged through Eli. His eyes drifted closed as he realized just how close to insane he'd been worrying about her. A girl that he hadn't seen in months should not affect him so strongly. But that was a thought for him to examine at another time.

After he'd gotten her to safety.

He straightened up and put his truck back in gear. Magnolia Avenue was just two streets over and didn't usually see a lot of traffic. Hopefully he could get over to her in five minutes or less. God help anyone who got in his way.

"I'm not that far from you, so I should be there in a few minutes. I'm on my way. Just hold on."

Chapter Three

THE NEXT FIVE minutes were the longest of her life.

Kay sat completely still and focused on her breathing. In. Out. In. Out. If she thought about things for too long, she'd start to freak out. She was trapped in her car with her daughter. On the edge of a ditch.

"Eli, I hope you're almost here."

Kay chanced a look into the back seat. Hope was staring out the window, two fingers in her mouth. She let out a breath. Everything was going to be fine. Eli would get them out.

It was completely irrational, but she always felt like nothing too bad could ever happen when Eli was near. He was strong and confident. Without a word, he could walk into a room and take charge of it. Just talking to him on the phone had made her feel better. All she had to do was follow his instructions and he'd get her out of this mess. Kay put a hand to her lips, not surprised to find that she was smiling.

I am so ridiculous.

She was stuck in her car on the edge of a ditch, but she was smiling because it meant she'd get to see Eli. There was really no reason for her to be happy. It wasn't as if Eli was going to be happy to see her.

Her smile faded.

He didn't like her much. She'd always thought it was the case but nothing had pushed the point home like their bungled overnight trip to D.C. last summer. Her friend Mara had wanted Eli to spy on her brother's new girlfriend, and Kay had somehow been roped into helping out. She rolled her eyes thinking of the crazy group of girls she was now lucky enough to call her friends. Mara had been friends with the Alexanders for years, and along with Eli's sister-in-law, Ridley Alexander, she'd come up with a surefire plan to force Eli into helping them. Ridley had booked a singing gig for Kay in D.C. so that Eli would have to follow her up there.

Things might have actually been okay if she hadn't trusted Ridley to make all the arrangements, too. Kay wouldn't have planned her gig so late, too late for them to drive back home. She certainly would have *never* booked them into the same hotel room.

They'd both been shocked to see that the room was not only tiny but didn't even have the usual two queen beds. The look on Eli's face would have been comical if his look of disgust had been directed anywhere but at her. He'd been *horrified* at the idea of sleeping anywhere near her. After the initial shock wore off, he'd been a perfect gentleman. He'd offered her the bed and then called the front desk to request a cot, but it was too late. She'd already seen his first reaction.

What had been only slightly obvious before was plain as day when they'd gotten to that hotel room. Elliott Alexander didn't like her.

She could have gladly lived her whole life never knowing that.

There was a loud rumble of an engine behind her and Kay's heart leaped. Eli was here.

She could see him in her rearview mirror. He circled the back of her car and then got back in his truck. Where was he going?

He drove his truck directly across the road from her. Then he got out again. She couldn't see what he was doing from her side mirror, but it looked like he was examining her tires. Kay rolled down her window as he approached the driver's side door.

"Looks like you really got yourself into a jam this time." His lips lifted at the corners. Not much of a smile, but about as close as Eli ever came to one. She couldn't say why but she immediately burst into tears.

"Aw hell, I didn't mean to make you cry." Eli looked alarmed at her outburst.

Kay shook her head. "It's not that. I'm just really glad to see you. Thanks for coming to get me."

"Anytime. Let's get you out of here." He reached for her door handle.

"No! Wait. You have to get Hope first. The car is really unsteady and keeps tilting. Get her out first."

He immediately nodded. "Okay, I will. Hold on tight. I had some old cables in my truck so I attached them to your bumper to hold you still. Even so, it's probably a good idea not to move. I don't want to test how strong those cables are unless we have to."

Eli opened the back door and climbed carefully into the back seat. There was another loud creak from the front end of the car and Kay tensed. She glanced into the back seat to see Eli examining Hope's car seat like it was an alien device. She suppressed a nervous giggle. He was a single guy. To him it probably was.

"There's a metal hook that latches into the top. Release that first." She waited while he did it." Now you have to push the big red button on the top to release her car seat from the base."

He nodded and then pushed the button. Once he was able to lift the seat up, he moved backward slowly, then carried the baby across the street to his truck. He jogged back and unhooked the base from the backseat and set it in the street.

"Now it's your turn. Grab my hand."

She placed her palm in his. His fingers gripped and held tight. "Now lean forward and grab your stuff off the seat. I'm holding you so it's okay to move forward a little."

Kay wasn't so sure about that, but she nodded anyway. She took a deep breath and leaned forward to grab her handbag. The car creaked a little, so she quickly leaned back, clutching her bag to her chest.

"It's okay. I've got you," Eli added.

Kay looked at the front of the car worriedly.

"I need you to trust me, angel. I'm not going to let you fall." He squeezed her hand. "I'm pretty strong." His lips lifted again in that maddening half smile.

His words gave her the courage to swing her legs out of the car and stand up.

"See, that wasn't so scary."

Kay let out a small breath. She was trembling so hard that he just picked her up and carried her toward his truck. "Eli! I'm too heavy for you to carry." Her face flamed as she imagined him pulling a muscle or getting a hernia from hefting her around.

Eli grunted. "Hardly. I think I can handle carrying a girl. Do I really look that wimpy to you?"

Kay giggled. He looked so affronted that she'd even suggested that he wasn't strong enough. But she was just trying to save his back the trouble. She wasn't exactly a small girl. Not like the girls he was probably used to.

"I'm sure you can carry anything, but you shouldn't have to. I'm fine. I can walk."

He set her down. "Okay, as long as you don't start crying again. I don't think there's a man alive who knows what to do with a crying woman."

Just then a horrible screeching sound pierced the air. Eli grabbed her and turned them away, shielding her with his body. Kay's ears were ringing but she still registered the firm muscles pressed up against her backside. Heat swept to her face.

She looked up from the cradle of his protective hold. Their faces were so close together. She'd never dreamed a man would put himself physically between her and harm. Even if he was just doing his job, it was more than anybody else had ever done for her.

"I'm sorry about your car."

Kay looked back and gasped. The cables holding her car had snapped. Now her sedan was completely in the ditch, tilted drunkenly on its side. This time when Eli picked her up, she didn't protest.

As he carried her away, she couldn't tear her eyes away from the sight of her totaled car.

*　　*　　*　　*　　*

ELI PULLED UP to his parents' house and turned off his truck. He'd already called his mom so she knew to expect them. He just wasn't sure what to expect from *himself*.

He hadn't asked Kay's opinion about what to do or even entertained the idea of taking her to her parents' house. His brain had been taken over by some dominant instinct to protect her. That meant he wanted her where he could keep an eye on her.

Kay took her seat belt off and turned to face him. He braced himself. She had every right to yell at him. They didn't even get along. He certainly had no right to make decisions for her.

"Eli, thank you for coming to get us. I honestly wasn't sure what I was going to do." She leaned over and squeezed his arm.

He looked down at her hand in surprise. She quickly took it back. "Sorry. Anyway, I just wanted to say thanks."

After a few moments of awkward silence, he could only respond with "You're welcome."

Kay pushed open her door and hopped down. There was a muffled curse as she half slid, then fell. He pushed open his own door and rushed around the truck to help her.

"Be careful. It's pretty high."

"Yeah, and I'm vertically challenged. I know." She shrugged and pulled open the back door. "Can you get her down? I don't want to take a chance that I might fall while holding the car seat. It's pretty hard to carry as it is."

Eli reached up into the truck and unhooked the car seat from its base. When she caught sight of him, Hope's eyes lit up and she let out a rousing squeal. Eli laughed, unable to help himself. When was the last time anyone was that happy to see him? He tickled her under the chin and lifted her down.

It was still startling to see how much Hope had grown. He was used to thinking of her as "the baby." But now she was so much bigger, with round cheeks and laughing eyes. Her brown skin was the same warm shade as her mother's, and her short, silky black hair had transformed into a wild curly mass. He'd always found it fascinating how quickly babies changed. How they looked at birth was usually nowhere close to how they looked just a few months later.

Just as they reached the steps, the front door flew open and his mother rushed out. Eli immediately felt bad. His mom must have been really worried the whole time he was gone. He opened his arms as she approached, but his mom bypassed him completely and enfolded Kaylee into a hug.

"You poor thing! We were so worried."

Kaylee looked just as shocked as he did, but she allowed his mom to fuss over her.

Eli just shook his head. "Gee, thanks for the concern, Mom."

Julia just sent him a chastising look. "Oh, hush. I knew you were perfectly fine. Now come in out of the cold."

As they bustled into the house, his mom shut the door behind them, cutting off the whistling sound of the wind. Julia took Kay's coat and then pulled her into another hug. After a moment, Kay melted into the embrace and let out a soft sigh. The sound hit Eli right in the center of his chest. It sounded like she'd had the weight of the world on her shoulders and just gotten out from under it.

He'd made the right decision to bring her here. If you needed comfort, there was nowhere else in the world better than his parents' house to get it.

"Now, let's get you settled."

"Thank you. I'm really sorry to barge in on you this way," Kay said.

"Oh, honey, you're not barging. You needed help. Everybody needs a little help sometimes," Julia replied.

Eli set Hope's baby carrier down gently. "Mom, can you get the baby settled while I show Kay to her room?"

Just as he expected, his mother's eyes went bright with happiness at the sight of the baby.

"Of course I can. I can take care of this little angel." She knelt next to the baby and tickled her belly while undoing the car-seat restraints.

Eli grabbed Kay's hand and pulled her down the hall that led to the bedrooms. He stopped at the first one on the left and pushed the door open. A light was already on next to the bed, casting a soft glow over everything. His mother had probably started tidying the room as soon as he called.

Kay sat on the edge of the bed gingerly. "This is your room?"

Eli shrugged. "It used to be. We all come home for Christmas and stay in our old rooms. It's nice for us all to be together again."

Kay picked at a small corner of the blanket. "Sounds nice. Having everyone together like that."

"Since Bennett lives in a converted barn out back, Mom offers his old room to guests. Mara's boyfriend surprised her with a trip to New York for Christmas so Matt and Penny are using his room this year. They're planning to head to Penny's parents before the New Year. According to Matt visiting his parents as well would have been more family time than he can handle. Last year, my mom's friend Miss Doris stayed over because her husband was in the hospital during the holidays. Mom didn't want her coming home to her empty house after visiting him each day."

"Your mom is wonderful." Kay crossed her arms, pulling the sleeves of her sweater down.

"Are you cold? I can get you another blanket." Eli moved to the closet and pulled down one of the spare comforters his mom kept on the top shelf.

"No, that's not it. I just need to feed the baby." Their eyes met and she dropped her gaze to her lap. Kay looked faintly uncomfortable. Probably because they were in his small room alone together.

Eli took a step back to give her some space.

"Mom can do that. I'm pretty sure she's got plenty of baby food here for Jada." His mother was probably planning on feeding the baby and putting her to bed. It was a good thing his younger brothers were happily married and willing to provide their mother with grandchildren. Eli was willing to do just about anything for his mother, but grandchildren was one thing he couldn't give her.

He dropped the extra comforters on the end of the bed.

"You don't want to deprive her of baby time, do you? She has to share baby Jada with the other women. Ridley and Raina have been hogging her apparently. They need another baby out there before they start fighting."

"It's not that. It's just—" Her cinnamon-brown skin turned slightly red at the top of her cheekbones. "I need to feed her. You know…" She pantomimed holding the baby to her breast.

"Oh! Right." Eli backed up so fast he almost tripped. "Uh… I'll go get her."

He couldn't meet her eyes as he left to find his mom. The thought of Kay holding the baby to her breast did something funny to his insides. His protective instincts were always in overdrive around her anyway, but the image of her feeding her baby made him feel like he needed to stand guard and protect her while she was so vulnerable.

Since he was clearly going insane already, it was best if he left to see about getting a tow truck out to pull her car from the ditch. Emotions weren't his area of expertise, but practical matters—those he could handle.

*   *   *   *   *

KAY SMOOTHED HER daughter's wild curls back from her forehead. A few minutes after Eli left, Julia appeared carrying Hope. She'd nursed the baby for half an hour and then changed her diaper. The house had been quiet when she'd arrived, but she'd heard an explosion of activity in the last ten minutes.

There was music and the sound of pots and pans clattering. They'd come so late and probably interrupted the family dinner. At the very least, she could offer to help Mrs. Alexander clean up.

When she opened the door, she was shocked to see Eli leaning against the wall outside.

"Eli? I didn't know you were out here waiting."

"I just got here a few minutes ago."

He didn't say anything else, just turned to walk down the hall. Kay followed, cuddling Hope higher on her hip. They walked through the kitchen and into the dining room. The table was set with delicate wineglasses and beautiful white plates trimmed in gold. Julia stood at the head of the table, carving a turkey that looked big enough to feed a village.

"Are you hungry, honey? I saved you a place right next to Eli." Julia looked up from her carving and smiled brightly at them.

Kay's mouth fell open. "I thought you would have already eaten dinner. It's so late."

"Oh, sweetheart, I held dinner when Eli went out to look for you."

Now she just felt completely self-conscious as everyone turned to look at them. "Oh no, I ruined your Christmas dinner. I'm so sorry—"

"Nonsense!" Julia interrupted. "You didn't ruin anything. We're all here now and ready to enjoy a nice dinner with family and friends. None of us could have thought about eating if we didn't know you were safe." She walked around the table and handed the carving tools to her husband. "Now, you two sit down. I'll just take this little angel so you can eat."

Kay watched, befuddled, as Julia plucked the baby from her arms and sat down with Hope in her lap. Eli nudged her gently toward the left side of the table. There were only two seats left. She sank down gratefully, Eli next to her.

Dinner was a raucous affair with eleven adults and four children all taking up space in the dining room. Mark and Julia sat at opposite ends of the main table. Jackson, Ridley, and Bennett sat on one side while Eli, Kay, Matt, and Penny sat on the other. She was sitting so close to Eli that their thighs brushed every time she moved.

Jackson and Ridley's two kids were seated at a smaller table. Nick and Raina sat with them, cutting up their meat and trying to keep them from knocking over their cups.

The babies were passed around until they ended up on someone's lap. Everyone talked at the same time, and Kay could barely keep up with who was saying what. Dishes were passed across the table and there were second and even third helpings dished out. When Eli saw her eyeing the mashed-potato bowl, he picked it up and put a huge serving on her plate.

"I'm sure I don't need that much," Kay lamented. At home, she'd get an earful from her mother if she ate this much, but she couldn't help it. Everything was so delicious and she needed comfort food after the day she'd had.

Eli gave her an appraising look. "Eat. You've got to be starving. Isn't nursing a baby hard work? Raina's always telling us how she's still got to eat for two since she's nursing Jada."

"Well, I don't look like Raina," she mumbled. Eli's sister-in-law was a bona fide supermodel and stick thin. She could probably eat everything on this table and still fit her whole body in one of Kay's pant legs.

"I'm glad you don't. Now eat."

Eli's voice was commanding and Kay shoveled a mouthful of potatoes into her mouth automatically, all while her mind raced over his words.

He was glad she didn't look like Raina? What the hell did he mean by that?

Kay looked up to see Eli still watching her. His dark, intense gaze didn't leave hers until she swallowed and took another bite. Kay shivered when he finally turned away. On her other side, Eli's father asked her a question about her upcoming album. She tried to focus on the conversation, but for the rest of the meal, her mind was on that one sentence.

I'm glad you don't.

Chapter Four

~

KAYLEE HAD ALWAYS secretly wondered how Elliott's mother had dealt with four children. There were days when she was completely overwhelmed taking care of Hope and she didn't even have any other children to worry about. But as she stood back and watched Mrs. Alexander turn down the bed and set up the spare playpen she kept for her granddaughter, she suddenly understood how she'd done it.

Julia Alexander was obviously a superhero.

"Thank you so much for setting this all up. I wasn't sure where I was going to put Hope tonight."

Julia waved away her thanks with an amiable smile. "It's nothing, sweetie. I always keep an extra playpen here just in case Nick forgets to bring one for Jada. It's just a simple model. No bells and whistles, but it gets the job done." She moved around the room, snapping her wrists briskly to open the clean sheets she carried under her arm.

"Oh, you don't have to do that." By the time Kay got the

words out, Julia had already spread the clean fitted sheet on the bed and was shaking out the flat sheet.

"Wow. You've got everything set up and it would've probably taken me twice as long to get things right."

Julia patted her on the arm. "Years of experience, dear. Now, let me know if you need anything else. Or if you need any help with the baby." She tickled Hope under the chin and the baby let out a gurgle of delight. "I really don't mind rocking her if she wakes up in the middle of the night."

Kay smiled at the hopeful tone in Julia's voice. Eli had warned her that his mom had baby fever and that she'd probably offer to help out with Hope. What he didn't understand was that she didn't mind at all. It had been ages since she'd slept soundly. She was more than happy to take any help she could get.

"I would love that."

Julia's face brightened and she squeezed Kay's arm gently. "Excellent. Well, once she's asleep come on out to the family room. It was an Alexander tradition when the boys were growing up to take a peek into our stockings on Christmas Eve. Since my boys are still *boys*"—she rolled her eyes affectionately—"they still do it to this day."

Kay grinned at the image of Elliott as a little boy taking a peek at his Christmas gifts. "That sounds like fun. I'll just rock Hope for a while and then I'll be out. She usually goes to sleep pretty quickly if I sing to her."

"Sounds good. I'll wait a few minutes before I put the hot cocoa on."

After Julia left, Kay bounced Hope on her hip gently, humming softly under her breath. Hope fidgeted for a while, then rested her head on Kay's shoulder. As Kay sang the familiar words of her favorite church hymn, the baby let out a wide yawn. When Kay looked down at her, she was fast asleep.

She continued walking and singing softly until she was sure Hope wouldn't wake up, then placed her carefully in the playpen. The plastic unicorn was already in there, so she placed it near the baby's clenched fist and then covered her with her blankie. Kay backed out of the room and closed the door quietly behind her.

"Is she asleep?"

Kay jumped and then let out a breath when she noticed Eli waiting for her in the darkened hallway. "You scared me. Yes, she just nodded off. She's had a long day."

Eli walked closer, coming out of the shadows. "So have you."

"Yeah, it's not every day I crash into a ditch. Thank God for that."

He grunted and took her arm gently. "That's why you need to sit down."

His words were gruff, but a small rush of pleasure made Kay shiver. Even when he seemed so remote and cold, he was still looking out for her well-being. Taking care of her.

"Your mom said something about hot cocoa?"

"There'll be plenty of that along with cider, eggnog, espresso, cookies, cakes, brownies, you name it. In case you hadn't figured this out yet, the Alexanders love a good party. Food is a big part of that."

They entered the family room, and Kay took a seat on the edge of the room. Julia brought them steaming mugs of cocoa filled to the brim with fluffy marshmallows. Plates of cookies were passed around, and after trying valiantly to ignore the delicious smell, Kay gave up on having willpower and took one. Warm chocolate melted on her tongue and she finally began to relax.

It was so surreal to watch Jackson and Nick fighting over the candy dish and to have a supermodel sitting on the couch talking about an acting role she'd been offered. This time last year she'd been pregnant and terrified, wondering how in the world she was going to take care of a baby by herself. Her own mother hadn't even been speaking to her at the time. Their dinner had been a tense, silent affair.

If things had gone to plan, this year wouldn't have been much better. She'd be shivering in her cold, empty apartment, worried about how to keep her daughter warm. Instead, Hope was safe and happy while she was sitting next to her secret crush and drinking cocoa. They were both safely tucked away in the warm interior of the Alexanders' living room, surrounded by happiness.

Everything was perfect.

* * * * *

"COME ON, EVERYONE. It's time to peek in the stockings." Julia herded all her children and grandchildren closer to the tree. Across the fireplace mantel, six stockings hung in a row, each one lovingly hand-knit by their Grandma Alexander, Mark's mother.

Ridley took a seat on the couch. Jackson sat next to her as Chris and Jase made a beeline for the Christmas tree. At Mark's suggestion, they'd started allowing the kids to open one present on Christmas Eve while the adults looked in their stockings. They usually hid candy and treats for the kids amongst the boughs of the Christmas tree as well.

It was a lovely tradition, one that Ridley looked forward to continuing for years to come.

"Hey, Mom, why don't you go first?" Jackson called out. He squeezed her hand and winked at her. He seemed just as anxious for her mother-in-law to find their surprise as she was.

"I would love to." Julia unhooked the stocking labeled "MOM" and rooted around in the bottom. The first thing she pulled out was a slim jewelry case. She turned to Mark, who was reclining in his favorite comfy leather chair near the fireplace.

"Mark, you didn't?" She popped open the case and let out a small sigh. "Would you look at that?" Her eyes were bright as she lifted the delicate bracelet out of the box.

"You always wanted one of those charm bracelets when we first got married," Mark grumbled. He looked abashed at all the attention.

"But we couldn't afford it back then," Julia whispered. Her eyes glistened with unshed tears as she walked over and draped herself across his lap. "It's never too late. Thank you, honey." She kissed him tenderly while her two grandsons made gagging noises.

"Ew, they're kissing again," Chris whispered. Laughter broke out as his loud whisper broke the silence.

"You'll understand one day." Nick pulled Chris into a hug. "I promise."

"Okay, enough of that," Jackson called out to his parents who were still snuggling. "What else have you got?"

"What more do I need?" Julia wiped her eyes with the back of her hand and then reached into the stocking again. She pulled out a small piece of blue fabric. Her brow furrowed as she stared at it. "It's a baby's hat. How did this get in my stocking?"

She glanced over at Nick and Raina who both looked just as puzzled as she did. Then she swung around to look at Jackson and Ridley.

"Oh! Oh! Does this mean what I think it means?" Julia jumped up and held out her arms to Ridley.

Ridley nodded shyly. Julia let out a whoop that startled both of the babies. Jada let out a disgruntled cry until Nick picked her up and rocked her.

"It's okay, baby girl. Grandma is just excited. And you're getting another cousin." He turned to Jackson and offered a hand. "Congratulations, little brother. I can't wait to meet the newest addition."

As Jackson accepted handshakes and backslapping from Matt, Eli, and Bennett, Ridley sat back down on the couch. She already could feel the changes in her body and she was only about four months along. Along with crying at everything from cute pictures of kittens on the Internet to Jase's drawings, she was also exhausted all the time.

"We're getting a baby?"

Ridley looked up when Chris sat on the couch next to her. He bit his lip as he glanced at her stomach. "Yes, we're getting a baby. Do you remember when Auntie Raina carried baby Jada in her tummy?"

He nodded. "Jada kicked my hand when I touched Auntie Raina's belly."

"Yeah, she did." She pulled him close and kissed the top

of his tight curls. He sat quietly for a moment and Ridley didn't push him. Chris liked to talk and ask questions, but she figured he needed time to process. They'd debated telling the kids first, but they'd been worried the boys would announce it as soon as they arrived.

Jase walked over to them. "RiRi, you've got a baby on your belly!"

The whole room laughed.

"Well, there's a baby *in* my belly. But that's close enough, sweetie."

Jase looked offended that everyone was still chuckling at his expense. Ridley pulled him onto her lap. He put his small hands on her cheeks.

"You're going to be the mommy." Since his own mother had died not long after he was born, Jase had long been fascinated by the concept of "mommies." She was sure he'd have many questions over the next few months.

Chris looked up then. "If the baby is going to call you mommy, can we call you mommy, too? Our first mommy is in heaven now, so maybe she won't mind." He looked down at his sneakers and then back up at her. The hope in his eyes made her feel like a big fist was wrapped around her heart.

Ridley glanced up to see Jackson watching them with a soft, indulgent smile. Tears sprang to her eyes. "Of course you can. I would love that. I love you both so much."

Chris grinned then. She realized that he'd been worried she'd say no. She held open her arms and hugged them both. After a few moments, Jase squirmed until she let him down.

"Okay. Bye, Mommy!" he chirped before running off. Chris jumped up to follow him. He turned at the last minute and whispered, "Bye, Mommy," before rushing off after his little brother.

Tears slid down her cheeks as she raised her hand to wave after him. "Bye, my sweet baby."

Jackson sat on the couch and pulled her into his lap. "Oh, to be as resilient as a four-year-old. Nothing fazes that kid." He squeezed her gently. "Go ahead and cry. I almost cried myself."

Ridley did just that, then buried her face in his shirt and smiled like a fool.

As Jackson laid a gentle hand on her still-flat stomach, Ridley whispered, "I never knew I could be this happy."

He tilted his head to one side, regarding Ridley silently for a moment. "You deserve to be happy. I'm going to do everything I can to keep you that way."

"Thank you."

"For what?"

Ridley shrugged. It wasn't something she could really explain. Even though she hadn't been that close to her own mother prior to her death, she'd felt the loss keenly every year since. There were so many holidays tied to family traditions. She and Raina had gotten used to doing things on their own. Then she'd met Jackson and everything had changed. Now they were a part of this amazing family and they would never be on their own again.

"For loving me. That's all."

*　*　*　*　*

AS EVERYONE CROWDED around Ridley, Eli edged closer to Kaylee. She sat on the floor near the door, obviously feeling a little left out.

She smiled slightly when Eli sat next to her. "Aren't you supposed to be right in the thick of things? You know, peeking into your stocking?"

He wasn't sure if she was kidding but just the mental image of him "peeking" into anything was a little too silly to be believed.

"Peeking is for little girls. If I wanted to know what was in there, I'd just dump the stuff out." He shot her a sardonic look. "Unless my mother was looking."

She laughed, just like he'd hoped she would. He didn't like how lonely and lost she'd looked sitting off to the side by herself.

"Besides, I already know what's in there. It's always a piece of candy, a silly card that made my mom laugh in the store, and a new pair of gloves or a hat." Even Eli could hear the affection in his voice. It was hard not to adore his mother when she so obviously adored each and every one of them.

"Sounds like you know your mom pretty well."

"I do. She's an amazing woman." He fidgeted, the small box in his pocket getting heavier and heavier by the minute. Finally, he gave up on trying to think of a smooth way to give it to her and just dropped it in her lap. "This is for you."

"You got me a gift?" Kay sat stunned, staring at the big bow on top of the box. Then she smiled, a genuine smile this time, her delight obvious in the way she attacked the wrapping paper.

He knew she hadn't expected anything. It had become clear to him in the time he'd spent watching over her that she didn't expect much from anyone. Far less than she deserved. It was foolish and a dangerous thing, but he just wanted her to know how much she deserved.

How valuable she was.

"It's not much." He was suddenly embarrassed that he'd purchased her something so personal. He'd been in the store trying to decide if he should get her a scarf or a sweater. He'd called Nick to ask for advice. Of course his brother the playboy had assumed the gift was for a girlfriend and had suggested jewelry.

Now when Kay was looking at him with her big, innocent brown eyes, it seemed inappropriate and a little pervy that he'd gotten her a necklace. What if her boyfriend had gotten her something similar?

That's what he got for taking advice from Nick. He should have gotten her the stupid scarf.

"It's beautiful, Eli." She lifted it out of the box and held it up to the light.

"It's a mother's pendant. That's Hope's birthstone, isn't it? I hope I got it right."

"It's a garnet, right? You got it right." She looked so happy with the gift that Eli relaxed a little.

"I hope I'm not stepping on any toes." When her brow furrowed quizzically, he added, "I'm hoping your boyfriend didn't already get you one."

"Boyfriend? If you're talking about Craig, we broke up at the end of the summer." She fumbled with the clasp of the necklace. "I hope I can get it on without breaking the clasp. Can you hook it?"

Eli just stared stupidly for a moment. His brain was still stuck on processing her words. He hadn't liked the slimy, girly-voiced singer she'd been dating over the summer, but he would never wish for her to be hurt.

"Sorry to hear that," he lied. She was still waiting for him to hook the clasp, so he moved closer and tried to focus on threading the minuscule loop onto the hook. Instead, he was so entranced with the curve of her neck and the fact that when she posed like that, holding her hair out of the way, it pushed her bottom and her chest out. It took him five tries before he managed to get the necklace fastened correctly.

Kay snorted. "I'm not sorry about it. Craig was too in love with himself to have much room for me to like him."

Her description was so perfect that Eli smiled. She stared at him. "You're smiling."

"I am," he replied.

"You have a really nice smile. You should do it more often."

Chris ran up and shoved his latest superhero toy in front of Eli's face. "Look what I got, Uncle Eli!"

He turned to his nephew and tried to show the appropriate amount of interest in the toy, but his attention was on the enigmatic woman sitting next to him. She wasn't intimidated by him and definitely got under his skin in a way that no one had in years.

If anyone was capable of understanding what it was like to make a mistake, it was Kay. Maybe it was time to allow someone to see him—the good, the bad, and the shameful.

For the first time in a long time, Eli wondered if it was time to come home in more ways than one.

Chapter Five

~⌒~

KAY WOKE CHRISTMAS morning to soft light coming through the blinds. Hope slept peacefully in the borrowed playpen, her bottom in the air as she clutched her blanket. Kaylee had been worried about how Hope would adjust to a new environment, but it looked like her daughter wasn't the one she needed to worry about.

Julia had been kind enough to offer her a pair of boy shorts with the tags still on that she'd purchased for herself just the previous week, a pair of pajamas, and a sweater to wear the next day. Kay had taken a shower the night before, so she stripped down to her new underwear and then dressed in the borrowed sweater and her jeans. She was really thankful for everything Julia had offered, but it was a little weird to be wearing Eli's mom's clothes.

Yeah, because that's totally sexy.

She cringed a little at the thought but shook it off. It wasn't much, but at least Eli hadn't looked at her the way he usually did, like he couldn't wait to get away. They'd had a lot of fun last night watching the kids playing with their toys, and she wasn't going to let anything ruin her holiday spirit. Especially not insecurity about her figure. She got enough of that from her mother—she didn't need to add to it.

Next week she'd be sure to stop by the mall and buy Julia something really nice to say thank you. While she was there she'd pick up something for herself, too. It was time she started loving the body she was in. It might not be perfect but it was hers.

There was a soft knock at the door. She rushed to answer it before the sound woke up Hope.

Ridley stood in the hall and turned when Kay opened the door.

"Merry Christmas," she whispered. "I heard you moving around and I wanted to ask what you like for breakfast. I'm trying to surprise Julia by cooking for her. She usually gets up before everyone else and makes breakfast, but I wanted to do it this year."

Kay stepped out into the hall, pulling the door closed gently behind her. "Oh, I think you've surprised her already."

Ridley flushed with pleasure. "I surprised myself."

They walked down the hallway and into the wide, open, eat-in kitchen. Raina and Penny sat at the dining table drinking coffee.

"Good morning. And here I was thinking I was up early," Kay joked.

Raina moved over slightly so she could sit down. "This is my usual hour now that Jada has decided she really likes play time at three a.m. She always goes back to sleep a few hours later, but then I can't go back to sleep."

Kaylee winced. "Sorry. Hope went through that phase, too. I think she actually had her nights and days mixed up at one point."

Penny looked between them uncertainly. "Now you guys are scaring me. I think I'll just pretend I didn't hear that."

"Me, too." Ridley pulled out a mixing bowl from beneath the counter. "I feel like I cheated a little bit since I got to be a mom without going through those rough early years. That'll all be changing soon."

Kay got up and stood behind Ridley as her friend pulled out pancake mix, eggs, and bacon. "What can I do to help?"

Ridley handed her the carton of eggs. "I'm putting you on scrambled-eggs duty. I would ask Raina, but the last time she made breakfast I think we were in high school."

Raina didn't seem offended by her sister's statement at all. "Hey, I'm good at stuff. Just not things that are useful most of the time."

"We all have our talents," Ridley replied, then turned to Kaylee. "So, I noticed you seemed pretty cozy with my buff brother-in-law last night."

Kay was in the middle of cracking an egg and missed slightly, dumping little pieces of shell into her egg yolks. With a sigh, she accepted the fork Ridley handed her and fished the pieces out.

"We weren't cozy. He was just keeping me company so I wouldn't be alone. That's all."

Penny and Raina exchanged glances over their coffee cups.

"What? He *was* keeping me company. There was a lot of family stuff going on and I didn't want to get in the way. I'm an only child, so I have no idea how this stuff works."

"We didn't say anything," Raina drawled. "But if I had said something it would be girl, are you sure you can *handle* Eli?"

"No, there's no Eli and me. There's certainly not going to be any handling." Heat rushed to her cheeks as she realized how that sounded. "No handling of anything. Definitely not... *that.*"

The other girls snickered, and Ridley fanned herself with an oven mitt. "Are you sure? Because it looked like you two spent a lot more time talking than he would bother with if he was just being polite."

Kay shook her head frantically, trying to get her thoughts together. "If there's anything there, it's mostly on my side. Basically our whole relationship is me drooling after him and hoping he doesn't notice."

Penny got up and poured herself another cup of coffee. Then she took another look at Kay and poured her one, too. "You look like you could use this."

Kay took a big gulp. "He picked me up," she blurted after a moment.

"What?" Raina stood too and leaned against the counter next to Penny.

Kay flushed. "It's just, when he came to get me. I was a little shaky and he picked me up. Like it was nothing."

"Eli's a take-charge kind of guy," Penny pointed out. "He reminds me of Matt in that way. He doesn't wait for you to ask for help, he just figures out what you need and does it."

"Yeah, but it's more than that. You guys are twigs, so a guy picking you up is no big deal. But I'm a big girl. Most guys don't even attempt it. I'd be worried they'd either drop me or end up with a hernia. But he could actually lift me. Not that I should be surprised. He looks like he could lift me."

Raina snorted. "He looks like he could lift a car."

All four women sighed appreciatively. Kay remembered how the hard muscles under his shirt had felt when she'd been cuddled in his arms. Why had she told him to put her down? She should have enjoyed the experience while it lasted.

"You know, Kay, I really think you should be one of my birthing partners. Raina will be there of course but it makes sense to have another mother there." Ridley whistled innocently as she whisked the pancake batter.

"That's good," Penny interjected. "It'll give her an excuse to be at the hospital with Eli."

"Oh, I couldn't. I'm not family," Kay mumbled.

Ridley put down the carton of milk she was holding. "We're all connected in some way to that gorgeous, loud, wonderful family in there. So that makes us a family of sorts, too. And it's the best one I've ever had." Her voice wavered a little at the end.

Raina plunked her coffee cup down on the table suddenly and swiped under her eyes. "Ri, you have to stop with the waterworks. Ugh, I hate this having feelings crap. I can't wait until I go back to my usual self. Then I can be a bitch

46

unrepentantly."

Ridley watched her sister with a knowing smile. "I'm afraid it's permanent, sister dear."

*   *   *   *   *

AFTER CHECKING ON Hope, Kay scrambled the eggs without any further incident. Ridley made pancakes and the family drifted in slowly, everyone coming in and grabbing a plate whenever they woke up. Julia and Mark came in first and Ridley made them both sit at the table so she could bring them their food.

When Julia tried to get up to help, Ridley sent her a stern look. "It's our turn to take care of you for a change."

Kay checked on Hope again and found the baby sitting up and having an animated babble conversation with herself. When she saw Kaylee, she got to her feet.

"Mama. Hi, my Mama." Hope danced on her toes happily and stretched her arms up toward Kaylee.

"Merry Christmas, baby girl." Kay snuggled her daughter closer. Hope wouldn't get her gifts until later since they were at the apartment, but she'd be getting something even better today. Breakfast with the Alexanders and then dinner with her grandparents. When she'd looked out the window earlier the roads hadn't been cleared yet, but she was sure they would be before long. Eli could drive her to her parents' house later so they'd still get to see them.

Hope would be surrounded by people who cherished her all day long. Kay couldn't think of a better way to spend the holiday.

She carried Hope to the bed and went through their usual morning ritual. After the baby was clean and dressed in the extra outfit Kay always kept in the diaper bag, they walked back to the kitchen.

"There's my other angel." Julia approached and this time Kay wasn't at all surprised when she suddenly found herself with empty arms. Hope didn't make a sound, just stuffed her fist in her mouth and allowed Julia to walk off with her.

Eli came in next and Kay stiffened. The other girls watched them closely. Kay felt like all the things they'd talked about that morning must be echoing around the kitchen and he'd somehow hear them.

"Morning. Did you sleep all right?" he grumbled.

She nodded. "Great. Hope did, too. Now she's getting spoiled some more."

He looked over to where his mom was lifting Hope in the air and blowing gentle kisses against her belly. "You've made my mom really happy, you know that?"

"She's made us really happy, too."

They ate breakfast together and then the family all gathered around the tree again. Kay watched the children shrieking as they tore wrapping paper off their gifts and tried to play with everything simultaneously. Raina plopped Jada down on the floor next to Hope. The two babies regarded each other with curious eyes before breaking into their excited baby chatter.

Still a little hesitant to get in the middle of their family time, Kay leaned against the doorframe leading to the family room and watched the chaos. It was like something from a movie, the extremely photogenic family all gathered around the huge eight-foot tree that twinkled with a multitude of lights.

Eli stood next to her and watched the scene with amused eyes. Then he leaned closer to her so she could hear him over the din. "I'm going to drive you to your parents later today. I'm sure they won't appreciate us keeping you all to ourselves on Christmas."

"They'll be grateful to you. Just like I am. I'm so glad you were there yesterday."

Kay wanted to say so much more. Not just to thank him for helping her, but for being the kind of person she knew she could count on. There were fewer and fewer of those people in her life lately.

Eli shrugged off her thanks. "I'm glad I could help. Actually, I've decided to move back home after the New Year, so I'll be around if you get the sudden urge to fall into another ditch or something."

Kay was startled into letting out a little giggle. "You made a joke!"

His lips pulled up just slightly at the edges. "It happens. Occasionally."

She could hardly believe it. It had to be the holiday spirit because she'd never seen Eli like this. Her eyes drifted up and she saw the sprig of mistletoe hanging over the doorjamb. He followed her gaze and his smile disappeared. Then his eyes dropped to her mouth.

Everything inside her softened. She wasn't sure if it was wishful thinking or if the mistletoe was actually having some effect, but in that moment, she closed her eyes and made a wish. *Kiss me.* She wanted it more than her next breath.

A second later, there was the soft brush of skin on skin as his lips whispered against hers.

Her eyes popped open and she sucked in a desperate breath before his mouth settled on hers again. His lips were warm and soft and perfect. Instinct, or perhaps it was just pure shock, was the only thing that allowed her to kiss him back. Her hand trailed up the incredibly tight muscles in his chest and settled against his cheek. When he pulled her closer, she melted against him, boneless. If he hadn't held her so tightly, she probably would have melted into a puddle at his feet.

It was way too soon when he pulled back and pressed a soft kiss to her forehead.

"Merry Christmas, Kay."

Then he turned and left her clinging to the doorjamb for support.

* * * * *

ELI HAD ALMOST made it out of the house when he heard someone calling his name. Jackson stomped down the back steps, pulling his coat on over his sweater.

"Hey, hold up." Jackson nodded at the barn where Eli was headed. "Are you going to get more wood?"

"Yeah. I noticed we were getting low." His shoulders sagged. As long as it wasn't Kay, he could deal with it. It had taken all he had to leave her with just a kiss. But he would never want to embarrass her.

"I'm glad I caught you alone. I wanted to talk to you."

They fell into step walking toward the barn, the newly fallen snow crunching under their boots.

"About?" Eli prompted.

Jackson shrugged, but he looked so uncomfortable that Eli suddenly knew the answer. He wasn't naive enough to think that no one in his family had noticed him kissing Kay under the mistletoe. In a family of busybodies, it was impossible to do anything without attracting attention.

"It's about Kay, isn't it?"

Jackson turned to him then. "This is going to sound weird, but I wanted to ask what your intentions are."

Eli let out a guffaw. "My intentions? Who are you, her daddy?"

Jackson chuckled along with him. "I know it sounds strange, but she doesn't have a lot of friends. Ridley and I have both grown really fond of her over the last year. She's a nice girl. I just don't want to see her get hurt. Even unintentionally. Or get pushed into anything she can't handle." Jackson narrowed his eyes.

Ahhh. That's what this was really about. His brother was referring to Eli's varied and experimental sexual background.

Eli wished he could tell his little brother not to worry, that he had absolutely zero interest in Kay and wouldn't hurt her. But he'd done enough lying to his family. There were so many things they didn't know about him. So many horrible things he'd done in his past. He couldn't face it if they ever learned the truth about him.

Or if Kay did either.

She looked at him like he was her knight in shining armor. For one magical moment, he'd been selfish and taken what she offered. It had truly been selfish, too because he knew if she ever found out the truth about him she wouldn't want him anywhere near her.

"Kay is a sweet girl and I like her a lot, but she's too young for me. I'm just sticking close to keep her safe." Eli almost choked over the words. But it was Christmas. It was time he thought about what was best for her. Best for them all.

"If anyone's a danger to her, it's you," Eli continued. "You guys spend a lot of time alone together. She looks up to you and that could easily turn into something else. She's been taken advantage of before. She needs to know someone will help her for the right reasons."

Jackson watched him for a long moment. "Oh hell, it's already too late."

"What are you talking about?"

"You already care about her," Jackson stated accusingly.

Eli stopped walking. "I told you, I'm just looking out for her. It's nothing."

"You wouldn't say that if you could see your face when you talk about her." Jackson clapped Eli on the shoulder so hard it almost knocked the wind from him. "I take back everything I just said. Instead I'll say good luck."

Eli held open the door to the barn where his parents kept their stash of firewood. "I don't need luck. But I do need your help with something."

*   *   *   *   *

KAY LOOKED UP anxiously when the back door opened. After Eli had left, she'd agonized over every little thing she'd done. Had she been too forward? Maybe she shouldn't have been so obvious, staring at the mistletoe. They'd just gotten on good footing, and maybe he'd felt obligated to kiss her.

He probably hadn't wanted to hurt her feelings.

She watched as Jackson stepped across the threshold. Then he closed the door behind him and headed straight for her. Her heart sank. Eli hadn't come back and Jackson had the carefully detached look she'd come to recognize as his *bad news* face.

"Hey there. Eli wanted me to tell you that something came up and he had to go. But I'll drive you to your parents' house later."

Kay nodded. "Of course. Thank you. I really appreciate it." She walked back to the hallway leading to the bedrooms, resisting the tears that burned behind her eyelids. She would never know how she managed it, but she kept it together until she got in the bedroom. As soon as she closed the door behind her, she let go and tears spilled over her cheeks.

It wasn't just that she was hurt and embarrassed. It was the fact that she'd really believed for that one shining moment that Eli felt the same way she did.

After a few more minutes feeling sorry for herself, Kay blew out a breath and wiped her eyes. As tempting as it was, she couldn't hide back here forever. Julia would wonder where she was, and it would put a damper on the atmosphere if they were all worried about her. They'd done more than enough of that for one holiday.

She opened the door to the hallway slowly. It was empty. Thank God. She didn't want anyone to see her with her eyes all red and puffy. She went to the bathroom and splashed water on her face, then returned to the family room.

The kids were still playing with their new toys, but the adults were trying to clean up. Mark walked around the room holding out a big black trash bag so they could all throw in the stray bits of wrapping paper.

Kay leaned down and scooped up some stray pieces near her foot. When she turned around, Julia stood next to her, holding Hope. She passed the baby to Kay.

"You look like you could do with a few baby hugs to cheer you up."

Everyone had probably figured out what had happened by now. They'd all seen Eli kiss her and then disappear a few minutes later. It had to be obvious that she'd chased him off from his own family celebration.

"You know, Eli found a stray dog when he was a boy," Julia commented. "He loved that thing. None of the other boys paid it any attention, but Eli spent hours finding him a bed and feeding him from his hand. He was devastated when we found out the dog had heartworms."

"Oh no. How terrible." Kay had never had a pet, but she'd always loved dogs. She couldn't imagine taking care of a pet only to learn that it wouldn't make it.

"Well, it's not incurable, but we couldn't have afforded those kinds of medical bills for a dog. Eli found a wealthy older couple in the church willing to take him on and pay for his treatment. I always wondered how he convinced Margie Herman to do it. She's hardly the charitable type." Julia made a face.

Kay smiled. Apparently Julia didn't like *everyone* in town.

"My point is, when people look at Eli, they see this big, strong tough guy. A warrior. They don't see that big heart. He's always been willing to sacrifice for those he cares about. He wants what's best for whoever is under his protection." She squeezed Kay closer and whispered, "Even if he thinks the best is someone or somewhere else."

Mark called out for Julia, so she gave Kay one last soft smile and crossed the room to where her husband stood with the rest of the family.

Hope pointed at the tree, and Kay moved a little closer so she could stare, enraptured, at the twinkling lights. As she watched her daughter's awestruck expression, a little bit of the warmth she'd felt earlier returned, seeping through her.

Maybe his mother was right and he'd left because he thought he was protecting her. From what she didn't know, but didn't she owe it to herself to find out once and for all?

Hurt feelings aside, Eli had proven he wasn't unaffected. She hadn't imagined that kiss nor had she been the instigator. He'd kissed *her*. And she definitely hadn't imagined how he'd pulled her closer. Kaylee grinned as she started making a whole new list of New Year's resolutions.

Ridley had tried to help her get Eli alone once before but Kay hadn't taken advantage of that situation. She hadn't been *ready* to.

But now she was.

As she watched the lights twinkling on the tree, she allowed herself to feel the first stirrings of that magical, elusive emotion that her daughter was named for.

Hope.

THE END

all
I need
is you

the Alexanders

NEW YORK TIMES Bestselling Author

M. MALONE

Chapter One

KAYLEE WILHELM STOOD at the window and watched the white, cottony flakes fall from the sky, blanketing the lawn of her childhood home. When she was a child she used to love the snow, running around and trying to catch the crystalline fluff in her mouth. It had felt like magic, like stardust on her tongue. Now that she was an adult, all she could think of was pollution and acid rain, of the inevitable mess, of shoveling and clearing off her car. There was no doubt about it.

Being a grown-up sucked sometimes.

Not that she'd had a choice. She unhooked her daughter from her car seat. Kay hadn't had the luxury of adjusting to adulthood. She'd been dropkicked into it with no safety net.

"And I wouldn't change a thing," she whispered and kissed her daughter on the nose. She stood, settling the baby on her hip.

"Did you bring her teething ring?" Her mom, Henrietta, pawed through the diaper bag, her usual pinched look in full force. Kaylee felt her good mood start to dissipate.

"Yes."

"What about her blankie?"

Kay bit her lip to suppress a huff of impatience. She'd been raised to be a good girl. To speak with care, to help those less fortunate, and above all else to respect her parents.

It was just really hard to do sometimes when no matter how great Kay was feeling, her mother had the ability to bring her down in sixty seconds or less. Especially when her mother was always impeccably groomed and Kaylee felt like such a mess.

Even now, just spending a quiet evening at home, her mother's black hair was styled in precise curls that formed a halo around her face. Her smooth brown skin bore few lines, and her makeup was perfect. Kaylee pulled her lip balm from the back pocket of her jeans and applied a thin layer, hoping the slight bit of color would keep her from looking like a twelve-year-old. She rarely wore makeup, and it usually didn't bother her.

Except when she was around her mom.

With laser precision, Henrietta's eyes narrowed and focused on Kaylee's bare face. Before she could comment, Kay answered her earlier question. "Yes, I brought her purple blankie and an extra one just in case she throws up on it again."

Her daughter, Hope, squirmed in her arms. Ever since the baby had discovered she could move around by holding on to the furniture, she didn't like to be held anymore.

"Oh, she wants to come to me. You want to come to Grandma, don't you? Yes, you do."

Her mom plucked the baby from her arms and carried her off toward the kitchen. "We're going to feed you. I know you're hungry."

"Actually, I already fed her." Kay sighed when her mom didn't slow down or even acknowledge that she'd heard her. As usual, her mom was going to do whatever she wanted.

After all, what did she know? She was just Hope's mother.

No big deal.

Kay looked around the living room. She'd grown up in this house, given her first performances on the shaggy brown rug in front of the fireplace, and brought her first boyfriend here to meet her parents. The familiar sight of the pictures over the mantel and the knitted blanket on the back of the sofa should have been comforting. Instead, it felt like she couldn't breathe in here sometimes.

"Don't let her get to you, pumpkin. You know how your mother is."

Kay turned at her father's voice. With his jet-black hair shot through with streaks of silver, Leeland Wilhelm was a striking man. To Kay, he was the most handsome man alive. He'd always been her champion and her protector. Even now when he didn't agree with the way she was living her life as a single mom trying to break into the music business, he was always in her corner.

Always on her side.

"Thanks, Daddy. I won't." She gave him a quick hug and then walked down the hallway and into the kitchen. Hope was already strapped into her high chair and eating a cup of yogurt. Half of it was on her cheeks and the other half was on the front of her bib. She gave Kaylee a big, toothy grin when she saw her.

"I'll be back around ten to pick up Hope. I'm sorry it's so late. I've just got a lot of catching up to do."

Her mom waved her apology off with an impatient flick of her wrist. "It's always something. They want you to sing it again, sing it differently, sing it better. They're never satisfied."

Kay swallowed her usual protests. She was tired of defending her profession to her mom. Especially since she should have understood. Her mom had been a jazz singer before getting married and had recorded a few albums.

"Okay, I'll see you then."

Kay kissed Hope on the top of her head and then left, her steps quickening as she approached the front door. There were days when it was harder than others to leave. Days when her mom made her feel guilty for having to work so late or days when Hope cried and clung to her. Those were the worst. Even though she knew intellectually that Hope was fine as soon as she left, it was still hard to leave when her baby girl was crying.

There were some days it was all she could do to get out while she could.

FOR NOT THE first time in the past few months, Elliott Alexander wondered if he was getting old. He was great at his job and that hadn't changed. But being the muscle had never been this exhausting.

"The senator has asked me to convey that he will answer questions at a short news conference after the hearing."

He ignored the riot of questions thrown out by reporters and blocked them from following his current client, Senator Ross Evans, up the courtroom steps. A particularly nasty reporter who'd been dogging their steps for days stopped short just before bumping into his chest.

Shame.

He wouldn't have minded knocking that little twerp to the ground.

The senator hadn't been sure about hiring a firm headed up by a former bouncer, but due to his connections from his younger brother his firm had an impeccable record when it came to protecting celebrities. Alexander Security Incorporated had started out providing protection for boy bands, but after his move to Washington D. C., they'd branched out to protecting the celebrities of the nation's capital: senators, congressmen, and influential businessmen.

"Hey, boss, I've got a message for you."

Eli turned to face one of his newest employees, Tank Marshall. He'd hired the young gun straight from the military. That was how Eli got most of his guys. They were tough, disciplined, and determined. Exactly what he needed.

"What is it?" He kept his eyes on his client as he responded. The senator was spearheading a controversial new bill about immigration. He'd contracted ASI because he expected threats against his life. He wasn't wrong. They'd intercepted several messages in the senator's mail that indicated he was a target.

Now they just had to keep him safe.

"Carly's been trying to get in touch with you. She has some stuff that needs your signature, and she also said you got a package."

Eli's brow furrowed. This was exactly what he'd been trying to avoid. Sleeping with an employee was the worst cliché in the book and for good reason. It was messy. It was complicated. And when it was over, it was awkward. His assistant had seemed fine with their no-strings-attached arrangement. Until she suddenly wasn't. Now he was ducking his own business affairs just to avoid dealing with her.

"Right. I'll take care of it. Thanks."

"Oh yeah, she said it had something to do with a prior case. K. Wilhelm."

Everything in Eli seized up in that instant. "Wait, which case?"

Tank backed up a step, which wasn't surprising if Eli's face looked half as tight as it felt. He tried to smooth his features into something resembling calm as Tank fumbled in his pockets. He finally pulled out a scrap of paper and offered it to Eli, who squinted to decipher the other man's crappy handwriting.

Package from K. Wilhelm. Received over the weekend. Already checked by security.

He looked up to see Senator Evans was entering the courthouse. He'd assigned a team of guys to shadow him, but he'd wanted to be personally involved in this case. Pushing papers behind a desk didn't suit him. The more he threw himself into work, the less he could obsess over how jacked up his life had become. He still remembered the soft, open expression on Kay's face when she'd realized they were standing under the mistletoe last Christmas. Kissing her was a luxury he shouldn't have allowed himself.

Especially since he'd had to witness the devastation on her face a short time later once she realized he wasn't coming back.

"Wasn't she one of the girls in the singing group? I was on that job last year. Do you need me to check on it?"

Eli shook his head and motioned for Tank to follow the senator. Even though her case had been closed, he didn't need anyone to check on Kaylee.

He always knew exactly where she was.

KAYLEE ADJUSTED THE microphone and nodded to Jackson, who was behind the glass in the control room.

"Whenever you're ready." Jackson's voice came through the headphones, a crisp whisper directly into her ear. His production assistant, Michael MacCrane, gave her the thumbs-up.

It was still a little weird to sing by herself. She'd grown up singing in the church choir and had performed with her friends for years. But it was only recently that she'd started singing solo. It was exhilarating and wonderful. It was also incredibly scary.

There weren't many things she was good at. Kay considered herself a good cook and great mother. But there was only one area of her life where she never entertained insecurity. One thing she knew she could do better than just about anyone else, without question.

Sing.

Kay knew she had the voice. It was all the rest she was worried about. She wasn't fashionable and she wasn't thin. These were things that shouldn't have mattered but did. People expected their pop stars to be glamorous. Kaylee wasn't glamorous.

But she knew what it was like to hope for something more. That was what her songs were about. It had taken months and her best friend Sasha threatening to do it herself before Kay had worked up the nerve to show Jackson any of her music. The songs she'd written were personal and it wasn't easy to open them up to criticism. But Sasha was right. Kay didn't want to record other people's songs. If she didn't put herself out there, she'd never know if she had what it took. More importantly, she wouldn't have an album that felt like it was truly hers.

The glass door to the recording booth opened and Jackson entered. He crossed the room and stood next to her for a few moments before speaking.

"Kay, we don't have to do this song if you're not ready. We're actually a little ahead of schedule, so if you need to just take a day, it's cool."

"No, I really want to record this today. It's just the first time I've sung it in front of anyone."

"It's a great song. The title, "Don't Stay So Far From Me"—I'm assuming it's personal?"

She couldn't look at him as she nodded. Sharing her voice was like breathing. It was as natural as talking and walking. She'd been doing it her whole life. But her songs had never been public before. She'd always written in the seclusion of her room, keeping her songs as a private record of her innermost thoughts and feelings. Sharing them now, even with people she liked and respected, was difficult.

"It gets easier, you know. Putting your heart on paper. I originally told Ridley I loved her through a song I'd written. I'm not even sure I knew what I was saying myself when I wrote it."

"She loves you just as much." Kay smiled thinking of Jackson's wife, a sweet girl who'd become a close friend over the past year.

Jackson inclined his head. "He cares about you, too. I can tell."

Kay pasted a smile on her face but didn't comment. She couldn't talk about Eli with him. It was his brother. Of course he would assume the best.

On New Year's Eve, after having a few too many glasses

of champagne, she'd made a list of things she wanted to change in her life. Her relationships with her parents were at the top of the list. Next was being brave enough to show Jackson some of the songs she'd written. She'd already accomplished that one. Jackson had done so much for her by giving her a chance and helping her at every stage of recording this album. She wouldn't badmouth his brother to him.

The last one was to open herself up to the possibility of love. Eli had kissed her on Christmas Day, and just like every other time she remembered it, her body flooded with heat. She shivered thinking about his strong arms around her. For one shining moment, she'd thought he wanted her.

But then he'd left and gone back to his house in Northern Virginia the next day. There were very few things he could have done that would have pushed his point home more clearly than that. Throwing herself at him had only embarrassed them both. She had been caught up in a fairy tale for the past year. Elliott Alexander wasn't interested in her. He never would be.

It was time to move on.

She looked out to the control room. Mac watched with sympathetic eyes. Did she really look that bad? Like a scared little girl afraid of what everyone would think? But she *was* scared. Scared that people would make fun of her, and worse, that no one would even care enough to do that and she'd just fade back into obscurity.

But fear hadn't gotten her anything so far. Maybe it was time to try bravery on for size.

"No, I'm good. Let's do this."

Jackson started to protest, but something he saw in her eyes must have convinced him she was ready. He left the room and took a seat behind the recording console again. He put his own headphones back on and then gave Kay the thumbs-up.

When the music playback started, Kay closed her eyes and pushed all the negative thoughts away. As she sang the familiar lyrics, all the rest of it ceased to matter. It had been really difficult to sing such personal music at first, but now it was easier than she could have ever expected. This song reflected her experiences and her pain. Singing about it was second nature at this point.

She sang throughout the first verse and then added a few new riffs to the chorus they'd already recorded. Every time she sang, it got easier to be in front of an audience. To be the one that everyone was looking at.

"That was amazing." Jackson's voice came through her headphones again and Kaylee smiled gratefully. He motioned for her to come in the control room, so she took off her headphones and walked through the glass doors separating them.

"Come here, I want you to hear this." Jackson moved over so she could sit next to him. He hit a few keys and playback started. Kay nodded her head to the beat as the familiar music came over the sound system.

"What you just did in there…" Jackson ran his hands through his hair. "We're about ninety percent of the way there with this track. I don't know how you do that. It's almost too easy."

Kay's smile felt like it would stretch around her head it was so big. "So we can finish the song tonight?"

Mac nudged her affectionately. "We can probably finish two songs tonight if you keep singing the way you have been."

Kay hopped up and headed back to the recording studio. "I'm ready if you are."

It was time she learned to focus on the things in her life that were real. She might not be in love, but she had something almost as good.

Music.

Chapter Two

THE NEXT AFTERNOON, Eli waited until the last client left the boardroom before he yanked his tie loose. He'd spent the morning in back-to-back meetings. Welcoming new clients was important work but tedious, and he was more than happy to get it over with.

"Please tell me I don't have anything else scheduled?"

His assistant, Carly, glanced over at him with a sympathetic smile. "No, that was the last one. I don't know why you don't let George handle the new clients. He's the vice president of the company. Why do you bother hiring executives if you won't let them do anything?"

Eli scowled. "What's wrong with having a personal touch? I like the clients to know that every contract will have my personal attention."

Carly harrumphed. "There's a fine line between a personal

touch and being a control freak. Anyway, I'm sorry I had to schedule all the new clients on the same day. It's just so hard to get you in the office."

Which was his fault. If he hadn't been avoiding her, he would have been in the office more lately. "Yeah, I know. That's my fault." He rubbed his temples.

"Are you okay? You don't look so good."

"Just a headache."

She eyed him suspiciously. "Is this your way of saying you won't be in the office this afternoon?"

"Yeah. But why don't you just bring me anything I need to sign? I'll be staying in Springfield tonight," he added before she could pout.

Just as he'd expected, her expression brightened. "Really? Okay, I'll get everything together and bring it over. You go ahead home and take some medicine. Maybe a cold compress will help." She brushed a hand against his cheek before gathering the folders containing the new clients' contracts.

Once she was gone, Eli walked back through the maze of cubicles to his office on the west side of the building. Even though he was here at least once a week, most of the employees didn't see him often. He was greeted with a chorus of "Hello, Mr. Alexander" and "Good morning, sir."

He nodded hello to everyone he passed but sped up so no one would try to talk to him. It was still a bit surreal to think that he was leading this diverse group of people. He'd started the company in the midst of personal crisis. It had been a lifeline when he was drowning. Carly probably thought it was an excuse, but he did like to look over every case personally. It was his way of saying thank you. His way of giving back to the company that had saved him.

He grabbed a client file he'd left on his desk and then walked to the elevators. Another pang shot him right between the eyes and he grimaced. It was going to take more than a few aspirin to get rid of this headache, especially since he was sure Carly was going to bring him more paperwork to look over later.

He stabbed the Down button several times impatiently.

11

The woman waiting there gave him a sideways glance and moved over slightly. He sighed.

Now he was scaring his employees.

After a long day, Eli was always happy to go home, but never more so than the days he spent at headquarters handling administrative work. Although home was a relative term for him as he rarely spent the night in the same location more than two days in a row.

His company maintained several houses and condos in the Washington D.C. area, which they used to keep clients safe. He usually crashed at one of them or in his office. However, he had to admit to harboring a particular affection for the little house he kept in the suburbs. It was the only one he didn't allow clients to use.

He guessed that made it as close to a home as he'd had in the past decade.

He rode the elevator down to the first parking level and managed to avoid seeing anyone on the way. He threw the client file on the passenger seat of his truck and then pulled out of the garage and onto the bustling streets of Fairfax.

Today what he needed was a beer and some peace and quiet. Carly kept the different houses stocked with the basics, so he figured he could take a load off and maybe order in. When his cell phone rang as soon as he pulled up to his Springfield house, he figured the second part of the equation would have to wait.

"Hi, Mom. How are things going back home?" Eli locked his truck with the remote on his keychain as he walked up to the house and opened the door.

"Oh, I'm just fine, honey. I saw the news. It looks like you have your hands full."

"I do, but you don't need to worry. People are riled up right now. But once congress has voted on the bill, things will slow down some. Tensions are always high this time of year." He kicked the door shut behind him and flipped the deadbolt.

She sighed, the sound coming over the phone and directly into his ear. "I know you've always had things well in hand; I just get worried about you, that's all. You work too much."

"I like working—you know that. Besides, I'll be home in a few weeks anyway."

"Good. I can't wait to spoil you a little bit. It'll be nice to have you back home. Things haven't been the same since you left." She fell silent on the other end of the phone.

"Is everything all right? Is Dad still having those chest pains?" Eli tensed, waiting for her answer. His mother had mentioned his father having chest pains on his last call and the thought of it had never been far from his mind.

His father had always been larger-than-life. This was the man who'd taught him how to ride his bike and given him the facts about the birds and the bees. The thought of anything happening to his dad made him feel ice-cold all over. Mark Alexander represented everything that held his family together. If there was something wrong, he wanted to know about it.

"No, it's nothing like that. We just miss you. I'm getting sentimental in my old age, that's all."

"You don't look any older than you did when we were kids, and you know it," he said, relieved when she laughed. He hated to hear her sound so depressed. His mom had always been the cheerful sort. It went against the natural order of things for her to sound so down.

"I just wish you were here already," Julia continued. "I've been worried about you. Working so hard, sleeping so little. I know you want to succeed and I'm so proud of you. But I also want more for you than just work. You're letting life pass you by, and I think it's time you face things head-on."

Eli gripped the edge of his cell phone as her words sank in. "There's nothing to face. I just need a vacation, that's all."

"Maybe you can lie to yourself but not to your mother. I don't know what sent you running all those years ago, but whatever it was cost me too. It made me lose my son. I think it's time I got him back."

An unexpected rush of emotion stole his voice, thickening his throat like he'd just swallowed a giant fist. He pushed back his shirtsleeve and stared at the tattoo he hated with a passion, a small number seven surrounded by several concentric circles.

In the beginning there was rarely a day that went by when

he didn't think about the things he'd done. His monumental mistakes. Then gradually he'd been able to go days, then weeks, and then finally months without flashbacks. He'd finally stopped looking over his shoulder every few steps, finally trusted someone else enough to invite them into his home.

His mother had no idea what he'd really been doing while he was "traveling the world." Worse, she had no idea that something he'd witnessed happening to her had been the catalyst to send him into his personal hell in the first place.

"Elliott Alexander, are you listening to me?"

"Yes, ma'am," he answered automatically. He had to get this under control. His mother sounded worried, and when she was worried, she got crazy ideas like coming to visit him. He adored his mother, but he couldn't have her here while he was in this mood.

"I'm doing fine, Mom. Seriously, I'll be home next week. Time will fly and before you know it, I'll be back under your feet again."

She sighed and Eli knew he might have avoided the lecture for now, but she'd ambush him with it later.

KAY UNWRAPPED HER sandwich and took a bite as she opened her e-mail. She glanced around to make sure Nick was still ensconced in his office before pulling up the photo Ridley had sent her from Christmas. It was a picture of her and Eli, standing under the mistletoe. It must have been taken right after he'd kissed her. The look on his face was a mixture of lust and longing.

If Ridley hadn't sent her the picture, she'd never have believed he could look like that.

After his abrupt departure following their kiss, she'd been through a gamut of emotions: hurt, embarrassment, despair, and finally anger.

She'd been *pissed*.

But ever since seeing the photo, her emotions had been in a blender. Everything around her was the same, but it was like viewing the world through tinted glass. Things took on new meaning through the lens of possibility.

The positive of the situation was the anger had finally pushed her to start making changes. She'd resolved to finally stand up to her mother, to share her music, and finally to get out more and start dating again. But if there was even a *chance* that Eli might want her, it made everything else fade into the background.

Her cell phone buzzed against the desk, making a clattering sound as it bumped around on the hard surface. Kay dropped her sandwich in her haste to pick it up.

"Oh, shoot."

"What happened?" Her best friend, Sasha, sounded like she had a mouthful as well. She called Kaylee on her lunch break most days, so she probably did.

"I just dropped my sandwich. It landed mainly on my lunch bag though, so I think it's okay."

A soft harrumph came over the line. "As long as it didn't hit the floor, it's fair game as far as I'm concerned. Food is too expensive to waste these days."

Kay picked up her sandwich and shoved the turkey back between the bread. "You're right about that. I'm not sure how I'm going to afford to feed Hope when she's older and starts eating more."

"I wish I lived closer. We could cook for each other. That's what my sisters and I do. Brenna is making lasagna tonight and she's going to bring half of it to me."

Kay would kill for someone to make her half of anything. Especially lasagna. She'd learned to cook at her mom's side, so she at least didn't have to spend a lot of money on prepackaged food. She bought in bulk and always froze her leftovers so there was no waste, but it was still a lot of time and energy to cook everything from scratch.

"You're not *that* far. Although I suppose driving over the bridge just to carry food back and forth is probably asking a lot."

"Are you kidding? I'll fight traffic if it means I don't have to eat my own cooking every day. Your macaroni and cheese has ruined me for life."

"At least I got you off that yucky boxed stuff."

"Whatever. Anyway, I was calling to see if you wanted to hang out tonight. I was supposed to be going on a date, but he canceled. Remember that new guy I'm dating? I think I told you about Devin?"

Her friend had a tendency to collect boyfriends just like she collected snow globes. It was possible Sasha had mentioned him and Kaylee had just forgotten.

"Yeah, I think you told me about him. How're things going?"

"Okay, he's just the commitment-phobic type, I can tell. But God, he's hot."

"I hope this one doesn't look like a felon. That last guy you introduced me to was a little scary."

"Yeah, he was." Sasha was silent for a moment and all Kay could hear was the soft crunch as she bit into something. "Speaking of tall, dark, and scary, have you heard when Eli's coming home?"

Kay's appetite immediately diminished. "No. Ridley said he hasn't told them a date. So I guess he's in no hurry."

"Sorry, sweetie. I know you were hoping—"

"I'm not hoping for anything. Because that would be stupid. As a matter of fact, I think us hanging out tonight is a great idea. Why don't you bring a movie or something and we can veg out after Hope's asleep?"

"That works for me. I'm getting off early today anyway. We've been working way too hard and I need a mental-health day. Basically, I need a *get-me-out-of-here-before-I-bitchslap-somebody* day."

"Isn't that pretty much your normal state of being over there? You can come by here and pick up my spare key if you want."

Since she didn't know any of her neighbors, Kay had decided to leave a spare key at the office. She spent most of her time at work or at the studio, so if she lost her main set of keys, it was easiest to have the spare somewhere she could easily get to it.

She pulled open the third drawer on her desk and shoved a few highlighter markers and a random receipt to the side. When her hand hit the key immediately, she leaned down and peered closer. She'd always put the key all the way in the back. She shrugged and pulled it out. It must have shifted around due to all the junk she kept in that drawer.

"Okay, I'll do that. I'll stop by the store and get some popcorn, too. That low-fat kind you buy is gross," Sasha added.

"Whatever."

Kay's smile faded as her eyes were drawn back to the picture still open on her computer. It was tempting to get caught up in the fantasy of what could have been. This was how she'd always lived her life, caught up in the clouds and high on the possibilities. She'd always played by the rules, done the safe thing. The predictable thing. She looked down at her sandwich. She even ate the same thing every day for lunch.

But she wasn't an impressionable young girl anymore. She was an independent woman. A mother. And the time for believing in fairy tales was gone. She clicked the x in the upper-right-hand corner of the picture to close it.

And dumped the last of her sandwich in the trashcan.

THE DOORBELL RANG and Eli jumped. "Mom, I have to go. I'll call you soon. Love you."

"I love you too, my darling. I hope you know how much."

Eli pocketed his cell phone as he walked from the kitchen to the entryway. A faint shadow hovered behind the glass in the brand-new front door he'd just had installed. Part of his preparation for moving back home was selling his current place. He'd made a lot of upgrades to the house over the past few months, including new carpet upstairs, wood floors on the entire main level, and energy-efficient windows. Now that he saw the place looking so good, he wondered why he hadn't done the improvements years ago. It seemed strange that he was doing all this work and wouldn't even get to enjoy the results.

He tapped the screen of the iPad installed next to the front door and, with just the push of a button, brought up the camera feed for the front door. All you could see when you looked out the peephole was the front stoop, so his cameras showed a panoramic view of the entire front of the house, including the areas to the sides of the door where an assailant could hide.

Carly stood on the doorstep, carrying a box and several shopping bags. Eli suppressed a groan. He hadn't thought she'd be there that fast. Apparently, they had different definitions of the word "later." He took a deep breath and then opened the door.

"There you are! I was trying to call you on the way to ask if you wanted me to bring you lunch." Carly pushed past him and strutted toward the kitchen. Eli followed and watched as she set the box and several letters on his kitchen counter. She dropped the shopping bags at her feet. "Having an assistant is useless if you don't answer my calls."

Eli held out his hand until she put the letters in his palm. "I was on the phone with my mom."

Carly grabbed his wrist before he could pull his arm back. "You wouldn't have answered anyway. You never do. I don't understand why you're being like this. We're good together." She came around the side of the counter and slipped under his arm. When their chests brushed together, she let out a soft sigh. "We're *really* good together. Not just anyone can give you what you need."

Her brown eyes were luminous as she gazed up at him hopefully. He let his eyes flow over her, the long dark hair, the sun-kissed skin courtesy of her Trinidadian ancestry. She was exotically beautiful and didn't have an inhibited bone in her body. He had no doubt she would do anything he asked of her. *Anything.* But the thing he needed most wasn't something she could give him.

Because as beautiful as she was, hers wasn't the face he pictured when he closed his eyes at night.

Eli pried her hand off his arm, squeezing until she loosened her grip. Her lashes fluttered and she looked up at him flirtatiously. "Mmm, yes. You always make it hurt so good."

He dropped her arm and stepped back. "I'll sign this stuff and bring it back later."

She pursed her lips in a well-practiced pout. "Fine. But I need those contracts signed before the end of the day. They're already late."

"Late. End of the day. Got it." He followed behind her as she walked out.

She stepped onto the porch and then swiveled on the heel of one of her extremely high, red-as-blood stilettos. "You can't avoid me forever. Some things are inevitable. You and I, we're the same. We need the same things. So whatever's going on with you, fix it." She pulled the collar of her jacket up and then strutted down the stairs to where her car was parked in the driveway.

Eli closed the door behind her and flipped the deadbolt. Carly had no idea how good he was at avoidance. If she was waiting on him to give in, he could only hope she wasn't holding her breath.

After a hot shower and several aspirin, Eli returned to the stack of mail on his counter. The first was a solicitation for money from his alma mater. He put that in the *Keep* pile since he usually tried to make a contribution several times a year. Next, he opened the smallest box. He pulled out the Wartenberg wheel and grinned.

He could imagine there was probably some confusion in the mailroom when they'd opened this one. He normally liked to buy his toys directly from a discreet shop in Georgetown, but he'd wanted to replace this quickly. Carly had broken the last one. Deliberately, he was quite sure.

Eli tucked the box under his arm and walked back to his room. It was the only area in the house that he'd taken the time to decorate. With deep plush carpet and midnight-blue walls, it was a sensual haven. He'd chosen white curtains to lighten it up slightly, but everything else in the room was a deep jewel tone. The color palette reflected his personality, he thought. Nothing was too bright or showy. It was a room for introspection and meditation. He looked up at the mirrors installed over the bed. And sex.

Hair-pulling, backbreaking, mind-numbing sex.

He crossed to the closet and pulled it open. "Hello, beautiful." Everything he needed to torment a woman into mindless pleasure lined the walls. He eyed the first row of vibrators—small ones, big ones, and waterproof ones.

Yes, he could do a lot of damage with those.

The second row held his instruments. Nipple clamps, feather dusters, clothespins, and zip ties lined the shelves. He pulled out his replacement Wartenberg wheel and placed it carefully on the shelf.

He couldn't imagine not wanting to make a woman beg or not wanting to control each and every aspect of her response. Watching that moment, when a woman looked at him with absolute and complete trust, it was better than a drug. He needed to feel that instant when they gave themselves over to his inevitable possession. Without it, sex was mechanical. An act between two bodies as opposed to the union of two people.

Sensation play was something he'd gotten into by accident. He hadn't been looking for a "lifestyle," but he'd happened to date a woman who was heavily into BDSM. To Elliott's surprise, his natural tendencies in the bedroom were apparently hard to find and in high demand. For him, it was just a natural part of his personality.

For women like Carly, it was a highly sought-out characteristic. Eli sighed and threw the empty box on his bed. His one night of stupidity had already complicated his life immensely. Women were such emotional creatures, something Eli feared and respected at the same time.

It had been obvious for a long time that Carly was willing to "assist" in more ways than one. She'd intercepted one of his packages he'd accidentally had shipped to the office. The order had been for a new flogger, a sweet brown cowhide that was only available online. He'd intended to ship it directly to the

Springfield house but had inadvertently put in the billing address, which was to his office. He'd told Carly to intercept the package and bring it directly to him. She'd caught the mailroom worker just as he was cutting into the packaging.

As soon as she brought it to him, he'd known she'd looked inside.

"You shouldn't have gone there." He blew out a breath and flopped down on his bed. His reflection stared balefully back at him. A late night when she'd stopped by to bring him his cleaning had turned into ordering dinner and then ordering her onto her knees.

He'd avoided female company for years and then had only allowed himself quick, impersonal encounters in clubs and hotel rooms. To allow her to come here and enter his personal space had been a mistake.

One he would pay for again and again.

Chapter Three

~⌒

THE SOUND OF the doorbell ringing was like nails on a chalkboard. Eli pulled out his phone and brought up the camera feed for the front door. Carly stood on the front step, holding a brown paper bag. He groaned and rolled over. Allowing her to come here again had been a mistake. She needed a firm hand, and any sense of softness on his side simply gave her hope of more.

No doubt she'd concocted some excuse for why she'd needed to come back. A document he'd forgotten to sign or something she'd conveniently left behind.

He stalked down the hall and to the front door. When he yanked it open, the smile on her face faded. "What are you doing back here?"

She looked down at the bag she held and then back up at him. "I forgot something. Since I had to come back anyway, I brought you dinner."

Eli accepted the bag. "Thank you, but you really shouldn't have." Guilt assailed him. She'd done something nice, and he'd bitten her head off.

"It was no trouble." Carly pushed past him and walked toward the kitchen.

He followed reluctantly. "You still shouldn't have." Eli held her gaze until he was sure she got the message.

Her shoulders drooped slightly before she picked up the purple gloves on the edge of the counter. "I really did forget something. See?"

While she yanked the gloves on angrily, Eli's gaze settled on a box at her feet.

"What's in the box?"

She glared at him and then picked it up and placed it on the counter. "I don't know. This is one of the boxes I left here earlier. You didn't open it?"

"I didn't see it."

"The mail room said it was some kind of present. Something personal from a former client."

Eli pulled the box toward him. Kaylee's name was on the upper corner of the label. His heart sped up a little at the sight. Why would she send him a gift? The only people who ever sent him gifts were his family members, and they wouldn't bother to mail it. They'd just wait until he came home and hand it to him. The last time he'd seen Kay had been at Christmas. He'd given her a present, just a necklace with her daughter's birthstone. He'd done it because he wanted to see her bright brown eyes light up. He hadn't done it to make her feel obligated to give him something in return.

He yanked at the tape on the box. Even though he'd long ago made the decision to have his mail checked at headquarters before he opened it personally, they still tried to give him some illusion of privacy by closing his envelopes and packages back partially and securing them with tape.

Inside the box there was an unsealed, padded envelope. He tipped it over and something slid out, weighty in his palm. Frowning, Eli turned it over, examining the ceramic cat figurine with interest. Why would she send him a knickknack? He wasn't the type of guy who collected shit. He glanced around at the barren decor of his house. Anyone who knew him—hell, anyone who'd ever met him—knew that dainty breakables weren't his style.

"So, this former client? Is she a little old lady or something?" Carly eyed the cat figurine with interest. "I think my grandma had one like that."

Eli ignored her and picked up the envelope included. It wasn't sealed and contained a single sheet of computer paper.

I wonder if she even noticed it was missing.

His blood chilled. Something in his face must have alerted Carly because she took the letter away from him and scanned it.

"When was this sent?" he barked.

Carly fumbled with the packaging. "It was postmarked a week ago but I only got it from the mailroom a few days ago."

Eli tucked the figurine back into the padded envelope and closed it. He wished now that he hadn't opened it with his bare hands but doubted it made much of a difference in the end. The types who were crazy enough to send threatening letters were rarely crazy enough to leave fingerprints. He tucked the box under his arm and grabbed his coat off the back of the kitchen chair.

"Wait, Eli! Where are you going?" Carly trotted behind him as he walked to the front door. She stepped out onto the porch and waited as he locked the door behind him.

He didn't look back as he got into his truck and started the ignition.

"Cancel all my appointments next week."

KAY WALKED BACK into the control room to a hearty round of applause. Jackson had called that afternoon and asked if she was available to record that night because one of his other artists had canceled. At first she'd said no because she didn't want to be one of those girls who constantly bailed on her girlfriends. However, when she told Sasha, her friend hadn't minded at all and decided instead to meet her at the studio. Now she was clapping and whooping the loudest.

"As many times as I've heard you sing, you can still bring tears to my eyes." Sasha swiped her cheeks with the back of her hand. Her long, glittery nails sparkled under the studio lights.

Her friend loved making a statement, which was obvious from the bold manicures she got every other week to the daring clothes she wore. Today her entire outfit was made of some kind of lime-green shredded fabric that hugged her hourglass figure perfectly. The color looked good against her cocoa complexion. With her hair elaborately braided and twisted up into a high ponytail, she looked like an Egyptian princess in a club dress.

Kay grinned as Sasha enfolded her in a hug. They'd just finished recording the first power ballad on the album, and Kay was quite sure she'd nailed it. Mac and Jackson both seemed really pleased with her, so she could only hope that meant they liked her songwriting. She'd been afraid they were only saying they did to spare her feelings.

"Thank you. I'm starting to get really excited about this. I mean, I was excited before, but it's different now. Having my songs out there."

She shook her head, not sure how to express what she was trying to say. Luckily Jackson seemed to get it.

"It's because these songs are yours. They represent you. It's great to have people love your singing, but it's better to have them love your style. To have them love *you*."

"Yes. That's it exactly."

Mac sat back in his chair, appraising her openly. "I have to say, I didn't know you had it in you, Kay. You're not singing like a church girl anymore."

Kay was about to respond when the outer door leading to the general office opened and Matt Simmons, her former bodyguard, strode in. His eyes swept over all the electronics in the room with a cursory glance before stopping on Kaylee.

"You're here. Good. I've been trying to find you for the past hour."

Kay jumped up, unconsciously responding to the urgency in his voice. "What's wrong? Are you all right?" She clapped a hand over her stomach. "Is it Hope? Did something happen?" She could hear her own voice rising with hysteria until Matt came forward and put a hand on her shoulder.

"She's fine." Matt squeezed her arm. "It's nothing to do with her. I just need to show you something.

Kaylee let out the breath she was holding. "Okay."

"Have you ever seen this before?" He held up his cell phone. There was a picture of a small ceramic figurine displayed.

"Yeah. I have a similar one." Kay leaned closer. It was hard to tell from just a picture, but the figurine looked almost identical to the one she had.

"That's what I thought. Uh, are you done for the day?" Matt glanced at the others uncertainly.

"Not really. Why?" Kay asked.

"Because we need to go. Now."

Even though it had been months since Matt was assigned as her bodyguard, some part of Kay still responded to his authority because she immediately turned and gathered her things. It had taken her a while to get used to someone shadowing her every move, but she'd gone along with it because it was for her own protection.

"Whoa, what's going on? Is she in danger again?" Jackson directed the question to Matt even as he stood and helped Kaylee with her coat.

Matt hesitated and the two men seemed to be having some sort of silent conversation. Kay rolled her eyes. This was exactly how things had been last summer, except then it had been Eli and Matt making decisions for her, treating her like she was a little girl who couldn't handle knowing the truth.

"Just tell me, Matt. What's going on?"

Matt finally looked at her directly. "I don't have that many details. Eli just called and said I had to find you."

"Well, I'm fine. I've been at the studio for the past two

hours and Sasha and I are going back to my apartment now."

Matt looked uncomfortable. "Uh, I'm supposed to bring you to the Alexanders' place and stay with you until he gets here."

Sasha appeared at Matt's side. "*Gets here.* Eli's coming back?"

At Matt's nod, Sasha turned to Kay, her eyes gleaming. "I don't mind if you take a rain check on our movie date. You should go, make sure everything's okay."

Kay narrowed her eyes at her friend. "I'm sure it won't take that long. You could come with me."

Sasha made a show of looking at the clock hanging on the wall behind her. "It's already so late. I'm sure you'll need time to get all this sorted out. I'll just call you later. Or tomorrow. In case you get home late tonight."

Kay grabbed her handbag. "I'm sure I won't be out that long." Although it would please her friend immensely if she was. Sasha had never agreed with her decision to give up on Elliott. If her friend had her way, Kay would have followed him to Northern Virginia and cornered him with an offer he couldn't refuse.

"A girl can always hope," Sasha whispered.

Kay pasted a smile on her face and zipped up her coat. "I guess we'd better go, then." She turned to Jackson and Mac. "Sorry to run out on you. Hopefully we can finish tomorrow."

"Whenever. Like I said, we're ahead of schedule." Jackson exchanged another one of those silent looks with Matt. "I think I'll come with you guys if you don't mind."

"I can close up, Jack." Mac offered her a sympathetic smile.

"Thanks, man. I'll see you tomorrow." Jackson retrieved his own coat and followed them out into the freezing night air.

He waved at them before getting into his sedan. Sasha gave Kaylee another quick hug. "Call me tomorrow with details. Hopefully something juicy."

"I doubt there will be anything good to report." She waited, Matt at her side while her friend unlocked her little economy car and got inside. Then she followed Matt over to his truck. He unlocked it with the remote on his keychain and she threw her stuff on the floor of the cab before hoisting herself up into the seat.

"So, are you going to tell me what's really going on now?"

Matt glanced over at her. His eyes were so dark she could barely make out the color in the dim interior of the vehicle, but she couldn't miss his smirk. "You thought I was joking before? When have you ever known boss man to be forthcoming with details?"

Kay couldn't argue with that. Eli Alexander didn't like unnecessary questions and rarely bothered with explanations at all. She was probably lucky he'd told Matt anything at all instead of just ordering him to drag her by her hair back to his parents' house.

"Hold on, I think this is him now." Matt pulled out his phone and turned on the speakerphone. "Eli, I'm here with Kay now."

"Good. I don't want to get into specifics over the phone, but I need to ask her a few questions."

"Okay, what do you need to know?" Kay asked.

"Are you dating anyone? Specifically, anyone with access to your apartment."

Kay flushed. Matt kept his eyes on the road, but there was no way she was imagining the sudden tension in the car. It had to be as awkward for him as it was for her.

"No. I've been too busy recording and working. The only men I see on a regular basis are your brothers and my dad."

Eli grunted on the other end of the line. "What about Hope's father? He hasn't come around recently has he?"

"No. That would require him to acknowledge her existence. Something he doesn't really want to do."

"Have you noticed anyone hanging around? Seen anyone who doesn't look right near the studio or anything?"

Kay exchanged a glance with Matt. He looked as worried as she felt. "Not that I've noticed. Am I in danger? I thought the guy who sent those letters was in prison."

"He is." Eli paused. "I just received something in the mail that makes me think we might have gotten the wrong guy."

KAYLEE SAT UP to accept the cup of warm cocoa Julia Alexander pressed into her hands. She'd already been wrapped in a warm blanket and given a plate of cookies to munch on. If Eli didn't get here soon, she was going to be delirious and in a sugar coma from all the mothering.

"Thank you so much, Mrs. Alexander. You really didn't need to go to so much trouble."

"Please, call me Julia. You're practically family." Julia fussed around her, adjusting the blanket and tidying the items on the side table.

Kay observed her over the top of the mug, wondering what it was about the woman that put everyone instantly at ease. It wasn't so much that Julia looked different from her own mother, it was that she *felt* different. She exuded a warmth that suggested she would always have a hug and a smile ready for anyone who needed them. Julia Alexander accepted people as they were. She wasn't looking for imperfections in the people she met or searching for things to criticize.

"Thank you, Mrs.... Miss Julia," she stammered. It was nearly impossible for her to call an older person by their first name. She'd never been allowed to growing up so now she found, it just felt wrong.

"Such a sweet girl. I can tell you were raised right. I still can't call Mark's mother by her first name, either. Now, you just drink your cocoa and relax. Hopefully Eli will be here soon." She patted Kay's knee and then walked back to the kitchen.

Matt stood by the window, his shoulders tense as he peered out the window into the night. It was disconcerting to see him so on edge. He wasn't exactly a happy-go-lucky kind of guy, but once she'd gotten to know him, she'd discovered he had a quick wit and a surprisingly similar sense of humor. Usually, he entertained her with stories about his other jobs and the changes his girlfriend, Penny, was making to his house.

So it was even weirder that he'd been so closed off and tense since picking her up.

"It's getting late. Can't Eli just meet us at my place? I'm really tired."

Matt's lips thinned before he glanced down at his cell phone again. "Eli is almost here. I think he wanted to talk to you first."

"Okay." There wasn't much else to say, so she sat back into the plush cushions of the couch and sipped her cocoa. Someone walked by and she looked up to see the lanky frame of Eli's older brother, Bennett. He was completely absorbed with reading something on his tablet and almost bumped into the doorframe. He did a double take when he saw Kay on the couch and glanced around as if unsure where he was.

"Oh, hello. I didn't know we had guests." He exchanged a handshake with Matt and then sat on the edge of the couch next to Kay. "How have you been?" He pushed up his glasses but didn't look directly at her.

The palest of the Alexander brothers, with his long slender body and hazel eyes, Bennett always seemed as though he'd accidentally wandered into the wrong family. Conversations with him were usually slightly strange, but Kay had come to enjoy their random interactions. He seemed interested in what she had to say no matter how inconsequential.

"I've been great. I was recording some new songs with Jackson tonight. But apparently Eli needs to talk to me, so here I am."

Bennett's brow crinkled as he considered her words. "That's strange. Why wouldn't he just call you? Or drive to the studio so he didn't have to interrupt your work?"

She glanced over at Matt again. "I'm not exactly sure."

Bennett crossed his arms. "If Elliott asked Matthew to bring you here, he must be concerned about your safety. I was doing some research but I think I'll stick around for a while and keep you company."

"Okay, thanks. That would be nice. Why don't you tell me about your research?"

Bennett sat back and placed the tablet in his lap. "Oh,

this? I'm just looking into recent legislation regarding GMOs. That's—"

"Genetically modified organisms, right?"

Bennett smiled then, a genuine smile, and looked at her directly for the first time. "Yes, that's right. There's been a lot of controversy surrounding their use and for good reason. However, I'm working on developing several vegetables that can grow under adverse conditions."

"You are? Geez, all I did today was sing a few love songs."

Bennett flushed. Even the tops of his ears turned pink. "The arts are a science unto themselves. We need things that make us happy just like we need food."

While Kay agreed, she was still a little flustered. He was so smart it was kind of scary. "Tell me more about the vegetables you're working on."

"Well, I've identified a few key crops that would benefit the most. Soy, corn, and wheat to start. Imagine what it could mean for people around the world to have food that grows even through periodic drought or extreme heat. We could end hunger. Or at least make a dent in it."

Kay tried to follow the conversation, but after too many phrases like *easy propagation, mediated transformation,* and *plant genome*, she gave up on understanding. Either way, it was a joy to see Bennett so passionate about something.

And it was definitely better than wondering exactly when Eli would walk through the door.

Chapter Four

NORMALLY ELI WOULD have ignored his cell phone while driving, but if there was a chance it was Matt calling, he didn't want to risk missing it.

"This is Eli."

"Hey man, it's Matt. I've got Kay and we're at your parents' house."

Eli let out a breath he hadn't realized he'd been holding. A million and one things had gone through his mind when he'd gotten that figurine. Mainly that this nut job had been in Kay's apartment. Could in fact be in her apartment at that very moment. All he'd cared about was making sure she was safe. He'd spent the last half hour worrying they'd be assaulted or run off the road before Matt could get them to his parents' house.

"How is she doing?"

"She's fine. Just a little annoyed that I interrupted her recording session. I know you wanted to talk to her yourself, but she keeps asking what's going on. What should I tell her?"

Now that he knew they'd reached his parents' house safely, he could take a step back and think. Who could have sent the figurine and more importantly, why? When she'd first started receiving threatening letters the previous year, they'd gone through her life with a fine-tooth comb. He'd scrutinized her family and friends, her acquaintances and coworkers. Anyone she came into contact with on a regular basis had been suspect. Everyone had checked out with the exception of the man who'd eventually been arrested. So Eli was forced to face an uncomfortable truth.

He must have missed something.

"Tell her I'll be there soon." He hung up and focused on the road. As he passed the familiar streets leading to his parents' farm, a sense of calm stole over him. By the time he pulled into the long drive leading to the ranch-style home, some of the stress he'd been carrying for the past few hours melted away. He parked behind Matt's truck and got out.

His father, Mark Alexander, poked his head out of the garage. "There you are. You made good time."

"There wasn't much traffic since it's so late." Eli averted his eyes. Even without traffic, he'd still arrived a half an hour faster than usual. He'd made excellent time because he'd been speeding most of the way. He doubted if his evasiveness fooled his father. Mark Alexander always saw way more than Eli would have liked him to.

"That's a nice girl in there. Is she in danger?"

Trust his dad to get right to the heart of things.

"I'm not sure yet. But I plan on protecting her until I know for sure."

Mark nodded and clapped him on the shoulder. "I wouldn't have expected anything less." Then he ambled back into the garage, no doubt to tinker with his old truck or one of the tractors.

Eli jumped over the few steps to the front of the house and then opened the door with his key. Light, warmth and the sweet scent of his mother's baking hit him all at once. Kay sat snuggled on the couch under a blanket next to his older brother, and Eli's eyes immediately homed in on her. When she saw him, she clutched the mug she was holding closer to her chest like a shield.

Bennett stood then and nodded at Kay. "Well, I'd better get going. It was nice to see you again, Kaylee."

He shook hands with his older brother absently before his attention was drawn back to Kay. She looked like a bundle of softness from the nubby texture of her soft blue sweater to the jumble of kinky curls she'd piled on top of her head in a bun. Her brown eyes sparkled as she took a small sip from her cup.

Eli yanked at the buttons of his coat and snatched off the knit hat protecting his bald head from the cold and wind. Kay watched him over the rim of her cup but didn't speak as he drew closer.

"We need to talk."

Matt stepped forward then and Eli realized he hadn't even greeted him. He stuck out his hand. "Thanks for getting to her so quickly."

Matt returned the handshake and glanced over at Kay. "I'm just glad she came easily. I thought she was going to deck me when I interrupted her studio time."

"I thought about it," Kay muttered behind her mug. "Am I in danger? What's going on?"

Eli retrieved the envelope he'd tucked in the inner pocket of his coat. He sat on the edge of the couch tentatively. "Does this look familiar to you?" He opened it and the cat figurine slid out and into his palm.

"Hey! I have one just like that." She reached out to touch it and then her gaze settled on Eli. "I have one exactly like that. What's going on?"

He held out the note next. "Someone sent this to me at ASI headquarters. It had to be checked by my mail department before I opened it, so I didn't see it right away. It was sent last week."

Matt leaned over and, after reading the note, shared a look with Eli. He then picked up the figurine and turned it upside down, peering into the tiny hole at the bottom. "He's taunting us. Showing off that we failed to catch him last time."

Eli agreed. They didn't have anything concrete that linked the two yet, but in his gut, he knew this was the same guy.

What did he miss last summer that could have kept her safe? They'd been so sure they had the right guy. The dumb ass had already had a warrant out for a drug charge, so he'd been picked up and was serving time. Could he have gotten someone else to pick up where he left off harassing Kay? But what would be the point if he was already in jail? He had to know that the police would immediately know it was him and give him more time. It didn't make sense.

Kay's safety hinged on something that was completely illogical.

"This note is sending a pretty direct message. He's right under our noses and he wants us to know it."

Kay read the note, her lips moving slightly as her eyes scanned the page. "I don't understand. What does this all mean?"

"It means we might have made a mistake last summer." Eli took the figurine from her trembling fingers.

"It means you aren't safe."

KAYLEE FOLLOWED RIDLEY into the kitchen, conscious of Eli's gaze on her back.

"I figured you could use a break," Ridley whispered as they sat at the small dining table in the kitchen.

"Thanks. A little space is much appreciated right about now." It had only been a few weeks since she'd last seen Eli at Christmas. So why was her traitorous body reacting like he was just coming home from war? Kay accepted another cup of steaming hot cocoa from Mara, who sat on her left. "Did Matt call you?" she asked the pretty brunette.

They'd spent a lot of time hanging out when Matt had been her bodyguard last summer. With her curvy figure, long dark curls, and sultry bedroom eyes, it would have been easy to hate Mara if she wasn't such fun. It was hard to believe she and Matt were related sometimes since their personalities were such polar opposites. She wouldn't have guessed that those two could have even come out of the same family, much less be twins.

"He did. He's worried about you. We all are." Mara took a sip of her own tea. "How are you holding up?"

Kay shrugged. "Okay so far. I'm just not sure why this is happening. I'm nobody. The album I did with Divine had lackluster sales, and I haven't released any music since. If it's true that the police arrested the wrong guy last summer, why would he suddenly start stalking me again now? It doesn't make any sense."

Mara regarded her over the rim of her mug. "Maybe this isn't a stalker. Well, not a random one. Maybe it's someone you've dated who is mad that you've moved on."

"That's just it. I haven't moved on. The only things I do are go to work, take care of Hope, and record music. Other than Nick's clients, I don't come into contact with many people."

"Well, that doesn't sound like much fun." Mara glanced over Kay's shoulder. Her eyes narrowed and then sparkled with a mischievous gleam. "You know what you need? You need a man. Penny told me what you guys talked about at Christmas. About how you're going to let us fix you up on a blind date."

Kay thought back to all the things they'd discussed on Christmas Day. Once she'd realized that Eli had left his own family celebration just to avoid her, she'd tearfully confided in the other girls. They'd rallied around her, supporting her decision to move on and start dating after the holidays. But she didn't remember agreeing to any setups. She *hated* blind dates.

"But I never said—" Kay's mouth dropped open as Mara kicked her under the table. "Ow," she whispered.

Mara typed something quickly on her cell phone and pushed it across the table. Raina, Ridley, and Kay all leaned forward to read what it said.

- - - *Eli is outside the door listening.*

"What?" Kay exclaimed. Then she crossed her arms. Pretending to set her up on a date to make Eli jealous was ridiculous. And childish. And unlikely to work since he couldn't seem to care any less about what she was doing.

Mara shot her an exasperated look. "So, who's up for a little matchmaking?"

Raina raised her hand. "I know someone who's perfect. He used to be a model but now he's an actor—"

"No models or actors," Kay interrupted. Just the thought of it made her feel squeamish. Blind dates were awkward enough. She definitely didn't want to deal with a guy who was prettier than she was.

"Oooo-kay then," Raina drawled. "What about bodybuilders? Who doesn't like a strong guy with lots of muscles, right?"

Kay had been pretty sure this was a bad idea from the beginning but she was especially sure of it now. A bodybuilder? Was Raina serious? She looked down at her own body, comfortably ensconced in her favorite pair of worn jeans and a soft sweater. She liked how she looked. Most of the time. But she had no illusions that a guy who spent most of his time in the gym would share her love of elastic waistbands.

"Um, I'm not sure if that would be such a good idea. I'm not that athletic."

Mara waved away her concerns. "That's okay. You shouldn't have to pretend to be something you're not. I'm not athletic either. We'll just find you a guy who appreciates other things. You've got a great rack. And plenty of guys are breast men."

Kay almost choked on her cocoa just as there was a soft *oomph* outside the door as if something had just knocked into the wall.

Mara tittered behind her hand. Kay dabbed at the spots on the front of her sweater with a napkin and glanced behind her at the doorway nervously. She wasn't so sure baiting Eli like this was the way to go.

"What about T.J.?" Ridley piped up, mentioning an R&B

singer that Jackson had recently signed to his label.

Kay shook her head. "I'm not dating another singer from the label. If it doesn't work out, it would be weird."

"Actually, he's perfect because he's only in town for a month or so to record his album. Then he's going back to L.A. because he has a condo there," Ridley said.

Kay looked around at the other girls, sure she was missing something. "Why would I date someone who'll be gone in a few weeks? What's the point?"

Mara hugged her. "Aw, you're so sweet and innocent. It's almost a shame that we're corrupting you."

Ridley finally took pity on her. "What Mara is trying to say is that sometimes you date guys just for the fun of it. Not because you plan on being together forever."

Mara pursed her lips. "Actually, I was trying to say she should date him because I heard he is *huge*. Like barely able to walk straight while carrying that—"

The door to the kitchen burst open. They all jumped, including Kay. Eli stood in the doorway for a moment before he crossed the kitchen to stand behind her chair. His fingers curled over the top of the wood so hard it creaked. Kay gulped when his eyes landed on her.

"We need to go now. I want to get to your place and make sure it's safe for the night."

Eli regarded his sisters-in-law with a scowl before turning his dark look to Mara. Kay shrank back into her seat, but Mara just grinned.

"Oh hi, Eli. Lovely to see you," she chirped.

"Um hmm," was all Eli said in reply.

"WE NEED TO get to your place." Eli ignored Mara and the other girls' knowing looks. He didn't doubt for a minute that they knew he'd overhead their conversation. Their amused grins told him that.

As far as he was concerned, he'd shown some serious

restraint so far. They were trying to set Kay up with some big-dicked player who'd probably use and abuse her. What the hell were they thinking? He was shutting that down.

Immediately.

Kay raised her eyebrows. "We?"

"I'm not letting you go there alone."

"I figured I wouldn't be going home alone, but isn't Matt coming with me?"

"No."

She made no move to stand up, so he pulled her chair out. It made a loud screeching sound as it dragged over the tile floor. Kay jumped up and gave him a dirty look before marching back into the family room. The other girls abandoned their drinks on the table to follow. Their expressions were a little too bloodthirsty in Eli's opinion. He had no intention of being the sacrifice.

Matt stood near the door, talking to Jackson. He looked up when they entered. "Hey, are you guys getting ready to leave?"

Kay turned toward him with what looked to be desperation. "You're not coming with me?"

Matt glanced at Eli before responding. "I was just assigned to a new client. I've been working with him all week. It would be unprofessional to yank me off his job and then force him to reacclimate to someone else. I thought Eli explained everything."

A strange sense of satisfaction came over Eli as he watched Kay's face. She was stuck with him and apparently didn't like it. He knew he'd hurt her. Their kiss at Christmas should have never happened. But he was the best man for this job. He hadn't protected her well enough last summer, obviously, or this dickwad wouldn't still be out there toying with her. This was his chance to make it right.

Eli wasn't going to leave her safety up to some new associate who might screw it up. Even if he hadn't gotten the right guy before, he'd kept her safe. They'd kept her security low-key since last summer, but it had been there. She didn't go anywhere without letting someone know and her cell phone and car were constantly being tracked. She also had a state-of-the-art security system at her apartment so she was safe while she slept.

"Is there a problem, Kay?"

She wouldn't meet his eyes. To his surprise, it was Mara who answered.

"It's no biggie. She's just nervous about her date."

Eli gritted his teeth at the reminder of the conversation in the kitchen. He was careful to keep his face neutral when he replied. "Her date? What date?"

"We're setting Kay up on a blind date. She's looking for Mr. Right. Or Mr. Right Now. Whatever. Either way, I know we can find the perfect guy for her."

"I'm sure Eli doesn't care about that." Kay grabbed her coat and slid her arms into it. "I'm sure he has a lot of important stuff to do running his company. In fact, maybe it would be better if Tank or one of the other guys stayed with me for a while."

"You don't want me on your case, Kay?" Eli tucked his hands in the pockets of his jeans, the better to enjoy watching her squirm as she tried to figure out how to respond.

"It's not that." Kay made several indistinct gestures while pointing at him. "It's just that, I don't know…"

"You're kind of scary," Mara supplied.

"Mara! I think Mara meant to say you're a little intense sometimes."

"And you'll scare her date away," Mara finished.

Kay dropped her head into her hand. Eli bit his lip to hold in a laugh. Damn if she wasn't cute when she was embarrassed.

"I've been in this business a long time. We're trained to be inconspicuous."

Kay sent him a disbelieving look as she grabbed her handbag. "So you won't interfere in any way?"

Eli made a motion as if he was crossing his heart. "You won't even know I'm there."

KAYLEE SHOVED THE books on her night table in the drawer. Her eyes swept over the rest of the room frantically. Hopefully she hadn't left anything embarrassing lying around. She wasn't used to having guys at her apartment. Especially not men like Elliott.

Big, masculine men that she fantasized about every night.

The hair on the back of her neck stood up and she didn't have to look to know that he was standing in the doorway. Her apartment wasn't that big, but it suddenly seemed exponentially smaller with Eli sucking up all her oxygen.

"Tank finished his assessment before we got here. We're all clear." Eli stepped in and looked around. "Where do you normally keep the figurine?"

Kay pointed to the top of her dresser. Eli walked over and looked down at her collection. He touched one and the sight of his thick fingers stroking the delicate china shouldn't have seemed erotic at all. But the image of this big, strong man handling tiny breakables with such care struck her as incredibly tender. Would that be how he treated a woman in bed? Like she was delicate, precious?

Or would he push her hard, demand things she didn't know how to give? Warmth spread to her face just thinking about it.

Not that you'll ever find out.

"There's an empty space here. He didn't even bother to push the others closer together to conceal what he took."

Kay hated to even think of it. Someone had been in her apartment, touching her things. Had he been here while she was home alone? While she was with her daughter?

While they were sleeping?

She shivered and grabbed the duffel bag she kept underneath her bed. Her favorite nightshirt was on top of the comforter, so she shoved that in the bag. Then she pulled open the drawers in her nightstand and added a big handful of underwear and bras. She didn't even look at how much she was taking, just grabbed blindly. Who cared, really, what she wore? All she cared about was getting out of here. Would she ever be able to relax in this room again without wondering if someone was watching?

She crossed to the dresser where Eli stood and yanked open the last drawer. In went several pairs of jeans, then she yanked open another drawer and added a big armful of sweaters.

"Kay, what are you doing?"

"Packing. I just want to get out of here."

She struggled with the zipper on the bag, almost breaking a nail on the metal teeth. Her breath came in harsh pants until little black spots danced in front of her eyes.

"Kay, calm down. Just hold on."

She struggled against his hold, but he held her securely in his grip, her back to his front. His arms wrapped around her, keeping her from moving but not holding her so tight as to cause pain. Eventually Kay stopped fighting and allowed her head to fall back against Eli's chest.

"Hey, hey. It's all right. Just calm down." He rubbed her arms gently, soothing her.

Kay finally stopped wrestling with him and allowed him to hold her. She closed her eyes and took a deep breath. It was a foolish moment of weakness, but for just a second, she soaked up the comfort and warmth of being in his arms.

"We're safe here. You've got a great security system. I already had Tank check it out and it hasn't been tampered with. I don't know how this guy got your figurine, but he didn't break in to do it."

Tears welled up, but she squeezed her eyes closed, swallowing back the sudden flood of emotion. There was no time for nonsense or feeling sorry for herself.

"Why would someone do this, Eli?"

"I don't know, angel." He spoke in a hush, the words flowing over her in a soft puff of breath.

His features tightened, and for the second time in recent memory, she allowed herself to soak up the masculine presence

42

that was Elliott Alexander: the smooth dark skin, the high cheekbones, the long straight blade of his nose, and the sinfully full lips. It was a harsh face, not quite as elegantly hewn as his brothers' faces, but one that she vastly preferred. It looked like safety.

It looked like strength.

"I'm okay now. I promise I won't freak out on you again." She stood reluctantly. As wonderful as it felt to be held in his arms, there was only so much she could take before she lost all sense of propriety and threw herself at him again. She already knew he wasn't interested. When you kissed a guy and he responded by leaving town, that was plenty clear enough.

"It's okay to be freaked out, Kay. As long as you know that I won't let anything happen to you."

Kay nodded and dropped the duffel bag on her bed. She didn't have enough room to put him up in style, but at the very least she could rustle up some extra pillows and a blanket for him.

"I'm sorry I don't have a guest room. Or an air mattress."

Eli gave her one of his trademark *are you kidding* looks. "I'm not supposed to be on vacation, Kay. The couch is fine. Now, what about Hope?"

Kay gasped. Shame flooded her face. She'd told her mom that she'd pick up Hope by eight o'clock and she was already twenty minutes late. She pulled out her cell phone and hit the first speed dial.

Eli walked away to give her some privacy. Luckily, her father answered, so she was able to explain things with a minimum of fuss. As expected, her parents were thrilled to keep Hope overnight.

When she turned, Eli was watching her with an inscrutable expression. Unsure what to make of his sudden change in demeanor, Kay pushed past him and pulled open the door to the linen closet in the hallway. Several towels fell out and hit her in the face.

"Don't worry about that now." Eli took the towels from her arms and shoved them in the closet. "We need to talk first."

"About what?"

"Everything. Clearly I missed something when I was digging into your life last year. It's time to rectify that."

"But nothing has changed. I don't do anything interesting. So what's there to talk about?"

Eli stopped and nailed her with an intense look. "I need to know who you've been with since last summer." He moved closer and Kay inhaled, immediately assaulted by his unique scent—warm and rich and disarming. She looked up at him, her senses swirling from the intoxicating blend of reactions that only Eli could cause.

"We need to talk about your lovers."

Chapter Five

ELI WALKED THE perimeter of the living room, checking the locks on the windows. It was unnecessary since he'd already checked them all when they'd first arrived, but it gave him a few moments to compose himself before they talked.

He'd need all the composure he had to listen to Kay talk about who she'd allowed into her body in the last six months.

His fists clenched at his sides and he forced out a breath. "Let's sit on the couch and talk."

Kay eyed him the way you'd watch a wild animal. Under any other circumstances it would be funny, but in this case, it just proved that she was as observant as he'd always suspected. She took great pains to stay in the background and not attract too much attention to herself, but it didn't fool Eli. She was smart. And savvy. He'd long suspected that she had a side she didn't allow many others to see. The only time he'd seen her stand with the type of confidence he knew she should have was when she was on stage.

To make her more comfortable, Eli perched on the edge of one of the sofa cushions. Kay sank down on the opposite end, clutching one of the throw pillows to her chest.

"Let's start with Craig." He bit out the name as he drew a pen and pad from the inner pocket of his coat. Despite his fondness for being in the gym, evidenced by him constantly walking around shirtless, the guy had seemed way too girly in Eli's opinion. There was just something weird about a dude who took more time in the bathroom getting ready than his girlfriend did.

"You know Craig and I broke up. I seriously doubt if he even noticed that I wasn't around for a while. He was too busy admiring himself to care what I was up to. I don't see him being a stalker unless he was stalking his own reflection." Kay rolled her eyes.

Eli secretly agreed with her assessment, but he kept that thought to himself. "What about after that? Did you date anyone else that summer?"

She shrugged and picked at a piece of lint on the edge of the couch. "I didn't really have time. That was right after Divine broke up, remember? Jackson had just offered me a solo contract, so I was spending a lot of time with him in the studio, coming up with ideas for the project." She smiled absently at the thought, and Eli's fingers tightened around the pen.

His little brother was devoted to Ridley, so he didn't entertain any thoughts that something was going on between Jackson and Kay. But the way she talked about him, the little smiles when she remembered something he'd done or said, all contributed to his worry that Kay was crushing on Jackson. When he'd kissed her at Christmas, it hadn't occurred to him until afterward that she might be projecting her fondness for his brother onto him.

He wasn't the type of man to play second string to anyone, but even more than that, he wasn't going to encourage a fascination that could ultimately end up hurting Kay. She'd given him only bare bones information about Hope's father, but it was enough for him to know that older men had taken advantage of her before.

He'd be damned if it ever happened again.

"I know you hate talking about him, but I need to know if Hope's father has done or said anything out of the ordinary in the past few months."

Kay immediately tensed and glanced down at her lap. "I haven't seen Tim in ages. Not that I saw him that much before. Remember when I used to waitress at that Italian restaurant? That's where I met him. I don't think I ever told you that."

She definitely hadn't told him that. Eli filed that bit of information away to examine later. Maybe it would mean something when he was looking at the big picture. He put an X next to the name Timothy Banner. He'd have one of his guys check on Mr. Banner's current financial situation later.

"So you didn't see much of him outside of the days you were working?"

"He used to wait for me after my shift," she whispered. "It seems so seedy looking back on it. All he wanted was someone to pass the time with when he was in town on business. We spent hours talking about everything. Or nothing. But then after I got pregnant…" She sighed and her fist clenched against her thigh. "I was so stupid to think we had a connection. I was just convenient."

Eli laid his hand over hers. "I'm sorry, Kay."

She looked up, seemingly startled by his touch. "It's okay. It's all in the past now. Anyway, I'm not even sure how long it's been since I've seen him. A long time. He doesn't care about Hope. Or me."

The last statement was said so matter-of-factly that Eli's heart broke on her behalf.

"He's a fucking idiot."

Kay's head lifted. She blinked a few times before a small smile spread across her face. "Yeah, he is. I'm just glad my mom convinced him to sign away his parental rights. He was so worried that I'd want child support from him, but he never considered that I might be a success."

"Like I said, he's an idiot."

She shrugged again.

"Okay, who have you dated since Craig?" He ran a hand roughly over his face. It was killing him to talk about it, but he'd do whatever it took to figure this thing out.

"No one," Kay whispered. She didn't look at him as she said it.

"What do you mean? There has to have been someone." He stopped at the stricken look on her face.

She'd moved back on the couch and wouldn't meet his eyes. It was obvious that this was just as uncomfortable for her as it was for him. He cleared his throat. A different approach was in order.

Light. Nonconfrontational.

"I get that it's weird and awkward to talk about sexual partners with me, but this is really important. Would you rather give this information to Matt? He could come over tomorrow and you guys could sit down and go over it all."

He hated to even make the offer, but if it made it easier for her to be honest, he'd do it. Matt had a way with her. They had a rapport. Maybe she'd tell him things she was too embarrassed to admit to Eli.

Kay finally looked up. "I don't need to pull Matt off his new job to tell him the same thing I just told you. How long does it take to write down nothing?"

Eli groaned. "Kay, you're basically saying no one's had their hands on you in more than six months. You're a vibrant, beautiful young woman. I find that a little hard to believe."

Kay stared at him for a long moment before she slid forward. "I didn't say no one had their hands on me in all that time. I just said I hadn't dated anyone." Her tongue darted out and wet her bottom lip before she lifted her eyes to his. Perched forward, her weight resting on her hands, caused her sweater to dip lower, revealing a shadow of lace at the top of her bra.

He swallowed, the sound loud between them.

"Okay. His name?" Elliott's stomach clenched but he lifted the pencil, poised to write the name of the lucky bastard she'd allowed to get close to her.

With a little lift of her chin that he should have realized spelled trouble, she leaned over his shoulder and pointed at his pad of paper as she spelled out "E-l-l-i-o-t-t."

TEASING ELI WAS probably a little like poking a lion with a stick, but Kay couldn't help herself. Especially since he was interrogating her like a criminal. How convenient for him to want a list of her lovers and not consider the fact that their kiss was the closest she'd come to intimacy in ages.

"This is serious, Kay."

"I know it is, Eli," she drawled in her best imitation of his deep voice. "When do you think I have the time to go out with a bunch of men? *I am a single mother.* I barely have time to take a shower and brush my teeth every day."

Eli looked chagrined. Maybe it was finally sinking in just how ridiculous his assumptions were. Although, she couldn't really fault him for assuming that she'd have had at least one other boyfriend since the summer. Most girls her age were out dancing and drinking on the weekends, picking up men at clubs, and having one-night stands they'd regret in the morning. There were times when Kay wondered what it would be like to have that much free time and be able to go out with her friends.

Then she'd look over at Hope and realize that she was exactly where she was supposed to be.

"I apologize if I've offended you. That wasn't my intention." Eli closed his notepad and tucked it in the interior pocket of his coat. "I'm just trying to figure things out. Like I said, your security system hasn't been tampered with and we went through this place, room by room. Whoever it was didn't break in." He turned to look at her directly. "It was someone you know. Someone you trusted enough to invite in."

Kay shivered. "I don't invite many people over. Just my family and a few close friends."

"Does anyone have a key to the apartment?"

Kay thought back to when she'd first moved in. She didn't know anyone who lived close by except her parents. She'd thought about giving a key to Sasha, but she lived too far away for it to be helpful if she got locked out.

"Just my parents."

Eli made a disgruntled sound. "Okay. I'm going to see if Matt remembers anything from when he was guarding you then. Maybe someone hanging around when you moved in or anything out of the ordinary. Whoever this is, they're smart. They're leaving no evidence of their entry, so we can't really go to the police until we have proof that a crime has been committed. They'd probably consider sending a cat trinket to be nothing more than a childish prank."

"But you don't think it is," Kay commented.

"No. I don't think it is." In typical Elliott fashion, he didn't offer any additional thoughts on the matter.

Kay got up and brought back a comforter and several pillows. "I appreciate you staying here with me. I don't think I could have stayed here alone knowing this guy has been in here."

Eli accepted the pillows with a nod. "You'll never be alone, Kay. Remember that."

His words warmed her as surely as a touch. Kay had figured any chance they'd had was gone when he disappeared after Christmas, but maybe he'd had a legitimate reason to leave town. Maybe his leaving hadn't had anything to do with her or their kiss.

"My mom considers you one of hers now. She'd kill me if I didn't take proper care of you."

Kay's heart sank. His mother. Of course.

She was just an obligation. She wasn't sure if it was better or worse than when he'd only been helping her because Jackson had hired him to.

"Of course. Good night, Eli." Kay didn't wait for him to acknowledge it, just walked down the hall to her room and closed the door.

KAY WOKE EARLIER than usual the next morning. The knowledge that Eli was in her living room had contributed to a long night of tossing and turning. At first, she'd just been on alert in case he needed anything. She'd heard him moving around, drawers and cabinets opening and closing and the hum of the pipes as he'd used the small bathroom off the hall.

Luckily, her room had its own connected bathroom so she didn't have to worry about any awkwardness there. She'd taken her shower before bed and changed into her favorite tank-and-shorts pajama set. It wasn't sexy by any means, but then she wasn't trying to seduce him. He'd shown less than zero interest when he'd been in her room and hadn't lingered when examining the "scene of the crime" as she liked to think of her collection of figurines now. He'd looked at the blank space in the collection and nowhere else. Not at the lingerie she'd been mortified to discover was hanging over the chair or at the romance books on her nightstand.

He'd just done his usual tough, gruff routine. It was too bad she found his deep, gravelly voice so sexy. It would be so much easier if she hated him. If she hadn't spent half the night wondering about what he was doing on her sofa. Whether he'd stripped off all his clothes to sleep or just gone down to his underwear.

Coffee. If she could just get some caffeine in her system, then maybe she could think practically. About anything other than what Eli wore when he was sleeping.

Kay spared a cursory glance at the clock, then decided it was early enough to chance making a run for it. Eli was probably dead to the world, so it didn't matter if she looked like hell. Turning on the coffeepot should take two minutes, max. She pulled on a short, silky robe and knotted it in the front. Even if he rolled over and caught a glimpse of her, he wouldn't see much other than a bunch of pink silk.

In the kitchen, she made quick work of measuring out the

coffee. The huge jumble of blankets on the couch didn't move, so she had to assume that Eli was a pretty sound sleeper. After adding water to the machine, she set the coffeepot to brew. She turned at the sound of a door opening. Startled, she glanced over at the couch. The jumble of covers still hadn't moved.

"Then where is—"

Kay squeaked in surprise when Eli walked past, a white towel wrapped around his waist. His skin was still damp, as evidenced by the beads of water clinging to his neck. Without the barrier of clothing, his muscles stood out in stark display. His chest was massive, and then there were the perfectly delineated abdominals. Once her eyes made it past those, they landed on the most interesting muscles on his sides, shaped like a *V* leading straight down to his—

At her gasp, he stopped and looked at her with raised eyebrows. "Morning. Everything okay?"

Stunned, it took her several moments to register the question. Then several moments more to realize she was standing in the middle of the kitchen gaping at him. Worse, gaping at the towel around his waist. The incredibly tiny towel.

"You're n...naked," she stammered.

"I am." Eli didn't bother to hide or run for cover. Oh no, the jerk had the nerve to come *closer*. "That's generally how I take my showers."

"And really..." She tried in vain to get her eyes to land anywhere other than the broad expanse of his chest. "Really, really big."

His lips curled up at that statement and Kay immediately realized what she'd just said. "I meant muscular. And really *muscular*. Is that an eight-pack? I didn't even know there were that many packs possible..."

There really ought to be some sort of law about how fine a man was allowed to be. Especially men who were gruff and difficult to understand. It was bad enough that she couldn't figure out his signals, but now she was supposed to think while confronted by a chest that looked like it had been chiseled out of concrete?

"Kay?"

"Hmm," she breathed.

He crossed his arms. "I meant to bring my clothes with me in the bathroom but I forgot. So I need to finish getting dressed."

"Right. Of course."

When she still didn't move, Eli grabbed the edge of the towel where it was tucked next to his skin. "I generally don't have an audience for this part, but if you want to stay... "

Now *that* got her attention.

"Oh my God. *Omigod.*" Kay stammered something that sounded vaguely like an apology and then ran for her room. She closed the door behind her and rested her head against the door.

Of course Eli was the type to be up at the crack of dawn. As if being built like a linebacker and covered in skin like dark chocolate wasn't sexy enough, he was an early riser who probably ran three miles every morning just for fun. Was there anything about him that wasn't completely intimidating?

Her phone beeped on the nightstand. With a sigh, Kay sat on the edge of the bed and leaned over to read the text message. It was from Ridley.

Give me a call when you wake up?

Kay quickly texted her back. A few minutes later, her phone rang.

"Hey! I didn't actually think you'd be awake this early. What's going on over there?"

"Nothing." Kay clutched the phone tighter as an image of Eli's perfect chest flashed through her mind. Suddenly she just had to tell someone. "I just saw Eli naked."

"What!" Ridley's shocked squeak was so loud Kay glanced behind her instinctively to make sure Eli hadn't somehow heard.

"It was an accident. Plus, he wasn't completely naked. Almost naked. He was wearing a towel, but it didn't cover much." Kay sagged back against her pillows and let out a long sigh. "I had no idea my towels were so small."

Considering that Ridley was married to an Alexander man,

she figured her friend would understand exactly why she was so affected.

"No wonder you sound so winded. Looking at that is enough to make any red-blooded woman lose her breath."

"I can't afford to lose my breath. I'm supposed to be looking forward, remember? Finding Mr. Right?"

"That's true. As a matter of fact, that's why I'm calling. I have some news that might take your mind off things."

"I seriously doubt that." Kay sighed.

"Mara found the perfect guy for you."

Kay cringed. Pretending to let the girls fix her up had been a ridiculous idea even when they were just doing it to make Eli jealous. There was no way she was actually going through with it. "I'm not sure that's such a good idea."

"Why not? Mara knows him from work and she says he's super smart and a great dancer. He's going to meet us tomorrow evening to hang out. There won't be any pressure. Just a chance for you to meet a nice guy."

Kay still didn't like the sound of it but figured it couldn't do any harm. Especially if they were surrounded by a group of people. If the guy was a weirdo, she wouldn't be stuck there alone with him. Maybe if she went this time, the girls would be satisfied and lose interest in fixing her up.

"Okay, I'll go. Just tell me where and when."

Ridley let out a little squeal. "This is going to be so much fun! Just meet us at the Alexanders' house at seven o'clock. We're not doing anything fancy, just going to The Rush for burgers. Julia volunteered to watch all the kids, including Hope, so we can all go out together and have a good time."

Kay smiled. The Alexanders really were just the nicest people. If she didn't already find Eli so fascinating, she'd probably like him just for his family.

"That's really nice of her."

"Raina and I definitely hit the jackpot when it comes to having the best mother-in-law ever. Oh, just one more thing." Ridley paused and then blurted, "Don't tell Eli. Okay, see you tomorrow!" There was an audible click as the call disconnected.

Kay stared at her cell phone in shock before a giggle erupted. She wasn't sure how Ridley thought she was going to go on a date without Eli noticing. The last time he'd been shadowing her, he'd followed her everywhere, to the point of driving her insane. She'd actually locked herself in the bathroom a few times to get some privacy.

"Oh Ridley, what have you gotten me into?"

Chapter Six

ELI LOOKED OVER at Kay playing with her daughter. After their awkward encounter that morning, they'd come to an unspoken agreement to act as though it had never happened. He'd accompanied her to her job as an administrative assistant to his younger brother, Nick, and then to the studio to record for an hour.

After that, they'd picked up her daughter from her parents' house. He'd watched in awe as she'd made dinner, finished some laundry, and entertained the baby all at once. In the time since they'd gotten home, Kay had yet to sit down for even a minute. She lived a quiet life but one that required a lot of stamina.

He was ashamed to admit that he'd never realized just how much work was involved in caring for a baby.

When he'd been protecting them last summer, Hope had been so small. She'd been attached to Kay the majority of the time. He wasn't used to thinking of Hope as a separate entity. Part of him figured that was because he didn't like to think about where Hope had come from. Thinking about that led him into the uncomfortable mental terrain of thinking about the man who'd hurt Kaylee.

Somewhere it was much better if he didn't allow his mind to go.

But now he was forced to view Hope as her own, well, *person*. He felt foolish thinking it, but she seemed like a tiny person with her big, knowing eyes and babbled phrases. She'd taken one look at him and broken out into delighted squeals. He hadn't thought she'd remember him even though they'd spent time together over Christmas, but apparently she did. Her tiny little face had lit up, and she'd started a long, animated conversation with him in what sounded like a mash of English and Klingon. Kay had seemed just as surprised as he had, so he could only assume the reaction wasn't typical.

"Eli, do you want something to eat?" Kay stood in the kitchen, a dish towel thrown over one shoulder. The sight sent a sharp stab of longing through him. It had been a long time since anyone other than his mother had been so concerned about his welfare.

"Sure. Whatever you have handy is fine. I'm not picky."

Kay grinned. "I'll make you a plate." She trotted over to where Hope was busy eating cut-up pieces of chicken from her high-chair tray, catching her before she threw a handful of food on the floor. Eli smothered a laugh. He was glad the incident that morning hadn't made things too awkward. Living in close quarters was bound to introduce strange situations such as accidentally seeing each other half-dressed.

Not that Eli regretted it, per se. Although he shouldn't want Kay looking at him like that—it was better for her sake if she didn't find him attractive—he couldn't deny enjoying her obvious admiration of his bare chest.

His phone buzzed in his pocket, so he turned back to the living room. "This is Eli," he barked without even checking who it was.

"Elliott. Glad I caught you. I have some information I'd like you to look over."

"Agent Harris. It's been a while."

"Things have been quiet. However, the group is recruiting heavily again and we've got leads. Word is that Zeus has made an appearance. We really need you on this one."

"I'd like to help, but I'm not sure that I can. I've told you before that I never met Zeus. I was just a low-level grunt. I did the dirty work, but I wasn't in the inner circle."

"I know, but it's imperative that you tell us immediately if he attempts to contact you. The agency considers capturing him a top priority. We have reason to believe he's trying to reassemble the old guard. The group has sustained a lot of losses over the past five years, and he's probably looking to regroup. Rebuild the ranks."

"I understand that and I wish I could help. However, I think you're wasting your time with me. The Circle always went for young guys. Strong, healthy, young. He's going to focus on college towns first. If he hasn't already left the country, that is."

Glad he'd stepped away so Kay wouldn't overhear him, Eli gripped the phone tighter. "Agent Harris, this really isn't a good time."

There was a pause. The other man obviously hadn't been expecting him to say no. "Mr. Alexander, I don't think I need to remind you that one of the conditions of your release was full cooperation with the FBI's investigation."

Eli gritted his teeth. "No, you don't need to remind me. Can the information be sent through e-mail, or do I need to pick it up?"

"You'll receive a secure e-mail in the next hour."

Eli hung up without bothering to say good-bye. It was his own fault that he was in this situation. The mistakes of his youth were going to haunt him forever it seemed.

A hand on his shoulder startled him out of his thoughts. He turned to see Kaylee standing next to him, her eyes narrowed in worry.

"Eli, are you okay? I called your name over and over and you didn't hear me."

He forced a smile. "Sorry, I'm a little distracted."

"Okay, well, your food is ready." She walked back to the kitchen and Eli had to force his eyes away from the sway of her hips. Even if he hadn't already known that taking their attraction any further was a bad idea, the call from Agent Harris was a sobering reminder. Until he'd atoned for the mistakes of his past, he was enslaved to the authorities, who held his freedom in their grasp. He had to continue to cooperate with them, and it was always on their timetable, not his. Kay needed someone who could put her first, be there for her whenever she called.

He wasn't free to be the man she needed.

ELI PARKED HIS truck on the side of the road the next afternoon and cut the engine. Kay was at work and he'd left Tank there in his place. She had no idea what he was doing with his afternoon off, and he hoped he wouldn't have to tell her. Any mention of her stalker was understandably upsetting for her, so he hadn't told her that Jeremy King had recently been released on parole.

He couldn't be the man she needed, but there was one thing he could do for her: help her get her life back to normal. The sooner he figured out who'd sent the figurine, the sooner he could make that happen.

He looked at the house across the street and two doors down. According to Jeremy King's parole officer, this was where he'd been living since his release. There was a pretty big chance that this was a waste of his afternoon. Taking the word of a known liar and a recovering drug addict was risky at best and downright stupid at worst. However, a year ago Jeremy King had claimed not to be acting alone. If Eli had taken him seriously then and pressed for more details, there was a chance he could have found the man's accomplice before now, and

Kaylee wouldn't be in danger again.

He walked down to the two-story house with the moss-covered siding and knocked. Grass was growing up around the cracked concrete steps, snaking over the edges of the small porch. The wood trim around the door was rotting and the house hadn't been painted in years. If Jeremy King had been paid to threaten Kay as he'd claimed, he'd clearly not gotten rich from the job.

"What do you want?" A haggard-looking woman with steel-gray hair glared at him from a crack in the door.

"I'm looking for Jeremy King. Is he home?"

"Who wants to know?"

"Elliott Alexander."

Her eyes narrowed. "You a cop?"

"No, ma'am. I just want to ask Jeremy a few questions. If he's honest with me, I may be able to prove that he wasn't stalking anyone."

She didn't look convinced, but the door was suddenly pulled all the way open.

"It's okay, Ma. Go back inside." Jeremy King stepped out onto the porch. He'd lost weight in the past year, and his skin was ruddy. His brown hair hung lank and lifeless around his thin face.

"I won't take up much of your time," Elliott promised.

"Ask whatever you want. I've got nothing to lose at this point." Jeremy leaned against the doorframe. His eyes narrowed on Eli's face. "I've seen you before."

"Last year, you said you were paid to send those threatening letters to Kaylee Wilhelm."

Jeremy stood up straight. "I was. Five hundred dollars per letter. I'm not proud of it but I needed the money, so I did it. All I had to do was stick them in an envelope and mail them to the address on the note. Once I did, I'd receive another note with money inside."

"You never saw the person leaving the money?"

"Nah. I didn't want to see him. I was hoping he'd bring me more letters to mail so I could keep getting paid. I made four thousand dollars in less than a month just for dropping a few envelopes in the mail."

For the first time, Jeremy's shoulders sagged. "I wasn't trying to hurt anybody. Kay was always nice to me in school. She was quiet. You know? Sweet."

Eli realized this visit was going to end up a bust. Even if he believed Jeremy's story—and he wasn't sure he did—if he hadn't seen who was leaving the money, this was all moot. He wasn't here to carry some deadbeat's apologies back to Kay. Then something Jeremy had said registered.

"Wait. You only sent five letters to Kaylee. So how could you have earned that much money?"

"By mailing the other ones," Jeremy said.

Eli blinked, sure he must have heard wrong. "*Other ones?*"

"Yeah. I told those cops that I was paid to send letters to a couple of people. There was Kay and then two other girls. One was named Tanya Cook and... what was the other one?" Jeremy's eyes rolled up as he looked to the sky for answers. "Oh yeah, Elise Able. That was the other girl's name."

"Do you know those girls?"

Jeremy shook his head. "Nah. That's why I thought it was weird that the police didn't believe me when I said I wasn't stalking anybody. I just sent a few letters. Why would I stalk some random chicks I never met?"

Elliott skipped down the steps, heading for his truck. "Thank you Mr. King for your cooperation."

"Hey!" Jeremy yelled after him. "Are you going to tell those cops that I'm innocent?"

"I'm going to try to catch the other guy. If I can catch him, that will only help your case."

Elliott jogged back to his truck and pulled out his phone as he swung up into the cab. Tank's voice mail picked up after four rings.

"Hey, it's Eli. I need you to run some names for me. Tanya Cook and Elise Able. Jeremy King claims he was paid to send letters to them, too. I want to find out everything about these girls. Where they live, what they do for a living, what they do for fun. If we can find a connection, maybe we can figure out why this guy focused on the three of them."

He hung up and put the truck in gear. Just before he pulled out, there was a flash of movement from his left side. A man, medium height and build, stood watching him from across the street. His oversized hooded jacket obscured his face completely. While he watched, the guy turned and started walking.

His head was down and he walked at a normal pace, but there was something about him that set Eli's instincts ringing. So he glanced in his rearview mirror and then pulled out, prepared to follow the guy. When he got a hunch, he always went with it. It had saved him more than once.

However, when he pulled out into the street, the guy was gone. He sped up and looked down the next street to see if he'd turned the corner.

Nothing.

If he told the story to anyone else, they'd likely think he was overreacting. A shadowy figure watching him. One that disappeared before he could get close. It sounded like a thriller novel. But Eli just *knew*. He'd started something by coming here. What, he didn't know. But whatever it was, he had to be ready.

He shook his head and then pulled off, driving a little faster than he would have normally. He suddenly needed to be near Kay, hear her voice and see her smile. He hadn't come here expecting to believe Jeremy King, but now that he did, it was more obvious than ever that whatever was going on was bigger than he'd imagined.

A FEW HOURS later, Kay examined her outfit in the mirror one last time. The flowing peasant top she'd settled on was feminine without showing too much cleavage. Something she always had to think about since her "girls" tended to struggle out of most tops. She sighed and tugged at the neckline again. Maybe she should have stuck with the black sweater she'd originally chosen.

She turned from the mirror, disgusted with her own indecision. It wasn't that she was nervous. Well, not that much. Ridley, Raina, and Mara would all be there. How bad could it be? It would be a low-key, no-pressure kind of date. Just dinner with a bunch of mutual friends was no big deal.

Although Kay had a feeling Eli wouldn't see it that way.

That afternoon, Tank had come to stay with her while Eli took care of something. Whatever he'd been doing must have really thrown him for a loop because he'd been distracted and distant ever since. She'd told him they were having a girl's night out and he hadn't questioned it, but she knew his distraction was only a temporary thing. Once he got past whatever he was brooding about, he'd start asking his usual questions.

Kay couldn't even begin to guess what he'd do when he realized their girl's night out was really just an excuse for the girls to fix her up.

Eli appeared in the doorway. "Are you ready to go yet?" He'd been waiting for her to finish dressing for the past half hour, but he seemed to have run out of patience.

"Almost. I just need to fix my hair." Kay avoided his eyes as she rushed into the bathroom. Curly black ringlets stuck out in every direction, so she pulled them into a high ponytail and fastened down any strays with pins. That would have to do.

"You look really nice," Eli commented when she rushed past him again. "Aren't we just hanging out with Ridley?"

Kay busied herself filling up Hope's diaper bag with the essentials. "Yeah, but it's been a while since I've gone out. Nick's got a new project, so we've been really busy working on that, plus I've been recording late with Jackson." Guilt kept her from looking him in the eye. "Your brothers have been keeping me busy!"

Eli chuckled. "You want me to beat them up for you?"

She tried not to stare, but it was hard not to be entranced by the rare appearance of his smile. It was still a novelty to see this side of Eli. He didn't joke around that often, so it was always a pleasant surprise when she could coax a laugh out of him.

"That won't be necessary. I'm kind of attached to them by now."

She grabbed the last of what she needed, then allowed Eli to take the bag from her so she could pick up Hope from her crib. A few minutes later, they were on their way.

Kay glanced over at Eli several times during the drive. He was in a strange mood, and she debated whether she should tell him to turn the car around and go home. But before she could make up her mind, they were pulling into the long drive of the Alexander farm. Just as she opened her door to step out of the truck, the front door opened and Julia Alexander came down the steps.

"There you are," Julia exclaimed. She held out wide-open arms for Kay. The red-and-white checked apron she wore was dotted with flour, and she carried the scent of warmth and sugar. After a round of hugs, Julia took the car seat from Eli and started back toward the house.

"I'm so happy to hear the girls found a nice young man to set you up with. And you look so nice, honey. I'm sure you'll knock him off his feet." Julia winked at them before starting up the steps.

"What is she talking about?" Eli narrowed his eyes as he looked at her outfit again, clearly seeing the clothes she'd agonized over and the makeup she'd worn in a new light.

"It's nothing. The girls just have someone they want me to meet."

Eli glared at her, but before he could say anything, Mara appeared in the doorway.

"Kay's here," she announced over her shoulder. "Now we can go. Hi, Eli. We'll have her back in a few hours."

"I know you will because I'm coming with you."

Mara stopped in her tracks. "You're coming with us?"

Ridley and Raina appeared in the doorway behind her. "Who's going where?" Raina asked, looking between Mara and Eli with confusion.

A slow smile spread across Eli's face. It was so unexpected, such an incongruous expression, that it took them all off

64

guard. "I'm going with you. Wherever Kay goes, I go. Bodyguard, remember?"

Mara nodded slowly. "Of course. Right. I forgot."

"I bet you did," Eli muttered. Kay covered her mouth with the back of her hand to stifle her laughter, and Eli turned his glare her direction before asking Mara, "So, what's on the agenda tonight?"

"Let's go, everybody!" Ignoring his question, Mara headed down the driveway toward her car. Ridley and Raina followed, sending worried glances over their shoulder at Kaylee.

Eli grabbed her elbow and towed her back toward his truck. "Where are we going?"

"The Rush. Eli, maybe we should—"

"Buckle your seatbelt." Eli helped her into the passenger side, then slammed the door. Kay shivered as he rounded the car and climbed up into the driver's side. She was going on a date. And the man she'd been crushing on for the past year would be there as a spectator. And he was armed.

Yikes.

Chapter Seven

THE RUSH WAS a small diner that had been in operation since the 1950s. Bright colors and waitresses on roller skates would have fit the atmosphere, but instead it was a plain white facade with a cherry-red awning. All the tables and chairs were a faded beige Formica that easily had fifty years of grease baked on.

Kay inhaled the familiar aroma of hamburgers and the sweet scent of milkshakes as they piled into a booth in the back corner of the restaurant. Mara's friend, Daniel, arrived several minutes later, sliding into the booth right across from Kay.

"Hi, everybody. Sorry I'm late." He smiled hello to everyone, making eye contact with Kay, including her in the greeting. His dark hair was cropped close on the side and stood up in disarray on the top, like he was far too busy to bother brushing it, and his brown eyes crinkled charmingly when he smiled.

She sat up a little straighter and smoothed her hair self-consciously. It had been an act of peer pressure that she'd agreed to do this, but in all of her mental preparation, she hadn't considered that the guy might actually be cute.

Mara caught her eye and winked.

"So, how have things been going? I haven't seen you since one of your clients sued one of our clients. Danny is a lawyer," Mara added dramatically.

Beside her, Eli groaned under his breath.

"Really? That must be challenging. What kind of law do you practice?" Kay leaned back when the waitress appeared to bring their water and take their orders.

Everyone except Eli ordered the special, the house burger and fries. Mara ordered a plate of cheese fries with her meal. Kay really wanted to order some too but figured chowing down on several plates of food was probably bad date etiquette. She could only hope she wasn't doing anything else wrong. She was so hopelessly out of practice with the whole man-woman flirting thing.

As soon as the waitress left, Danny said, "Disability."

"Huh?" Kay took a sip of her water as she tried to remember what they'd been talking about before.

Eli leaned over and whispered, "Disability. I think he's an ambulance chaser."

Kay spluttered, the water going down her throat the wrong way as Eli's loud whisper carried across the table.

"Actually, Danny works on disability cases for people who have been denied coverage by their insurance companies." Mara shot Eli a death glare.

To his credit, Danny didn't show any reaction. "It's true. Although I wouldn't have turned my nose up at ambulance chasing a few years ago. I had law-school loans bigger than the national debt."

The tension around the table went down a notch as they all laughed. Kay smiled at him gratefully.

"So, is this your brother?" Danny gestured to Eli. Kay

slapped a hand against Eli's chest before he could say anything.

"Oh they're no relation. He's actually our brother-in-law," Ridley said.

Danny didn't look convinced, but he nodded. "So, Mara tells me you're a singer. I couldn't carry a tune even if I strapped it to my back, so I think that's pretty amazing."

Kay had gotten used to answering questions and being interviewed more over the past year. She'd never love it, but it had definitely gotten easier.

"I'm really lucky. I used to sing as part of a group, but now I'm going solo. My album should be out in a few months. We're halfway finished recording."

Danny looked impressed. "Wow, congratulations."

"You should go visit her at the studio," Mara piped up. There was a round of agreement from Ridley and Raina.

"Can I? That would be really cool."

Kay shrugged. It was hard to believe he was really interested in coming to watch her work, but he seemed completely earnest. Plus, he hadn't seemed disappointed when he saw what she looked like. As far as blind dates went, they were probably already doing better than average.

"I guess so."

Next to her, Eli tensed and then slid out of the booth. "I think I'm going to order something to eat as well. I'd better go find the waitress. Do you guys want anything else?"

Kay shook her head then said, "Well, maybe some coffee."

Danny looked up. "Coffee sounds perfect. I'll have one, too."

Although he'd offered, Eli looked like he was chewing nails as he asked, "Sugar or creamer?"

"No, I don't take anything in it."

"Interesting. I would have pegged you as a low-fat, half-caf, soy-only guy." Eli walked off and left them all staring after him.

After a few awkward moments, Kay finally said, "I am so sorry about that."

"It's okay." Danny leaned forward, his eyes amused. "I'm not the easily offended type."

"I can tell." In his place, she doubted she would be so calm. He'd been invited here to meet her and Eli had been treating him with disdain the entire time. His laid-back nature was definitely attractive. She smiled at him. "You should definitely come and watch me record something. It'll be fun."

"I would love to. But are you sure your boyfriend won't mind?"

"He's not her boyfriend. He's her bodyguard." Ridley gave Kay a sympathetic look. "Singers have weirdo fans sometimes. He's just here as a precaution."

Kay sighed. "He's just a little overprotective. We're friends. He doesn't want me to get hurt. That's all."

A coffee cup clattered on the table in front of her. Eli set down the second one in front of Danny, spilling a few drops over the edge. "We're not exactly friends. Friends don't normally see each other naked."

Everyone at the table stopped moving and the diners at the next table looked over. Kay sucked in a shocked breath as heat flooded her cheeks.

Finally Danny stood and asked the closest waitress, "Where's the bathroom?"

After he was gone, Kay turned to Eli and punched him as hard as she could in the arm. "Ow, damn it." She held her sore hand close to her chest. She was raging mad, and now she couldn't even concentrate on her anger because she'd almost broken her hand on Eli's freakishly big biceps.

"Let me see it." Eli tugged until she allowed him to examine her hand, spreading the fingers and then closing them back into a fist. "Don't do that again, you could seriously hurt yourself."

"Ugh, you are awful. Let me out."

Eli moved out of the booth. "Where are you going?"

Kay turned to Mara. "I am so sorry. Please tell your friend it was great meeting him."

Then she ran out of the restaurant.

ELI GLANCED OVER at Kay, who was silently glaring out the window as he drove them home. The tension in the air was a tangible force. He gripped the steering wheel, the memory of how he'd behaved eating away at him. He hated it when she was mad at him. Something about it just tugged at his conscience. She was softhearted, so he knew if he apologized she wouldn't hold a grudge.

But he just couldn't do it. He couldn't pretend he was sorry for something he knew he'd do all over again in a heartbeat.

As soon as they pulled into his parents' driveway, Kay had her seatbelt off and was halfway out of the car. Eli trailed behind, waiting on the sidewalk while she rang the bell. His mother gave him a curious glance when she opened the door. He shook his head slightly so she wouldn't ask any questions. His best bet was to get Kay in private before she blew up at him.

"Thank you again, Mrs. Alexander. I really appreciate it." Kay carried Hope's car seat in one hand and the diaper bag in the other.

Eli reached out to take the diaper bag from her and was left hanging as she brushed past him angrily. His mom narrowed her eyes. Eli waved and rushed back to his truck. He was already due for a tongue-lashing from one irate female tonight; he didn't need to add to the pain.

As soon as they got back to Kay's apartment, Eli keyed in the security code and quickly looked around. Kay continued ignoring him as she unhooked the baby from the car seat and took her to the bathroom. There was the distinct rush of water hitting the porcelain of the bathtub, and then came Hope's happy squeals and the sound of splashing.

Eli smiled at the sound before he sat down in the living room to wait for the inevitable fight. The couch was obviously older, but it was comfortable. That described most of the apartment, actually. Kay seemed to favor warm, muted colors and soft textures. There were also books everywhere. He leaned closer to read the spine of the book on the coffee table. *You Get So Alone At Times That It Just Makes Sense* by Charles Bukowski. He picked it up and started reading.

He hadn't realized it was quiet again until Kay emerged, wearing a clean T-shirt and soft lounge pants. She didn't look at him.

"Are you still not talking to me?"

He let out a sigh when she ignored his question and sank down on the couch. "You have scary taste in books. I literally have no idea what this one is about."

Her head whipped around. When she saw the book he was holding, her lips tightened. Then she turned her head in the other direction again.

Eli closed the book and set it back on the coffee table where he'd found it. "You can't ignore me forever."

"Oh yes I can," she muttered.

"I'm sorry, okay. I was rude and I apologize." He had to force the words out, but Eli figured it was a small price to pay. This tense silence was painful.

"I'm not the one you need to be apologizing to."

"There's no way in hell I'm apologizing to Mr. Saving-poor-disabled-people Guy. No way."

Kay turned on the couch to face him. "See! That right there is why I'm so angry. You're not even sorry. You don't think you did anything wrong."

Eli agreed but figured that wasn't the response she was looking to hear.

"I was just trying to look out for you."

Kay's eyes nearly bugged out of her head. "Look out for me?" She squeezed her eyes shut, her hands clenching into fists. "You embarrassed me! Not only were you completely rude to Mara's friend, but you humiliated me. Did you really need to tell the entire restaurant that I saw you naked? If I wasn't sure I'd hurt my hand again, I would punch you for that. Maybe you don't care what anyone thinks, but I do."

Eli felt the first stirrings of true remorse. Hurting Kay had never been his intention. "You're right. I shouldn't have said that, but I was just trying to protect you. That guy... he was just trying to get in your panties."

Kay looked like she was fighting for control. "Did it not occur to you that maybe I *wanted* him to get in my panties? Hmm? That's usually why people go on dates, isn't it?"

Eli stood and wandered over to the kitchen. He couldn't look at her just then. Not when she was talking about making it with some other guy. He shoved his hands in his pockets to prevent him from breaking something. "So that's what you want? Some guy who just wants to get his rocks off?"

Kay stood and walked over to him. He backed up until he was leaning against the counter. She was so close she almost stepped on his foot. He realized then that her feet were bare. It was such an odd thing to notice in the midst of an argument, but somehow it bothered Eli that she looked so vulnerable when he really wanted to pick her up and shake some sense into her.

"I want someone who wants to get off *with me.* Someone who likes *me.*" She took a deep breath and he could see her fighting for control. "I don't need you to protect me all the time, Eli. I know what I'm doing."

"What about when you kissed me at Christmas? Did you know what you were doing then?" Eli tensed as her gaze slid downward, her eyes eating up the view of him, lingering on his lips, then his neck, then lower.

She let out a soft sigh and then glanced up at him from beneath her lashes. "I did. Just like I know what I'm doing right now," she whispered.

"Do you really, angel? Because I sure as hell don't." Eli grabbed her, his hand sliding up into the soft curls at the base of her neck. She made a soft murmur of protest at the contact, but then she melted against him. It set off every dominant instinct he had when she collapsed against him. Nothing could have stopped him from scooping her up and setting her gently on the counter. He pushed forward, parting her knees, making room for himself between her thighs.

She went rigid as a board when he pressed forward. Her

eyelids fluttered shut and her head tilted back. Eli tugged her closer so his lips could explore the soft skin of her throat. She was so soft, he thought, and absolutely perfect. He rained kisses along the skin leading to her collarbone, lost in the scent of her skin.

There was a roar in his blood, to take her, lay her out on the counter, and spend the rest of the night exploring her from the inside out. But she wasn't ready for the things he'd require, would in fact be shocked or even frightened by the things he wanted to do to her.

"Kay... We shouldn't be doing this."

"Yes," she breathed, too far gone to hear him, the perfect weights of her breasts rising and falling with her frantic breaths. Her hands came up, settling gently on his shoulders before skimming over his head.

Eli's fingers clenched against her thighs at her touch. The sensation of her fingertips dragging over his bare scalp was almost orgasmic. His control snapped and he tugged her up, supporting her with a strong hand in the center of her back.

He took her mouth gently at first, just a soft press of their lips before he took her deeper, sealing his mouth over hers. She cried out, but the sound was swallowed up between them. Then her fingers tightened against his skin as she finally, *finally*, opened her mouth.

She accepted the first stroke of his tongue with a breathy little sigh. The sound wrought something in him, an emotion he couldn't define. It was like something awakening, something that wanted to own that sound so she'd only make it for him. Tentative and unsure, she seemed to have no idea what to do with her tongue. It was obvious to Eli that Kay hadn't had many lovers. A rush of satisfaction went through him at the thought.

She gripped his biceps and held on as he coaxed her tongue into his mouth. Before long, her legs were crossed behind his back, and he was snugged up right next to her core, rubbing tight circles in rhythm with the sensual thrusts of their tongues.

"Oh, I can't breathe," Kay panted. She arched her back,

the move pushing her breasts right up in his face. With any other woman, he would have thought the move was deliberate, but Kay had no idea how desirable she was. He growled and buried his face in all her lush softness. A shot of arousal zinged through him, making him still his movements. If he didn't slow things down, he'd end up taking her on the kitchen counter. She deserved soft sheets, not a quick tumble on a tabletop.

There was a loud crash behind them and they jumped apart. Kay's eyes were dazed but cleared quickly.

"Hope," she whispered. She hopped down from the counter and Eli followed on her heels as she dashed down the hallway. She opened the door to the baby's room. Eli slipped inside behind her, blinking quickly so his eyes would adjust to the dim interior of the room.

Hope stood on tiptoe, peering over the railing of her crib. "Mess, Mama! Make a mess!" She pointed across the room. Her purple teething ring was lying in front of the dresser along with several picture frames.

Relief swept through him when he saw that she was unharmed. Despite the bad timing, Eli couldn't help but be amused. "She's got a good arm."

Kay picked up the teething ring with an indulgent smile. She left the room and came back a few minutes later, wiping it down with a paper towel.

"I had to wash it off just in case there was any glass on it." She gave it back to Hope, who promptly stuck the end back in her mouth. The broken pieces of the picture frames were deposited in the waste bin.

"That'll do it for now. I'll vacuum tomorrow."

Eli left the room so she could soothe the baby back to sleep. He walked back to the kitchen and planted his hands on the counter. The salt and pepper shakers were overturned, and there was a dish towel on the floor. He picked it up and cleaned up the counter. Now that his blood pressure had normalized, he was glad they'd been interrupted. His behavior that evening had been borne of jealousy, but it hadn't been in Kay's best interest.

She wanted to find Mr. Right and settle down. Kay

deserved that life. She was an amazing mother and she deserved someone who could give her the life she was meant for. Eventually she would find that guy. A nice, normal guy with a sense of humor and a nine-to-five. Not an antisocial workaholic with a shady past. He wanted that for her, even if the thought of it was like swallowing knives.

If he wanted to do what was best for Kay, he'd leave her alone.

KAY PULLED THE door to her daughter's room shut behind her. She clasped her arms around her body. Her nerves were still humming like they were remembering Eli's touch, the hair on her arms standing on end.

The lights in the living room were low, and she looked around in confusion as she observed the perfectly tidy kitchen. She walked a little farther and then stopped abruptly. Eli lay on the couch, wrapped in the comforter.

Snoring.

She stood there, stunned, for a few moments before the hurt moved in. He'd just had his tongue all over her skin a few minutes ago and now he was asleep? She eyed the lump on the couch suspiciously. Then her hands clenched into fists.

"Don't you dare pretend to be asleep!"

When he didn't move, she stalked over to the couch and yanked the top layer of the comforter back. Their eyes met and Kay's heart sank. Just as she'd suspected, Eli was fully dressed and wide-awake.

Disappointment lanced through her. It was always one step forward and then giant leaps back with Eli. Any time she thought she'd made progress with him, he ran the opposite direction. Then, just when she was finally making an effort to get on with her life, he kissed her like he couldn't help himself. Like he wanted nothing more than her.

He was leading her on in so many directions she had emotional whiplash. She was sick of it.

"Is this what you do? Kiss a girl and get her all riled up, then roll over and go to sleep?"

Eli's eyes narrowed at her scathing tone. "I was trying to do you a favor. There's only one place that little make-out session was going, and you aren't ready for that. Not by a long shot."

Kay bristled. "I know exactly where it was going. I was hoping it was going to my bed."

Eli sat up then, pushing the comforter back. Kay backed up at the dark desire in his eyes. She thought he was annoyed, but as he got closer, his shoulders and thick arms seeming even bigger as his chest heaved with his breaths, she realized she'd misread him.

Badly.

He wasn't annoyed. He was aroused. The thick length pushing at the front of his jeans proved it. She shivered, remembering how that thick flesh had felt when she'd been wrapped around him. It had been like being caged in by a wall of muscle. She'd never felt so safe and yet so in danger at the same time.

Even when she'd been too boneless and limp to move, she'd never worried about falling. All it took was one of Eli's hands on her back and she'd felt cradled in safety. He would never let her fall. He would never let her down.

Or so she'd thought. Because his running act made it seem that he was willing to let her down in one way.

"I don't understand. You know I want this."

Eli skimmed the back of his hand over the tip of her right breast. His eyes narrowed, watching with obsessive interest as the tip tightened under his touch. Kay bit her lip as a whimper escaped her throat.

"If you keep pushing, we'll end up sleeping together. Some men would be fine with that except I know that you want more. You want someone you can have a future with. That's not me. No matter how much I want you."

It was hard to equate the harsh words coming out of his mouth with the intensely erotic look on his face. But then that was part of her problem, wasn't it? Any other guy would have told her this after they'd woken up in bed together the next morning. Eli was just nice enough to tell her up front. She wasn't able to separate sex and love and he could tell. He knew her and knew this wasn't something she did lightly. Whereas he was no doubt used to casual flings. With a body like his, she wasn't fooling herself that he'd been saving himself for her. If she even knew how many women he'd been with, she'd probably be shocked.

She was operating way out of her league.

"You're right. I want it all. I just don't understand why we can't have it."

His face tightened and then his arm slid around her back. "Not possible. No matter how much I might want that, too." He pulled her closer until her cheek rested against his chest. He gazed down at her and Kaylee wondered what he saw when he looked at her. A client? A friend? An inexperienced girl?

Whatever he saw, it obviously wasn't enough.

"I want so much for you, Kay. One day you'll meet the right guy and have the life you deserve."

"I don't want to date some other guy." Kay squeezed him around the waist. His arms tightened around her for a moment, then he let go.

"You don't want to now, but in time what you're feeling will fade. You don't really know me. If you did... Well, anyway, one day you'll meet someone worthy of you. You should make another date with that lawyer guy. He seemed like a pretty cool dude. I treated him like shit, and he took it well. That's a good sign. I won't interfere this time. I promise."

He let her go and walked over to the alarm panel next to the door. A series of loud beeps told her he'd set the alarm. Without another word he lay down on the couch and wrapped himself in the comforter.

Chapter Eight

~⌒

OVER THE NEXT few days, Eli tried to stay in the
background. Kay ran errands, spent time with her daughter,
and went to work. She kept to her usual routine. The only
thing that was different was Eli shadowing her.

He settled himself in the waiting room at Nick's office,
watching Kay handle the constantly ringing phone. Whatever
project his brother had her working on was taking up all her
time. She'd been rushing in and out of Nick's office all
morning. She hadn't even taken her lunch break yet.

He'd taken advantage of her being distracted to finally dig
into the e-mails he'd been ignoring. He pulled up the e-mail
he'd received from Agent Harris. It linked him to a secure
website. He entered his password and then the e-mail opened.
He scrolled through pictures of mug shots and scrutinized
grainy images of tattooed arms and legs. It was hell being

forced to revisit a period of his life that he'd rather forget, but it was the only reason he wasn't currently in jail. He had knowledge that was invaluable to the authorities. So he was an asset.

One they would use until he ceased to be of value anymore.

He'd just finished college when he was approached by a man named Justice about an opportunity to work in private security. An opportunity to help victims of kidnappings and violence. A chance to help right wrongs and be useful.

Things he'd desperately needed to feel.

Caught up in the young man's seductive stories of battles fought and won, Eli had joined the secretive vigilante group called the Circle of Seven. After witnessing the inability of law enforcement to help a lot of victims, especially women, he'd believed in their cause wholeheartedly. Working outside the law, they were able to help whoever they deemed worthy. The power had been like a drug, a potent drug that kept him enthralled and unable to see the truth of what he'd become. It wasn't until he'd seen his friend and mentor almost kill an innocent girl that he'd been forced to acknowledge they were no better than the criminals they'd claimed to fight against.

He'd become one of the monsters he'd worked so long to eradicate.

After he'd finally seen the truth about the Circle, he'd been offered amnesty in exchange for working with the FBI to uncover the leaders of the vigilante group. Despite his claims to the contrary, they were convinced he knew how to reach the group's elusive leader, known only as Zeus. In the beginning, he'd had to physically meet with the agent in charge on a regular basis, and every meeting had felt like an interrogation.

No, I haven't been contacted by anyone in the organization.

No, I haven't had any contact with any foreign nationals lately.

No, I'm not plotting against the United States.

He'd slowly reintegrated back into normal society and tried to atone in his own way for the atrocities he'd allowed to happen under his watch. He sat back, stretching his arms overhead. At least he was allowed to conduct his business and move around freely now. After seven years, he still wasn't living a "normal" life. But it was better than being in jail.

Anything was better than that.

His phone buzzed in his pocket and he pulled it out. The display read *Tank Marshall.*

"What have you got for me?"

He'd assigned Tank to track and observe Kay's ex, Timothy Banner. Tank was an interesting character. Quiet. Methodical. Thorough. He was a former Army sniper, so he was trained not only in marksmanship but also in reconnaissance.

"He's back in town."

Eli sat up, the tablet on his lap almost sliding to the floor. "Since when?"

"Credit-card activity places him at a deli in D.C. yesterday morning and then a gas station in Williamsburg last night. He just checked into the Stanton Hotel in Virginia Beach."

Eli gripped the phone tighter. "Interesting coincidence. He hasn't been in town for a while right?"

"Not for a few months."

It wasn't that unusual for a businessman who traveled a lot to be out of town for long periods of time. Eli had noticed Banner tended to spend the majority of his time on the West Coast since a few of his local business ventures had failed last year. However, it was incredibly interesting that he was suddenly back in town just a week after the suspicious package was sent.

Coincidence or premeditation?

"Great work. Keep tabs on him and we'll see if he tries to make contact with Kay. I'm not sure why the package would have come to me, though. Why not send it directly to Kay?"

"Makes no sense to me. But I'll let you know if anything changes. Also, I ran a search for those names you got from Jeremy King and I found one of the women he claims he sent letters to. Actually I didn't have to dig far. She's in our database."

"Wait? You're saying one of the women he stalked was under our protection?"

"Yes. Weird, right? Tanya Cook is a lawyer whose firm hired private security after they lost a high-profile case. It appears he sent letters to Tanya right before he sent the letters to Kay. The bad news is there seems to be no connection to Timothy Banner. He's never used her firm and they don't have any common associates. It's like they live on different planets completely."

"What about the other girl?"

"I still haven't found any leads on Elise Able, but I'll keep looking."

A dark feeling settled over Eli. This didn't fit the profile of a stalker at all. Obsession didn't leave much room for alternates. If this guy was obsessed with Kay, then he wouldn't have been following and harassing other women at the same time.

"Keep looking. These women may be our only lead on figuring out whether Banner is our guy. Maybe they're old girlfriends or colleagues. Cross-reference them against his family members and known associates. If there's a connection between Banner and these women, I need you to find it."

Eli thanked him and then hung up.

He pulled up the e-mail he'd been looking at again and sighed. It had been so long since he'd been a member of the Circle that a lot of his intel was no longer applicable. However, he recognized their MO for recruiting new members. Find guys who are slightly isolated, strong, healthy, and with a need to belong to something.

His desire to make a difference, to make a mark, had been exactly what the group had used against him. He'd been so starved for purpose that he'd been willing to accept any facsimile of it he could find. Now he could only hope to help the authorities catch as many members of the Circle as possible.

Maybe it would prevent another young man from losing his soul the way he had.

AFTER THE DISASTER of their first meeting, the last thing Kay expected to see in her e-mail inbox was a message from Danny. Apparently Mara had explained everything and he wanted to take her to dinner.

That night.

She got a curl of embarrassment in her stomach every time she thought of their last date. Despite that, she wished she could have been a fly on the wall when Mara had told him what was going on. What could she possibly have said to explain that train wreck of a date? Hopefully no one her mother knew had been in the restaurant. Otherwise, she'd be hearing about it soon since Eli had announced to the entire room that she'd seen him naked.

She glared at him as he sat in the waiting room looking at something on his tablet. He'd claimed he could be inconspicuous, but he didn't exactly blend into the background. Every client who'd come in so far had done a double take when they'd seen him sitting in the corner. He looked dangerous.

And way too sexy for her peace of mind.

"Kay. Kaylee?"

She snapped to attention to see her boss, Nicholas Alexander, waving a hand in front of her face. Instantly, Kay was ashamed. How long had she been sitting here daydreaming?

Nick tucked his hands in his pockets as he regarded her. "Are you okay? You know, no one would blame you if you wanted to take some time off."

"No! That's not necessary. I'm fine. Really," she added when he looked doubtful. Staying at home was not an option. Twenty-four hours a day with Eli? She fanned herself absently with her hand. She'd spend her days locked in the bathroom trying to avoid him and her nights delirious from sexual frustration. Being at work was definitely preferable to that.

"I sent you a calendar reminder for two meetings I set up for next week," Kay reminded him, determined to keep her mind on business.

"I got them. Except they were set up for last year."

Kay's mouth dropped open and she turned to her computer. A few key taps later, she had his calendar open. Sure enough, she'd set the correct month and day on both events but with last year's date.

So much for being fine.

"I am so sorry about that. I'll fix them immediately."

"No worries. To be honest, I think I'd rather these appointments be last year anyway."

Kay smiled weakly when he turned to talk to Eli. She had to get it together. The last thing she wanted was to let Nick down. He'd hired her as a favor to Jackson, but surprisingly, they'd turned out to be a great team.

Nick was sometimes a ball of energy as he paced around his office tossing out ideas for his charity foundation, other times quiet and contemplative when running numbers for his financial clients. She could never predict what her job would be from day to day, but it was always interesting and never predictable. Plus, he didn't expect perfection. When she made mistakes, he was patient enough to teach her how to correct them.

He was also very understanding when she needed time off.

"Actually, I think I'll take you up on the offer for time off. I'm a little tired. But I finished that memo you needed." She pulled it from her outbox and held it out to him.

Nick looked up in surprise. "Of course." He took the page she held out and scanned the front page quickly. "It's perfect. Thanks. Take as much time as you need. I'll hobble along without you for a while."

Kay smiled at the image of Nick being helpless without her. She thought back to their early days working together when he'd often forget to get his cleaning or missed appointments because he was so engrossed in his work. He really did need her. It was a nice feeling.

"I'll be back tomorrow."

Nick sent a casual wave in Eli's direction. "See you guys later."

Eli stood and tucked his phone into his back pocket. "Taking off early?"

"Yeah, I think I've done everything I can handle today." She pulled out one of her drawers and her eyes landed on the spare key. Since she'd ended up recording the night Sasha was supposed to come over, the key was still in her desk drawer. Her brow furrowed when she remembered how it had seemed to be in a weird place the last time she'd looked.

"You asked me if I'd given my key to anyone. But I forgot to tell you that I keep a spare here at the office."

Eli rounded the desk and looked down at the open drawer. "How long has it been here?"

She did a quick mental calculation. "I think it's been about six months."

"Who knows you keep a key here?"

"No one. Well, my best friend Sasha knows because I've given it to her before so she could wait for me at home. Sometimes she comes over so we can hang out and watch movies."

"Does she have your security code?"

"No. You told me I have to change it monthly, remember? Whenever I give her the key, I give her the current code. But it changes so often that she couldn't use it to come when I'm not there."

At his disbelieving look, Kay shook her head. "I've known Sasha since elementary school. She's the sweetest girl ever and we've been through way too much together. She would never hurt me."

"People do things that would surprise you."

She gave him a pointed look, remembering his *friends don't see each other naked* comment. "Believe me, I know. Now, it's time for me to go home. It seems I have a date."

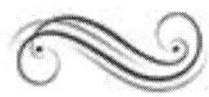

THE RESTAURANT DANNY had chosen was an Indian place nestled in the Harper's Creek neighborhood of Newport News. As Eli pulled into a space on the far end of the parking lot, Kay turned in her seat to face him. This time she'd gone for the basic black dress she wore whenever she needed a confidence boost and had pulled her hair back in a loose knot. She hadn't spent much time primping, instead going over security protocols with Eli. There would *not* be a repeat of last time.

"You're going to wait at the bar, right?"

He nodded wordlessly.

"And you won't use that listening device unless you really have to?"

His head dipped in another barely perceptible nod. "I plan to have my eyes on you the whole time, but if anything obstructs my vision, I'll listen periodically just to be sure you're okay."

Kay relaxed slightly.

Danny was waiting for her at the front of the restaurant. He looked more like a lawyer now in a crisp gray suit, and his brown hair appeared to have been tamed with a brush and some gel. She accepted a quick hug and then they walked into the dim interior of the restaurant together.

"I've never been here before," she commented.

He stopped right before they reached the hostess stand. "Wow. I probably should have asked if you like Indian food before I made the reservation. I really hope you don't have a sensitive stomach."

Kay waited as he gave his name to the hostess. They followed the waitress to a booth in the back. She slid out of her coat and folded it on the seat next to her. Once Danny was seated, she answered him.

"I love all different types of food. There's a tiny Indian restaurant in Norfolk that my best friend loves. She orders takeout from there all the time and got me hooked on it."

He visibly relaxed and sat back in the booth. "Great. I didn't even think. I guess it's obvious that I don't get out much."

"I don't either. Don't feel alone."

After the waitress told them about the specials, Kay allowed Danny to recommend a few things. She'd only had a creamy butter chicken dish that Sasha favored and something made with curry.

"This is going to be fun. My friend always orders the same things, so it'll be exciting to try a few new dishes."

"I usually order the same things, too. I'm feeling adventurous lately." His eyes settled on her again and it wasn't at all unpleasant. Then he broke off a piece of the naan bread on the table and popped it in his mouth. "So, tell me about the album you're working on."

Kay relaxed as their conversation turned to the places she'd had singing gigs, which segued into a conversation about travel. Not that she had much to contribute on that topic, but Danny had lots of fun stories about his last visit to his grandparents in Poland and a drunken bachelor party in Vegas. Their food came and he offered her samples of the various items on his plate.

I could really like this guy, she thought.

The possibility would definitely have been there under different circumstances. Especially if she weren't pining after someone else who might or might not be listening to their entire conversation.

Kay turned her head slightly, then tensed when she noticed Eli sitting at the bar. He lifted his chin slightly when their eyes met. She whipped around and hoped that Danny hadn't noticed. After what she'd put him through last time, the least he deserved was to have her full attention tonight.

"So, who is he?" Danny scooped up a bite of food and then looked at her quizzically. "Someone you loved and lost or someone you never had?"

"What?" It was a struggle not to spit out the bite of spiced chicken she'd just taken. Kay chewed carefully and then took a sip of her water.

"The man you've been thinking about this entire time. Who is he?"

Kay started to protest but stopped when Danny propped

his head on his fist and smiled at her. "It's okay. You don't have to answer if you don't want to."

"How did you know?" Kay finally said.

His eyes returned to his own plate. "Like recognizes like. There should be a club for the heartbroken."

Kay craned her neck slightly until Eli came into view. He still sat at the bar. He'd promised not to listen in unless it was absolutely necessary and she believed him. There was never any doubt in her mind that she could trust him. He would do what he'd said he would.

"The guy you met last time."

Danny's eyes lit up with recognition. "Ah. That makes sense. I figured there was way more behind that story."

Kay stabbed a piece of chicken. "I'm not sure there is a story at all. I just can't seem to stop hoping for something that will never happen, that's all. I'm not sure I'd call that a story. Unless it's a tragedy."

Danny leaned forward. "Look, I'm not exactly the right person to give out relationship advice, but do you love that guy?"

Her eyes were drawn back to Eli again. As her gaze soaked up his familiar profile, the wide breadth of his shoulders, the intense set of his jaw, she shivered. Was this love? How could she possibly know that? Tim had made her feel special, had seemed to appreciate the things about her that no one else cared about. She'd thought that was love. Look where that had gotten her.

But had she ever felt this strongly for Tim? She couldn't imagine him throwing himself in harm's way to protect her. But, without a doubt, she believed that Eli would always put himself between her and danger. Not just because it was his job to protect others, but because he cared about her.

"I'm not sure," she said finally.

Danny didn't look convinced. "But the fact that you had to think about it tells me that you probably care about him a lot."

Kay shrugged. "Yeah, but that doesn't make it any easier to figure it out."

He pointed at the breadbasket. "Eat. Trust me, the feelings aren't going away overnight, so we might as well try to enjoy our lives in the meantime. Even if we're both thinking of other people, it doesn't mean we can't have a good time."

That was a philosophy that Kay could get behind. She broke off a piece of bread and chewed methodically. She was going to have fun on this date if it killed her.

Chapter Nine

ELLIOTT TOOK ANOTHER sip of water and tried not to choke. He'd had Indian food a handful of times before, but he didn't remember it being quite this spicy. Although, the churning in his gut could just as easily be jealousy as indigestion.

Kay and her date were in the midst of spirited conversation. They seemed to have hit it off if the guy's wide smile and animated hand gestures were any indication. The sinking feeling in his chest was almost as hard to ignore as the burning sensation on his tongue.

Too bad a cold glass of water wouldn't help soothe his heart.

A waiter appeared at his elbow. "Excuse me, sir. Are you the owner of a black Yukon?"

"Yes, I am."

"Is this your license plate?" He held out a piece of paper with a number jotted down in blue ink.

Eli recognized his plate number and grimaced. "Yes it is. Am I parked illegally or something?"

"No, sir. Your lights are on. Another patron noticed it in the parking lot and let us know."

Eli nodded his thanks. It was incredibly odd because his truck had automatic lights. He rarely turned the lights on manually unless he needed his brights on one of the dark country roads bordering his parents' property. There hadn't been any reason to use them on the way here.

Reluctantly, he stood and activated the audio feed. Instantly Kay's voice was in his ear. He folded his napkin and placed it in his seat. When the waiter moved to leave, he held up his hand. "Actually, could I order another dinner? Something less spicy this time. Can you just do a plain chicken-and-rice deal?"

"Of course, sir. I'm sorry the meal wasn't to your liking. I'll bring another right away."

Eli tried to tune out Kay's voice, but it was nearly impossible. They were discussing books. Lawyer dude was talking about a literary festival coming up in the springtime. Eli swallowed, trying not to feel bitter. He hadn't even been able to get through more than a few pages of that book on her coffee table, so he doubted he'd be able to talk with her about anything she'd find interesting. He wasn't exactly good date material. All he'd be able to do was take her to the gun range and teach her to shoot. Hardly the stuff of romantic fantasy.

In the parking lot, Eli narrowed his eyes as he approached his truck. The lights weren't on. In fact, there were no lights anywhere in the back section of the lot. When they'd arrived, he'd deliberately parked directly beneath the light. Now that same light was conspicuously dark.

Still, he figured it couldn't hurt to check and make sure that nothing else was on. The last thing he wanted was to come out here in the next hour to a drained battery. Just before his hand connected with the door handle, Kay's voice blared though his earpiece.

"Oh no! Get it off me!"

He spun around and dashed for the door of the restaurant, cursing himself the whole way. He shouldn't have left Kay behind, even for a moment. Then behind him he heard a curious ticking. Instant recognition flowed though him and he threw himself to the side behind another parked car.

The air behind him exploded and it sounded like the world was being ripped apart.

Eli had instinctively dropped into a ball, but he tugged his jacket closer over his head as debris, metal, and ash rained down. His hearing cut out for a second as the air grew hot, then came back in a roaring wave. A flaming piece of debris floated down to land right next to his hand.

After a moment, he chanced a look around. The door to the restaurant burst open and people streamed out, cell phones held aloft to capture pictures of the scene. A mother held her children closer, trying to soothe their cries. A distant siren approached. All Eli could think of was getting to Kay. He pushed his way through the crowd, fighting against the tide of people trying to get out of the building.

The same waiter who'd brought the message stood in the middle of the bar area. Waiters scurried back and forth between them, yelling things to the man behind the bar. Eli pointed at him and yelled over the chaos, "You! Who gave you that message?"

The waiter looked frantic for a moment, then turned to run. Eli sprang forward and grabbed him by the collar. "Who gave you the message? Start talking."

"I don't know, I swear," the man babbled. "I didn't even answer the phone. One of the other servers gave me the message. We were all supposed to ask our tables and since I was working the bar, that's why I asked you."

Eli pushed him away and ran toward the back of the restaurant where Kay had been sitting. His eyes scanned every face until he saw her. His heart stopped for a moment, then it beat once, twice. Finally he could breathe again.

"Eli! What just happened?" Kay stood on the seat of her booth, trying to see over the crowd of people. Her date watched him with barely veiled curiosity. Eli nodded hello and then turned back to Kay.

"Some kind of explosion." He tugged on her hand until she hopped down. He reached into the booth and grabbed her coat and bag. "*Our car.* We need to leave."

Kay followed him as he dragged her by the hand toward the back of the restaurant. "Where are we going?"

"Back way. Come on."

He dodged fallen chairs and frantic people and pushed through the doors leading to the kitchen. It was a den of chaos, people running in every direction. They moved through the narrow lanes until they reached the back door. He shoved his shoulder against the heavy door and they stepped out into the cold air. The door led to an alley with a few dumpsters. He glanced in both directions and then pulled her to the left.

"If my memory is correct, we should hit a major road if we go this way."

Kay didn't speak, just trotted to keep up. A few minutes later, they emerged onto Jefferson Avenue.

"I must have touched the door handle."

"What?"

"The handle. I was given a message that my lights were on. I was walking to the car to check it out. But just as I touched the door handle, I heard you say "Oh no" and so I turned and ran back to the restaurant. That's when it blew." The bomb must have been on a pressure sensor. If he'd taken Kay back to the truck, they'd be dead.

Kay stopped walking suddenly. "Someone blew up our truck?" Her voice wavered a bit before she brushed her hand against her cheek. "Someone wanted to blow us up?"

He recognized the beginning stages of shock. He put his arm around her and steered her in the right direction. "We have to keep moving, angel." He pulled out his phone and sent a message to Nick. His brother responded immediately and his shoulders sagged.

"Our ride is on the way."

They needed time to get to a safe location, and he needed to start making calls. It wouldn't take local police long to figure out who the car belonged to, but Agent Harris could shut the investigation down all the way from the nation's capital. Then he could start the important work of unraveling Kay's life to figure out what the hell was going on.

One thing he knew for sure was they couldn't stay in Kay's usual environment. They didn't have the advantage here. They needed a place to hide out and regroup. This guy would start to make mistakes when he was forced out of his comfort zone.

It was time to take things to Eli's turf.

ELI FORCED THEM to keep walking, pulling the hood up on Kay's coat to shield her face. His phone buzzed in his pocket. "Yeah."

"I'm right around the corner. Where are you?"

Eli glanced behind them, looking for Nick's dark sedan. It was early evening and there was a respectable amount of traffic. It was impossible to tell who was near them. The thought made him pull Kaylee a little closer. Anyone could be out here. He'd deliberately left through the back of the restaurant, but he had no idea who they were dealing with. Or *how many* people they were dealing with. It wasn't out of the realm of possibility that they'd been followed.

"We're walking east on Jefferson Avenue." He glanced up and rattled off the street number of the store next to them.

"I'm right there. Hang tight."

They weren't far from Jackson's studio. He'd briefly considered walking over to see if Jackson or his assistant was there but in the end decided against it. For whatever reason, this battle had just been kicked into high gear. He didn't want anyone he cared for caught in the cross fire.

Kay shivered next to him, tremors wracking her body so hard Eli could feel them through the layers of their coats.

"Hey, it's going to be all right. Come here." He rubbed a brisk hand up and down her back. She'd been quiet the whole time they were walking.

Too quiet.

"Kay, I'm not going to let anything happen to you. As soon as my brother gets here, we're going into hiding."

She nodded against his chest, her face brushing against the exposed skin of his neck. "I know. I just can't believe this is happening. I've never hurt anybody. But someone out there wants me dead enough to put a bomb under our car."

Eli's arms tightened around her. He pulled out his cell phone.

Agent Harris had been the bane of his existence for years, but there were certain advantages to being on the FBIs radar. They'd used him for information for years, and it was only recently that they'd made significant progress locating members of the Circle. The group was now suspected of being a huge part of the influx of cocaine into the country, and his intel had helped them find several cells and infiltrate them. They needed him alive. He wasn't above using that if it would help him keep Kay safe.

He dialed and Harris answered on the first ring. He didn't bother with a greeting. "I don't know if this is related to what you sent me, but someone just blew up my car."

"Your location?"

"My hometown. I need you to keep my name out of that police report." The last thing they needed was the New Haven Police Department splashing his name and picture around as a person of interest in a bombing case.

"Done. Did you see anyone beforehand? Or notice anything out of the ordinary?"

"No. But then again, you and I both know if this is our friends, then I wouldn't have seen anything. They're too good."

"You need somewhere to stay?"

"No. I've got that covered." Eli hung up as a black Mercedes sedan pulled up to the curb next to them. Kaylee inched behind him, her fingers digging into the sleeve of his jacket. The window rolled down and Nick's face appeared. "Need a ride?"

Kay let out a soft sigh. "Hi, Nick."

Eli opened the door for her and ushered her into the back. He glanced behind him, his eyes roving over the people and buildings on the street. Was someone following them even now? A woman walked by with several shopping bags, and Eli peered at her. When she noticed his gaze, her fingers clutched her bags tighter as she scampered away. He ducked his head and folded himself into the front seat.

"Still driving this clown car, I see." Eli rolled his shoulders in the tight space, feeling like he'd bump out a window if he raised his arms too high. His brother liked his toys. Eli preferred his truck any day. The truck which was now blown to pieces in a restaurant parking lot. He sighed.

Nick patted the steering wheel as he pulled out into traffic. "Don't talk about my baby that way."

Eli snorted and then turned to look into the backseat. Kay sat behind Nick, curled up against the window. When their eyes met, she smiled tremulously, almost as if trying to reassure him. His chest tightened. She was holding up better than he'd expected, but she shouldn't have to be this strong. She was the kind of woman meant for cozy nights by the fire and cuddling under soft sheets. Not running from danger and matching wits with criminals.

It was no doubt going to come back to haunt him asking for Agent Harris' help, but if making them think he was the target meant they'd use their resources to find the guy faster, so be it. He had no problem with a little creative restructuring of events if it meant Kay was safe. What if she'd gone out to the car with him? She could have died.

More blood on his hands. Another life he couldn't save.

LATER, KAY WOULDN'T be able to recall exactly how she'd spent the next few hours. She remembered Nick picking them up and Tank being at the Alexanders' house when they'd arrived. It had crossed her mind then just how calm everyone else seemed. Nick hadn't acted as though anything had occurred outside of the ordinary. They could have been calling him for a ride for any reason. Tank was polite and direct, just as he usually was, although he'd seemed to have a gentler manner when speaking to her than usual.

Eli himself had been at his gruff best, barking out orders on his cell phone to she could only guess who. There seemed to be no end to what he could make happen with just a phone call. Within a short period, he had a new black SUV delivered to them along with a suitcase full of clothes for Kaylee. She'd opened the bag, shocked to see her own things. Whoever had packed her stuff had also included things for Hope, including pajamas, diapers, and wipes.

They'd driven to her parents' house to pick up Hope. She definitely remembered her mother's shock and dismay at the news that they were leaving town.

"We don't even know this young man. I know he's been working to protect you, but this seems so drastic."

"Mom, we have to take drastic steps. Someone put a bomb under our car. It's not safe for me to stay in the open." Kaylee had reached over to take Hope from her mother.

"And where will you be sleeping?"

"Mom! I'm sure there will be plenty of room wherever we're going. This isn't… it's not like that."

Henrietta had placed her hands on her hips, making Kay feel like a teenager who'd been late for curfew.

"I'm not so old that I don't know what's what," she scolded. "A man and a woman alone together is just asking for trouble. Think about how this looks. You're just so impulsive, Kaylee. I don't want you to do something else you'll regret."

Kay hadn't had the mental energy to reassure her mother. Their car had just been blown up. Something her mom didn't seem to be taking all that seriously if her only concern was whether Kay was running off to "shack up" with some man.

No matter what she did, her mother would always assume the worst. She shivered and pulled her coat closer. In her mother's eyes, her life was defined by her mistakes. She'd trusted the wrong man and ended up pregnant and unmarried. In Henrietta's world, that was something shameful. Something to be hidden. Nothing she could do now would ever make up for embarrassing her mother in front of her conservative church friends.

It was a chilling thought to realize that she'd never be good enough.

"Are you cold?" Eli turned up the heat and pointed the air vent in her direction.

"I'm okay," she whispered. Hope had been restless the first hour of the trip, whimpering and crying the entire time. She'd finally settled for banging her teething ring against the side of her car seat. Kay was afraid to talk too loud and attract the baby's attention again. Her head was still ringing from the past hour of crying.

"Who knew about your date tonight?" Eli took her hint and lowered his voice to a near whisper as well.

"No one, really. Danny, of course. I told Sasha and I also e-mailed Mara and Ridley about it, too." She fell silent. It wasn't hard to understand why he was asking the question. It would have taken some planning to put an explosive under their car in the short time they were in the restaurant. Someone had to have known where they'd be and planned ahead.

Only she hadn't even known about her date until today. It had been a last-minute thing, after all.

"Danny asked me to dinner over e-mail today. It wasn't something we'd planned in advance. What if I hadn't gone tonight? Would they have blown up my apartment, instead?"

"It's possible." Despite his harsh words, Eli's face was gentle as he turned to her. "I'm sorry, Kay."

Tears welled in her eyes. She'd initially balked at the idea of going into hiding. It was so drastic, to just up and leave her job, family, and friends.

But Eli's argument had been simple yet persuasive. If she stayed, her family and friends would be in the crosshairs.

Leaving was safer for them.

Kay turned her face to the window, watching the faint shadows of the trees pass by in the darkness. She wasn't entirely sure where they were, just that they were on Interstate 95 on the way to Eli's house in Northern Virginia. With every mile they traveled, they drove farther away from all the things she knew and cared about.

Just a few days ago, her biggest worry was finishing her album and saving enough money to start a college fund for Hope. There were days when she'd grown frustrated, of course, but she had so many things in her life that kept her grounded. Her daughter, her friends and family. Her songwriting. Now she had no idea what she was. Rootless. Homeless. With one act, some faceless person had taken away her foundation.

She'd been working on lyrics in the car on the way to the restaurant earlier. All she could think about was that notepad, blown to ash and scattered to the wind.

Just like the rest of her life.

Chapter Ten

~⌒~

WHEN THEY PULLED up to the single-story bungalow with blue shutters, Kay's first thought was that Eli was stopping at a friend's house. It wasn't until he grabbed their bags and then pulled out his keys that she figured out where they were.

It had to be Eli's house.

She carefully unhooked Hope's car seat from its base and followed him, eager to see the inside. When she'd imagined Eli at his place, she'd expected something more modern. A cool condo or one of the newer-construction homes that all looked the same with perfectly square lawns. This little house looked homey and inviting. It looked like a family with a toddler and a dog should live there, not a bachelor.

Then Kay realized with a chill that perhaps Eli'd had a family at one time. She'd never asked him if he'd been married or engaged before.

After opening the door, Eli keyed something into a security panel next to the door. Then he motioned for Kay to follow him inside. "Home sweet home. Make yourself comfortable."

Kay set the baby carrier next to the stairs and shrugged out of her coat. Eli took it and hung it on the banister. After whimpering in the car for the first hour of the trip, Hope was finally sound asleep, so Kay wasn't in any hurry to disturb her just yet.

"So this is your house."

Eli grunted a reply and walked off, leaving her by herself. Kay huffed out a breath. Then she pulled out her cell phone to call Sasha. If she didn't let her friend know she was out of town, she might come by the house or her job. She didn't want her to worry. After a quick conversation, she hung up and looked around.

If Eli wasn't going to offer her a tour, she would just be nosy and show herself around.

The dining room had a simple table and chairs but no mirror on the wall or decorations of any kind. There was a small living room on the other side of the stairs, similarly barren of furniture and decorations. It smelled like it had been recently painted. She turned around and followed the sound of Eli's voice until she found him in a bright, modern kitchen. Kay perked up at the sight. The surfaces gleamed and the appliances looked brand new.

"Wow, this is a nice kitchen. Do you like to cook?" Kay hopped up on one of the barstools at the island.

Eli looked amused at the question. "Not really. It's more of a necessity than a joy. I just redid the kitchen because I plan on selling the house soon."

"Oh. You mentioned you were moving back home at Christmas, but I wasn't sure how soon you were planning to come back."

"As soon as the house sells."

He didn't offer any other information so Kay shifted uncomfortably on her stool.

"Let me show you how the security system works."

Kay hopped down and followed Eli to a small panel in the living room, next to a hallway. It looked just like the one near the front door. Her arm accidentally brushed up against him and he shifted slightly, bumping against her full breasts. Eli looked pained.

"Sorry. Um, anyway this is where you enter the security code. I'm an early riser, so you won't have to disarm it most of the time. The only time you should have to worry about it is if you need to get something from the kitchen in the middle of the night. The motion detectors cover the main living area and the kitchen. If you don't disable the alarm first, you'll set it off."

Kay nodded and repeated the code aloud several times. "I really hope I don't forget it."

"I'll quiz you later today to make sure you remember it. Now, let's get your bags and get you settled in your room."

Eli retrieved her bags from the entryway and then walked down the hallway that she assumed led to the bedrooms. Kay followed silently, peering into the open door of the first room they passed. It was a nice size. She could put Hope in there. Eli stopped at a door at the end of the hall and opened the door. She followed him into a room with a queen-sized bed, a dresser, and a night table. He set her bags on the floor.

"I'm right across the hall if you need anything."

Kay turned and stared at the closed door behind her. "Oh, that's close. Do I get a tour?"

Eli's lips curled up. "No." Then he walked out.

Typical Eli.

A soft cry rang out from the front of the house. She trotted back up the hallway and reached her daughter just as she scrunched up her face to let out a full-on wail.

"Let's get you settled so you can stretch out." She checked Hope's diaper and then carried her into the family room. Mrs. Alexander had given them a portable gate system to take along, so a few minutes later she had a sizable section of the room blocked off.

After settling Hope in the middle of the gated area with her teething ring and a set of soft, squishy blocks, Kay looked in the refrigerator. She pushed aside a six-pack of beer and a package of browning celery. "Okay then. I guess I'm not hungry."

"My assistant is bringing groceries. I asked her to pick up the basics for us. I was expecting her to do it before we arrived." The doorbell rang. "This should be her now," Eli said and walked up front.

Kay heard the door open and felt the telltale cold draft of air. She heard the other woman before she saw her, her voice soft and husky as she fussed at Eli about something or other.

When she entered the kitchen, Kay's heart sank. The other woman was beautiful. Not that she'd expected anything different. Slim with long, toned legs and large breasts, she was exactly the type of woman a man like Eli would go for.

When she looked at Kaylee with assessing eyes, it became clear exactly why she hadn't delivered the groceries earlier.

"Kay, this is my assistant, Carly. Carly, this is Kaylee Wilhelm." His phone rang and he snatched it off his belt. "Excuse me for a moment." Then he disappeared into the front hallway.

Carly didn't speak, just stood staring at Kaylee. After a few awkward moments, Kay pulled the first grocery bag toward her. It was filled with all the staple items like milk, bread, eggs, and raw ground beef. She'd even purchased snack food. When Kay pulled out the package of chocolate-chip cookies, she decided she didn't even care that the other woman was obviously lusting after Eli. After all, it wasn't as if she could fault the girl for her taste.

"Thank you so much for bringing the groceries. It would have been hard for us to go out with the baby." Kay grabbed a few more items and started stacking things in the empty refrigerator.

"Baby? What baby?" Carly eyed her suspiciously.

Kay pointed to the living room where Hope was standing on her tiptoes, trying to see over the side of the baby gate. "Peek-a, Peek-a!" she squealed when she caught sight of the newcomer.

"She's trying to say peekaboo, I think. She always does

that when she sees someone new." Kay pulled out the nonperishable items and stored them in the small pantry.

"Oh, well that's adorable," Carly admitted grudgingly.

Eli appeared in the doorway then. "Thanks for bringing the food, Carly. Is there anything you need me to sign?"

Carly glanced back at Kay once more before she pulled a sheaf of papers from her tote bag. "Yes, just a few things."

Eli scanned each page before scrawling his name at the bottom. When he got to the last page, he signed it and handed the whole stack back. "That should do it. Remember, I don't want anyone at HQ to know I'm back in town. It won't be for long."

"Oh? You're going back home again then?" There was no disguising the disappointment in the other woman's voice.

Kay turned back to the refrigerator and fiddled with the containers she'd just placed in there. Even though she didn't want to leave the other woman alone with Eli, it didn't mean she didn't empathize with her. She knew exactly what it felt like to want a man, all the while knowing he was way out of your league.

Although she didn't really understand why the other woman was acting threatened by her being here. His assistant was slim and pretty with the kind of body that Kaylee could only wish for. If that wasn't good enough for Eli, then her own chances with him were officially less than zero.

"I'll be going back home soon, yes. I'm not sure when though. Either way, I won't be accessible by phone or e-mail for a while. Just tell everyone I'm on vacation."

"Vacation?" The incredulity in her voice was hard to miss. "But you *never* go on vacation. Not really. You were checking e-mails on Christmas." There was a long silence before she said, "I guess you really are going home."

Kay didn't turn around until she heard the front door close quietly. Eli still stood at the counter, his shirtsleeves pushed up to reveal his thick forearms. His eyes rose to hers. "Sorry about that."

"When did you guys break up?"

A small smile tugged at the edges of his lips. "Was it that

obvious? I should have known you'd catch on. Smart girl."

Kay ignored the sharp thrill of pleasure his words brought. She shouldn't care so much that Eli thought she was smart. "I have some experience with being rejected."

Eli stood up straight, his jaw tight. "I hope you're not comparing me to the asshole you were dating last summer?"

"No. You're nothing like Craig. I'm just saying that even when the guy is trying to let you down easy, it still hurts to want something you can't have."

Eli came over and planted a hand on the counter next to her, blocking her in. Kay took a deep breath and then immediately regretted it. He was so close and he smelled so *good*. Now she would have his scent on her brain for the rest of the night.

"Kay, about the other night—"

She held up a hand to stop him. "I think we've already said all we need to say. You're not interested in settling down. I get it."

He opened his mouth to protest, then seemed to think better of it. "Like I said, it's just not possible."

"I think we have different ideas about what that word means. You say not possible, but I say not interested. And that's okay."

Eli regarded her with a tense look before he finally gave a sharp nod. "I set up the playpen in the third bedroom already. My mom sent along some sheets and baby blankets in case you need those."

"Thank you. I've just been putting her in warm pajamas. Then I don't stay up all night terrified that she'll get tangled up in a lot of bedding."

Eli followed behind her as she carried Hope down the hall.

"I'm going to rock her for a while. It'll probably take her a little longer to fall asleep since we're in a new place."

"Okay. Don't forget, the motion detectors will be on tonight, so you'll need to disable it to walk around during the night."

"I doubt I'll be walking around. I didn't realize until just now how tired I am."

"Goodnight, Kay."

He stood in the hallway watching her until she closed the door.

ELI TURNED OVER for the hundredth time and punched the pillow on the empty side of the bed. This was the only one of his residences where clients weren't allowed. What the hell had he been thinking to bring her here?

Oh right. He hadn't been thinking. That was it. He'd been running on pure, unbridled instinct.

It had been late by the time they'd arrived, so he hadn't expected Kay to ask to see his room. Now he had to field her questions about everything. She'd want to know why there were no decorations anywhere. Why he didn't have any personal items in the house.

Why he kept his bedroom door locked?

"Damn. I might as well get up at this rate." He shoved the heavy comforter back and swung his legs over the side of the bed. Shadows fell across the bedspread. He'd opened the curtains before going to bed to allow the silvery light of the moon to illuminate the room.

A black robe hung over the end of the bed, so he stuck his arms through the sleeves and belted it at the waist. She'd said she wouldn't be roaming the house, but he'd wear it just in case. He'd held himself in check when she'd caught him half-naked at her apartment. It wouldn't be so easy for him to do that in his own space with an inviting king-size bed only a few feet away.

The hallway was quiet and dark, the only sound the pad of his feet as he walked. He punched in the security code and waited until the lights flashed green before he entered the living room. It was colder out here, the wood floor under his feet like a block of ice. He crossed the room quickly and entered the kitchen. Carly had brought a wide range of items, so he could always make himself a sandwich or at the very least have a glass of milk. He opened the refrigerator and pulled out several items.

When he looked up, Kay stood at the entrance to the kitchen. He took a step forward and then stopped. She wore a long T-shirt and nothing else. As his body tightened at the sight of her legs, he was suddenly immensely happy he'd worn the thick robe.

"Sorry, did I wake you?"

She shook her head and walked into the kitchen. "No. I couldn't sleep. Then I heard you moving around. You can't sleep either, huh?"

"No. But then again, we did narrowly miss being blown up, so it's not that surprising that we're both still a little wound up."

Her sigh could be heard from across the room. "Yeah, there is that." She pulled at the edges of her T-shirt, frowning down at it as if suddenly aware that she was talking to him while only half-dressed.

It hit him then, why she was standing there in his kitchen wearing nothing but a T-shirt. She wasn't trying to drive his libido crazy or mess with his head. Kay wasn't the type to play those games. She was sweet. She was honest.

She was also probably scared out of her mind.

He dropped the milk carton on the counter with a thump. "Kay, I'm going to figure out who is behind this. I'm going to figure it out, and then I'm going to nail the bastard. He won't touch you or Hope."

She nodded, but her smile didn't quite reach her eyes. "I know."

"You're safe here. You don't have to be afraid," Eli continued. It was one thing to know intellectually that you were going to be okay, but knowing it and feeling it wasn't the same thing. He knew that from experience. Sometimes you just needed to hear someone say it.

Suddenly she sprang forward and curled against his chest. He forgot all his prior warnings and rules and resolutions to stay away from her. In that moment she needed comfort, and he'd give her everything he had if it would make things right.

"I know things are happening really fast. This is scary and everything seems out of control. But I want you to know that I won't let anybody hurt you."

She looked up at him, her brown eyes wide. "Can we just sit out here on the couch for a little while?"

He grinned. "Yeah. I'm not tired anyway."

They sat on the couch and Kay curled against his side and tucked her legs underneath her. He turned on the television and they laughed along with the old *I Love Lucy* reruns playing on one of the cable channels. She fell asleep against his chest, her hand curled in a fist right over his heart.

When he carried her to the guest room bed, she never woke up.

THE NEXT DAY, to Kay's surprise, Eli didn't mention their late-night cuddle fest. She'd emerged from her room in the morning, sure that things would be awkward, but he'd simply said good morning and offered her some toast. It was strange that he was acting like it hadn't happened, but she couldn't deny that she was grateful because she still wasn't sure exactly what had happened. One minute she'd been in her room staring at the ceiling, and then she'd suddenly needed to see him. Needed to know she wasn't alone.

She certainly hadn't meant to fall asleep on him.

After breakfast, Eli had shown her where everything was and took her and Hope for a walk around the neighborhood. Kay was surprised that he was allowing them out of the house, but he said it was important for her to know her surroundings. Later, Kay made a quick pot of spaghetti for lunch and then started prepping the ground beef to make meatloaf for dinner.

Eli had disappeared after their walk to make some calls. She'd tried to find some music to put on to give her something to listen to instead of the oppressive quiet of an unfamiliar house but couldn't find a stereo system. There wasn't much in the house in the way of personal items at all. No books on the coffee table, magazines in the bathroom, or shoes under the table.

Eventually she'd stopped her shameless snooping and just turned on the television in the family room to give her some background noise. They hadn't brought a high chair for Hope, so she'd held the squirming baby on her lap and fed her.

A door opened in the hallway and Kay looked up eagerly when Eli appeared at the edge of the kitchen.

"Something smells good." He sounded so bewildered by the fact that Kay smiled.

"Yeah, it's meatloaf. It should be ready in a few minutes. Actually, you can take it out of the oven now."

Eli picked up the oven mitt she'd left on the counter and pulled the pan from the oven. He set it on the stovetop carefully.

"I haven't had meatloaf since I was a kid."

Kay settled Hope back in her play area and then walked over to the stove. She stuck a knife in the top, relieved when it slid out easily.

"Your assistant brought several pounds of ground beef, so I figured we'd better use them."

He helped her set the table and she filled their plates. Sitting across from each other at the table, they ate in silence until Eli finally spoke.

"I didn't know meatloaf could be this good. Don't tell my mom I said that though."

Kay grinned, ridiculously pleased when he stood to get a second helping. "Thanks. It's one of my favorite things to make when it's cold outside. It's filling and hearty. My dad always said you need to eat food that sticks to your ribs in the wintertime. Not that I need anything else on my ribs."

Eli frowned at her. "Your ribs are perfect."

Her smile stuttered and melted under the force of his gaze. Good grief, the man had the ability to freeze her in her seat with those eyes.

"I'm going to have to plan some gym time this week. I'll definitely need it. I didn't know you were such a good cook." Eli sat down next to her again and shoveled in another mouthful.

Uncomfortable with the praise, Kay shrugged. "Yeah, I'm good with food." She looked down at her stomach. "Obviously. I probably need some gym time, too."

Eli put down his fork and grabbed her chair, dragging her closer. Kay squeaked at the sudden movement, then again when he put a gentle but firm finger under her chin. "Don't do that. I don't like it."

"Do what? I was just joking." She met his eyes, surprised at the barely concealed anger on his face.

"No, that's not joking. That's putting yourself down. My cousin Laura used to get teased a lot when we were kids. They called her awful names. One of them taped a picture of Miss Piggy over the mirror in her locker so it was the first thing she saw that morning. If she was having dinner with us, would you make that joke about her?"

Kay sank down in her chair, his gruff tone making her feel about two feet tall. She gulped and pushed the remaining scraps of food on her plate around with her fork. "Of course not."

He leaned closer. "Then don't say it about yourself."

Kay looked up at him then and nodded. "It's funny how it's so much easier to be nice to others than it is to be nice to yourself."

"I'll help you remember," he stated.

She had no doubt he meant every word. Thinking of herself negatively was second nature, but she'd have to make an effort to watch what she said around Eli.

He seemed to sense her discomfort because he forced a lighter tone when he said, "If I can make Walter Herman apologize to Laura, then I think I can handle you."

"How did you do that?"

"My fist in his face a few times took care of that problem." He held up his closed fist and shook it comically.

She giggled. "I definitely don't want that."

He started when she wrapped her fingers around his wrist. She rubbed the vein that stood out on the back of his hand, stroking over it a few times and trying to force it down. Now that she was so close, she could see that he had prominent veins on his arms, too.

Kay gulped. She wasn't used to seeing men with this much muscle up close. He looked like those guys on the fitness magazines. She pulled the edge of her sweater down to cover her belly and thighs. Eli's eyes narrowed at the action, then zeroed in on her neckline. She glanced down and saw that her tugging was exposing a shocking amount of cleavage.

"Oh, I should clean up." She popped up and started stacking their plates and the spare plate she'd used to hold bread. Eli stood too, silently helping her clear their drinking glasses and the silverware. They worked side by side, loading the dishwasher and wiping down the counters until finally the kitchen was clean.

"Where do you keep these cups?" Kay turned to Eli.

He turned around at the same time and they ended up face-to-face. She sucked in a breath as his lips brushed her forehead. They both froze, shocked into stillness at the sudden intimacy. Her body instantly warmed, all her nerves suddenly hypersensitive. A heavy fullness settled in her breasts, her nipples tightening almost to the point of pain. If he moved any closer or brushed up against her, she'd go up in flames. Or melt into a puddle.

"The universe is conspiring against me," Eli whispered.

Kay smiled, inordinately pleased at the idea of tormenting him. Why should he get off easy? She was walking around as a mass of shivery, fluttery hormones whenever he was near. It was vindicating to her feminine pride to see that he was struggling too. Although it would be so much more satisfying if neither of them had to struggle. If they could just...

Give. In.

Kay leaned forward slightly and sucked in a long, slow breath as she brushed up against him. He made a sound, a low growl in the back of his throat that made her panties go instantly damp.

"I'm going to go shower. And pray the water is cold enough," he muttered. "Good night, Kay."

"Good night, Eli." She didn't look at him as she said it. If she looked at him, she wasn't sure if she'd be able to keep it together. One look at that fierce face and she might decide she didn't give a crap about pride and beg him to put her out of her misery.

Or at the very least to give her another taste of what she was missing.

Chapter Eleven

THE NEXT DAY, Kay was in the kitchen cleaning up after breakfast when Eli found her. He'd changed into sweatpants and a tight muscle tee. His arms flexed against the thin fabric, straining the edges until they looked like they'd cry out for mercy. Kay almost dropped the dish towel she was holding. Heat swept through her as she tried desperately to look anywhere but at him. No one needed that kind of muscle. He was like an action figure come to life.

"I'm going to ask Tank to stay with you for a while. I really want to get a workout in."

Kay nodded. That made sense. A body like his required maintenance. And worship. She blew out a breath.

"Could I come with you? I'd love to get some exercise too. I can't do all the stuff you do, I'm sure, but maybe they have yoga. Or dance classes."

Eli looked surprised. "They do. They also have a daycare, so we could bring the baby. They give you a wristband that will vibrate if you need to come back to the nursery."

"That's pretty handy."

"I know." Eli shrugged. "It's one of the things I recommended they do when I redesigned their security system last year."

Kay felt a burst of pride. "Well, I feel completely safe taking Hope there, then."

His eyes flashed at her words. "Okay, meet me back here when you're changed and ready to go."

Kay dashed down the hall to her room. Since she hadn't packed her own bag, she had no idea if she had anything appropriate to wear for exercise. However, her purple fleece sweatpants were rolled into a ball and tucked into the corner of the bag along with a few sports bras and some T-shirts.

She sent up a silent prayer that whoever had done the packing had included several sports bras instead of just one. Due to her size, she always needed a double layer. Otherwise she wouldn't be able to do anything high-impact without putting out an eye. She giggled at the thought.

Eli was waiting for her in the kitchen. He looked up when she entered. "Ready to go?"

"Yeah, let me just grab some stuff for Hope." The diaper bag already had diapers and wipes, so she just added another outfit and a blanket. Then she leaned down and scooped up her daughter.

Eli appeared at her side with the car seat.

Kay smiled appreciatively. "You're getting the hang of this baby thing."

"I have a new respect for my mother after these past few weeks. And for you."

Kay's stomach tightened. "Thanks."

She buckled Hope into her seat and allowed Eli to carry her out to the car. He settled her car seat into the base like a pro and then rounded the car to the driver's side. Kay was fastening her own seatbelt when he spoke again.

"I'm glad you're coming with me. An old high school

friend teaches a dance class at this gym. If you want to learn about fitness, Janet is the perfect person to ask. She's got a great body."

It was impossible to miss the affection in his voice. Probably because he was so serious most of the time, it was even more obvious to see him light up now. Eli apparently still had a thing for this Janet.

"Let me guess, an old girlfriend?" Kay tried and failed to keep the interest out of her voice.

Eli's laugh rumbled through the interior of the vehicle. "I wish. She was way out of my league in high school. And she's happily married now. But I have no shame admitting that if she hadn't married her high school sweetheart, I would have eventually made a move. She's exactly my type."

Kay swallowed against the sudden lump in her throat. Why should she care if Eli was carrying a torch for some old classmate? A classmate who was apparently gorgeous and a great dancer. It wasn't like he was her boyfriend or even a casual date.

He was there with her because protecting people was his job. She was just the unlucky duck who'd attracted the attention of a psycho and needed protection. It shouldn't matter to her one way or the other if Eli thought this Janet was the best thing since sliced bread.

Right. Nothing to be jealous about at all.

KAY WALKED INTO the studio, shocked to see that the room was almost full. It was a wide space with bamboo flooring and large, open windows. Multicolored strobe lights pulsed with the beat of the salsa music blaring from the speakers.

After signing her in under a guest pass and getting Hope settled in the nursery, Eli had given her a quick tour of the multistory workout complex. By the time they looked at the schedule, he realized they were going to be late for the class she'd wanted to take. He'd seemed excited that it was one of Janet's classes and promised to introduce her afterward. Kay wasn't sure if she'd mustered up the appropriate level of faux-enthusiasm.

Just one more thing to look forward to, she thought. Not only was she going to dance around until she was a sweaty, exhausted mess, but she'd have to meet the perfect Janet afterward. Maybe she should have just stayed home.

Tank would have left her in peace to read a book.

"Okay class, let's get started," a voice yelled out. The other students lined up in rows. Everyone chatted excitedly as the music turned up even louder. After storing her things in one of the cubbyholes at the back of the room, Kay took a place off to the side. Several students were stretching their arms overhead and doing dance steps to limber up. Kay hadn't checked to see if this was a beginner's class, so she could only hope she'd be able to keep up. She wasn't much of a dancer and definitely wasn't a triathlete like some of the other women in the class appeared to be.

"Welcome, ladies, to Zumba!"

There were three teachers at the front of the room. The instructor who spoke was thin and blond with very perky breasts. The one to her left was curvy with wild, curly hair. She looked biracial like Ridley and Raina. The one on the right was the same shade of skin as Kaylee and had a similar body shape with full breasts and wide hips. Even though it shouldn't have mattered, the sight made Kaylee feel better. At least this dancing stuff wasn't only for skinny girls. Maybe she could do this.

"It's time to move those feet. Let's warm up." The blond instructor started stretching right to left. The class mimicked her movements.

Kay clutched her towel and energy drink in trepidation as she copied the movement. This was a lot more intimidating than she'd expected. She'd envisioned a few people in a room dancing. Not a huge crowd that looked like extras from a music video. At least she was in the back, so hopefully no one would notice her awkward moves.

Absently Kay wondered if the blond woman was Janet. Eli had made a comment over Christmas that he was glad she didn't look like Raina, so she assumed the girl on the left wasn't his type. However, she'd caught him checking out her chest more than once, and the blond woman looked like she'd had some surgical enhancements in that area. Plus the blonde had that perfect, thin body with the gap between the thighs. She looked like she spent as much time in the gym as Eli obviously did.

Exactly the kind of body that Eli would think was perfect.

The tempo of the music picked up and Kay stumbled as the whole class executed a turn. She picked up her feet and tried to emulate the way the person in front of her was moving. Was it left, right, left? Or right, left, right?

Just when she thought she had it, the whole class turned in the opposite direction and Kay stumbled into the person next to her.

"Sorry!"

The girl didn't even seem to hear her because she was turning in the other direction. Her breath was coming faster now and not just due to embarrassment. Her lungs burned and her thighs ached. How was everyone else moving their feet so fast?

Kay moved to the side to get a better view of the instructors. To her shock and surprise, the teacher on the right was moving and shaking better than the skinny instructors. Kay watched, mesmerized, as she executed each step with perfect grace. Her hips seemed to have a seductive sway to them. Kay looked down at her own body and swung her hips. Some of the steps were easier when she put her hips into it.

Maybe she could enjoy this after all.

ELI WAS IN the middle of a dead lift when the first call came in. After several rings, it went silent. He blew out a breath and squatted again. The phone beeped, indicating he

116

had a new voice mail. He ignored the sound and tightened his abdominals as he stood back up.

Eli gritted his teeth, relishing the burn and stretch of his muscles as he worked his back. He considered his body to be a machine, a tool in his arsenal just like his Beretta or his SUV. Honing it was part of his job and necessary so it would perform as needed. There were other "performance" benefits of a healthy body, as well. Not that they'd come in handy any time soon. Kay couldn't handle seeing his kind of endurance.

All the more reason he needed to work out his tension in the weight room.

When the phone started ringing again, he set the bar back on the rack and rummaged in his gym bag. He pushed aside a towel, an extra weight-lifting belt, and a change of clothes before he found it. He'd missed the call again. When he saw the caller ID, he hit the button immediately to call Tank back. He'd asked the man to contact him with any news about Hope's father. If he was calling now, it meant he must have found something.

"What have you got for me?"

"Hey, boss. I've been keeping tabs on Banner and something finally popped. It appears our guy thinks he has what it takes to be a senator."

Eli planted himself on an empty weight bench. "That's quite a jump for a guy who owns a bunch of strip malls."

"Exactly. The guy has no background in politics and few connections. What's a second-rate businessman doing running for congress?"

"I don't know, but I'm less worried about his chances in the polls and more concerned about what he's willing to do to make himself look good. Maybe he's worried about Kay running to the press with stories about him once he's in the public eye?"

"That seems likely. He hasn't announced his bid officially. This is all based on communications between him and his assistant."

"As soon as it's official let me know. He might step up his efforts to scare Kay into silence once he's officially running.

Maybe we'll get really lucky and he'll give us the evidence we need to hang him."

"Will do."

They hung up and Eli dropped his head into his hands. A quick glance at the time told him he only had about twenty minutes before the end of Kay's class. Not enough time for him to do much other than some curls. He usually only worked one body part at a time, but since his workout schedule had been so disrupted lately, maybe he could fit in some leg work as well. He was hampered by his need to stay within sight of the dance studio. From this part of the gym, he could see everyone going in and out. There was no way he'd have allowed Kay to go otherwise.

Now that he knew her ex had some pretty good reasons to want her out of the picture, he definitely wasn't leaving her alone. It would be pretty risky for him to try to hurt Kay when he was about to be in the public eye, but he'd seen people do crazier things. Especially when they saw someone as an obstacle to getting what they wanted.

Eli shook his head in disgust at the thought of a man trying to terrorize the mother of his child because she was inconvenient. His job had stripped away many of his illusions over the past decade, namely that anyone in politics had good intentions. He'd seen far too much of the ugly side of the political game.

There was no way he'd allow even a fraction of that to touch Kay or her daughter.

"Excuse me. Are you done with this?"

Eli turned, startled, at the voice next to him. An older man pointed at the machine he'd just finished using. He'd been sitting on the weight bench next to it, staring into space.

"Yes, sorry. Let me get these."

Eli lifted the heavy plates off the bar so the other man could get started, then moved to the next machine. He only had a short time until Kay's class was over, so he'd better make the most of it.

TWENTY MINUTES LATER, all Kay could think was that Zumba was a tool of the devil. Huffing and puffing, she edged her way to the corner of the room and slid down the wall into a heap. The rest of the class continued turning and stepping while she sucked on her energy drink and tried to pull more oxygen into her lungs.

It was tempting to just sneak out, but she didn't want Eli to see her and feel compelled to cut his own workout short. He'd been looking forward to this. His routine had been destroyed by protecting her. The least she could do was stick it out for the entire class.

Ten torturous minutes later, the class was over. Students milled around chatting. A few people smiled at Kay where she was still collapsed in a heap next to the wall.

She looked up to see Eli in the doorway. He'd pulled on an oversize sweatshirt, but he still looked like he was all muscle. The teachers all greeted him, but the blond one especially looked like she wanted to gobble him whole. Eli smiled at her and she placed a hand on his arm and leaned forward. She couldn't have gotten any closer unless she crawled inside his sweatshirt with him.

Guess I was right.

Eli motioned her over. Kay struggled to her feet, too tired to even care if they saw. She crossed the room, dodging the other students who milled in small groups, chatting and laughing.

"Kay, I want you to meet someone." Eli took her arm and pulled her against his side.

She immediately tried to pull back, not wanting him to feel how sweaty and gross she was. The blond instructor was still hovering near his elbow, so Kay fixed a smile on her face and turned toward her, ready to do the whole *hi-how-are-ya* thing, but to her surprise, Eli steered her in the opposite direction.

The brown-skinned girl with the seductive hips stepped

forward and pulled Eli into a hug. "Where have you been, stranger?"

Eli shrugged. "Around. I've had a couple of jobs in the southern part of the state. You know how it is."

"Unfortunately, I do." The girl turned to Kaylee with a friendly smile. "This must be the friend you were talking about. Hi, I'm Janet Reed." She stuck out her hand and Kay took it automatically.

"Um, hello," Kay said finally, sure she sounded like an idiot. But the other woman wasn't paying attention, already absorbed in a conversation with Eli about the recent changes he'd made to the gym's security system.

They tried to include her in the conversation, but Kay couldn't do much more than smile and make appropriately vague noises of agreement. Her mind was in too much of an uproar for her to make conversation. She surveyed the other woman with open curiosity. *This was Janet Reed?* The girl with the big hips and the even bigger smile? She glanced up at Eli. He didn't seem to notice her befuddlement because he was too busy chatting with Janet.

Finally Janet hugged Eli again and waved good-bye to Kay before trotting over to one of the other students. Eli watched her go with a wistful smile before turning to Kay. "Are you ready to go?"

She shrugged and took another pull of her energy drink, trying desperately to get her thoughts together. As they walked out of the gym toward the nursery to pick up Hope, she finally said, "So, that's *the* Janet Reed, huh?"

He winked and leaned down to whisper, "I told you she was perfect."

Chapter Twelve

~

"SO, DID YOU enjoy the class? It's pretty intense at first,"
Eli asked as they drove away from the gym, Hope safely
buckled into the backseat.

Kay shot him an incredulous look. "Intense is walking up
a few flights of stairs. That was taking my life in my hands. I
could barely breathe, and I didn't even do the whole class. It
was still fun though."

They shared a chuckle at the thought. He'd noticed her
slumped down in the corner when he'd first entered the studio
but had chosen not to mention it. He'd assumed she hadn't
enjoyed the class due to her murderous look when he'd first
seen her.

"Janet's been teaching dance classes for years. She always
loved to dance, even in high school."

He could feel Kay's eyes on him, but he didn't dare turn to

look at her. Just the heat of her gaze on his skin was dangerous enough.

Eli knew he'd shocked Kay. Her face was so expressive. She'd been completely stunned when he introduced her to Janet. She'd also seemed a lot more relaxed and comfortable after meeting her. Janet had given him a sly look behind Kay's back and a thumbs-up. She'd apparently figured out the real reason he'd wanted her to meet Kay. Not that he minded.

"That's your idea of perfect, huh?" she whispered.

He knew what she was really asking. If that was his idea of perfect, then how did he feel about her? Was she perfect?

"It is. Healthy, strong, curvy, and loving life. It doesn't get any better than that." His fingers tightened around the steering wheel, the truth making him feel uncharacteristically vulnerable. His answer was way too revealing, but Kay needed to hear it more than he needed to protect himself.

Kay was quiet for a few minutes. They turned off the highway and onto the quiet residential streets leading to his house.

"I need to understand why."

Her quiet plea got his attention. "What?"

"The why of it. I need to know why we can't be together. You can't just keep telling me that you're not good for me. Because as soon as you do that, you turn around and do things like this. Perfect things. Things that make me fall for you all over again."

Eli's heart banged an extra rhythm in his chest. The ache in her voice was a killer. Second only to the tears sparkling in her eyes.

"*Kay*—" Her name from his lips was a ragged plea. For her to stop, for her to keep going. Hell, he had no idea.

"Do you know what Danny and I were talking about in the restaurant that night? Before everything happened?" she interrupted. She turned from the window to face him. Damn, she was magnificent, so strong and resolute as she faced off with him.

He shook his head.

"We were talking about how much it sucks to have your

heart held hostage. To be stuck in a holding pattern, waiting to see if the person you care for will ever see you the same way. Will ever want you the same way."

"Wanting isn't the problem, Kay. It never has been. You know I want you. More than my next breath."

"Do you honestly think that helps? Knowing that you want me as much as I want you, but I still can't have you. It's torture, Eli. Telling me to move on doesn't make me forget. If you want me to have even a chance to move on, help me understand. Tell me what you've done that's so horrible." She looked at him and the tears in her eyes almost broke him. "It would be so much easier if I could hate you. Even just a little."

Eli realized then that he'd made a mistake keeping her in the dark. It had been nothing more than his own narcissism, his own egotistical desire to keep her love, to have her look at him like he was her hero, that had kept him silent. He had the means to help her get over him, and he'd just been too selfish to use it.

The truth. All he had to do was tell her the truth. She'd never look at him the same way again.

"You're right. I've been keeping things from you and that ends tonight. I'll tell you everything. Then you'll understand."

And she'd finally be free.

DINNER WAS MAINLY a silent affair. Kay shoveled in the chicken breast she'd sautéed, trying to hurry up and get to the part where he told her his story. They'd both showered and changed clothes as soon as they got home, and then Eli had disappeared while she made dinner. They hadn't spoken the entire time. Hope seemed to sense the tension because she was cranky and cried off and on while Kay was trying to feed her.

"Do you want some of mine?" Eli held out a small piece of chicken on his fork. To Kay's surprise, Hope immediately leaned forward.

"Careful," Eli crooned. He allowed Hope to take the bite

and then pulled back. "It's just a small piece. That's okay, right?"

Kay nodded. "I'm just surprised she took it. I always have to trick her into eating when she's cranky like this."

"I think it's just the novelty of having me feed her. Here, let me try." He held out his arms and Kay allowed Hope to crawl into his lap. He grinned down at the baby and fed her tiny pieces from his plate. Hope stared up at him the entire time, seemingly fascinated.

"Whoa, what is she doing?" Eli struggled to keep a grip on the baby as she squirmed in his arms. Finally, she turned over and then stood up, her tiny feet balancing on his thighs. She slapped two hands on his bald head and squealed. Delighted with this new toy, she patted his head again and then tried to move his head backward and forward.

Kay giggled along with her daughter. "I think she's fascinated with your head."

"I never thought I'd hear that from a woman." A rare smile crossed Eli's face and his deep chuckle rumbled through the room, the sound causing a bubble of joy to escape her own mouth.

How beautiful a sound to hear him laugh. It was the kind of thing dreams were made of, to have her daughter and the man she loved laughing and happy.

And she did love him, she thought. No matter what he told her, it wouldn't take away that obvious truth.

She loved his gentle heart, his tender way with her daughter, his firm refusal to allow anyone to put her down including herself. In that moment, Kay knew for certain that nothing he could tell her would change that.

They worked together, cleaning the table and the kitchen. By tacit unspoken agreement, neither brought up the conversation they knew was coming. It was like a last moment of calm before the storm. She just wanted to enjoy it. Because even though she knew it wouldn't change her feelings, there was no denying that whatever he'd done might impact their future. It was impossible not to speculate on what it could be. What if he was a drug addict? What if he'd killed people?

Kay bathed Hope in the hall bathroom and then rocked her until she fell asleep. She kissed the baby on her soft, fragrant cheek and then placed her carefully in the playpen. For a moment, she watched her sleep, her tiny features so peaceful. Peace was hard to come by lately.

When she left the room and emerged into the living room, Eli had dimmed the lights and a fire crackled cheerfully in the hearth. The flames threw soft light and shadows across the room.

Kay sat on the edge of the couch and waited. She heard Eli before she saw him. He entered the room from the kitchen and sat on the other end of the couch. It dipped under his weight, bouncing Kay slightly.

"I had just finished college when I met him," Eli said.

Kay turned her head at his statement. She was afraid to move or breathe wrong for fear that he'd stop. So she said nothing and just waited.

"I was only twenty-two. Only a little older than you are now. Thought I knew everything." He chuckled but she could tell he wasn't at all amused. There was a wealth of pain in the sound.

"His name was Justice. Or at least that's the name he went by then. There was nothing exceptional about him at first glance. He could have been anyone. He could blend into any crowd, fit in with any group. It wasn't until later that I learned it was a skill he'd learned and developed over the years. A skill that I would learn and develop as well."

He was quiet for a time, gazing into the fire and twisting his hands in his lap. There was just the soft crackle of the flames and the creak of his knuckles as he clenched and released his fingers.

"The first time I went with him on a mission, it was to break into a local gang's hideout. They were into running just about anything you could think of. Drugs, booze, women. If they could make money from it, they were doing it. Our job was to get the girls out. To set them free. And we did. Or at least I thought we did."

He turned to look at her and Kay shivered. There was

nothing of the man she knew in that gaze. He looked like he was a million miles away, reliving whatever it was he saw in his head. And whatever he saw was bleak.

"We did this many times," he finally continued. "Breaking into criminals' homes and places of business. Taking their money and destroying their stashes of drugs and weapons. We were like modern-day Robin Hoods, stealing from the rich to help the poor. It was a powerful feeling."

Despite his strong words, Kay could sense his fear and his shame. He glanced over at her then, and she leaned forward, worried that he'd stop talking.

"What happened then?"

"It was about six months after I'd joined the group that I discovered the truth. We were living in this hovel on the south side of D.C. I hadn't seen anyone in my family during that entire time. The group discourages you from staying in contact with anyone you knew before. The Circle becomes your family. You live together, work together, and play together. It was hard, but we were doing important work. The police couldn't help people the way we did. We weren't bound by the rules of law. If a woman got beat up by her pimp, what was she going to do, call the cops? She'd end up getting arrested. But we could help. I regret a lot of things from back then, but not that. Beating the hell out of any man who puts his hands on a woman is something I'll never feel guilty about."

Kay agreed. She wrapped her arms around her middle. He looked so fierce while he was telling his story, but this was the side of Eli she was used to. The protector. The one who took care of her and would never let her come to harm.

"You shouldn't. It sounds like you were just trying to protect people."

He cringed and ran his hands over his head. "Yeah, I'm making us out to be real heroes. See, the thing is while we were playing Robin Hood, we had no idea what was going on behind the scenes. The girls we liberated? They were simply sold to someone else. The drugs we stole? They weren't destroyed the way I thought. That was how the group leaders made enough money to fund our activities. I thought I was taking from criminals but I was *working* for criminals. I was a foot soldier in a war that I wasn't even aware of. When I think of the girls I delivered to them..."

His voice broke and he pressed his palms over his eyes. He turned in the opposite direction and wouldn't look at her for a minute. Tears welled in Kay's own eyes, but she dashed them away with the back of her hand, afraid that if he saw them he'd interpret it as horror at what he'd been a part of.

Or worse. *Pity.*

He cleared his throat and glanced at her before continuing. "We were busted by the FBI and I was picked up in the raid. Most of the guys I'd lived with and trained with were killed fighting back. I was captured alive and held for weeks while they tried to ferret out the head of the group. Once they realized they'd captured a lower-level member, I was able to cut a deal. In exchange for telling them everything I knew and cooperating with their investigation, I was able to avoid jail. I'm still helping them to this day. It feels like I'm still under investigation sometimes."

"That sounds miserable. Isn't there a time limit that you can be held accountable?"

"There is no statute of limitations on domestic terrorism charges," Eli stated.

"Oh, I see."

"Do you?" Eli got up and then knelt on the floor in front of her. "My life isn't my own. I work and I sleep. I spend each and every day trying to make up for the consequences of a decision I made almost a decade ago."

She squeezed his hands. "It sounds like you've done everything you could."

"No matter how much I've done, it'll never be enough."

KAY SAT QUIETLY, watching him with her big innocent eyes. It was a killer to have to be this close to her and not touch her. But he didn't want to scare her or make her feel uncomfortable, especially now that she knew everything.

"You can ask questions if you want to," he offered. It would probably be easier to get it all out at once.

"What happened to Justice?" She reached over and grabbed his hand. "Did he survive?"

"Yeah. He was picked up by the FBI and held for questioning, too. I ask about him sometimes. Check on him." Even though he had to do it discreetly. One of the major provisions of his release was having no further contact with anyone in the organization. If Agent Harris ever found out about it, he'd probably assume that Eli was still a member and ferrying information back and forth.

"I'm not surprised. Even though he got you into something horrible, you still thought of him as a friend."

"Yeah, I did. Stupid, but I did. He wasn't cooperative with the authorities, so he ended up serving jail time. He won't get out until next year." He squeezed her hand, stunned that she still wanted to be close to him.

"What about your family? You said you left them behind."

"My parents thought I was traveling. To this day, they have no idea what happened to me during that 'lost' year. I never told my brothers either. They all probably think I had some kind of breakdown."

"That's not what I meant. I was asking *how* you could leave them. What could have possibly happened to make you want to leave your family behind?"

"You're the first person to ever ask me that. The only one who could see inside me and figure out that there was more to the story."

Kay smiled and put a warm palm on his cheek. "I've seen you with your family. You adore them. Especially your mom."

"Yes. I do." Eli's throat tightened. Images of his mom, frightened and hurt, flashed through his mind. "I saw something happen to my mom... Has Jackson ever mentioned our cousins? The ones that live on the west side of New Haven?"

"I've met a few. The tall, handsome one that's a doctor

was at the Memorial Day party."

Eli gritted his teeth. "Handsome, huh?"

Kay bit her lip and grinned at him. He could tell she was trying to defuse the tension in the room. "Well, you Alexanders are known for having pretty good genetics."

Eli grunted. "Yeah, yeah. Anyway, we all grew up together. Uncle Stewart is the oldest. My father was the second child, then Aunt Maria, and last is Uncle Gordon. He's the drifter. Every five years or so, he'll blow through town and then back out again just as fast."

"If your father was the second son, why did he inherit the farm?"

Eli raised his eyebrows. "Your guess is as good as mine. Apparently Uncle Stewart felt the same way because they haven't gotten along since. However, for the sake of us kids, they always tried to keep their feud as civil as possible. We played together on the weekends. Grant was as much of a tool then as he appears to be now."

Kay slid forward until she was perched on the end of the couch. Her breath fanned across his cheek when she exhaled. "So you used to spend time together. What changed?"

"My parents don't speak of it. I just know what I saw. Uncle Stewart kissing my mom."

Kay's hands tightened around his. "No! Your mother wouldn't do that."

"It wasn't her choice, believe me. She slapped him so hard it left a handprint on his face. I was only seventeen when it happened, but I ran up and fought him off. My mom was crying. I wasn't strong enough to fight him the way I wanted to back then, but I was like a beast possessed. My dad came in then and once I blurted out what happened, he punched my uncle in the face. That was the last time our families got together."

"I am so sorry," she whispered.

"She wouldn't press charges. I couldn't understand it. I pleaded with her and my dad, but they wouldn't do it." He covered his mouth with his hand. He needed to stop talking. Some of the secrets he was telling weren't his to share. But now that the dam was open, it was like a gaping hole that he couldn't cover. Everything came spilling out, and he couldn't hold it back. "It broke something in me, knowing that he could do that to her and get away with it."

Eli was startled when Kay pulled him closer and pressed a soft kiss to his forehead. "No wonder you feel so strongly about standing up for women. Because of what happened to your mom."

"All I could think about for months afterward was what if I hadn't heard them? What if I hadn't been near the barn that day? He could have—"

"Don't even think about it." Kay caressed his face. "You were there and that's all that matters. Just like you were trying to do the right thing when you joined that group."

Eli blinked a few times. "Apparently you haven't heard a word I've said. We were criminals, Kay. We stole and hurt people. The women we saved from the gangs ended up being sold into prostitution somewhere else. We were monsters."

"Did you know ahead of time that this group was doing bad things?"

Eli sighed. "No, I didn't, but that's not the point."

She moved closer, snaking an arm around his waist. "Would you have joined if you knew the things you know now?"

"Of course not."

She squeezed him, her arm pulling him against her hip. Her hand rested lightly on his chest as she gazed up at him. "I know that. I wasn't asking for me. I was asking for *you*. Because I think you needed to say it out loud. You made a mistake, yes but it wasn't something you did purposely. I know you'd never want to hurt anyone if you could help it."

He swallowed against the giant lump that had formed in his throat. Talking her out of her hero worship wasn't something he wanted to do, but it was the only fair thing. There was so much available to her; the entire world was wide open at this point in her life. She'd never have to know the despair of losing her sense of self or being afraid to look in the mirror because you didn't like what you saw. She was pure and good. He wanted her to keep that sense of peace, and she wouldn't be able to with him in her life.

"You always look at me like I was the hero. But I'm not the good guy. I'm just a guy who's trying to make up for doing bad things."

"That's just it, Eli. You're trying to make it up because you care. Only good guys care about atonement."

Eli wouldn't have thought it possible for love to be as evident as it was in her eyes just then. The way she looked at him, damn if it didn't make him feel invincible. Like he could do anything, bear anything, for her sake. To protect her.

Now she knew the good, the bad, and the unforgivable, and yet she still *saw* him. Still wanted him. He couldn't believe it.

No one was this blessed.

"Kay, you can't have the kind of life you deserve with me. The government monitors me. The people I used to associate with are the kind who hold grudges. I usually don't sleep in the same location more than a few nights in a row just in case. This is not the kind of life for a family."

"Tell me one thing. If it wasn't for all of this, would we be together? I mean, would you give us a chance?"

He would have given anything to be able to lie to her. To tell her what she needed to hear to let him go. But he knew then that he was just as selfish as he'd always been because he couldn't do it. He couldn't say the words that would allow her to walk away.

"Nothing would be able to keep me away."

As soon as their lips met, he knew it was over. She clung to him so sweetly, pressing soft kisses over his face, his lips, his throat. Anything she could reach. Eli gave up and kissed her back, the cold reserve he kept in place melting beneath the warmth of her embrace.

He vowed then and there that he'd never hurt her or give her any reason to change her mind. His mind flashed to all the stuff in his closet before he could shut the thought down. Kay would freak out if she knew about the things he liked to do. He could find other ways to get the control he needed. He'd have to.

Having her in his bed would be enough. It filled him with a possessive satisfaction, the thought of her in his bed, wearing his clothes with his scent all over her skin. There were other ways he could get inside her mind, possess her thoughts, and control her body. She liked the way he touched her, he could tell. Over time, he could introduce her to new things, slowly push her boundaries. As long as she never knew how deep his desires ran, how all-consuming his need to control and possess her was, then she'd stay with him.

She'd never have to know just how twisted he really was.

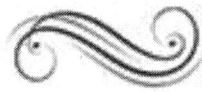

KAY COULDN'T TELL what changed, but something did. Suddenly, Eli wasn't just in front of her but he was *there with her*, looking into her eyes like he wanted to climb inside her skin. He turned and nuzzled his face into her palm and she knew. After tonight, there was no going back.

He was going to make love to her and she'd be forever changed by it.

"I will never hurt you," Eli whispered, his voice carrying the weight of a sacred vow.

"I know that. I've always known that."

Kay shivered as he buried his face in her neck. She felt like every touch, every whisper, held secret meaning, and she could barely contain herself. It had been almost two years since she had gotten pregnant with Hope, and that had been the end of any semblance of romance she had shared with Tim. She had a feeling that her lackluster experiences with her ex would pale in comparison to the erotic promises she saw reflected in Eli's eyes.

Her breath caught as he dropped a wet kiss on the curve of her collarbone. The hair on her arms stood up as he trailed his fingers gently over her skin. She inhaled and let her breath out in a quick gush as his arms encircled her. His warmth seemed to pervade every inch of her until her skin was on fire.

He stood in a swift motion, scooping her up in his arms. She gripped his neck, expecting him to carry her back to his room. Finally, he would let down the walls he'd erected between them and allow her into his private space. But he didn't carry her to his room. Instead, he dipped his knee next to the fireplace, laying her gently on the rug. The heat of the flames fanned over her skin, ratcheting the burn in her blood even higher.

He eased down on the floor next to her, cradling her head in his hand. She relaxed into his hold, allowing him to pull her closer and fit her body to his. He didn't speak, instead using those quiet moments to look at her. It should have been uncomfortable, lying in his arms while he drank in every inch of her skin with his eyes. But every sweep of his gaze, every glance contained such reverence. *Such heat.* As if what he beheld was the most beautiful thing he'd ever seen.

No woman could feel anything but perfect when a man looked at her like that.

"You take my breath away," he whispered. He lifted his hand, slowly, like he was afraid to spook her. He popped the first button on her shirt, his eyes fixed on the line of skin revealed. Finally, the two sides of her blouse fell apart and he was practically nose deep in her cleavage.

Kay tried to close her arms over her chest, self-conscious now. Gravity wasn't her friend.

"Oh no. You can't hide these from me." Eli slid an arm under her shoulders and held her still. Then he grabbed one of her bra straps with his teeth and slid it down.

"Wait. What about you?" If she was going to get naked, she wasn't doing it on her own. Plus, she wasn't going to deny that looking at Eli naked would definitely distract her from her own insecurities. She couldn't think much at all when looking at him.

"You want me to take my clothes off?"

"Yes, please."

Eli grinned and yanked his shirt over his head with one hand. "Whatever the lady wants."

She looked down at his jeans and quirked an eyebrow. He

threw his head back and laughed, the full, rich sound turning her on even more. He stood and pushed his jeans down. The front of his boxers stood away from his body. Kay gulped.

"I think I'll leave those on for a while yet."

"Okay," she squeaked.

Eli knelt beside her. "Your turn."

She lifted her hips obediently and allowed him to slide her jeans off and over her ankles. He looked up at her, his features pinched with strain, and then back at the lacy panties he'd just revealed. Kay thrilled at the possessive look in his eyes. He wanted her.

Their lips met and before long she forgot about being self-conscious or who was wearing what. His fingers trailed over her skin, slow circles that were driving her insane. Every touch was so careful, so tender, that Kay finally just grabbed him and pulled him on top of her. His lower body pressed onto hers until the fullness between his legs settled into her thighs. His groan came out as a harsh sound in the quiet room, and she glanced up at him uncertainly.

"Easy, now." He kept most of his weight on his arms and smoothed her brow with his free hand. "We've got all the time in the world."

Relief and joy bloomed in her chest, the emotions so big she wondered how one person could contain them. Everything she'd ever dreamed of was finally happening, and she was on the verge of passing out from oxygen deprivation.

Going completely on impulse, Kay leaned up and kissed him. He smiled, his lips moving under hers, and it only made her want him more. She wanted to be filled with him in every way but didn't know how to ask for what she wanted.

Luckily Eli seemed to know without words.

His knee inched between her thighs and parted them, and she felt completely exposed. Despite her vulnerability, she wasn't afraid. She was more excited about the things he had in store for her. Sex with Tim hadn't been anything to write home about. She had a feeling making love with Eli would surpass anything she could dream up.

His gentle fingers caressed the insides of her thighs, tracing their shape all the way down to her calf. A few seconds later, his lips followed the path of his fingers. She closed her eyes against the assault of sensation. It was too much to take in, too hard to breathe.

"There were so many nights I dreamed of this. Of touching you. Tasting you. Making you scream."

Kay's breath caught as he moved higher and his lips dragged over her belly button. "You did?"

He looked up at her. The sight of him hovering between her thighs was so erotic but also so shocking that Kay instinctively tried to close her legs. The action accomplished nothing except locking him closer to her core. He looked down, his lips curling up in a private smile.

"I think you'd be worried if you knew some of the things I've dreamed about you," he muttered. Then he leaned down and dragged his teeth over the lace between her legs.

Chapter Thirteen

~⌒

KAY TENSED AS the first shock of sensation flowed through her. A scream rose then stopped, trapped in her throat as he lapped at the wet satin. She shivered beneath him, the motions of his quick tongue setting off a wave of convulsions. She grabbed at his shoulders, tried to move away, and then tried to move closer. Eli ignored her moans, her cries, and her fingers tugging at his ears. He gripped her thighs, his strength evident in how easily he held her still while she shook and trembled beneath him.

When she could breathe again, Kay looked down and couldn't believe he was watching her, a look of intense satisfaction on his face. She instantly tensed and tried to cover herself with her hands. Wordlessly, he grabbed her hands and held them out of the way as he dipped his head and licked her again.

"Oh my," she sighed and allowed her head to fall back.

"Kaylee. I need you to know something."

"Yes," she mumbled.

"I want you with an intensity that might be a little frightening. I don't ever want to do anything that scares you. But when I want something, I take it. And there haven't been too many things I want the way I want you."

Kay let out a breath, overwhelmed and overjoyed by his words. "I want this. I want you."

Her words unleashed something in him, a wildness evident in the unbridled desire in his eyes and the firm grip of his fingers as they tightened on her hips. His thumbs slipped beneath the sides of her panties, and Kay huffed out a shocked breath at the first brush of his fingers on her bare skin.

He pulled back and reached over to where his jeans lay crumpled on the floor. When he pulled the silver packet from his wallet, her heart drummed a sudden insistent rhythm that echoed all the way to her ears. This was it.

He wasn't going to stop this time.

Their eyes met and he dropped it on the floor next to her. Then his hands were on the sides of her face and his tongue was in her mouth. She wrapped her legs around him, holding his big body against her, reveling in the sensation of all those muscles rubbing against her. He ground his hips between her thighs, getting into a rhythm that had her crying out for him. She needed him inside her, would die if he didn't soothe the ache he'd created.

He grabbed the foil packet and ripped it open. Then, his eyes holding hers the whole time, he pulled his boxers down. Kay's breath left her lungs in a soundless huff. She watched, fascinated, as he rolled the protection over his thick shaft.

"Are you okay?" he whispered, stroking a hand gently over her stomach.

At her shaky nod, he flexed his hips, pushing deep. A ragged groan escaped his lips as he slid home until he was so deep that Kay couldn't feel anything but him. She rubbed her hands over his bald head and arched up against him. He seemed to like that because his fingers tightened on her hips.

She thrilled at the thought of making him lose his careful veneer of control and ran her hands over his head and down his shoulders. The movement pushed her breasts against his chest.

He dipped his head and laved a nipple before he took it between his lips. She cried out as he sucked it deep. It was too much, the gentle suction at her breast as he moved inside her. Everything about the way he touched her was so primal and erotic. He pulled things out of her that no one else could see.

Tears sprang to her eyes as her pleasure hit its peak, her body clamping down on him, trying to keep him deep inside her as she came. Long moments later, she realized that he'd stopped moving.

And he was still achingly, breathtakingly hard.

"You aren't… I mean, you didn't…" Kay flushed and pushed her hair out of her face. She couldn't even say it out loud. Had she done something wrong?

"We aren't done yet, angel." He kissed her on her right breast and gently helped her turn over.

She flushed at the thought of what the view from behind must be like. But somehow with Eli, even when she was bashful, she never felt like she needed to hide. Maybe it was the way he looked at her or the fact that he'd made a point to tell her that he loved her body just the way it was. Either way, she'd never felt so powerful in her life, knowing that her curves were exactly the kind he preferred.

"I love the way we fit," Eli whispered. He leaned over her, his chest warming the skin of her back. She purred when he nipped the lobe of her ear just as he slid inside from behind. "Tell me how it feels."

Kay grabbed at the carpet, her fingers searching for something to hold on to as he used her hips to leverage her back and forth. "Full. Thick. Good." Her words sounded almost slurred. She was drunk on pleasure.

"Do you want me to tell you what I'm feeling?" Eli asked. When she nodded, he continued. "I feel soft skin. Lush curves." His hand slipped under her, pulling her upright until she rested against his shoulder, his hand resting lightly at the base of her throat.

"And all of it's mine. All mine," he rasped in her ear. His tempo increased until he suddenly stilled, his hands tightening slightly around her waist and her neck.

As his breath came hard and fast in her ear, Kay tumbled over the edge again, feeling every tremor centered in the fingers resting on her collarbone. It was frightening, this hold he had on her. It made her feel like he could make her do anything. Even control her breathing. He'd warned her that he liked things a little rough. That he took what he wanted. Pushed hard and demanded much. She'd thought she was ready. But it couldn't prepare her for the reality of being held by him.

It couldn't prepare her for the dark desire unfurling from a place she didn't recognize. A place that reveled in this frightening loss of control, in the rush of pleasure from being taken by him.

From being his completely.

WAKING WITH AN armful of softness was a new experience. Eli gathered Kay closer, burying his face in her neck. It had been a long time since he'd considered himself green, but the previous night had made him feel like a teenager copping his first feel. After telling her his story, he'd expected sympathy, even a little understanding. What he'd received was complete acceptance. She'd seen him, the good, the bad, and the worse and loved him anyway. Then to have her give herself so completely... His mind was blown. She'd melted beneath his touch and, in doing so, melted his heart.

Afterward, she'd slumped in his arms, boneless and replete. Her complete trust in him to take care of her had been just as fulfilling as the sex. He'd carried her to her bed and then cleaned her up with a warm washcloth. Those intimate moments had humbled him. He'd never particularly liked sharing his bed, but last night, the thought of leaving her alone hadn't even entered his mind. It was only right that he keep her near while he slept and warm her with his body heat. It was only right to wake up and have her face be the first thing he saw.

Reluctantly, he climbed from the bed, tucking the covers around her so she wouldn't feel a draft. He'd asked Tank and Matt to both come over so they could compare findings. Matt had been assigned to look over the financial records of Kay's family and friends. Tank had been busy keeping track of her ex-boyfriend and monitoring the security system at her still-empty apartment in case anyone tried to get in. As he showered, Eli thought of what Tank had mentioned the prior day. If Timothy Banner was planning on cleaning house before he ran for office, why hadn't he contacted Kay? Wouldn't it be easier to sweet-talk her into signing an NDA? Or try paying her off before resorting to violence?

The thought bothered him as he went about his morning routine—shaving, dressing, and preparing a quick breakfast of whole-wheat toast and two hard-boiled eggs. He passed the coffeepot and stopped. Although he didn't drink coffee most of the time, he knew Kay lived and breathed for it in the mornings. Before he could overthink it, he measured out coffee, filled the unit with water, and set it to brew. He was still standing there brooding when Kay found him ten minutes later.

"Good morning." Kay entered the kitchen hesitantly. When their eyes met, she bit her lip and her hand fluttered to her throat. Eli's eyes narrowed on the action. She was thinking about last night, remembering the things he'd done. The things they'd done to each other. Just thinking about it made him hot again.

"Good morning. Do you want coffee?"

"Oh yes, please." She let out a grateful sigh when he pointed to the full carafe he'd brewed for her. She stood on tiptoe to grab a coffee mug, and the hem of her T-shirt rose up, giving him a peek at her panties. When she turned around and saw where his eyes were, she immediately tugged her shirt down lower.

"Hey, you can't blame a guy for appreciating the view."

She came over and stood on tiptoe to plant a kiss on his cheek. "After how well you appreciated things last night, I'm not blaming you for anything from now on."

Eli reached out to grab her when the doorbell rang. "Damn it, the guys are here. I called a status meeting for this morning. I'm going to cancel it."

Kay kissed him on the nose. "You can't cancel it."

He pulled her closer and then ran his hands over her curvy bottom. "Yes, I can. I *definitely* can."

"Uh-uh. Don't you dare." She danced out of his reach and then poured her coffee. "I'm going to get dressed. Answer the door."

Eli waited until he heard the guest room door close before he moved. He opened the front door and let Tank and Matt in, then motioned for them to go in the dining room. "We'll have more room to spread out on this table."

Matt took the chair at the end and put the stack of folders he held on the tabletop. Tank took a chair in the middle. Eli sat at the other end of the table from Matt.

"All right. Let's get started. Tank, anything new from our senator-to-be?"

"Yeah. It's official. He's running."

"So, it's confirmed?"

"It is. He's having some benefit in a few weeks to raise money for his campaign."

"Matt what about you? Anything unusual with Kay's friends?"

Matt opened the first folder. "Her parents just paid off their mortgage, so I did a little digging to see where they got the money. It turns out her mom got a small inheritance from an aunt who just passed away. So that turned out to be completely on the up-and-up."

Eli's shoulders sagged. "Good. I would have really hated to tell her someone in her family was dirty."

"Tell me what? Hey, guys." Kay appeared in the doorway and they all sat up straighter. Matt closed the file folder.

"Nothing. We're just going over some strategies for your case," Eli replied.

She nodded. "Right. Well, I'd love to hear what you come up with."

Not happening. Eli didn't want her anywhere near this tangled web of deceit. She didn't need to hear them debating which one of her acquaintances had sold her out.

A cry in the background had Kay on her feet. "Oh, baby's awake. I'll be back." With a little wave over her shoulder for Tank and Matt, she was gone.

"I'll talk fast before she comes back. Because I don't think you'll want her hearing this next part." Matt opened his folder again.

"Well, I don't want her mixed up in any of this. So what did you find?" Eli sat forward.

"It's about her friend, Sasha. You mentioned her once before as someone who had a possible motive to want to hurt Kay."

"I think so. She was in the same singing group, and Kay was picked to go solo instead of her. I'd call that a motive for jealousy."

"It might be a motive to pass along information as well. I started digging into her financials. She has large cash deposits that started last year. They're never the same amount and there seems to be no pattern to them either. I've got one a few days ago for two thousand dollars. That's a lot of cash for a girl who works as a data-entry clerk in a warehouse."

"What are you thinking?"

Matt shrugged. "This guy has to be getting his information from somewhere. We've been operating under the assumption that he's in close contact with Kay since he seems to know so much about her, from her daily routine to when she's going on a date. That got me thinking, what if he doesn't know her that well, but he's in contact with someone who does?"

"Aw, hell." Eli pinched the bridge of his nose. "I really don't want to tell her that her best friend might be dirty."

Tank leaned forward. "Maybe you don't have to. Just give Kay some bogus information and then we'll wait and see if it gets passed along. Something we can control. Maybe tell her you're taking her back to her apartment tomorrow and then

142

we can send someone else in disguise. Then we'll see what happens."

Eli didn't like it. The idea of sending his people into what could be a trap felt wrong in every way. However, Tank's plan made the most sense. It would give them the chance to draw out the danger and keep it contained. Maybe it would be better to force a confrontation now when they were ready for it.

"Let's see what we can dig up first. Maybe it won't come to that. But if we can't rule her out, then we'll do it. But let's see what pans out with Banner, first. He seems our most likely suspect."

Tank flipped a page on his notepad. "This guy is a real piece of work. Typical rich shill who thinks he can buy anything he wants, including a senate seat."

Eli wondered if this was it. The turning point where things would heat up. Every case seemed to have one, the moment when he knew shit was about to get critical.

"We need to talk to him. Before he goes public."

Tank made a face. "If we talk to him, we risk tipping our hand. He probably has no idea he's even on our radar."

"Yeah, but there's also the chance he'll give us something we can work with. Catching him off guard has advantages. People give away so much more when they're trying to act innocent."

"When are you going to do this?"

Eli cracked his knuckles and regarded Tank. "I want you to do it."

The other man couldn't hide his surprise. Eli knew he had a reputation as a control freak. He liked for things to get done and proper. But in this case, he couldn't be objective. There was no chance of it. Sitting down and having a civil conversation with the man who'd gotten Kay pregnant and then ditched her was one big journey to *never-going-to-happen-land*.

"I can't be objective in this case," Eli admitted. "And we need him alive after the conversation is over."

Matt and Tank exchanged glances.

"Of course. Whatever you need," Tank finally replied.

"However, I haven't even told you the best part yet. Guess what his party platform will be?"

At both of their blank looks, Tank held up a photocopy of a flyer. "Family values."

Matt scoffed. "An old girlfriend with his illegitimate baby would probably be an inconvenience, wouldn't you say?"

Tank slapped the flyer down on the table between them. "You said it. This guy is looking dirtier and dirtier by the minute."

Eli's eyes locked on the flyer and the black-and-white image of Timothy Banner and his all-American smile. This guy had a track record for lying and hurting Kay. He would probably look at stalking and attempted murder as collateral damage on his way to the top.

"Go find this fool, Tank. Find him and get him to talk. The sooner we can put this to rest, the better."

TANK MARSHALL LOWERED his binoculars and then stashed them in the center console of his SUV. Timothy Banner was checked into the Ritz-Carlton. He snorted. Of course he was. Guys like him, with more money to spend than brains, tended to stay in flashy places. They liked to see and be seen. Tank preferred to see and remain invisible.

He'd just seen Banner and his mini-entourage walk into the hotel. Now he just had to follow and wait. So much of what he did involved patience. Not unlike his work as a sniper. He could watch. And wait. Then at the perfect moment, take his shot. He wasn't taking any chances on screwing up this assignment.

Security wasn't something he'd have thought would be a great fit, but Eli trusted his guys and gave them the leeway they needed to do their jobs. If he needed equipment, he got it. If he had a hunch, Eli trusted him to follow it.

So if his boss needed him to interview some wannabe politician, he could handle it.

He'd met Elliott Alexander at the gun range. They'd gotten to talking and before he knew what was happening, he'd had himself a job. He'd given ten years to Uncle Sam, and when he got out, he'd had a lot of plans for what he wanted to do. Travel. Spend more time with his family.

Nothing had worked out the way he'd planned.

His mom was still doing drugs and wouldn't go into rehab. His little brother was in the midst of a deep depression and hadn't left his apartment more than a handful of times that he knew of in the past year. His life was going to shit and there was nothing he could do about it. Except work.

The job was all he had some days.

He walked through the lobby, his shoes squeaking slightly on the marble floor. Banner and his entourage were about to get on the elevator. He sped up. A couple walked in front of him and he allowed them to get on the elevator first, keeping his head down. The couple exited at the fifth floor and the doors to the elevator slid closed, sealing him in the small space with Banner and his men.

He kept his eyes on the electronic counter which announced each floor. They didn't seem to notice him. The doors opened with a subdued chime and he turned left, waiting until he heard the group exit and walk in the other direction. He waited a few moments, then turned around and followed.

The door to room 9804 was just closing. Tank glanced around to make sure nobody was in the hall before he knocked on the door.

"Yes." The older man who answered the door resembled the pictures he'd found of Banner's campaign manager, Robert Dooley. He looked Tank over from head to toe, his eyes lingering on his blue jeans. His mouth puckered like he'd just tasted something sour.

"Tank Marshall to see Mr. Banner. I sent him an e-mail message earlier today."

The man's expression got colder if it was at all possible. "Mr. Banner isn't here."

"Tell him it's about Hope. I'm sure he'll want to know, Mr. Dooley."

The eyes widened a fraction at Tank's use of his name. "A moment, please." The door shut in his face.

Tank leaned against the doorframe and waited. He wondered if Old Sour Face was really going to deliver the message. Then he heard it. A raised voice and the sound of a scuffle.

A few minutes later, Sour Face was back and holding the door wide. "Mr. Banner will see you now."

You bet your ass he will, Tank thought. *Can't have anyone finding out about the dirty laundry.*

He was led to a living room that was bigger than Tank's apartment and took a seat on the sofa. Someone with an eye for fine things would probably appreciate it more, but to Tank it just looked like the kind of stuff you weren't supposed to actually sit on. He took a mental note of everything in the room. Eli would definitely ask. What did you see? Who was there? Thorough was his boss's middle name. Usually, anyway. He'd been different lately. Distracted.

He wasn't sure what had happened to his boss over the past few weeks, but he hadn't expected to be going in alone. Eli was usually a pretty scary SOB, so it was a huge deal that he trusted Tank to handle this interview alone. But he'd seemed different lately. More open. More human. He supposed the right woman could do that to you.

He liked Kaylee, too. She was a nice girl. He liked the way she looked at Eli. So he really wanted to get this right for her sake, as well. If this guy was the one threatening her, then Tank wanted a part in taking him down.

"Mr. Marshall. I wasn't expecting you." Timothy Banner emerged from the bedroom connected to the suite. Tank stood.

"I know, but there are some things better said in person."

Banner inclined his head and then sat on the couch across from him. "I agree. I just don't know what more needs to be said. I don't have contact with Kaylee or... our daughter."

Interesting, Tank noted. He either didn't think of Hope as his child or he was purposefully trying to distance himself from her in his mind. Tank decided to go with the direct approach. He was a pretty good judge of character and could usually tell when someone was lying. If Banner had nothing to do with the threats against Kay, hopefully he'd be able to tell so they could move on.

"There have been some developments recently. Someone has been threatening Kay. She received a package recently containing something stolen from her apartment."

Banner leaned forward. "That's terrible. Is she all right?"

Tank dipped his head slightly. "She's fine."

At Tank's continued silence, Banner sat back with a knowing smile. "I'm beginning to see why you're here. I have no reason to hurt Kay. Things ended badly between us and that was entirely my fault. I was going through some things. But I'd never want to hurt her."

"I understand, Mr. Banner. I'm not here to cause trouble. On the contrary, I'm here to prevent it. All I want is to be assured that you mean Ms. Wilhelm no harm. With your move into politics, you have motive to want her silenced. Especially running as a conservative."

"What I'm about to tell you isn't public knowledge." Banner stood, adjusting the lapels of his jacket. "I'm running as an independent, but my platform is a conservative one. So it'll be something of a shock to some that I'm running as the first openly gay conservative."

Tank leaned forward. "Say what now?"

Banner gave him a thin-lipped smile. "I'm not worried about my image. Not in the way you think. I never planned to hide that I'd fathered a child. People who are scandalized by sex outside of marriage aren't going to vote for me anyway."

"Huh." Tank couldn't think of anything else to say.

Banner took a seat on the couch across from Tank. "Look. I'm sorry for how things ended with Kaylee. But her mother made it clear when I signed away my parental rights that they didn't want anything from me and would prefer it if I stayed away."

"I see. That's all I needed to know. Thank you for your time." Tank rose and Banner stood, too.

"If you see Kay, would you tell her I'm sorry about the way things ended and that if she needs anything, feel free to call."

Tank nodded but didn't make any promises. He wasn't sure how Eli was going to feel about this visit. It was good to know that Banner wasn't a threat, but that conversation had just wiped out their best lead.

Chapter Fourteen

KAY WALKED BACK and forth across the floor of the small bedroom for what felt like the hundredth time, Hope whimpering softly in her arms. Tank and Matt had been at the house, clustered around the dining room table with Eli for most of the day. Even Carly had come by with stuff for Eli from the office. Tank had left for a few hours and then come back again. Every time she entered the room they'd stopped talking, so she could only assume they were talking about her case.

She hated being kept in the dark. She had the right to know if she was in danger or if they'd found new leads. But she already knew what Eli would say, that he was just trying to protect her. Ugh!

Save me from alpha males, she thought.

Matt and Tank had finally retreated to their hotel around

ten o'clock. Kay had hoped to finally get a little time alone with Eli, but Hope was refusing to settle down for the night.

Hope let out another whimper and rubbed her eyes with her fists.

"You are just determined to stay up so you won't miss anything, huh?" Kay whispered.

They'd had a house full of people for the first time, and Hope wasn't used to so much noise. She wasn't either, come to think of it. She was an only child, and since it was just her and Hope, her apartment was usually quiet after nine o'clock in the evening. She'd assumed the baby was just cranky from being up late and being overexcited.

But the crying hadn't stopped. Nothing Kay had tried so far had helped, between rocking her back and forth, singing to her, and rubbing her back. Kay wasn't sure what to think. Each and every one of her daughter's cries tore at her heart. Wasn't she supposed to be able to know what was wrong? What if her daughter was ill and she couldn't tell?

A soft knock sounded on the door before Eli's head appeared. "Do you need some help?"

Kay wanted to say no. It was on the tip of her tongue. She didn't really want Eli to see her looking like this, all frazzled and exhausted. But he must have seen something in her face that indicated just how close to the edge she was because he pushed the door open and came in.

Eli crossed the room and put his arms around her, enfolding Hope into the hug as well. Kay let out a sigh and relaxed back against his strong chest.

"You've been walking her for a long time. Let me try. You need a break, angel. Your arms have to be tired." Eli's lips brushed the shell of her ear.

Her arm muscles gave a slight twinge in agreement. She shifted Hope to the opposite hip. "It's okay, you don't have to. I think she's just cranky from having so many unfamiliar faces around."

Eli slid a hand between her and Hope, taking the baby into his arms as easily as if he was picking up a book. Hope curled against his chest immediately, snuggling her face into his shoulder.

Kay looked down at her clothes. She'd changed into a nightshirt before coming in to rock the baby. It was stained with drool on the shoulder and wrinkled in a million places from all the times Hope had grabbed it.

So much for romance, she thought. The sleep-deprived mommy look was hardly sexy.

"I'll just go make her a bottle. Maybe something warm will calm her down enough so she can sleep. She usually doesn't take a bottle before bed, but I'm willing to try almost anything at this point."

Kay walked down to the kitchen. She grabbed the baby formula from the pantry and added some distilled water from the refrigerator. She didn't have a bottle warmer, so she heated it in the microwave, shaking it thoroughly afterward.

She tested the temperature on her inner arm, then shook the bottle again and did a second test just to be sure. On the way back to the room, she grabbed an extra baby blanket from the diaper bag. After she drank the bottle, Hope would need to be burped. It couldn't hurt to have an additional barrier over her clothing in case she spit up.

In the hallway outside the room, she took a moment to pause, listening to the soft rumble of Eli's deep voice through the door. Her feet were exhausted from walking the baby around, and she was so tired it was a wonder she hadn't fallen asleep standing up. But at the very least, she knew she could take this last moment of calm because she trusted Eli had everything under control.

This must be what it was like to have a husband. Someone who loved you and whom you trusted completely so you could feel safe leaving your baby in their care. Someone to carry part of the weight.

Finally, she pushed the door to the third bedroom open slowly. Eli stood next to the window, talking to the baby in a low voice, his deep baritone rumbling across her worn and weary nerves. Hope was cuddled up on his shoulder, contentedly snuggled against his wide chest.

As the rumble of his deep voice carried across the room,

Kay's heart melted observing them. Her gentle warrior. She didn't blame her daughter one bit for her fascination with Eli. She knew from firsthand experience that it was pretty much impossible not to feel safe when being held in those strong arms. When he saw her in the doorway, he waved her away. Startled, she backed out of the room and eased the door closed.

It looked like he didn't need her help.

In the living room, she collapsed on the couch. She massaged the tender balls of her feet before propping them up on the other end of the couch. A ragged sigh escaped her lips. She would just rest her eyes for a moment. Eli would probably be out soon. Hope had looked to be halfway to la-la land already.

ELI WATCHED THE gentle rise and fall of Hope's back, waiting until her breathing was deep and even before he moved closer to the playpen. After spending most of the day going over strategy with Matt and Tank, he was exhausted and had been looking forward to a beer and bed. Kaylee had looked just as wiped out after a day entertaining the baby.

It was amazing how such a tiny person could get into so many things. It was hard to stay in the house as an adult, so he could imagine the forced seclusion was taking its toll on the baby as well. He resolved to find a safe way to get them out of the house. Even if he took them to headquarters with him for the day, that would be better than being in hiding all the time.

He looked down at the baby and then smiled triumphantly. She wasn't asleep yet, but she was almost there. She was a gentle weight on his shoulder, her fingers curled against his neck. So peaceful. So trusting. He had a real knack for this baby stuff.

Then she opened her mouth in a wide yawn and let out a high-pitched screech guaranteed to raise the dead.

"Oh no. Don't do that. Please don't do that again." He

bounced her gently, looking around the room for something to distract her. Unsure what to do, he picked up the small notebook on the dresser. Every page contained lines of poetry in Kaylee's careful handwriting.

"Maybe your mom's poetry will calm you down. Let's try reading some. Would you like that?" She seemed to enjoy it when he talked to her, so Eli opened the book to a random page and started reading.

Don't stay so far away from me
It hurts when you stay
It hurts when you leave
Don't stay so far away from me
You, and only you
Are all that I need.

Hope stopped whimpering and relaxed against his shoulder again. A few minutes later, she was asleep.

Eli set the notebook down, then moved closer to the playpen, slow and easy. He eased her down, afraid to move too fast and jostle her awake. Remembering Kay's words about the blankets, he didn't cover her, just let her curl on her side. He'd accomplished a lot of things in his life, but none felt as monumental as coaxing a cranky baby to sleep.

This was what it truly meant to be a man. To have the love and trust of the people who needed you. He'd spend the rest of his days being the man they needed him to be.

He left the room, turning the knob all the way so the latch wouldn't catch as he shut the door behind him. His breath left his lungs in a satisfied rush when the door closed without a sound. Now that the baby was asleep, he could have Kay all to himself. Maybe he'd get a fire going and see if he could get her down on that rug with him again. A little quality time with his woman was exactly what he needed.

He turned the corner into the living room. "Are you warm enough, angel? I can start the fire—"

Kay lay asleep on the couch, snuggled up with one of the accent pillows under her head. Her feet were bare and the nightshirt she wore had ridden up to expose the temptation of her thighs.

He bent at the knees and gathered her gently in his arms. Even in sleep, she turned to him so trustingly. Even in sleep, she reached out for him.

"Eli? Where are we going?" She asked the question even as she wound her arms around his neck.

He kissed the top of her head. "To bed, angel."

He carried her to the guest bedroom, placing her on top of the comforter so he could pull her nightshirt over her head. His own clothes followed and then he had her under the covers, tucked against him. The bed in this room was smaller than his and for the first time, Eli was glad. Nothing could feel as natural as having the right to undress her and tuck her against his side.

He didn't want to let her go.

USUALLY KAY WAS a pretty patient person, but as one week passed and then another, she finally broke down and begged Eli to get her out of the house. She'd caught up on all the back episodes of her favorite television shows, and she'd written several new songs. It had been time very well spent, but it still felt like she was stuck in some sort of time capsule, frozen while everyone else lived their lives unaware.

Eli had decided taking them along when he went to his company's headquarters wasn't too risky. He'd been absent longer than usual and there was apparently a ton of paperwork waiting on his signature. His phone rang incessantly, and she could always tell when it was Carly.

It was the only time he left the room to take his phone calls.

Kay pushed the negative thoughts out of her mind, determined to enjoy her first outing in weeks. Alexander Security Incorporated was housed in a moderately sized building in central Fairfax County. Kay leaned closer to the window to take it all in. She felt a huge swell of pride for the company Eli had built from the ground up. Especially since she knew he viewed his work as atonement for the mistakes of his past.

"I'm really sorry about this. Human Resources only needs me to meet a new employee and sign some documents. It shouldn't take long. I wanted to get you guys out of the house, but I'd hoped to find something more fun than this."

"Trust me, I'll take it. We've been in the house so long I'm starting to forget what the outside looks like."

"I thought I was doing a pretty good job of keeping you busy," Eli said, reaching a hand over to caress her knee.

Kay grabbed his hand before it could reach its intended destination and squeezed it, satisfied when he gave her a lascivious look. "As much as I'm enjoying your *distractions*, we have to come up for air sometime. Plus, I want to see where you work. You've spent so much time following me around at my job, so turnabout is only fair."

He grinned and put his hands back on the wheel. They pulled into an underground parking garage and followed it around, going lower and lower until Eli pulled into a parking space marked with red lines.

"I guess there are some perks to being the boss, huh?"

Eli grinned and got out. This time she knew enough to wait until he rounded the car and opened her door for her.

"There're a few benefits, yes."

She lifted Hope carefully into her arms, deciding to leave the car seat behind. They rode the elevator up to the fifteenth floor where he held the door so she could precede him. Directly in front of them was a gleaming glass-and-chrome receptionist's desk.

"Good afternoon, Mr. Alexander." The receptionist seemed startled to see them.

"Afternoon, Marcy." Eli nodded and then turned to the right.

Kay followed him, conscious of the older woman's curious stare. They passed cubicles and small offices. Most of them were empty, but they passed quite a few people in the hallways who spoke to Eli or nodded.

"This is my office."

He closed the door behind them and led her over to this desk. It was a massive piece of wood with two black leather chairs in front. Kay sat down and shucked off her coat.

"I need to go down to the HR department. They just hired someone new and for management-level employees, I like to introduce myself right away since they'll be reporting directly to me."

"Well, you can go do whatever you need to do. I don't mind waiting. Actually, if there's anything you need me to do, just let me know. I want to be useful. In case you didn't know, I'm pretty good at keeping Alexander men on task. Just ask Nick."

Eli chuckled, his deep baritone washing over her, rumbling through her and leaving a trail of goose bumps in its wake. "I believe you." He gestured toward a stack of files on his desk. "If you're determined to help, there is something you can do. I need these to be put in alphabetical order so they can be filed. Also, I need you to pull out the ones that have incident reports because I need to sign off on those."

Kay looked down at Hope, who was regarding the new surroundings with interest. "I should have brought her car seat after all. I guess I'll have to hold her on my lap."

"She can come with me. What do you say, princess? You want to take a ride?" He held out his arms and Hope immediately leaned forward.

"How quickly she deserts me for a handsome face." Kay winked at him.

Eli held Hope protectively against his shoulder. "She knows I'm a sucker for that smile and she can get away with anything."

Kay's heart flipped over when he looked down at Hope so affectionately. Hope had been up late again the prior night but amazingly, Eli didn't look as though he'd stayed up rocking a cranky baby. He looked like he belonged in a fashion magazine. She'd never seen him in a suit before and the result was shockingly arousing. Eli looked up and caught her staring, so she covered it with a cough.

"So, you need me to look for incident reports and set those

aside. Then I can file the rest. Anything else?"

"No, that's it."

Kay pushed up her sleeves. "I can do that. Don't worry about me. Just go do... boss stuff."

Eli watched her with amused eyes as she plopped down in his chair and opened the first file folder.

"Okay. I won't be gone long." He kissed her lightly on the cheek and then he was gone. She could hear him talking to Hope all the way down the hall.

She let out a breath before turning her attention to the mountain of folders. It shouldn't be that difficult to scan through each file and see if there was anything Eli needed to sign. It was the type of work that wasn't difficult, just tedious. She scanned through the first stack and then filed them. By the time she got to the next stack, she was actually enjoying herself. Some of these case files read almost like fiction.

"What is going on in here?"

Kay looked up from the file she was reading. Carly stood in the doorway, her hands on her hips.

"Eli asked me to help him get his desk in order."

Carly marched over to the desk and snatched the pile of papers from her hand. "That's my job. I'm his assistant. I keep his desk in perfect order, thank you."

Kay snatched the file back. "I'm sure you do, but he's the one who asked me to help him with this stuff. Maybe he thought you were too busy working on something else."

"I'm never too busy for him. For *anything* he needs me to do." Carly crossed her arms and raised an eyebrow.

Kay shook her head. "Really? You don't think I already know that? I figured that out about ten seconds after we met."

Carly's eyes narrowed. Before she could respond, Kay held up a hand. "Whatever. I couldn't care any less about your past with Eli. Based on your behavior, I'm going to take a wild guess that he was the one who broke it off? Which means he made his decision before I came along. So, like I said, if you have a problem take it up with him."

Eli entered the room then and stopped short when he saw Carly. "Hey, what are you two doing?"

Carly whirled around. "Nothing. I was just welcoming Kay to headquarters."

Kay looked at her in disbelief. Her voice had switched from furious to saccharine. Carly sashayed across the room toward Eli. "I'll just go back to my desk. Let me know if you need anything."

Kay blew out a breath and told herself to let it go. It wasn't even worth mentioning to Eli. He'd probably assume she was taking it out of proportion or just being a typical jealous female. Men were so clueless about that kind of thing. She definitely wasn't going to give the other woman the satisfaction of driving a wedge between them with her antics.

His past interactions with his assistant were clearly not being repeated, otherwise Carly wouldn't feel so threatened by her. So there was that.

Tank appeared in the doorway. "Boss, can I talk to you?" His eyes landed on Kay briefly before they skittered away.

Right.

"I'll just wait outside." She took Hope and then left, pulling the door shut behind her. Eli smiled at her gratefully right before the door closed.

"Kicked out already?" Carly sneered.

She let out a long breath and hugged Hope closer to her side. She was way too tired for this nonsense. Of course, Carly looked perfect, slim and beautiful and she didn't have bloodshot eyes from exhaustion. The world really wasn't a fair place most of the time.

"Why do you stay? Working for your ex has to suck."

Carly seemed shocked at her statement. "I don't know. It's a good job. I like my job. Or I used to anyway."

"You could always get another job somewhere else."

"Look, I'm not just being bitchy here. You seem nice enough and I'm trying to warn you. Don't get too comfortable. As soon as he gets bored with the good-girl routine, he'll come back where he can get what he really needs."

"What does that mean?"

Carly's eyes narrowed. "Have you slept in his room yet?"

Heat rose to Kay's face as the other woman's lips curled

up in a satisfied smile. "I didn't think so. Because you don't look like the freaky type and there's no way he's getting what he needs from you."

The door opened behind her and Kay whirled around. Tank and Eli emerged, still talking quietly. Kay looked back at Carly, who simply shrugged.

"Are you ready to go?" Eli asked.

"I'm not sure."

Eli looked at her strangely but didn't comment. "Well, let's go then. There's time for me to give you a quick tour."

Kay followed and was extremely proud of herself for not looking back even once.

Chapter Fifteen

~⁓

AS SOON AS they pulled into the garage, Kay unhooked her seatbelt. She could feel Eli's eyes on her as she fumbled with the door, but he didn't comment. He waited for her to get Hope out of the car and then held the door open for her.

Once they made it into the house, Eli entered first and disabled the alarm. As Kay got Hope settled in her play area, her mind swam with questions that had no answers. She should be thinking about what to make for dinner or enjoying a few stolen moments with Eli while the baby was distracted, except all she could think about was Carly's words.

Have you slept in his room yet?

What was so special about his room? And how had Carly known that he hadn't let her back there? As determined as she was not to let some bitter, jealous ex-girlfriend get to her, she couldn't deny that her curiosity was now at a peak.

She had to get in that room.

"Would you mind keeping an eye on Hope? Just for a second while I use the bathroom."

Eli nodded and stepped over the gate into the play area. "Of course. We'll spend a little time building a tower with these ABC blocks. It's never too early to start teaching her to read."

Hope toddled over to him and he picked her up. She squealed as he swung her around and then sat with her settled in his lap. Once they were absorbed in what they were doing, Eli reciting the alphabet while Hope knocked over the blocks with destructive glee, Kay slipped down the hallway to the bedrooms.

Eli's room was directly across from hers, but she rarely saw him in it. He got up so early that the door was always closed by the time she woke up. He'd been sleeping in her room every night lately so she could only assume he was going in there to get clean clothes every day.

She hesitated, her hand hovering over the knob. What was she doing? This was his personal space and she was about to sneak in and trample all over his privacy.

Because you don't look like the freaky type and there's no way he's getting what he needs from you.

The memory of Carly's taunt made her turn the knob. It held fast under her hands. She looked down in shock. It was locked.

What in the world was so important that he felt the need to keep it under lock and key? Before he could get suspicious, she whirled around and ducked into the bathroom, flushed the toilet, and then came back out.

"Okay, thanks for watching her. Does pasta sound okay for dinner?"

He looked up from where he was sitting and smiled at her. "It sounds great."

The locked door was on her mind as she made a quick dinner of fettuccine Alfredo, while they ate, and while she got Hope ready for bed. When she emerged from the third bedroom, Eli was sitting on the couch. A bottle of wine sat in an ice bucket on the floor next to him. He poured two glasses and held one out to her.

"I figured we could use a little relaxation."

Kay sank down next to him and accepted the glass gratefully. She took a big swallow and then another. Eli watched, bewildered, as she set her near-empty glass down on the side table.

"I'm guessing you really needed some relaxation. Was Hope cranky again? You know I don't mind walking her around."

Kay instantly felt guilty. He was trying to reassure her while she was thinking of ways to break into his bedroom. "No, she was fine. I'm just on edge. I think this whole situation is finally catching up with me."

Eli nodded. "That usually happens after a few weeks. Your whole life has been disrupted. It's okay to be pissed off about it. You have every right to be."

"Yeah, I'm feeling a little down. That's all."

He set his glass on the side table next to hers. "Maybe I can help with that." A soft kiss on her cheek. Then another on the curve of her earlobe.

"Hmm, that's definitely not helping me relax. I think that's having the opposite effect." She climbed in his lap and looked down at him. In that moment, she wanted to hear him moan with abandon. She wanted to be the one to put a smile on those delicious lips and know she held his complete fulfillment in her power. Shifting, she pulled his shirt up until she could run her fingers down his muscled chest.

"I will never get tired of this," she whispered.

He chuckled and tugged the shirt over his head. "Glad you approve."

She waited as he lifted the hem of her T-shirt, helping her draw it over her head. His eyes fixed on her cleavage spilling out of her bra. She shivered at the frank and open possession in his gaze. His obvious approval gave her the courage to stand up and take off the rest of her clothes. If anyone had told her she'd be undressing in the middle of the living room with the lights on, she'd never have believed it. But with Eli, it gave her a sense of power to see how her body affected him. He tugged her closer and took a playful nip at her stomach.

"I was trying to do the romance thing, but then you distracted me." Eli surveyed her nude body with a gleam in his eye that Kay had come to recognize as his "caveman" look.

"Oh my God!" She clutched at his neck as he lifted her into his arms. "What is your obsession with lifting me all the time?" She scolded him, but truthfully she was thrilled. It wasn't often that a man was strong enough to make her feel dainty.

"Because I can. And because it's so much fun." He leered down at where her full breasts were pressed up against his chest.

Kay laughed. "Such a guy."

"Through and through, angel."

Seeing his reaction gave Kay courage to be more aggressive. Once he lowered her to the rug in front of the fireplace, she ran her fingers down his chest to tentatively touch the bulge at the front of his pants. He stilled and she raised her eyes to his and found herself caught in his tortured gaze. A groan escaped his clamped lips and she delighted in the sound. He covered her lips in a quick, hard kiss. Then he stood to remove his own clothes.

Every inch of him was a visual delight. Had she ever wanted to just stare at a guy before? It was impossible not to marvel at how utterly masculine he was, from his incredible physique to the deep voice that sent shivers down her spine. Then there was the obviously male part of him currently trying to escape the confinement of his boxers.

She licked her lips and his eyes narrowed. Scooting closer on her knees, she nuzzled his lower belly. He'd left the boxers on more for her benefit than his, she was sure, but she wanted them gone. All it took was a gentle tug and he popped free, huge and hard and ready. *For her.*

Wrapping her hand around his hardness, she licked up the length, enjoying the feel and scent of him. It was so intimate, to have him in her mouth, to have his scent in her nostrils and his rough moans in her ears. She'd never thought she could enjoy doing this, but it was such a turn-on to look up at him and see his head thrown back, eyes squeezed closed, teeth bared in a grimace.

His barely restrained moans told her he was close to the edge. She sucked him deeper and his hands clenched against his thigh. What a rush to give him the same abandon that he had given her.

"Kay, I can't wait. I need to be inside you now," he growled.

Nodding her head, she gave a final suckle to his hot tip, smiling when he clamped his lips against a groan. Stretching out her hand, she found the packet he had removed from his pants a few moments ago and handed it to him.

Eli stroked the condom on quickly and then lay back, folding his arms behind his head to allow her free rein over his body. Heady with the power she wielded, she straddled him. His breathing roughened and she could feel the moisture between her legs signaling her readiness.

Crawling up his body, she laced her arms behind his head and sank into his kiss. His arms grasped the fullness of her hips, caressing them, and she didn't miss his sigh of appreciation. He made her feel womanly and luscious, and she wanted to show her appreciation the only way she knew how. Settling herself over his erection, she slowly sank down, taking each inch of him in. She wanted to go slowly, but the unbearable ache between her thighs had her bearing down with all her weight, crying out with relief when they were finally joined.

His hands grasped her waist firmly and pulled her into a rocking motion that made the friction almost unbearable. Digging her nails into his shoulders, Kay struggled to keep up with his frantic pace, delighting in every groan and cry she wrenched from his lips. She had never known how empowering it could be to take control, but she found herself savoring the ability to drive Eli over the edge.

She began varying her speed, luxuriating in the powerful feel of him inside her, around her. The tension grew to unbearable proportions until she finally succumbed to the flood of desire and allowed climax to overtake her. She heard Eli's shout of abandon a few moments later.

"I am never getting rid of this rug."

Kay snorted out a surprised laugh. "Sentimental value, huh?"

"You bet."

Her heart rate finally slowed and she propped her head up on her fist. "Let's sleep in your room tonight. Isn't your bed bigger?"

He tensed beneath her and Kay wished she could call the words back. Hadn't she just decided to leave it alone? Apparently her subconscious had its own plans.

"It's kind of a mess in there. I'd rather stay in the guest room. There's more space, and I won't have to be embarrassed by how sloppy I am."

"I wouldn't care about that. Besides, are you telling me you normally slept in the guest room with your prior..." She stopped, at a loss as to what to call herself. Lover? Girlfriend? They hadn't really progressed to the labeling phase of the relationship yet. "With other women," she finally finished.

"I never stayed overnight with them," Eli replied. He shifted and Kay moved over so he could sit up.

"Never? Why?"

He looked uncomfortable. "I don't usually like sleeping in the same bed as anyone, but with you it's different. You're different."

She wanted to ask him more but stopped when she saw the look on his face. He looked so trapped and uncomfortable. He was hiding something else, but what could be worse than what he'd already told her?

He'd once been considered a domestic terrorist by the FBI. If she could handle hearing that, what in the world was he worried about?

ELI SWALLOWED, FEELING like a total ass for lying to

her. He needed to turn the conversation to something else. Anything else. "Are we ever going to make it to a real bed, I wonder?"

She shrugged, but there was a shadow of hurt in her eyes. "I didn't mind. Although I'm sure I won't mind in a bed either."

"You have something of a dirty mind, angel. I would have never guessed."

She laughed softly, and the crease in her forehead and the tension lines around her eyes eased a bit. "I'm full of surprises, lately."

He extended a hand and pulled her to her feet. They gathered up their discarded clothing, and he set the alarm for the night before they walked down the hall and into the guest room. He waited until she switched on the bedside lamp.

"I'm not sleepy." Kay's eyes fixed on his nude body and he instantly got hard.

Eli leaned down to kiss the flush in her cheeks. It touched him that she was still so bashful about his response to her. "Neither of us will be sleeping for a while yet."

He walked closer. Kay met him halfway and when their skin met, she gasped.

"Just let me take care of you, angel. Lie down on the bed."

She scrambled to obey him. A bottle of lotion on her nightstand gave him an idea. "Turn over. I'm going to give you a massage."

She rolled to her stomach, resting her head on her bent arms. He reached over and grabbed the bottle of lotion and pumped a small amount in his hands. Starting with her back, he smoothed the lotion on in broad strokes. She let out a little sigh and her eyes fluttered closed.

"That feels wonderful."

He took his time massaging the dips and curves of her shape. The lotion he'd smoothed on eased the way as he trailed his fingers over the muscles of her back, in the indentation of her spine, and then down, down, down to the enticing curve where her lower back flared out to her hips.

He took his time, tracing gently over the sensitive skin on

the sides of her rib cage and on her bottom, then—

Kaylee reared forward, turning to look at him over her shoulder. "Eli, you accidentally... I mean you almost touched..."

He stared at her, not speaking, then brushed his thumb between the cheeks of her ass in a deliberately slow, dragging caress. Her breath left her lungs in a sudden whoosh. *"Oh my."* She collapsed down on her arms, her head hanging loose on her neck.

Eli leaned over her, the skin of her back warm against his chest. "You have no idea what you look like. You're so beautiful, baby, lying there so trusting while I touch you. Every bit of you is open and ready. You'd let me do anything to you, wouldn't you?"

He grasped her head gently, turning her so he could look into her eyes. "But you're not ready for that. Not yet."

She whimpered at his words, her eyes telling him the truth. Their mouths met in a soft brush of lips. Then he threaded his fingers through her hair, holding her still as their tongues dueled.

He pushed his thigh between her legs and gently turned her over. She was completely at his mercy, her legs forced and held open by his wide stance. He'd never hurt her, would rather cut off his arm than cause her even a moment of fear. Still, the knowledge that he could do anything he wanted to her, that she'd *let* him do anything, was heady.

"You have no idea what you do to me, do you?"

He slid his middle finger deep and then pulled out to massage around the ring of her opening. Kaylee moaned, a soft, vulnerable sound in the back of her throat as he slid two fingers inside her, teasing her warm, snug flesh until she panted his name.

Then she shuddered as a massive orgasm crashed over her, her core clenching around Eli's busy fingers. He positioned himself at her opening, no longer able to hold back, and thrust inside, holding still to allow her time to adjust.

She shrieked, first in surprise and then in pleasure, as he pulled out and then thrust forward again. He groaned. She was so wet, so hot.

Then her back bowed and her inner muscles clamped down around him. Her eyes flew open and he saw it, the moment she lost control of herself. The squeeze and pull of her muscles stole what little control he had left and he followed her over the edge.

She let out a soft sigh and wrapped her arms around his neck. He reveled in the feel of holding her so close to him and buried his face in her shoulder, inhaling the warm scent of her skin and letting it drug him into exhaustion. She patted his chest and pushed him over so they lay on their sides with her leg thrown over his hip. She made no move to get up, content to rest there in his arms.

The gesture was so trusting, and he had never wanted or needed a woman to trust him this much before.

Normal people didn't lock their partners out of their bedrooms, so of course she'd find it odd that they never slept in his room. The only reason she'd waited so long to comment on it was because she trusted him. He was glad she did, because he cared for her too much to hurt her. He wanted only to make her every fantasy and dream come true.

He curled around her, tucking her head right below his chin. Right then and there, he decided that he would clean out his closet the next day. He could get rid of a lot of it and put some in storage. He wouldn't need it anytime soon, if ever. There was no guarantee that Kay would ever be open to that level of experimentation. He needed her more than he needed control.

He hadn't been in a normal relationship, well, *ever,* so it wasn't surprising that he was already screwing it up. But after what she'd already been through, she needed stability and normalcy. Plus, after everything else he'd told her, she probably thought being locked out of his room meant he was hiding something else.

And she was right.

THE NEXT MORNING, Kay woke to the annoying sound of her alarm. She slapped it off and then sat up in bed, every muscle protesting the motion. Heat climbed to her face. The tight ache between her legs and behind her thighs reminded her of why she was so exhausted. They'd used muscles last night that hadn't seen a workout in a long time.

She needed coffee. Immediately.

There was still a slight indentation in the pillow on the other side of the bed, so she figured Eli hadn't been up long. She grabbed her nightshirt from her bag and then her toothbrush before tiptoeing over to the door. There was no sound in the hallway, so she cracked the door slightly and peered out. She ran her hands over her hair and straightened her shirt. Knowing Elliott, he was probably running five miles before breakfast or something equally hardcore. Whereas she just wanted her caffeine injection and something filled with lots of carbohydrates.

After cleaning her teeth and washing her face, she finally felt human again. Today was going to be a different day, Kay decided. It was silly to let anything Carly said get under her skin. She already knew the other woman wanted Eli for herself. Plus, it wasn't as if Eli didn't already know that she was inexperienced in the bedroom. He'd made her give him a list of her lovers, after all. Clearly, he'd made his choice and she had no doubt that he was up to the task of teaching her anything she wanted to know in the bedroom.

She walked down the hallway and as soon as she entered the living room, a blaring siren pierced the air.

"Oh no, the alarm!" Kay whirled around and raced back down the hallway. Her heart was pounding so hard it felt like it was in her throat. All she could think was *get to Eli*. Even though she'd been careful to give him his privacy, at that moment she didn't care. She burst into his room.

Eli was standing near the closet wearing a pair of jeans

and nothing else. Dimly, she thought it was a good thing that she'd already seen him naked, otherwise the additional shock would have probably stopped her heart.

As it was, she launched herself into his arms without a thought or care. "The alarm!"

"It's okay, angel. I've got it. Just wait here." He somehow managed to untangle her arms from around his neck and Kay sat on the floor at his feet. He walked out into the hallway, and a few moments later, the shrill sound stopped.

Kay let out a sigh of relief. She had completely forgotten about the alarm since he was usually up early and disabled it before she even woke up. Her alarm at home was only on the front door, so she'd never had to worry about it when walking around inside her apartment.

A glint of light caught her eye. Eli's closet doors were open. There were rows and rows of shiny and colorful objects. There was something hanging near the door that looked like a long belt. She leaned closer to see what it was.

"Oh my God." She almost fell forward when she realized what she was looking at. It looked like some kind of torture device, made from leather with a multitude of long, flowing strips at the end. With a small gasp, she stood and walked closer. One shelf held small metal instruments. Kay couldn't even begin to imagine what some of them were for, but they looked painful.

And scary as hell.

The second shelf held things that she could at least identify. Kay blushed all the way down to her toes as she looked at the row of vibrators. Sasha had always kept hers in her bedside drawer and loved to mortify Kaylee by whipping it out. Kay had always been curious about them and wanted to get one, but every time she decided to do it, she chickened out. It was so childish, but she couldn't help wondering what if her mother ever came over and stumbled across it. She would instantly die from the embarrassment. Plus, she wasn't entirely sure what to do with it, and that wasn't the kind of thing you could ask someone.

"It's okay now. I called headquarters so they'd know it

was a false alarm." Eli appeared in the doorway to the room. When he noticed her staring into the closet, he stiffened.

Kay backed up a step and looked down at her feet. "Sorry about that. I wasn't thinking."

Eli came into the room and shut the closet door. She sneaked a glance in his direction to see him watching her, his eyes guarded.

"Well, I should go take a shower."

"Kay, wait."

Eli took a step in her direction and she couldn't help but shrink back. His eyes fluttered shut for a moment, and when he opened them, the pain on his face made Kay instantly sorry.

"I would never hurt you, angel."

"I know. I'm so sorry. I was just shocked by... everything. I didn't mean to snoop, I swear. It was just the closet was open—"

"You don't have to explain anything. I just wanted you to know that what's in there doesn't change anything between you and me. It doesn't matter."

Kay let out a half sigh, half sob. "*It doesn't matter?* Of course it matters. Eli, I don't even know what half that stuff *is.*"

Eli ran his hands over his bald head. "You don't need to know what it is because I was never going to show it to you anyway."

Fantastic, Kay thought. She wasn't sure what his deal was, with him kissing her, calling her his angel, and teasing her until she was so hot that just the brush of her thighs against each other was enough to set her off. He'd trusted her with so much, telling her things she was pretty sure no one else knew. She'd definitely trusted him with everything she had.

Had he been planning to hide this part of himself forever?

"I want you to forget about it. Okay? I know it upset you, but if you could just pretend you never saw it, we can go back to the way things were." Eli watched her closely, like he was afraid she would break at any minute.

The problem, Kay thought, was he was probably right.

Chapter Sixteen

ELI STOOD AT the mantel in the living room, staring into the flames dancing in the grate. When he'd done the upgrades to the house, he'd converted the fireplace to an automatic. All you had to do was flick a switch. Standing there, awash with anger and regret, he found that he missed the old way when you had to go out in the cold and chop wood. It would have given him something to do with his hands. And something to hit.

A door slammed in the hall and he looked up. A second later, another door closed. Then it was silent again. He hung his head. Kay was probably going to spend the rest of the day in her room, hiding from him. She probably didn't feel safe being alone with him now.

He yanked his cell phone from his belt, desperate to do something useful. A few minutes later, Tank answered.

"Hey, boss."

"Where are we with Banner? Have you found anything to connect Jeremy and Timothy Banner?"

"No. Although Jeremy claims he was always paid in cash, and I believe him. Everything he's told us so far has been true, so I can't think of any reason he would lie about that one detail. Banner was also telling the truth about his campaign platform. He's already scheduled several interviews to talk about alternative family values and the need for diversity in the senate. So he wasn't just blowing smoke to throw me off."

Eli pinched his nose, massaging the tension between his eyes. "So your hunch was correct. It looks like Banner isn't involved."

A sound at the doorway drew his attention. Kay peered around the doorjamb.

"Tank, I have to go. Let me know as soon as you find something."

"Wait, boss. Have you decided when we're doing our test? You know, the bait and switch? Matt and I are both free starting tomorrow."

"Tomorrow it is, then. In the morning." He ended the call and put his phone back in his pocket. "Hey. You can come in."

She didn't come any closer. "I'm sorry. I didn't want to interrupt."

"You're not."

"I just wanted to apologize again."

Eli took a step closer, hoping she wouldn't run away. "I'm the one who should apologize. I never meant for this to happen."

"It was my fault. I'm the one who invaded your privacy. At least I know what she was talking about now."

"Who?"

"Carly," she whispered.

Eli held in a curse. *Of course.* She'd been different yesterday, edgy and irritable. Why hadn't he thought that Carly would say something? It honestly hadn't occurred to him she'd be so reckless. There was nothing to indicate that Kay was anything other than a client. Carly was usually very discreet, which was part of why she was such a great assistant.

But she was also a woman used to getting her way.

"Look, I don't know what Carly said to you, but I'm sure it was meant to scare you off."

"She said that you'd get tired of my good-girl routine and come back to her. She said that if you hadn't let me into your room, then I didn't really know you. That only she could give you what you really need."

"She's wrong," Eli said. "The reason I'm not with Carly is because she couldn't give me what I need. Because what I need is you."

Her face fell. "I'm not what you need. Clearly."

"Please don't say that."

"I just need some time. To think about things. This is a little overwhelming."

"I know. Take all the time you need. First, though, I need to tell you something. It's about Timothy Banner."

Kay nodded shakily. "What about him?"

"We just found out he's running for office as the first openly gay conservative. We thought it was possible he might be behind all this since he's running on a family-values platform. However, he's obviously not courting the usual conservative votes. Tank talked to him and he seems to have no ill will toward you."

"What? Tim is running for office? And he's gay?" Kay temporarily seemed to forget her fear of Eli because she moved to the couch and sank down.

"So, you didn't know?"

"No, I had no idea. About any of it. I guess that explains a lot." She looked down at her hands.

Eli sighed. She looked so lost that he hated what he was about to do. So many people had already lied to her and here he was about to do the same thing. But now that their best lead had evaporated, their next best bet was Sasha. He needed to know if she could be trusted.

"I know things are a little strange right now, but we're going home tomorrow. I need to meet with someone in that area, so you'll get a chance to visit with your family. Matt will stay with you while you're there."

"When are we going?"

"Tomorrow. First thing in the morning."

She didn't answer, so he left her there sitting alone. She wasn't ready to talk to him, and he was willing to give her space. The only thing he could do for her now was figure out this mystery. Once she was free, she could decide what she wanted to do with an open heart.

KAY WAITED UNTIL she heard the bedroom door close, then got up and went back to her room. Her head was spinning from all the impossible things she'd seen and heard that morning. Her ex-boyfriend and the father of her child was gay? Eli, her sweet, gentle warrior, had some kind of scary torture chamber hidden in his closet?

Everything she thought she knew was a lie. Either that or she'd just been walking around with blinders on. Neither option was all that comforting.

Despite the fact that it was only seven o'clock in the morning, she dialed Sasha's number. Since they'd been in hiding, Eli had asked her to limit her phone calls. But she decided this counted as an emergency. Finding out that the man she was in love with had a closet full of whips and chains was worth bucking the rules to call her best friend.

"It's too early," Sasha's voice sounded like she was hungover. Her friend could be something of a party girl, so Kay figured it was a distinct possibility.

"Wake up, Sasha. I need your help."

"Wait, what? What do you need?"

"I need an intervention. Or a rescue."

Sasha sounded slightly more alert when she asked, "Aren't you with Eli? You're already being rescued."

"Well, I need a rescue from my rescue," Kay snapped. "I need something."

"Okay, what has got you so worked up? The last time we talked, you were floating on a cloud of orgasmic bliss. What did he do?"

Kay sank down on the mattress and buried her face in her hands. "It wasn't what he did. It was what I found. In his closet."

"Oh boy. That's the kind of sentence that never ends well. What did you find? Naked photos of his last girlfriend?"

"Uh, no."

"Naked photos of his last five hundred girlfriends?"

"Sasha, seriously?"

"Hey, it happens. He's got the body for it. If it's not other women, then what could be so bad? I hope you're not freaking out because the dude has a porn stash or something. Every guy has one whether he admits it or not. It's not that big of a deal."

"Does every guy have a closet full of whips, vibrators, and scary-looking metal torture things?" Kay whispered.

"Whoa? Are you serious? Girl, you have all the luck. It's always those quiet, intense types that turn out to be undercover freaks."

"Sasha! This is not helping. I have no idea what to do."

"Baby girl, you don't need to do anything except *enjoy*. A man who actually knows enough about sex toys to use them properly is a rare thing. My ex acted like my vibrator was an insult to his masculinity or something."

Kay flopped on her back and stared at the ceiling miserably.

Sasha cleared her throat. "Okay, look. I know this is scary and new to you. You haven't been with many guys. But do you really think Eli would hurt you?"

"I didn't say that. But what if he wants to hit me with one of those things?"

"Uh-uh. Just answer the question. Has he ever done anything to you against your will or ever tried to push you into something that made you uncomfortable?"

Kay fidgeted. "No, of course not. He was trying to talk me out of liking him."

"That's because that man cares about you. I'm a little jealous to be honest. The way he looks at you... I get a proximity hot flash every time I see it."

"What do I do, Sasha? I need you to tell me what I should do."

"I can't do that. All I can say is that good men are rare. I certainly haven't met any lately. Even if it's kind of scary that he's into some freaky stuff, which I need to point out is not a bad thing, he's a good guy who cares about you. Don't you think he should at least be given the opportunity to explain what you saw?"

Kay thought back to him standing next to his closet, jeans low on his hips. He was perfect naked. Like a marble statue come to life. It was already intimidating to take her clothes off in front of him, but now she had to worry about all the other stuff he might want to do. Stuff she wasn't sure she could handle.

How could she ever compete with someone like Carly? She wasn't even sure what half that stuff was used for and was more than a little freaked out by the items she had recognized.

"You're right. I'm going to try to talk to him about it. Although the thought is already embarrassing. Maybe I'll cook up some chili and then if the conversation is too embarrassing, I can claim I have heartburn and leave the table."

"Chili?"

"Yeah, it's supposed to snow later today. So I figured I'd make chili or maybe some kind of stew."

"Hmm, girl that is not sex food. That's a little gassy, isn't it?"

Kay giggled. "That's why I love you. Always practical."

"I know. I miss you, Kay. We've never gone this long without seeing each other."

"I miss you, too. But I'm coming back home tomorrow morning. Eli just told me. So meet me at my parents' house for lunch. I can't wait to see you and catch up. I feel like I've been hidden away in a cave for the past few weeks."

"Yes, but you're in the cave with a sexy guy. So get off the phone with me and go talk to him. The sooner you talk, the sooner you two can make up and then he can show you some of his freaky stuff. And if you don't want him, send him my way."

"Sasha!"

"Just kidding. Or not. Bye!"

Kay hung up, still chuckling. She glanced at the time. Maybe if she started now she could come up with something suitably sexy for a romantic dinner. Sasha was right. They needed to talk, and she was ready to hear what he had to say with an open mind.

KAY DIDN'T HAVE long to obsess over things. A few minutes later Hope woke up, so she spent the rest of the morning entertaining the baby. When Eli emerged from his room around lunchtime, she was too embarrassed to look at him or even try to engage him in conversation. He'd looked at her cautiously and then gone into the dining room with his laptop. She could hear him clicking away, typing on the keyboard.

She chewed on her thumbnail and then scowled at the ragged edge. That was a habit she'd broken back in high school. But she was completely nervous, and there was no point pretending otherwise. Despite Sasha's early-morning pep talk, she still hadn't come up with a way to approach Eli about what she'd seen. Sasha seemed to think she should play it cool and act like a closet full of sex toys wasn't at all intimidating.

Although it probably wasn't to a lot of women. Women more sophisticated than her, obviously. She thought of Carly and scowled again.

She could talk about this rationally. It might be slightly awkward and embarrassing, but she could do it.

"Mama. Want more?" Hope waved her sippy cup in front of Kaylee. She grabbed her and planted kisses all over her face.

"Mommy's not much fun today, is she? I'm sorry," she whispered. She'd been so preoccupied thinking about Eli that she'd just been sitting in the play area in a daze. Resolved not to think about it anymore until that evening, she got up to refill Hope's cup with juice.

Eli stood in the doorway watching them. When she caught sight of him, she stumbled. He sprang forward, picking her up and lifting her over the gate. As soon as she had her footing again, he stepped back.

"Sorry, I didn't mean to startle you."

"You didn't. I'm just clumsy, that's all." Kay avoided his eyes and walked into the kitchen. Hope's giggle floated from the living room. She leaned back until she could see into the room. Eli was in the play area with Hope, dancing around and making silly faces.

She turned back to the refrigerator and pulled out the apple juice. The steaks she'd taken from the freezer to thaw that morning didn't look as though they'd be ready on time.

She sighed. She might have to go with chili for dinner, gassy or not. Sasha would be appalled.

"Wait, don't climb on that... Oh shit!"

Kay turned from the open refrigerator in time to see Eli dive forward and the bookcase fall on top of him.

"Oh my God! Eli, are you okay?" She dropped the sippy cup and ran back to the living room.

The bookcase lay on top of Eli's back. He wasn't flat on the ground however, but up on his arms.

"Kay, grab the baby."

Her eyes almost bugged out of her head when she saw Hope's face peek out from under Eli's arm.

"Hope!" She dashed forward and pulled her daughter from under the shelter of Eli's body. As soon as she stepped back, Eli dropped to the ground and the bookcase fell flat against him. He then rolled to his side and edged out from under it.

Kay watched, stunned, as he stood and shook himself off. His shirt had a dark smudge on it and there was now a long scratch on his arm. A small drop of blood welled up and then smeared when he wiped at it.

"Is she okay? I didn't fall on her, did I?" Eli walked closer and looked Hope over from head to toe.

Still in shock, Kay couldn't even speak, so she just did the first thing that came into her mind.

She hugged him.

He stood, stiff and unyielding, in her embrace for a moment before his arms came up and around her back. Hope stuck her fingers in her mouth and then looked up at Eli. Then she patted his cheek with her damp hand. He burst out laughing.

"I guess she's okay then."

Kay lifted her head and looked up at him. "I think she knew she was safe the whole time."

Eli disappeared through the door leading to the garage. Kay sat on the couch, Hope still clutched in her arms. So many conflicting emotions raced through her mind. It was irrational, but she wasn't ready to put Hope down yet. Her eyes went back to the overturned bookcase and she closed her eyes and hugged her daughter tighter.

A few minutes later, he came back with a drill and a small toolbox. Kay watched from the couch as he pushed the bookcase back up against the wall. The picture frames and candles that had fallen off the shelves he set to the side in small piles.

"It's a good thing there wasn't much on this bookcase," he said. Then he rummaged in his toolbox.

The loud sound of the drill made Hope jump. She turned to Kaylee and pointed.

Eli turned and saw her pointing. "I'm making a lot of noise aren't I, princess? But I need to make sure this room is safe for you."

He drilled inside the bookcase on the left side and then the right. He did this on the second to last shelf and then the middle one. After that, he pulled on the bookshelf to see if it would move. Once satisfied, he picked up his toolbox and the drill and carried them back to the garage. He came back in and stepped carefully over the gate, then sat next to Kay on the couch.

"I'm really sorry, Kay."

Shocked, she stared at him. "Sorry? For what? You just saved her from being seriously hurt."

"It's my fault she almost got hurt in the first place. I should have blocked off an area that didn't have stuff she might try to climb. Or bolted that bookcase to the wall as soon as you got here."

Kay shook her head. "It's not your fault, Eli. You don't have children. I wouldn't expect you to know about child safety hazards."

"You don't have to be a parent to know that bookcases are heavy and that a baby can't resist trying to climb everything in sight," he said.

Kay regarded him silently. This was the kind of man who took the care and shelter of everyone around him personally. He considered it his duty to help and protect others. Was that the kind of guy she needed to be afraid of? In any way?

Her heart sang out a resounding *No.*

"I think you're amazing. Thank you." She didn't qualify her statement or explain anything else, just rested her head on his shoulder.

"No thanks are needed. I would never let anything hurt you or Hope."

She smiled against his shoulder, even though he couldn't see her. He'd unwittingly just made her decision for her. No matter how scary things might seem, Eli would never harm her. He wouldn't do anything she didn't want him to do.

If only she knew exactly what that was.

Chapter Seventeen

~⟳

ELI WATCHED KAY from the corner of his eye as she stirred the pot of soup she'd made for dinner. Every few minutes her eyes would drift over to him. He could feel the heat of her gaze on his back, but when he looked up, she'd glance away. She clearly wasn't ready to talk about things yet, but at least when she looked at him now it wasn't with the shocked disgust he'd seen in her eyes earlier. It was with confusion. With questions.

It was only a matter of time before she got around to asking him whatever was on her mind.

Eli sat on the living room floor playing with Hope. Every time he tried to leave, Hope followed him to the gate and held up her arms. The bookcase falling had really scared her, and he blamed himself for the oversight. Even though he didn't have children, he knew that bookcases were a safety risk. He should have bolted it to the wall the first day they were here. That kind of lapse could lead to a serious injury. Hope toddled over to him and handed him one of her alphabet blocks.

"This is an *A*. For apple," he recited.

She clapped her hands, her eyes dancing with glee. "Abba!"

His heart turned over in his chest as she toddled over and brought him another block. When he took it, she patted his cheek as if congratulating him on a job well done.

"You know exactly how to wrap me around your little finger, don't you?" Eli tickled her under the chin.

Kay appeared at the edge of the gated area. "Dinner's ready." She lifted Hope over the gate and placed her in her booster seat at the table.

"It smells great, Kay. Thank you." He smiled at her and then took his seat next to hers.

"You're welcome." She ladled soup into both of their bowls. For Hope, she'd saved some of the chicken and diced it. She also gave her some cooked carrots she could eat with her fingers.

They ate in relative silence except for Hope's random squeals. Afterward, they cleaned up the kitchen together while Hope played unaware in the background. He wiped off the counters and the table while she packaged up the leftover soup and put it in the refrigerator.

She took a seat at the table. Eli sat, too, choosing to remain quiet. It was obvious she was working up the nerve to say something.

"Do you hurt them?" She looked down at her lap before continuing. "The women you use those things on, I mean."

Eli froze, his hand suspended over the table. He slowly set his drink down again. "It depends on what they want."

"Who wants to be hurt?" There was no vitriol in her voice, just pure curiosity. Kay twisted her hands together in her lap. "I'm not trying to pry. I'm just trying to understand."

"I know. It's not the kind of thing that's easily explained." He reached over and picked up her hand. She tensed and then allowed him to lace his fingers through hers.

"There are some sensations that you can't understand unless you've experienced them." He drew his finger down the delicate skin on her inner arm. She glanced at him, a quick flash of her eyes before she fixated on her lap again.

"Experienced?"

His finger continued its trek from her inner arm to her wrist. She had small hands, the contrast between their sizes more noticeable as he held her hand cradled in his. Not wanting to shock her out of the moment, he continued his gentle massage of her wrist. When she let out a soft breath, he stroked his thumb into the center of her palm.

"Oh, I... what are you doing?" Kay tried to pull her hand back, but Eli encircled her wrist and held fast.

"Just wait."

He continued his path, digging his thumb deeper, massaging the fleshy skin from the center of her palm to the crease between her thumb and forefinger. Once her hand relaxed again, he dragged his nails over the heart of her palm. She let out a soft moan and then snatched her hand away.

He didn't try to hold on this time. After a few moments, Eli asked, "Did I hurt you?"

Kay nodded and then shook her head. "Not really. Maybe a little."

"But it felt good in a way, too. Didn't it?"

She stared at him for a long moment before dipping her head. "Yeah. It did."

The rest of the evening passed agonizingly slowly. They both took seats on the couch and took turns playing with Hope. Kay disappeared around eight o'clock to bathe the baby and get her ready for bed. The television was on in the background, but he couldn't have named a single one of the shows that played to save his life.

Would she go to her room alone and shut the door? Or would she come back and see where things might lead? Would she trust him to take her to a new place?

When he looked up and saw Kay standing in the doorway, wringing her hands uncertainly, his heart leaped.

"Good show?" she asked, nodding at the television.

"I have no idea."

She let out a small, surprised laugh. "I'm glad it's not just me who's feeling a little awkward about this."

"It's definitely not just you." He held out a hand, relieved when she walked forward and grabbed it. "Let's just sit for a while."

"No."

He flinched, startled at the suddenly vehement tone of her voice.

"I want to go to your room." She glanced behind her nervously. "I want you to show me… everything. I want to pretend for just a little while that I'm sexy enough to know how to use that stuff."

He stood then and came around the couch to hold her in his arms. "It's not about being sexy. Knowing or doing certain things doesn't make you sexy. It's your attitude. It's that stubborn tilt to your chin when you stand up to me and give me hell. That's sexy. All the rest is just a little fun and games."

She eyed him, a sudden gleam in her eyes. "Well then, teach me how to play a game."

His blood heated as he imagined her spread on his bed, all her lush curves his to tease and torture. "You want to play?"

She bit her lip and nodded. "I want to try. I just don't want to disappoint you."

"Not possible. Just being with you is satisfaction enough. Looking at you, touching you." He ran his hands up her arms. "I wasn't sure if you'd allow me anywhere near you after this morning."

He took her by the hand and together they walked back to his room. She glanced back at him once before her hand curled around the doorknob. Then she pushed it open and stepped into the room. He'd left the small lamp next to the bed burning, so most of the room was in shadow.

"First thing, I want to show you something." He took her hand and led her to the closet. "On the left wall, there's a panel here. When you put in the right code, it opens the door to the panic room. I want you to come here immediately if the alarm ever goes off and you don't know where I am. Come here and stay here until I come get you."

"Okay. What's the code?"

He slid open the closet doors, just enough so the left wall was visible. She tensed as several rows of vibrators appeared. But she didn't move back. He glanced at her before typing in the code, 1-2-2-5. A small panel in the wall slid open. He typed the code again and it slid closed.

"Twelve twenty-five?"

"Christmas Day," he clarified.

Her eyes softened. "The first time we kissed. That's a good code. I definitely won't forget that one."

"I'll never forget it either." He stepped back and slid the doors to the closet closed.

Once the contents were covered up again, Kay visibly relaxed. She crossed to the bed and sat down on the edge, then peeked up at him with a mischievous smile. "I feel like I'm not supposed to be in here."

He grinned at her. "You can go anywhere you want to go. Why don't you lie back?"

When she did, she let out a small gasp.

He climbed up on the bed next to her and reclined, looking up at their reflection on the ceiling. "Yeah, I wasn't sure if you'd noticed this last time. The closet had all your attention, so I figured this wasn't a top priority."

She turned to him and buried her face in his shoulder. "I like this part," she whispered.

"Oh yeah? My angel secretly likes the idea of watching? What a bad girl."

She peeked up at the mirrors again. "I do. I really *really* do."

He rolled over and propped himself above her. "Well, I'm happy to provide some entertainment for your viewing pleasure."

KAY STRETCHED LANGUIDLY, loving the way her body

sank into the mattress and even more how she was trapped by the weight of Eli on top of her.

"I'm going to do some things to you, angel. Dirty things. Shocking things. Things that good girls don't do. Are you okay with that?" Eli raised his head from where he'd been nuzzling her neck to look at her.

Kay shivered at the stark, raw need reflected in his eyes. How heady, how thrilling to know that she pushed him to the brink of insanity. That she put that look on his face. That fierce, possessive look that told her he'd do anything to have her. To take her.

It was madness. It was thrilling and primal and wild. She loved every minute of it.

"I don't want to be good when I'm with you. I want to feel. And I want to make you feel things, too."

His arms slipped under her shoulders, holding her caged in his embrace. He was huge and hard between her thighs.

"I'm pretty sure you already know that I feel a hell of a lot when I'm with you."

She wrapped her legs around his hips, thrilled at his sudden hiss of breath. "Good. I want to be the one who drives you crazy."

Her words were cut off when he kissed her, a rough dance of tongues and lips, hands and hips. Her skin heated and she pulled the edges of his shirt up frantically. He needed to be naked. Skin. She needed to feel his skin.

"Lift up, angel."

She obeyed instantly, allowing him to draw her jeans down her legs. He followed the path of the fabric with hot, wet, suctioning kisses. She yanked her sweater off in record time as he kicked out of his jeans and underwear. It was strange and thrilling to see their actions reflected back above them. Her eyes drifted closed as his mouth went to work on the front closure of her bra.

"I can't seem to move fast enough. I want you, all of you, now but I also want to go slow. Savor you. You make me want it all. Everything. All mine."

She wasn't sure if he was aware of the things he was saying.

He was rambling, a stream-of-consciousness flow of love words that made her feel like she wasn't the only one who was going crazy.

She wanted to experiment. She'd never tried anything adventurous. Never had the opportunity to try anything. Now she had a man she trusted with her life who could teach her things. Delicious, sensual things. She wanted to know it all.

But she wasn't the first woman to look up at this reflection.

Jealousy swept through her. Carly's words had been the catalyst to get her thinking, but it was more than just envy that the other woman had clearly experienced everything Eli had to offer. It was knowing that she wasn't afraid to do or be whatever he needed. That was the kind of woman Eli needed. Someone who was courageous and strong.

Kay wanted to be that woman.

Eli framed her face with his hands. "What's wrong?"

"I want to know how to please you, too. And don't say just being here is enough. I'm serious. Show me what you like."

He narrowed his eyes. "Are you sure?"

She nodded. He got up and walked over to the closet. Kay sat up on one arm and watched in trepidation as he selected something from one of the shelves and walked back to the bed. She couldn't see what he'd taken, but it had to be small enough to fit in the palm of his hand. He climbed up on the bed, straddling her.

Lifting her arms over her head, he pressed them back. "Keep these here." The movement forced her breasts up and in his face. He buried his head between them.

At her shocked look, he grinned. "You thought I was kidding when I said I love your body. But I wasn't."

Kay blushed, feeling like her face was on fire. "I didn't think you were kidding. I just didn't think you meant you loved to look at it up close and personal. Plus, I thought you'd want to tie me up or something."

"Not all bonds are physical. The most arousing bondage of all requires no props. Do you remember this?" He touched her neck, his fingers wrapping slightly around her throat. Instantly Kay's thoughts flashed to the first time they'd made love, when he'd held her there. She'd felt the ghost of his touch on her throat for days.

"Yes, I remember."

"The sensation of being collared or controlled can be very arousing. But not just for the reasons you think. It represents trust. You trusted me enough to let me do that. You're trusting me now even though I'm much stronger than you. It's the most beautiful gift, the way you look at me."

He flicked the tip of her nipple with his index finger, teasing it into a sharp point. Kay moaned and bit her lip to hold in the sound. He dipped his head and finished the job with his tongue until he seemed satisfied that she was at the point of insanity. Then Kay felt a tug of sensation that made her inner muscles clench against a throb of need. She looked down. Eli had attached a small metal clamp to her nipple. Little rhinestones dangled from the clip, catching the light.

"I love your breasts. I could play with them all day." His tongue curled around the other peak until it stood up. Then he attached the other clip.

"Beautiful," he whispered.

He lowered himself on top of her and she wrapped her legs around his waist. Their lips met again and they didn't break apart even to breathe until Eli slipped a long finger into her heat, coaxing a startled cry from her lips. He grabbed at the nightstand and sat back long enough to roll on protection. Then he raised one of her legs and wrapped it around his hip, using it as leverage as he thrust into her.

Her hands curled around each other, forming a tight knot against the sheets. He'd taken her slowly and sensually, but this was hard and fast, her breasts rocking in time with his powerful strokes. His eyes fixed on the movement of the little tassels, watching as they bounced and swirled with every thrust.

Kay looked up at their reflection in the mirror and was shocked by the erotic tableau reflected back. Was that really how she looked? All flushed and tousled and... sexy? Eli's muscled back moved over her, his ass flexing as he pushed deeper and deeper.

That was when she lost it.

"Eli, *oh God.*" She exploded in a burst of light and sensation, shuddering as waves of pleasure radiated through her. Eli growled her name and buried his face between her breasts, his deep groan muffled against her skin.

When she finally had enough energy to lift her eyelids, she was startled to see him gazing at her with such affection.

"What?" she asked.

"Look at your hands," he ordered.

She glanced up to see that through it all, she'd kept her hands exactly where he'd put them.

"I'm not sure why I did that."

"Because you wanted to please me." His gaze held hers. "That pleases me most of all."

ELI PULLED HER hands down and massaged her arms. He'd been shocked that she'd kept her hands in place. Even more so that she'd looked so aroused by the notion of being held captive, even if the bonds were mental.

And the way she looked... His whole body tightened as he remembered her captive beneath him with her eyes closed and her mouth partially open. She'd panted and whimpered, every one of her little sounds making him even hotter. It was such a high, watching the moment she realized her body was no longer her own and that her cells and nerves responded to his will alone. It was everything he'd ever dreamed love could be.

He loved her.

It was a terrifying moment and also one of the happiest of his life. He adored her, and she actually seemed to feel the same way about him. Never before had he wished he knew poetry or wished he'd paid closer attention when they'd been forced to read that sappy Shakespeare stuff back in school.

But he wanted the words to express his feelings. Needed to tell her all the ways she was perfect. If he could, he'd wrap her in verses and odes to her loveliness. Crown her with sonnets of her beauty. But in the end, he wasn't a poet or even a romantic.

He was just a guy in love with a girl.

"I have a surprise for you." He moved off her, allowing her room to stretch out.

"You do? You didn't have to get me anything."

"I know. I wanted to. It'll be here tomorrow." For a moment, Eli wished he'd gotten her a real present. Something expensive and shiny that he could present to her while down on one knee. He'd never understood the need some men had to shower their women with monetary gifts, but he could understand now that it was just a reaction to overwhelming feelings. It was difficult to express how you felt and buying jewelry was easy. Hopefully the gift he'd gotten her would mean more.

Kay's eyes lit up. "What is it? Tell me?" She tackled him and he staggered back, laughing as he tried to keep them upright.

"I'm not saying a word. Now, is there anything you need from the other room for the night?" He deposited her back on the bed and kissed her on top of the head, breathing in her scent.

"So, I'm sleeping in here from now on?" Kay hugged her knees to her chest. She looked so cute with her curls standing up on top of her head and a bashful smile on her face.

"Damn straight you are. I love this room. Every single thing in here I picked out personally. I love sharing that with you. I just couldn't show it to you before."

"Because you were worried about how I'd react to your freak supplies?"

He pushed her back on the bed, covering her with his body. "Oh, you're going to pay for that one."

"Am I?" She giggled.

Her laughter rang out and filled all the empty spaces in his heart.

Chapter Eighteen

KAY OPENED HER eyes the next morning and let out a startled shriek. Her reflection blinked back at her. The blankets were twisted around her legs and her hair was wild around her head. Her horrified expression perfectly matched how she felt inside.

"Okay, that was sexy at night. Not so much when I have bed head and morning breath."

Eli mumbled something in response and rolled in her direction, his eyes half-lidded with sleep. He looked mouthwatering in the morning, wearing nothing more than muscles and a smile. His arm darted out and dragged her against his chest, his head immediately moving to the curve between her neck and shoulder.

Kay's thoughts blurred as his tongue dragged up the side of her neck. She was plastered against him, the curve of her bottom pillowed against the hard muscles of his abdomen. One of his thighs came up between her legs, and she shuddered when it pressed right between her thighs.

"You're beautiful in the morning," he muttered. His right hand meandered lazily down and stroked her over the cotton panties she'd worn to bed.

She gasped. The man was a menace, and he wasn't even fully awake.

She swatted his hand away. "Oh, no you don't! You're just trying to sweet-talk me into morning nookie."

His deep chuckle in her ear was almost as arousing as the hard length pressing against her bottom. "Is it working?"

Just then Hope's plaintive cry echoed down the hallway. Kay immediately sat up. Eli did, too. He pressed a quick kiss to her shoulder before he climbed out of bed.

"You're exhausted. I should know since I'm the one who exhausted you. I'll get her."

"Are you sure? She needs a diaper change." Kay didn't doubt that he had the best intentions, but morning diapers weren't for the uninitiated.

"I may not have kids, but Jackson's two boys used to produce diapers that looked like toxic waste. I think I can handle it."

"Okay. She'll only eat dry cereal in the morning. She can eat it with her fingers."

"Got it," he replied. His voice was muffled since he was in the middle of pulling on a sweatshirt. He stepped into the pair of jeans he'd left on the floor the prior night, then he leaned over the bed to give her another kiss.

"Sleep in a little bit. We'll be fine." He tapped the end of her nose and then he was gone.

Kay flopped back down in the bed and listened with half an ear to the familiar sounds of morning. Hope's chatter was easily distinguishable from Eli's deep rumble. Then there was the clanging of cabinets and the soft thunk of Hope hitting the table as she ate her cereal. It was comforting, these sounds of home and family. Before she knew it, she'd dozed off again. When she awoke, it was quiet.

She took a shower and dressed before going up front to look for them. When she got there, she stopped short at the sight of the man and woman on the couch.

"Jackson! And Ridley! What are you doing here?" Kay clapped her hands over her mouth.

"Surprise," Eli whispered. He came up behind her and kissed her on the side of the neck. "I know you've been lonely and feeling stuck in the house, so I asked Jackson if they could come by."

Kay turned to him and kissed him, not even caring that they had an audience. "I can't believe you did this for me."

Ridley pulled her into a hug. "I am so happy to see you."

Her friend had announced her pregnancy over Christmas, and she wore it well, glowing and happy. "You look fantastic. And you haven't gained an ounce. How is that possible?"

Ridley shrugged. "I just hope I don't have as rough of a time as Raina did. Although, she wasn't a healthy weight when she got pregnant. She's been living the model life so long she thinks it's normal to eat lettuce and breath mints as a meal. I need food!"

"We can certainly make that happen." Kay followed Ridley into the kitchen. Apparently her friend had brought along a bunch of food because the counter was covered with Tupperware containers and takeout boxes.

"Did you guys bring us dinner?"

Ridley blushed and looked at the boxes ruefully. "No, that's just the food I brought along as snacks. I told you I was hungry!"

They laughed and linked arms as they walked back to the couch. "I want to hear everything that you and Jackson have been up to lately."

Ridley glanced back at Eli. "I think I'd rather hear what you've been up to."

MARA SIMMONS TUCKED her tote bag under her arm

and rushed to catch up with her twin brother. She'd brought along several of her favorite movies, a couple of library books, as well as a pack of playing cards and some snacks. All Matt had told her was that Eli and Kay were in hiding but that Eli had asked him to drive up. She'd jumped at the chance to come along, and not just because she figured poor Kay had to be going crazy stuck in a house with Eli for the past two weeks.

There was a good chance she might need Eli's help with something soon. Now was as good a time as any to start building up brownie points.

"So, why did we park so far away?" Mara huffed, already irritated that she had to lug her heavy tote bag so far.

"I don't want to park right in front of the house. They're trying to keep a low profile, not advertise that there's a bunch of people there."

"Oh, right. That makes sense."

They crossed through several yards. Matt seemed like he knew where he was going, so she kept her mouth shut and followed his lead. It occurred to her then that he knew the way because he'd lived here for a few months last year. It was so weird sometimes to think that there were stretches of his life she wasn't a part of. For years they'd shared so much that it was a foreign feeling to not know something about him. It made her feel distant and more than just a little lonely.

"We're here. Approaching from the back." Matt had his cell phone to his ear. He held up his hand to halt Mara's steps. A few seconds later, the curtains on the back windows of the house in front of them moved to the side slightly.

"Okay, thanks." Matt hung up and then twitched his head toward the house. "Come on. They're waiting for us."

"This is all very cloak-and-dagger. I had no idea your life was so mysterious."

Matt scoffed and gave her a sardonic look. "There's nothing mysterious about it. I just had to call ahead and warn them so they won't shoot us."

"What?" Mara stopped walking again.

Matt smirked.

She pursed her lips and shook her head slowly. "Ha ha.

195

Very funny."

"Thanks for coming with me, by the way," Matt said. "Kay is probably feeling pretty isolated right about now. I think she could use a little girl talk."

Mara suppressed a twinge of guilt. It wasn't that she didn't want to see Kay. She did. Of course, she wouldn't have been quite as eager to give up her weekend if she didn't need to ask Eli for a favor. She hitched her bag higher on her shoulder. To be honest, she was probably in need of girl talk just as much as Kay. Once she asked Eli for help, she wouldn't be able to take it back. And it wasn't something she felt comfortable discussing with her brother or any of their other friends.

But Kay was a relative newcomer to their group. She could give an unbiased opinion on the whole mess.

The back door opened and Matt stepped back to allow her to go first. As soon as she crossed the threshold, she was grabbed by the arm.

"Mara! I'm so glad you're here, too!"

Her breath left her lungs as Kay tackled her in a hug tight enough to almost knock the wind out of her. Ridley gave her a hug, too.

"I am so happy to see you guys." Kay looked between her and Ridley with a big smile.

The poor girl, Mara thought. She'd probably been going crazy out here with only Eli's gruff company for the past few weeks.

"Don't worry I came prepared for us to have a girl's night right here. I brought movies and snacks." Mara held up her tote bag.

The guys were already huddled around the kitchen counter, looking at a bunch of files. Tank was on the end, looking somber as usual. Matt stood next to Eli. They both looked tense.

"I want to hear what the guys found out first." Kay sat down in one of the kitchen chairs and crossed her legs.

Eli's lips tightened. "You don't need to stick around for this."

"I want to know what's going on. If I'm in danger, I

should be aware of it."

Matt glanced at Eli, then brought the files over to her. "Eli asked us to go over all our cases that had incident reports to look for commonalities. Then we can hopefully spot something that will give us a clue."

Tank stood in the corner, not speaking.

She didn't know him well, but he'd always seemed like the kind of guy who spoke his mind. "So, who do you think is behind it," Mara asked him.

"It had to be someone who knows Kaylee. Really well."

Eli grimaced. "Tank, a word outside."

Kay looked at her before jumping up. "Wait a minute. I want to know who he suspects. I'm not that fragile, Eli. I can take it." She looked at Tank. "Who do you think it is?"

"Your friend. Sasha."

Kay gasped. "Why would you think Sasha has anything to do with this?"

Matt cleared his throat. "She's been depositing large amounts of cash for the past year. There's no way she's earning all that money at her job."

Kay suddenly became very interested in her toes. "Oh, about that. I might not have been totally honest about her job."

Eli suddenly looked murderous. Mara took a step back. "Maybe we should come back later."

Kay sprang forward and grabbed her arm. "No, don't leave. It's not that big of a deal. I just didn't want to tell you because, well, because Sasha's still a little embarrassed about it. She's been singing at this club lately and the owner pays her in cash. Under the table."

"What club?" Eli demanded.

"The Black Kitty," Kay mumbled.

Eli cleared his throat.

Tank suddenly looked like he was trying not to laugh. "So she's a stripper."

"No, Sasha isn't a stripper. She just *sings* at a strip club. And I don't believe she would ever hurt me. Not her. We've been friends too long. I would know if she was capable of something like this. We know each other too well to hide things."

"So, she'd know that Tim gave you that figurine?"

Kay glanced up at Eli again before she sank back into her seat. Her shoulders sagged slightly before she answered. "Yeah, she'd know that. I showed it to her after he gave it to me."

"I'm sorry, Kay. But until we know for sure that she's not involved, I need you to avoid talking to her. Just until we sort this out."

"But I already told her we were heading back today..."

Matt looked at her, his eyes full of sympathy. "Why don't you girls relax a bit? Watch some of those sappy movies you like so much, huh?" Matt squeezed her arm before following Eli and Tank out of the room.

Mara smiled back as she watched them disappear into the next room.

Kay looked devastated. That just wouldn't do. She reached into her tote bag and pulled out the movies she'd brought and a chocolate bar.

"You have every right to follow them and kick their butts until they tell you what you want to know. But if I was in your shoes, I probably wouldn't want to know every detail. So if you want, we can ignore it all and distract ourselves with chick flicks and chocolate."

Kay reached for the chocolate bar immediately. "No contest. Come on, I need to medicate."

"NOW THAT THE girls are occupied, let's talk for real." Eli sank down in one of the dining room chairs, Hope perched on his knee. Matt and Tank sat on either side of him. Jackson took a seat in the corner. He looked up to see his brother watching him, a silly little grin on his face.

"What are you smiling at, runt?" he teased. His brothers were all taller than he was, but he had them all on muscle mass.

"You. You're holding a business meeting with a baby bouncing on your knee." Jackson pantomimed wiping away a tear. "I'm so proud."

Eli chuckled. "I learned from the best. You always made it look so easy." He looked down at Hope, who was happily shredding the pages of the agenda he'd printed out for the meeting.

He could only hope to be the kind of father Jackson was and that their own father had been. It was one of the most important roles he'd ever play.

"I had a lot of help. You guys have been there every step of the way," Jackson admitted.

"Yeah, yeah enough of the trip down memory lane," Eli grumbled, determined not to get all emotional in front of his brother and two of his employees. A man had to have some standards. "Who's up first?"

Matt spoke, templing his hands in front of him like he was in prayer. "I went to headquarters like you asked and we got a team ready to ride down to New Haven. They drove the same model SUV that you drive and the female agent was a similar height and weight to Kay. They even took along a car seat filled with blankets to make it more realistic. The ride down was uneventful, but as soon as they crossed into New Haven, they were followed."

"Did you get any plate numbers?" Eli asked.

Matt shrugged, frowning. "Yeah, but they were all stolen."

"That's what I figured. But at least we know. Sasha is definitely involved. She's the only one Kay called yesterday."

"What do you really think about Kay's friend? Do you have any reason to think she's dangerous?"

"I'm not sure. She's always appeared to have Kay's best interests at heart, but at the same time, Sasha knows a lot about Kay. Also, I find it hard to believe that there were no hard feelings when their group broke up. Kay got a solo contract and Sasha is now singing in some strip club. What if she thought 'Why Kay? Why should she have all the luck?' and took things into her own hands?"

Matt didn't look convinced. "That's a lot of *what-ifs.*"

"True, but I'm not suggesting we indict the girl yet. I'm just saying we should keep an eye on her. Maybe she's selling Kay out, or maybe it's just a coincidence. But either way, she bears watching."

"Fair enough," Matt conceded.

Kay appeared in the doorway with Mara behind her. Eli held up a hand to halt any further conversation. "Hey. Are you guys okay?"

"Yeah, we just paused the movie so we could make more popcorn. Ridley's having pregnancy cravings and just inhaled the first bowl. Don't stop the meeting just because I'm in here." She made a show of going back into the kitchen.

Eli raised his eyebrows. Matt and Tank nodded. Any further discussions of Sasha could wait until Kay was out of earshot.

"Have we made any progress finding out who Elise Able is?" Elliott asked.

"Ellie Sable? I know that name." Kay poked her head back into the room. "I remember from when I was filing things at your office."

"Ellie Sable? You saw that name on one of the files at my office? So she's one of ours, too." He looked over at Tank. "Jeremy must have gotten the name wrong. Can you run it and find out what kind of job it was? It has to share a connection with the other case. Maybe this guy was a client at one point and he's fixated on women with a certain profile."

"I wish I'd known that file was important. I would have pulled it out and brought it home," Kay said.

Tank held up a finger. "It's okay. I've got it here. Ellie Sable is a six-year-old girl. She's the daughter of a reality-TV-show star who hired us to supplement his personal security last summer."

"What does a six-year-old girl have to do with any of this?" Kay rubbed her arms.

"I'm not sure yet, but we will figure it out. Everything indicates that the person we're dealing with is intelligent and highly calculating. There is nothing random about this case. We just have to put the pieces together."

"Was there anything unusual that happened on that job?" Matt asked.

Tank hit a few more keys. "Actually, there was. Not that it's a big deal, but one of the guards was injured in a minor scuffle and Eli took his place."

"I remember that. I didn't want anything going wrong on that case."

Matt leaned forward. "What about Tanya Cook? Did anything out of the ordinary happen then?"

A few key taps later, Tank looked up. "No, nothing. Although Eli was on that job, too. Maybe you're bad luck, boss."

"Wait, what was that?" Eli asked suddenly.

"I was just kidding," Tank deadpanned.

"I know, but you may be on to something. I don't go on every job, just ones where we've had problems or if the client is influential."

It was quiet as Tank tapped keys. He looked up a minute later. "I ran a search for all the jobs you've been on in the past year. A month before Kay got the first letter, there was a spike in incidents. But only high-profile clients, the ones where Eli showed up. Ones where he was photographed."

He turned the laptop around. There was a picture of Eli standing next to Tanya Cook. It was grainy but it was obviously him.

"After that, the threats seemed to slow down and focus on one target. Kaylee."

"What does that mean?"

"He was targeting jobs that you were associated with. Then he focused on Kay when you took over her case. Maybe that's how Sasha originally got involved. Maybe he targeted her since you were guarding all the girls in the singing group."

"I don't believe Sasha has *anything* to do with this," Kay said.

Tank winced and then sent an apologetic look to Eli. "Sorry. I, uh, well I shouldn't have said that."

Eli took her hand and tugged her closer. He could tell she didn't want to come but did it because she didn't want to make a scene.

"Kay, remember yesterday when I told you we were going home so you could visit your parents?"

She shrugged. "Yeah, but Jackson and Ridley came up here instead."

"I only told you that because I figured you'd tell Sasha. This morning, we sent two agents down in a SUV similar to mine. I wanted to see what would happen. As soon as they got to New Haven they were followed."

"That could just be a coincidence. Or maybe they just thought they were being followed."

Matt spoke up then. "We ran the plate numbers on the car that was following them. It was stolen. As soon as they tried to lead the guy into our trap, he took off."

Kay crossed her arms. "That doesn't mean it was Sasha. Maybe my cell phone is bugged or something."

"Maybe." Eli didn't look at her. He figured there was no point explaining that it was simply more likely that Sasha was telling someone else things about her in exchange for money.

Matt stood and leaned over to see the picture on the laptop. "So basically the point is that this guy targeted our cases and then whenever Eli showed up, he stalked those women."

"So, he's got it out for me? That's what you're saying?"

"It's not your fault, but maybe you're the reason he's doing it." Tank closed the laptop. "He's not stalking Kay. Or at least, he wasn't in the beginning. He's stalking you. And he's using her to find you."

Chapter Nineteen

~⌒

KAY SAT BACK on the bed, watching as Mara fiddled with the DVD player. She was trying to keep her mind on their conversation, but all she could think about was Eli. If Tank was right and someone was really after him, then that meant he wasn't safe. Had he put himself in more danger by sticking around to protect her?

Hope yawned in her arms.

"Excuse me, ladies. I'm going to put her down for a nap. I'll be right back." Kay carried Hope into Eli's room, where he'd placed her playpen. Hope didn't even protest when she laid her down, just clutched her teething ring and rolled onto her side. Kay watched her for a few minutes to be sure she wouldn't wake up again and then left the room.

The distinctive rumble of male voices coming from the front of the house brought her mind back to Eli. Not only was she worried about his safety but also about Tank's allegations against Sasha. She hadn't called anyone else to tell them about their surprise trip home. If someone had followed their decoys, then there was no other explanation. No one else could have passed that particular message along. With a sigh, she plopped down on the end of the guest room bed. Ridley moved over slightly to make room.

"Are you okay, Kaylee? Things were pretty intense in there." Mara placed the DVD they'd just finished watching back in its case.

"I bet I seem really stupid, huh? For not wanting to believe what they're telling me."

Mara pushed a few buttons on the remote to start the next movie. "Not stupid. Loyal. You want to believe the best of your friend. There's nothing stupid about that."

"She's right," Ridley added. "But Eli and the guys have to assume that anyone is capable of doing this. If they didn't, they wouldn't be doing their jobs."

"I know. It's just hard. We've been friends since the third grade."

Mara sat on the end of the bed and tucked her long legs beneath her. "You're lucky. We were military brats. It's pretty much impossible to have long friendships when you're moving around all the time."

Ridley promptly grabbed the spare pillow Kay handed her and shoved it between her back and the wall. "Thanks. I love movie marathons, but it's hard to find a comfortable position."

Kay understood completely. She'd gained a lot of weight while pregnant with Hope, and it had been like trying to maneuver around with a beach ball under her shirt. "I appreciate you coming. I'm sure this has been hard on the Alexanders, too, having Eli gone all the time."

She turned to Mara. "So, how did Matt rope you into coming? Did he bribe you? Hold some of your stilettos hostage?"

Mara grinned. "He'd be taking his life into his hands if he went anywhere near my closet. But he didn't have to bribe me.

I wanted to come. I figured you had to be going a little stir crazy stuck here with just Eli for company."

Kay blushed and avoided Mara's eyes. Images of just how crazy Eli made her flashed through her mind.

"Wait a minute? What is that look?" Mara sat up straight and peered at Kaylee. "Are you blushing?"

"No! I'm not. It's just warm in here," Kay insisted.

"It's like twenty degrees outside," Ridley teased.

"Well, we aren't outside."

"Oh, give it up. You are practically glowing. Oh my God." Mara squealed and bounced closer on the bed. "I *thought* you two were acting really cozy. What happened?"

"It's nothing."

"That smile on your face doesn't look like nothing. I guess that means Eli has been treating you right?"

Kay finally gave up trying to suppress the large, cheesy grin trying to take over her face. " *Very* right."

"Good for you. You both deserve to be happy." Mara's face fell slightly and she turned back to the movie.

"Are you okay?" Kay asked.

"Huh? Oh yeah. Of course." Mara swept a stray lock of her dark, wavy hair behind her ear. "I was just thinking how lucky you are. Enjoy this time you have together when everything is new and exciting. It's a really special time. You need these memories to get you through the rough patches."

Mara blew out a breath. They were all ignoring the movie playing in the background. Kay and Ridley exchanged a look. Ridley shrugged. Apparently she didn't know why Mara looked so down either.

"I have to confess I did have an ulterior motive for coming up here this weekend," Mara said suddenly.

"You did?" Ridley asked.

Mara shrugged. "I might need Eli's help with something soon. But it's nothing you guys need to worry about. You've got plenty of your own troubles—you don't need to hear mine."

"It's better than thinking about the fact that Eli suspects my best friend of conspiring against me. Besides, I'm glad you're here. You might be able to help me figure this thing out. I know they suspect Sasha's behind it, but I just can't believe that. Maybe if I can put the clues together, I can figure out what's really going on. Whether he's ultimately after me or just using me to get to Eli—either way, if I can figure it out, maybe we can catch him."

"I'm happy to put my diabolical mind to good use. There is nothing like the mind of a woman scorned." Mara's words were upbeat but her smile lacked its usual cheer.

"Scorned?" Ridley asked. "But Trent adores you. It's so obvious how he feels about you."

Mara let out a little sigh. "But am I the only one he feels that way about or am I just one of many? He's been flying so many places lately. Denver, Illinois, California. He claims it's all for business, but his company doesn't have offices in those locations."

"Maybe he's visiting clients?" Kay suggested.

Mara shook her head, sadly. "He designs financial models. He's more of a behind-the-scenes geek. Why would he need to meet with clients, anyway?"

"There has to be a reasonable explanation." Kay hoped there was. She didn't know Trent that well, mainly just what she'd heard from Jackson and Ridley. But if he was lying to Mara, he'd be hurting a lot of people. Her thoughts turned to Matt. He'd be caught in the middle, between his sister and his best friend.

"You're probably right. I'm just overreacting. I've always had an active imagination." Mara leaned her head back against the wall and stared at the television.

Eli poked his head around the doorjamb. "Ridley, Jackson said you guys need to go check into the hotel."

Ridley patted Kay on the knee. "We'll be back later. After we check in, I'm going to take a nap and then we'll be back for dinner. Eli agreed it's safe to go out to eat as long as we pick a restaurant he's familiar with and we don't tell anyone in advance."

Kay clapped. "I never thought I'd be so excited just to go out for dinner."

Mara waved good-bye as Ridley left. Then she turned back to Kay. "Well, Matt and I are staying here. So, that means we can watch movies and eat chocolate all day."

AFTER JACKSON AND Ridley left, Eli pondered the best way to convince Kay to leave, too. If he was the guy's target, then it wasn't in anyone's best interest to stay near him. Jackson hadn't wanted to leave, but fear for his pregnant wife came first and foremost.

Eli wished he could wave a magic wand and move them all to a safe place. If he told Kay what was going on, she wouldn't want to leave him behind either. He wasn't sure what he'd done in another life to deserve all the people in his life who loved him so much, but putting them in danger seemed like a crappy way to repay their loyalty. The only thing he could do was leave without telling her. Tank and Matt could stay behind to protect her. This guy clearly knew Eli well if he'd figured out that hurting Kay was the best way to get to him.

He shouldn't be surprised, really. He'd known it would only be a matter of time before his past caught up with him. Considering the types of guys he'd run with back in the day, it was only surprising it hadn't happened sooner.

Tank appeared in the doorway. "We've set up a surveillance van. What should we tell the girls?"

"Nothing right now. Eventually I'll figure out a way to get Kay out of here without arousing her suspicions. If I'm the one he's after, then I'm the one he'll get. No one else."

Tank and Matt left so Eli could start getting his things together. Leaving Kay wasn't what he wanted to do, but it was inevitable. Being together was a dream. Reality was that he was a hazard. She'd come into his life and brought joy, laughter, and light. He wouldn't repay that by knowingly putting her in danger. He would make some calls, get things in order. She would be protected always.

But not by him.

The sounds of feminine laughter floated through the walls. Mara and Kay were still in the guest room watching a movie. He moved around quietly since Hope was asleep in the corner. After he'd put together a week's worth of clothes, he zipped them into a duffel bag, then walked over to the playpen and looked down at Hope. She was asleep with her bottom in the air and her blanket clutched in her fist. The sight filled him with a bittersweet longing.

For a short time he'd been a part of their lives, and he would cherish the memories they'd given him forever.

He carried the duffel bag out to the garage and stashed it in the back of his truck. Over the years he'd learned to function with the bare minimum, so he had no doubt that what he'd packed could stretch for a month if he needed it to. There were several safe houses he could retreat to, but it was tempting not to bother. Maybe he should just check into a hotel under his real name. Bring the fight to him.

If the Circle was truly intent on rounding up former members to bring them back into the fold, it wasn't the kind of invitation you could turn down without expecting a fight. But the FBI was determined to bring in as many members as possible, and he would be effective bait. He could draw them out and possibly get them closer to the core of the organization. All it would take was for them to capture the right member. Someone who would crack under pressure and give them useful info.

He walked back through the house and out the front door, setting the alarm behind him. Tank had set up a surveillance van and parked it across the street and down a few houses. He'd need to get either Tank or Matt to relocate to the house before he could leave. As he got closer, the back door opened. Matt peered out from the doorway.

"You needed to see us?"

Eli hopped up in the van and pulled the door shut behind him. "I think I should just leave. You two can stay here with the girls. This has gone on long enough. I'm kind of ready to get off the ride."

Matt whistled. "Are you sure?"

"I'm tired of always waiting for something to happen. Maybe it's time to just let the other shoe drop. Get it over with. If they're going to come for me, I probably have a better chance when I'm ready and waiting for it."

Eli was just about ready to go back in the house when Matt suddenly hit a key and brought up one of the images from the video screen.

"There's someone approaching the house from the right side," he muttered.

Tank leaned over his shoulder and squinted at the image of the small figure creeping along the side of the house. He climbed over Matt and then opened the back doors of the van. "I've got it."

Eli and Matt watched on the monitors as he crossed the street and then disappeared behind the house. A few minutes later, he reappeared dragging a small figure with him. From the size of the guy, it was only a teenager.

"He's got him." Matt slapped his knee triumphantly.

The back doors of the van swung open again. A burst of cold air flowed into the van as Tank climbed in.

"Look who I found sneaking around the back." Tank yanked the small figure forward and when she pushed her hair back from her face, Eli instantly recognized her.

"Sasha? What the hell are you doing here?" He moved aside to make room for her and Tank. The surveillance van was only designed to fit two or three people at a time, so it was a tight fit. It wasn't intended to be a party bus.

"More importantly, how did you know how to find Kay?" Tank slammed the doors of the van behind them and pushed Sasha down onto a seat.

"Ow! Let me go, you big bully!" She smacked him with her purse a few times before Tank reached up and grabbed it.

"I'll tie you up if you don't behave. I just caught you trying to sneak into a safe house. You're lucky we don't call the cops right now."

Sasha's eyes rounded with horror. "But I didn't do anything! I was just trying to see if Kay is even in there. I had to warn her. Devin is looking for her, and it won't take him long to figure out that I'm gone."

Eli crossed his arms. "Explain."

She shrank under his glare. "I was at home yesterday waiting for my boyfriend, Devin, to pick me up. We were supposed to be going to the movies, but then he called and canceled. He said he had a business meeting up north that he couldn't miss. Well, I've been catching him in lies lately, so I didn't believe him."

"I'm going to need the CliffsNotes version," Eli growled.

"I'm sorry. I'm just not exactly sure what all this means," she wailed.

Matt put a hand on her shoulder and she instantly calmed. "Take a deep breath, Sasha, and start from the beginning. Your boyfriend suddenly decided to take a weekend trip, and so you followed him?"

She twisted the strap of her purse between her fingers. "Yeah, I did. He was pissed, too. I could tell he didn't want to let me in the room. I was convinced he had another girl in there, but I was wrong. So I just figured I was being paranoid. But then this morning I found a slip of paper in the bathroom with all these words on it." Her hand slipped into her pocket and pulled out a small scrap of paper.

"Long drive. Night. Dollhouse. Blue shutters. Gym. Dance. Snow. 116," Eli read. "It's just random words and numbers."

Sasha shook her head. "It's not random. Each of those words corresponds to something Kay said to me when she called. The first time she called, she told me how it was a long drive and you drove at night. She thought your house was so cute. Like a little dollhouse with blue shutters."

"They're descriptors," Tank said. "He was pulling out keywords from your conversations to see if he could identify where she was staying."

Eli turned back to Sasha. "Who is this guy? Does Kay know him?"

"No, they've never met. Not to my knowledge anyway. I've tried to introduce them several times, but he always has an excuse. He even met me at Kay's apartment once. We were going to order pizza and watch movies, but he got a phone call and left before she got home."

Eli closed his eyes. "And that's how he gained access to her apartment to steal the figurine."

Sasha nodded. "It must have been. He said he had to go to the bathroom. I never thought he'd take something." She swiped at the tears on her cheeks.

"It's not your fault, Sasha. What happened earlier today?"

She looked down at her hands again. "He told me he needed to go out, so I decided to follow him. He drove down this street, and I could tell he was checking out each house. When I saw number 116, the cute little dollhouse with the blue shutters, that's when I figured out what he was doing. That he'd somehow figured out where she is. I went around the side of the house to look in the window, just to see if I was right."

"Where is he now?"

"I don't know. He drove off, so I figured he was on his way back to the hotel. This might be my only chance to warn Kay before he figures out that I know."

Tank suddenly leaned forward, his attention fixed on the surveillance screens. "We've got action on the back of the house. Someone coming in fast."

On the screen, a black-clad figure emerged from the trees behind the property. With no hesitation, the figure headed straight toward the house. A chill ran up Eli's spine. He'd only seen that kind of single-minded determination a few times in his life. Paid assassins and sociopaths.

Eli sprang forward. "I have to get back in there."

KAY AND MARA both sighed as the credits rolled on the romantic comedy they'd just finished watching. The hero of the movie had been a little too Hollywood-perfect, and of course the actress in the lead had been perfect and thin and blond. In other words, *so not her life.* But it had still been the perfect combination of sappy and funny. Exactly what she'd needed.

"I'm really glad you came," she told Mara. They were both backed up to the wall with their feet dangling over the edge. Mara had ditched her socks an hour ago and her bright orange toenail polish was on display. Kaylee looked with dismay at her own feet, covered in thick black socks. She couldn't remember the last time she'd had a pedicure. A little me-time was long overdue. Especially now that there was someone to admire the results.

"Me, too. I was sitting at home alone, feeling sorry for myself. This is way better. I think I know what I'm going to do now."

There was a loud bang and then the sound of glass shattering. A few seconds later, the alarm screamed out its distinctive warning.

"What is that?" Mara asked, sitting upright.

Unlike the last time the alarm went off, Kay instantly knew something was wrong. She sprang forward off the bed and grabbed Mara by the arm. She pulled her out of the guest room and into Eli's room. Her eyes fell on the playpen in the corner of the room.

"Hope's still asleep. Grab the baby!" Kay turned to lock the bedroom door behind them. It wouldn't stop someone from getting in if they wanted to, but hopefully it would buy them a few extra seconds.

Mara rushed over to the playpen and leaned down to pick up Hope while Kay pulled open the closet doors.

She came up behind Kay and then let out a soft gasp. "Holy mother, are those what I think they are?"

"I'll tell you later," Kay yelled over the sound of the siren as she hurriedly typed the code into the keypad next to the door. A small section of the wall moved aside and she ducked inside. Mara followed and Kay slapped the button next to the door and the panel slid closed. Immediately, the sound of the siren was muffled.

"Where are we?" Mara asked.

Kay stood up and pressed her hands over her rapidly beating heart. "Eli's panic room. He told me if the alarm ever went off again, this is where I should go."

Mara looked around with wide eyes. "A panic room. Really?"

"Yeah. I just hope it was a false alarm."

Kay looked at the panel in the wall that concealed the hidden door. She could only hope that if someone had broken in that they wouldn't know how to break into the panic room as well.

She turned around and surveyed the room. Eli hadn't shown her the inside when he'd given her the code and she hadn't given it much thought. Now she was here and she had no idea what she was supposed to do now. It was a small room, about the same size as a bedroom. In the far corner there was a desk with two computer monitors and a phone. The sight of the phone made her realize she hadn't brought her cell.

"Do you have your cell phone?" she asked Mara. She thought of hers, sitting on the night table next to her bed. If only she'd thought to grab it.

"I do. Should I call Matt? Or should we wait until they contact me? I'd hate to break his concentration at a critical moment."

"Let's wait and see what happens. Maybe this is a false alarm."

Eli had told her to go straight to the panic room if the alarm ever went off again and to wait for him to come and get her. But how long was she supposed to wait? What if Eli was outside the door and needed help? How would she know?

"Wait, I just got a message from Matt." Mara peered at the screen of her phone and then started typing. "I'm letting him know that we're safe in the panic room." Her phone beeped again. "They've got help on the way. He said for us to stay where we are until they come and get us."

"Thank God!" Relief flooded through Kay's veins, so fast and potent it made her dizzy.

She tiptoed closer to the door and placed her ear to the wall. Maybe if she could hear something it would tell her what was going on. Mara came closer, cradling Hope in her arms and rocking her slightly.

There were several loud pops similar to the sound of firecrackers. Except Kaylee was pretty sure no one was celebrating.

"Did you hear that?"

Mara looked back at her. The fear in her eyes echoed the rising hysteria Kaylee felt. They both backed away from the wall.

"Gunshots. It sounded like gunshots to me," Mara whispered.

Kay took Hope from Mara and held her close. Hope peered around them curiously but didn't cry. Kay buried her face in the baby's soft curls. Even though help was on the way, she had no idea where Eli and Matt were or whether they'd been in the house when those gunshots had been fired. All she could do was hope and pray they were safe.

"Please let them be all right. Please. *Please.*"

Chapter Twenty

AT THE SOUND of gunshots they all stopped and turned in unison. "Oh my God. What was that? Did he shoot Kay?" Sasha whimpered.

"Pull up the video feed," Eli growled as he pushed to the front of the van. He wasn't even sure he believed her story, but it was just crazy enough to be true. Either way he looked at it, Sasha had led trouble right to their doorstep. Even if she hadn't meant to, if Kay got hurt then none of that mattered.

"He's in the house. He broke the glass on the back door," Matt said. He pointed to one of the screens. It was a grainy picture, but he could clearly see the entire back sliding glass door had been smashed in.

"I have to get in there." He pulled out his weapon, satisfied that he at least hadn't walked out of the house unarmed, then checked the clip. "I need more firepower."

Tank took the Beretta he held and handed him the Glock 23 he always carried. "What's our plan?"

"The plan is for me to go in there and put a round in whoever the hell just broke into my place."

"You can't go in there alone," Matt said.

Eli climbed to the edge of the van and shoved the doors open. "Kay is in there and so is your sister. Do you want to sit here and talk about plans when they could have a gun to their heads right now?"

Tank grabbed him by the back of the collar and yanked him back into the van. His grip felt like iron. Eli was a solid 220 pounds of muscle, so it wasn't often he was manhandled like a rag doll.

"Maybe you're going to fire me after this, but I'm not letting you go in there alone," Tank growled. "I get it. Your girl is in there. But you're not doing her any favors by charging in with no plan in place. Kaylee is smart. I'm sure she heard the alarm go off."

Tank let go and Eli rolled his shoulders. Adrenaline flowed through his system, and he checked his natural instinct to go for the other man's throat. He was talking sense; intellectually he knew that. But Kay could be in trouble right now and he was standing outside *talking*. He needed to get in there. He needed to save her.

"Just let me go in and distract the shooter. You guys can come in after me."

Tank clapped a hand on his shoulder. "If you go in there with no plan, you might as well just shoot yourself right here and now. Just wait."

Matt's phone beeped and he snatched it off his belt. "It's Mara. The girls are safe in the panic room."

"Tell them to stay there," Eli ordered.

Matt typed out the message, his thumbs flying over the screen. Then he handed Eli an earpiece. "Put this on. We need to be able to communicate."

Tank took the other one and slipped it over his ear. "I'll go around back. All you have to do is get him near the back door. Since he already broke that glass, I should have a clear shot."

"And I'll take the front," Matt added. "We've got this covered. Let's nail this bastard."

Tank loaded his rifle ammunition into a bag and hopped out of the van. He looked both ways and disappeared around the side of the house into the trees. There were plenty of places he could take cover back there.

He pulled out his phone and sent Agent Harris's number to Matt. "Call this number and tell them what's going on. I don't have time for questions right now, but we'll need them as backup."

Matt looked at the information that had just popped up on his phone's screen. "The FBI?"

"Yeah. I've been consulting with them on a case. If this guy has been looking for me, then they'll want to know about it." He glanced at Sasha. "And what about her?"

"I'll take care of her, don't worry about it."

Sasha shivered and pressed back against the wall. Eli nodded at her and then walked to the front of the house. The wind lashed his face, but he couldn't feel the cold, just the tears it brought to his eyes. His focus was on one thing—getting inside the house. He couldn't think about what he might find when he opened that door or whether Kay might be injured.

The front door was slightly open. He pushed it open the rest of the way and it gave a long, extended whine. He pulled his Glock as he stepped over the threshold. The front hallway was empty. He crossed to the entry of the kitchen and entered low. The floor was covered in glass, the shards glittering on the wood like diamonds. A brick lay in the middle of the destruction. He took a hesitant step forward, and glass crunched beneath his shoe.

"I've been waiting for you."

He turned at the sound of the voice, his gun at the ready. The man standing in the doorway to the room wore black from head to toe. The hood of his jacket obscured his face.

"You were watching me the day I talked to Jeremy King."

The hood nodded. "I've been watching you for a long time. You're a hard man to catch up with." He raised a hand

and pushed the hood back. It fell away and his face came into view.

And Eli felt the years fall away.

MARA HAD NEVER considered herself to be that calm under pressure, but when Kaylee started praying, she found an inner well of strength she didn't know she had. Her brother was out there, possibly in danger, and if there was anything she could do to help, she'd never forgive herself later if she didn't do it.

"We are not just going to sit here and wait. There has to be something we can do." Her eyes landed on the computer in the corner of the room. It looked like a general workstation but this wasn't an office—it was a panic room. If it was there, there had to be a good reason.

"The computer. Eli wouldn't have put that in here for no reason, right?" Mara didn't know Elliott that well, but from her brother's descriptions of him as a boss, he was exacting and thorough. Everyone respected him because he took his job seriously. So she had to assume that would carry through into every aspect of his life.

Kay's head snapped up and her eyes followed Mara's. "Eli doesn't do anything for no reason. Maybe there's some kind of program on there that will tell us what to do." She smiled tremulously and, for the first time, looked hopeful.

Mara could only hope the computer would help them because otherwise she had no idea what to do.

She sat down in front of the desk. "Let's see what we've got here." As soon as she shook the mouse, the monitor on the left flickered to life and she was presented with a screen filled with icons.

"Oh crap. Where do I start?" She decided to just click on the first thing that caught her eye. The program loaded and she was faced with something that looked like a legal contract.

"Okay, that's not any good."

"This is going to take forever," Kay said. She was walking around the room, bouncing the baby in her arms. Her eyes reflected her worry.

Mara quickly clicked on another icon and then another. She figured process of elimination should eventually bring her to something useful.

"Wait! What's that?" Kay moved closer to peer over Mara's shoulder.

The second monitor displayed an image of a house. The color wasn't very good, so Mara wasn't sure if she was looking at an older home or just a faded picture.

"I'm not sure, but it looks familiar." Mara hit another key and the image changed to a street with several cars parked alongside the road. There was a white van on one side of the street. She hit another key and got an image of an SUV.

Kay gasped. "That's our car!"

Mara wasn't sure how she could tell because the image was so dark and grainy. "Are you sure?"

"Yes. It even has the little triangular-shaped air freshener Eli hung over the rearview mirror."

"This must be the security system. The car is in the garage, right?"

"Yeah. Maybe if we keep going, we'll see the guys and whether they're safe. For all we know, they might have already caught the guy and we can come out now."

Mara tapped the Enter key a few more times, scrolling through images of the back of the house and several empty rooms. She had a feeling that this situation wasn't going to be resolved so easily.

FOR ELI, TIME fell away and it was seven years ago. He was young and hopeful. Things weren't so complicated, and all he knew was the Circle. He was staring into the face of his best friend, his mentor, and his fellow soldier. He was staring into the face of his past.

"Justice."

The other man's head dipped in acknowledgement. "Knight."

Eli grimaced. "I don't go by that name anymore. It was a lie just like everything else."

Justice moved closer and Eli raised his gun higher. "Stay where you are." It horrified him that his hand shook. His arm felt only loosely connected to his body, like whatever held him together most of the time had gone liquid.

"Are you going to shoot me now? After everything we've been through together? After all I did for you?" The voice that came back to him was just the same as he remembered. Everything about Justice was the same as he remembered. It made him angry that time hadn't stamped the evidence of his treachery on his face.

"You told me we were going to help people. That we were making a difference."

Rage rose in Eli's chest, an inferno that burned through his veins and made his trigger finger itch. It would be so easy to end this. To pull the trigger and take him out. But there was a small, traitorous part of him that couldn't do it. Didn't want to.

Because then he would never understand *why.*

"We did make a difference. All those people we saved appreciated the things we did for them. I didn't see them complaining afterward." Justice gave him a long-suffering look.

It was so familiar, so much like the looks he'd often given him back when they were training together. The sense of familiarity only enraged Eli further. He shouldn't feel an affinity toward the man who'd been systematically tormenting him and the people around him for months.

"Sure, it was fine as long as we got some money and some drugs out of the deal, right? You never gave a shit about helping people. I just want to know if you're here, then who the hell is the FBI holding?"

"They're holding someone willing to pretend their name is Justice. I'd used that identity too long anyhow. It was time for it to die a valiant death."

Eli wondered if the FBI knew they'd been wasting their time on a decoy. Although, considering the things he'd learned that day, it was time to start reexamining all the information he'd taken for granted as fact over the last few years.

"Why would someone do that? Take the fall for you?"

"Sometimes you have to sacrifice a few pawns to protect the king." Justice watched him with knowing eyes. He waited patiently, his lips fixed into that infuriatingly smug smile.

Eli's finger flexed against the trigger slightly. It was a frightening thing to feel your universe realigning around you. Even more so when you realized that so much of what you thought you knew was a lie.

Or if not a lie, at least not the whole story.

Agent Harris had seemed so sure that the leader of the Circle would be in contact with Eli. Maybe he'd known that the Justice they'd captured wasn't who he'd claimed to be.

Maybe he'd known all along that Eli had been far more connected in the organization than even he had realized.

"You're the leader. You're Zeus."

The other man's eyes glittered in triumph. "To think, all that time you were at the right hand of the gods. I was going to bring you in—you would have been in the inner circle. Unfortunately, I had to leave the country for a while. Spent some time in Cambodia and Indonesia. Lovely places. More importantly, non-extradition countries. I figured I could hang out for a few years until the heat died down stateside."

"So I was here taking the blame while you were vacationing," Eli spat.

"I came back as soon as I could. I figured five or so years was enough time for memories to get fuzzy. When I came back to the States, I started rounding up as many of my old comrades as I could find. Imagine my surprise to find you in bed with the FBI. I would have thought it of anyone but you. You narced on us and got dozens of my best guys killed."

"No, I didn't. I was pulled in from the same sting and had no idea what was going on. But I'm glad it happened now. Otherwise, I would have never known the truth. I'd have wasted my life helping a drug kingpin build his empire on the backs of the very people I was trying to save."

Justice bared his teeth. "Look at you. So righteous."

"This is a game to you, but it's my life," Eli snarled. "You turned me into a criminal. Then you put everyone around me at risk. But why spend all this time playing with me? Hurting innocent people and dragging this out? You could have just come straight at me months ago. Ended it all."

It would have been so much easier that way. Eli could have put them all out of their misery if he'd had a chance to take Justice out months ago.

"I had the misfortune of being picked up by the cops last summer on a minor drug charge. It was almost funny. The FBI has been looking for me so long and the local police in a podunk North Carolina town are the ones who managed to hem me up."

"You were arrested? And they let you back out?" Eli almost laughed it was so ridiculous.

"I served eleven months and then got out. They never even suspected they had the head of one of the most notorious gangs in their midst." He chuckled at his own joke. "So due to those unforeseen circumstances, you got a reprieve. Then once I got out and headed back up here, I had to start all over. You're not the easiest guy to catch up with. Your schedule follows no discernible pattern, and you've got all those eyes on you."

"Obviously not enough."

He waved his gun crazily in Eli's direction. "Enough that I couldn't get close. I knew I'd taught you something all those years ago. So I had to find a way to get you away from those FBI agents. The only thing that worked was going after your clients. You'd fly out and they wouldn't always follow you. But you never stayed long enough. Except for with *her*."

"That's why you focused on Kaylee." Elliott's chest tightened. All this time she'd been in danger. How many times had she been in the crosshairs when Justice was aiming for him? His stomach revolted and for a terrifying moment, he thought he'd vomit right then and there. All he'd ever wanted was to protect her, but his adoration of her had almost gotten her killed.

"She was the only one you consistently showed up for. Any hint of a threat on this girl and there you were, and you'd stay for days." Justice's eyes gleamed over the barrel of his gun. "Pretty thing, too. Innocent. You always did have a thing for saving the defenseless."

Eli growled, his dominant instincts set into overdrive at just the thought of Justice anywhere near her.

"All I had to do was watch and wait. Those two things can give you an opportunity, even against someone as careful as you. The bomb was a mistake. I got frustrated. I realized then that if I killed you, I'd never know why you sold us out or how much you told the FBI. It was just that every time I thought of all those years on the run..."

His arm rose and Eli dove to the side, chunks of plaster exploding from the wall beside his head.

"I already told you it wasn't me!"

Justice made a small sound of disagreement. "I don't believe you. And now I'm done talking."

Eli fired back and used the opportunity to double back and hide in the dining room. There were two ways into the room, but he would be able to hear Justice approaching from either side.

"You can't hide." The voice floated from his right. He must be in the front hallway.

Eli edged to the side slowly, then stopped, his instincts ringing when he didn't hear the telltale squeak the wood floors made near the front door. He spun around, dropping low at the same time. He got off several shots before he fell backward, his arm suddenly numb.

Then he was engulfed in pain.

Chapter Twenty-One

AT THE SOUND of more gunshots, Kay and Mara both turned around. Hope let out a small whimper, and Kay wanted to cry along with her.

"We have to do something," she moaned. She moved closer to the door.

"We can't go out there. Matt told us to stay in here." Mara crossed her arms.

"He's going to get shot protecting us. I can't just wait here." Kay walked back to where Mara sat in front of the computer. She was clicking through each of the menus at the top of the program.

There had to be a better way to view the security cameras. Scrolling through all the images one by one was taking too long. Suddenly the screen split and they could see four images at once.

"Is that them?" Mara leaned closer. An image of two men circling each other was on the uppermost left.

"Yeah. That's the living room, and look…" Kay pointed to the upper-right screen. "That's the bedroom. Right outside the door." She wished now that she'd insisted on knowing more about the security system. Eli had given her the password to disable the alarm and the separate passcode to the panic room, but he hadn't shown her how to operate any of this stuff. If he had, she might be able to help him somehow. "I wish I knew how to work all this. If I did, we could set the alarm off or maybe cut out the lights. Something."

"Just look around and start clicking. That's what I did. It can't be that difficult to figure out," Mara suggested. She stood and held out her arms to take Hope.

Kay plopped down in the seat and scanned the main screen. It looked like the desktop of any computer, filled with icons and folders. She clicked on things at random until something popped up with images matching the ones on the other monitor.

"Found it. This must control the cameras."

"Great. Maybe we can create a distraction of some kind. Like cutting the lights off so Eli has time to run away."

"But what if we cut the lights and the other guy shoots?"

Mara's shoulders sagged. "Yeah, or that could happen. What are we going to do? Matt said help is coming, but by the time it gets here, it might be too late."

"I wish I had my cell phone. I could call Tank or one of the other guys. But I don't know their numbers by heart."

Kay started clicking through the different menus in the program. Camera feeds, windows, doors, fire alarm. She stopped. Fire alarm? "Maybe I can set off the alarm and the noise will give Eli enough time to get away." She clicked the button next to the icon.

"I didn't hear anything. Are you sure it worked?"

She squinted at the icon. "It says *Test* so maybe this isn't how you're supposed to set it off. Go stand near the door and listen. Maybe you'll be able to hear it over there."

Mara walked over to the door and pressed her ear right up

against the wall. "Okay, hang on."

Kay clicked the button and looked at Mara expectantly.

"Nothing. Try again."

Kay minimized the screen she was looking at just in time to see Eli duck out of view.

"I lost him!" She clicked through the video feed images until she found Eli again. He was in the dining room, his back against the wall. She clicked through to another screen. The other man was walking down the hallway. Then he turned around and went the other way. Her skin chilled. He was going to enter the dining room from the kitchen.

"What's he doing?"

Kay shook her head and pulled up the menu she'd found earlier again. "He's trying to find Eli. I have to do something. Maybe I should cut on the sprinkler system or something."

"Wait, look. Oh no." Mara gasped.

Kay looked up to see the other man sneak up behind Eli with his arm raised. Eli turned, a look of shock on his face, then fell to the ground.

Her heart in her throat, she started clicking every icon she could.

A SCREECHING ALARM blared above their heads and they both covered their ears. Eli used the distraction to run out of the room and into the hallway. He collapsed against the wall and clutched his arm where the first bullet had grazed him. It was just a flesh wound. The thick leather of his coat had taken the worst of it. The alarm fell silent and then blared again.

"What the hell is that sound?" Justice screamed from the other room.

Eli was grateful for the erratic noise because it was the only way he'd known that Kay was safe. Unless someone had his password to get on his laptop, the only other way to control the system was through the computer in the panic room. He wasn't sure exactly what Kay was doing, but her messing with the security system could give him an opportunity.

That's my girl, he thought. It sounded like she was running a system test. Even if she didn't know how to operate the security system properly, she could create enough distraction for him to have an advantage.

"Boss, I need you to get him closer to the back doors." Tank's voice startled him. Eli had forgotten he was wearing the earpiece. "I've got rounds that go through glass, but it'll be easier if I have a clear shot."

Eli ran into the kitchen and behind the island. If he was going to get Justice in position, he'd have to back himself into a section of the kitchen behind the counter and hope he followed.

It was a risk. It would leave him vulnerable because he'd have the oven at his back, so he'd have to take a leap of faith and trust that his guys would come through for him.

"You know, I was going to let her live," Justice mused, his voice thoughtful. He sounded close. Eli peered around the island, taking note of the other man's position at the entrance to the kitchen. He stood slowly, his weapon on Justice the entire time.

"Who?"

"Your girl. *Kaylee*. Such a pretty name. And that voice. *Mmm, mmm*." Justice ran his tongue over his lips. "I've never been into thick girls like you are, but I'm starting to see the error of my ways. I bet she tastes like heaven."

Eli's fingers tightened around his weapon. "You're going to stay the hell away from her, that's what you're going to do."

Justice laughed. "You're not in the position to tell me what I'm going to do. That was always your problem, you know. You never knew when to accept that you'd been beaten. One of the most stubborn trainees I ever had. It's what made you so tough, but it's also what made you so easy to track. You never could let go of the things you couldn't have."

"I don't like letting go, but we all have our faults. Yours

was always your arrogance. That's what led you here in the first place. This revenge you've spent the last year seeking, and it was all for nothing. I wasn't the one who betrayed you. I was just a stupid kid who thought you were my friend."

"It *really* wasn't you?"

"No, it wasn't me. But I'm sure as hell glad it happened because I've learned something over the past few years, too. I've learned about friendship and trust. You were always so sure you were smarter than everyone else, and you couldn't trust anyone to have your back."

"Trust is for fools."

"It's the one thing you can't understand, and it's the reason why I've won."

"You haven't won shit. I'm still holding a gun pointed directly at your heart."

Eli shrugged.

Justice's eyes narrowed, rage all over his face. "You think I won't shoot you?"

"I know you will, but I'm not that worried about it. Because I know something you don't know."

Eli stopped moving and Justice did, too. He stood directly in front of the gaping hole in the sliding glass door.

"Oh and what's that?"

"That the guys I employ are better shots than I am."

A second later there was a soft thud, and Justice dropped to the ground. Eli dove to the side, covering his head with his hands as the cabinets where he'd been standing were plastered with bullets. There was a soft moan and then the sound of the front door being kicked in.

"FBI, show me your hands!"

Eli dropped his weapon and put his hands on top of his head. The SWAT team fanned out, yelling instructions as they secured each room. A moment later, he saw Agent Harris. He lowered his hands and let out a heavy breath. He'd been strangely calm until this moment, but now his heart was racing and his pulse pounded like a drumbeat in his head.

"Good work, Elliott. We've got him."

Suddenly the room was swarming with people. The SWAT

team, FBI agents, and then a team of paramedics barreled in. He watched as they loaded Justice onto a stretcher.

One of the paramedics spoke directly to Agent Harris. "He'll be okay. It was in the shoulder. But the bullet needs to come out."

Eli crossed to the french doors. Tank stood on the lawn of the house behind his. He raised his hand in greeting and Eli waved back.

Agent Harris approached. "Great work here, Elliott. Since Zeus is still alive, hopefully we can get all the information we need from him."

Eli nodded, his thoughts still jumbled from everything that had happened. Everything he'd learned. "Did you know he was behind all this?"

Agent Harris's lips thinned. "I'm not at liberty to say. So I'll just say again, good work."

Eli pushed away from the counter and headed toward the back of the house.

"Where are you going, Mr. Alexander? We need to debrief you."

Eli didn't even slow down. "Consider me debriefed. My woman is stuck in a closet. I need to get her out and to a safe place."

WHEN THE DOORS to the panic room slid open, Kay and Mara both scrambled to their feet. Eli's head appeared in the small entryway. Kay's heart leaped.

"It's safe to come out now. It's over."

She ran across the room and collided with his chest. He lifted her off her feet. "It's all over."

They followed him back out to the living room. Mara ran to her brother and jumped into his arms. Kay surveyed the damage done to the room. It looked like the aftermath of an earthquake in the kitchen. There was glass over the floor and the back door was smashed in.

For the next two hours, they waited as the police questioned them about everything that had happened. Kaylee was already tired of telling the story, and she hadn't even told anyone she knew yet.

Just then, the doors to the house opened and she heard a familiar voice. "Where is my baby? Young man, I don't care if you're FBI or DIY, you'd better get out of my way. Elliott!"

Eli got up from the couch where he'd been talking to one of the FBI agents he'd introduced her to. "Mom? Is that you?"

Julia suddenly appeared, pushing past all the FBI and ATF agents in her way. "Of course it's me."

"What are you doing here?"

Jackson appeared behind her, followed by Mark Alexander. "I called her. Matt called to warn me not to return to the house. Once I realized what was happening, I called Mom as soon as I hung up. I knew she'd want to know."

"Of course he called me. We came straight here. I was so worried." She grabbed Eli around the waist and didn't let go. He held her, letting her sob openly on his shirt.

When her tears subsided, she wiped at her cheeks. "That's it. You're definitely coming back home now where I can keep an eye on you."

"Yes, ma'am." Eli pulled her in for another hug, which apparently shocked Julia but made her very happy.

"We came with the Wilhelms. I knew they'd want to know their daughter was all right."

Kay's heart sank. "You brought my parents with you?" As soon as the words left her mouth, her mother's face appeared amidst the crowd. She skirted around the policemen and agents, looking like she was afraid they'd contaminate her if their bodies touched.

Oh no.

"What is this I hear about you all being shot at? And where was the baby during all this?" Henrietta exclaimed as soon as she reached Kaylee's side. She took Hope from Kay's arms and hugged her.

Kay pulled her mother away from the crowd so everyone else wouldn't have to hear her mom's criticisms. "She was here, too. I had her safe in the panic room with me the whole time."

"This is just too much. You should have just left Hope with us. You know I would have kept her. Why didn't you call if you thought you were in this kind of danger?"

"I didn't know we'd end up being shot at, Mom. And you know what? I don't call or come by more often because I can't take hearing what a screwup I am every single time. Or seeing that look on your face that shows how disappointed you are in me."

Kaylee registered the shock on her mother's face, but she was on a roll now and couldn't stop. All the things she should have said over the years tumbled out in a big, jumbled rush.

"All I ever hear from you is how badly I'm ruining my life and Hope's future. How I make stupid decisions. I know I'm an embarrassment to you. I'm doing the best I can, but it's still scary. It would be really great to have you hold my hand and tell me that you understand and that you're there for me."

Her mother's face had hardened and she handed Hope back with stiff arms. "I don't know what I've ever done to deserve this. I've tried to be there for you, Kaylee. I really have."

"I know you've tried. But you know what I really wish? All this time I wished you could stop being embarrassed by me long enough to just be my mom."

Eli put his arm around her shoulder and pulled her to his side as her mother turned and walked away.

Her father looked between them awkwardly before he squeezed Kay's arm. "I'm sorry, pumpkin."

She pulled him into a quick hug. It wasn't his fault that she and her mother couldn't get along. "I'm sorry too, Daddy. Go ahead and follow her. You'll never hear the end of it otherwise."

Eli rubbed her arm as they watched them go. "She'll come around. You've never stood up to her before. I think she'll need a little recovery time before she learns to deal with it. But I'm proud of you."

Kay hugged him back, his words reassuring her. She hated

to think of having a rift with her mother, but she'd finally learned that others could only treat her the way she allowed them to treat her. She'd been through so much lately. She was proud of how far she'd come, and she wasn't accepting put-downs anymore.

From anyone.

"Can we get out of here?"

Eli looked back at the cluster of agents behind them. "Gladly. I've had enough of this scene to last a lifetime."

Chapter Twenty-Two

~◦

OVER THE NEXT few weeks, Elliott learned the true meaning of family. After a long discussion with Kaylee about it, he'd decided to tell them the truth. Family was about people who accepted you, warts and all. He'd been afraid of their reaction to his failings, but in the end, they'd rallied around him in a way that humbled him.

Mara had gotten a recommendation from her friend Danny for an attorney who specialized in criminal law. It turned out Agent Harris had counted on Eli not being aware of all his rights. Since he'd never been formally charged with anything, his new lawyer was going over the details of his case carefully to see what obligations he had, if any, to continue being involved in the FBI's case.

Now that it was all over and he had some distance from the situation, he realized he was happy to help out. However, if he did, it would be because he wanted to, not because of a threat hanging over his head. His lawyer thought he had reason to be optimistic, and he felt lighter than he had in years.

"Do you want another biscuit, Eli?"

He looked up to see his mother offering him a plate of homemade rolls. His stomach growled and he grabbed another one off the plate. His mother had insisted he stay at their house when he moved back to town. It seemed that after years of him being absent, she wasn't ready to let him out of her sight yet.

"Thanks, Mom. You don't have to cook all this food every day."

She beamed at him. "I like cooking for my boys. I haven't had enough chances to feed you lately. I'm not sure where I went wrong that only Nicholas absorbed my cooking lessons. The rest of you are a fire hazard in the kitchen. Although now that you have Kay, I know you won't starve. She'll take good care of you."

"We'll take good care of each other." He glanced behind him instinctively to where Kay was sitting on the couch with Ridley.

Ever since the day of the shootout, she'd been right by his side as he'd taken every step in his new life. She'd come with him to the lawyer's office. She'd ridden up to headquarters for meetings so he could turn over control of the day-to-day operations to his vice president, George Callahan.

"She thinks that I should talk to you. About that day in the barn. When I was seventeen," he clarified.

Julia's face paled slightly. He covered her hand with his and squeezed. "I'm sorry, Mom. I hate to bring up something so painful, but I need to talk about it. How it affected me."

"All right." She squeezed his hand back gently.

"I was really angry," he admitted. It had taken a lot of introspection for him to come to terms with that.

"At me?" Julia's voice wavered slightly.

"Yeah. A little. I shouldn't have been, but I was confused. I couldn't understand why you wouldn't press charges. I wanted to hurt him. I wanted him to pay. I think that's why I joined the Circle. It was stupid, but I felt like I was helping *someone.* Even if I couldn't help you."

Julia sighed. "I am so sorry for... a lot of things. But Eli, things are so much more complicated than you know. It's not what you think. It's just... not what you think."

Eli saw it in her eyes then and suddenly didn't want to take the conversation any further. "You don't owe me any explanations, Mom. I just wanted you to know that I'm here if you ever need me. A really smart woman is helping me see that it's time to move on. I'm excited about the future for the first time in a long time."

"She's good for you." Julia stood and kissed him on top of his head before picking up the plate of leftover biscuits.

He walked over to Kaylee and sat next to her on the couch. He pulled her into his arms and she purred and snuggled up next to him.

"You two are just so cute." Ridley sniffled. "I'm so glad you found each other and now you're so happy," she said and looked at Eli. "And I'm so happy."

Jackson appeared. "What did you do to my wife? I finally got her to stop crying."

Ridley waved her hand at him. "I'm not crying. I'm just misty-eyed, that's all. Leave a girl and her hormones in peace."

Eli breathed in the scent of Kaylee's hair and held her close. They'd spent a lot of time together over the past few weeks and now he couldn't imagine how he'd lived so long without her. Now that he wasn't working sixteen-hour days, he could see just how barren his life had been before she and Hope had barged into his house and heart and brought them both to light.

It was long overdue for him to delegate so he could live a little. He'd always be grateful for and proud of his work because it had given him a productive outlet for his anger and frustration. Through it he'd been able to realize his purpose of helping people. But it was no longer the main focus of his life.

His family was.

KAYLEE STOOD ON the doorstep of her parents' house and rubbed her arms. It had been a few weeks since they'd gotten back in town and her mother hadn't called her once. She was definitely still angry.

But Julia had stepped into the void and helped Kaylee out in more ways than one. Not only was she supportive of her relationship with Eli despite their age difference, but she'd given her encouragement and reassurance about how she was raising her daughter. Things Kay hadn't realized she'd needed so badly until she had them.

Then there was Eli.

She looked over at him and everything inside her went gooey. The last few weeks had been challenging for him. She'd done everything she could to support him as he'd started untangling the legal mess from his time with the Circle of Seven and from his defiance in walking off the active scene of a crime at his house a few weeks ago.

Danny had found him a great lawyer, which she thought was amazing considering that his only introduction to Eli had been less than complimentary. Even Hope's father had called to offer support. Not that she needed it, but it was nice to hear anyway. He wasn't going to be a part of their lives and Kay was at peace with that.

Finally at peace.

She hadn't told Eli about the call from Tim. He'd just go crazy and she'd have to pretend to be upset on principle. Truthfully, she kind of liked it when he got a little jealous. Eli treated her like the focus of his entire world, which was great because he was the center of hers, too. She loved every inch of her exasperating, overprotective, dominant alpha male.

The only thing that still hurt her heart was that Sasha wasn't speaking to her. Her friend had been hurt and embarrassed when she'd realized Eli had suspected her of being the stalker. Kay had tried to explain that she hadn't believed it, but Sasha had left in tears. She left messages on her friend's cell phone every day, but she probably wasn't even listening to them. Kay sighed.

"Don't be nervous. It'll be fine," Eli said as he rang the bell. "I'm sure she's not still angry. She's your mother."

"Oh, I wasn't even thinking about that. I'm sure my mother is still angry. I don't expect anything less. You have no idea how stubborn she can be."

"I wondered where you got it from," he muttered.

She was saved from responding when the door opened. Her father stepped back so they could come in. "Hey, pumpkin. I was wondering when you'd finally come by. You know we've missed you something awful."

"Sorry, Daddy. I know I should have called, but with the way I left things with Mom, well, I wasn't sure my call would be welcome."

He enfolded her in a hug. "You're my daughter. You are always welcome."

She snuggled into the embrace, soaking up the flow of love and acceptance. "I missed you."

Her father pulled back and his eyes landed on Eli. "Mr. Alexander. Thank you for keeping my baby girl safe. I hope you won't be taking her away from us again anytime soon."

"Well, about that..."

"So, you've finally decided to come visit. We've been worried sick."

They all turned around. Henrietta stood in the doorway, her arms crossed. Kay's heart sank. She knew her mother's body language, and she wasn't giving off a forgiving vibe.

"I'm sorry, Mom. Things have been really hectic."

Kay handed Hope to her father. He carried her into the kitchen and Eli followed with a sympathetic smile.

Kay sucked in a breath to steady herself. "Actually, I needed some time away. From you."

Her mother took a step forward, her eyes wide. "Kaylee! What an awful thing to say."

"I'm sorry, Mom, but it's true. For a long time, I've tried to be smarter, thinner, just *better* so I could finally make you proud. After all this time, I've realized that it's never going to happen. I didn't go to college, I got pregnant and embarrassed you in front of all your church friends, and I'm singing pop music. But I'm proud of my life. I've made mistakes, but I've learned from them, too."

Henrietta crossed to the couch and sat down. "I'm a horrible mother."

"I didn't say that. I just think you want something from me that will never happen. You wanted a perfect daughter. That's not me. That will never be me. And I'm okay with that."

She was shocked when her mother pulled her into a hug.

"You are perfect. Exactly as you are. I'm the one who is a failure for not letting you know that."

"Mom? But you always seemed so disappointed that I wasn't singing in the choir anymore."

"I wasn't thrilled that you went into popular music because I know how rough that industry is. I recorded a few albums, so I know what it's like. They demand your all and then if you don't live up to their expectations, they'll grind you up and spit you out. I was just worried for you, Kay. I didn't want them to break your spirit the way they broke mine."

Stunned, Kaylee allowed her mom to pull her closer. For years, she'd thought her mom's criticisms were because she was disappointed in her. Not because she was worried *for her.*

"And I was upset when you got pregnant because I wanted to string that no-good man up by his gonads for how he treated you. I was disappointed because I want the best for you, Kay, not a lifetime of struggle. Of course, you proved me wrong as usual because you didn't struggle, you thrived. I am truly awed by you."

Kay sat back, stunned. "I never knew. I guess we could both do better at communicating what we really feel. I'm sorry I didn't call. I hate to think of you being worried. I was safe the whole time. Eli would never let anything happen to me."

Henrietta wiped the tears from her eyes and stood. "Yes, well, I'd like to hear what happened from him. I think he has some explaining to do." She marched into the kitchen where

Eli was standing next to her father.

"Now, I'd like to hear directly from you, young man, about what happened. You show up on our doorstep one day and then the next thing we know, our daughter is gone for a month. I'd like an explanation."

"Mom! I already told you everything." Kay groaned. She walked over next to Eli, as if she could shield him from her mother's wrath. It seemed their mother-daughter truce didn't extend to being nice to her man.

"I am so sorry about this," she whispered to Eli. She supposed she couldn't expect her mother to break all her old habits. *All things in good time*, she thought. But at least they'd made a start to patching up their relationship.

He pulled her closer and grinned. "It's fine."

"Now, pumpkin, your mother has a point. We're your parents. We can't help but worry. I didn't protect you from that last fella, but I mean to do so now. I think a man who's got nothing to hide shouldn't mind answering a few questions."

"I agree," Eli added.

Kay turned to glare at him. "Whose side are you on?"

"Yours. Always." Then he turned to her parents. "I have no problem answering any questions you have. I love your daughter and I'm not going anywhere. I want to marry her, if she'll have me. I hope we'll have your blessing."

Henrietta covered her mouth with her hands. "Marry her? Well, this is unexpected."

"Yes, ma'am. I realize you don't know me that well, but I plan to rectify that real soon. There's nothing more important than family."

Her father looked at Kaylee and winked. "A straight shooter. I like this one."

"Well, come on in, Mr. Alexander. Come in and sit down." Henrietta beamed up at him as she took his arm and he followed her into the living room.

"Call me Eli, please."

"Do you work here in town, Eli?"

"I own a security company headquartered in Northern

Virginia, but I'm moving home. I'll open a secondary location in New Haven."

Henrietta looked back at Kay. "*He's a business owner, Kaylee.*" She didn't let go of Eli's arm as she led him into the living room. Probably figured Kay would never bring home such a good catch again.

Kay shook her head as Eli effortlessly charmed her parents.

When the doorbell rang, Henrietta looked over her shoulder. "Get the door, Kaylee. It's for you."

"How do you know it's for me?"

But as usual, her mother wasn't paying any attention, instead smiling up at Eli and hanging on his every word. Kay snickered. She wondered what her mother would think if she found out that *good catch* was thoroughly corrupting her daughter every night and introducing her to things that were illegal in some states.

She peered through the peephole and then pulled back in surprise. Her hand fumbled with the knob as she struggled to turn it. The door swung open and Sasha looked up.

After a few moments, they each reached out, ending up in an awkward hug.

"I am so glad to see you."

"I'm so sorry I didn't call you back."

They both spoke at once and then ended up grinning at each other. Kay pulled her friend back into another hug. "I wasn't sure if I was going to see you again. I'm so sorry about everything that happened."

"Me, too. I was just hurt. And embarrassed. But I know it wasn't your fault."

"I knew you'd never hurt me." Kay pulled her friend inside and then shut the door.

"Not me, just my crappy taste in men." Sasha's face twisted and tears welled in her eyes. "I didn't know what he was doing, I swear."

"I know." Kay hooked an arm around her friend's neck. "My life isn't right without you in it. Don't go away again, okay?"

Sasha nodded. "Never again."

Kay wiped the tears from her cheeks. "We don't need to talk about that anymore. I have something better. Let's go watch Eli charm my parents."

Sasha's eyes sparkled gratefully. "Tall, dark, and scary meets the parents, huh? I'm in."

Epilogue

In the not-so-distant future...

"I CAN'T BELIEVE this day is finally here. Thanks for hosting this party for me." Kaylee could have danced in place with excitement. Her album was releasing the following day and her friends were hosting an album-release party at Sweeties, an exclusive restaurant, just for her. She'd done several so far, including one in L.A. and another in New York, but this was the one that mattered most to her.

The private party with all her family and friends in attendance.

"Of course. We're happy to do it." Ridley swayed back and forth, her hands on the small of her back, her pregnant belly extremely evident even under her loose maternity dress.

"It feels like a dream, being here. Like, what did I do to deserve all this?" Kay shrugged, sure she sounded maudlin.

"No, I understand completely. Sometimes I still pinch myself and can't believe this is my life. I just roll over and watch Jackson sleeping next to me and think it's all been just a dream. Then the boys come crashing in and I know it's real!"

The two women chuckled as they glanced over to where Chris and Jase were helping themselves to the buffet. Ridley's friend and neighbor, Katie Mason, was behind the buffet handing out drinks.

Kay looked down at the sparkling stone on the third finger of her left hand and said a silent prayer for all the blessings she'd received over the past few months. She had discovered the true meaning of friendship, fallen in love, and now she was releasing her first solo album.

She'd also become a part of the best family in the world. Jackson had offered to sing a duet with her on the album. It was getting a lot of buzz just because it had been years since anyone had heard him sing other than in the studio or privately. Then there were the rest of the Alexanders. They'd embraced her and Hope as if they'd always belonged.

Her new cousin, Laura, had organized this party for her and it had been perfect down to the last detail. Things were obviously a success as she looked around and saw guests contentedly sipping champagne and munching on various items from the sumptuous buffet. Early industry buzz was very positive about the album, and Kay had even gotten a few inquiries about writing songs for other artists.

She was on top of the world.

Glancing to her left, her gaze landed on her fiancé. Elliott stood with Matt near the doors, scrutinizing everyone who entered the party. Even though there hadn't been any reason to fear lately, he took her security seriously. He took everything to do with her seriously, actually.

Including her introduction to the naughtier items in his sensual collection.

Maybe she'd never be into all the same things he was, but she'd surprised herself. She blushed. He probably hadn't expected her to enjoy wielding his favorite brown leather flogger quite so much.

"There's mommy! Let's go say hi." Sasha appeared, Hope in her arms. "I was introducing my goddaughter to the concept of bad fashion. Because there are some ladies here who need a little help. And a new mirror, because the ones they have are telling lies!"

Kay giggled. "Sasha. What are you teaching her?"

"Life lessons, girl. These are things she needs to know." Sasha looked around at the people dancing in the center of the room and the tuxedo-clad waiters gliding through the crowd. "Can you believe this, Kay? Look at all this. This is all for you."

"I feel like I shouldn't get too excited, you know. Like all this good fortune will disappear if I'm too happy." Kay wrapped her arms around herself and rubbed the goose bumps that had suddenly appeared on her skin.

Sasha bumped her arm. "You deserve all the good things in the world, Kay. You've worked hard and come through some hard times. This is your time to shine. I'm so proud of you."

"I'm proud of you, too. For hanging in there."

Jackson had agreed to listen to some new songs she'd written for Sasha, specifically to complement her friend's distinctive, husky alto voice. Sasha had been making waves on her own lately, and Jackson had agreed to release her new single under his label. She was going to perform the new song tonight. Kay had no doubt that once she was given a chance, her friend would set the industry on fire.

Laura ran up to them then, her long red dress swirling around her legs. Her long hair was styled in long barrel curls like a pinup girl. "It's almost time for you to go, Sasha."

"Can you take Hope for me? I need to get ready to perform." Sasha handed Hope over, gently disentangling the baby's hands from her hair. She waved gaily before rushing off backstage.

Kay gently cradled her daughter in her arms, savoring the

sweet scent of baby powder and what smelled like applesauce. Hope clung to her and contented herself by sticking two fingers in her mouth.

"Enough room for me in here?" Elliott sidled up behind her, running a hand quickly over the curve of her bottom. He lifted her hair off her neck and kissed the sensitive skin behind her ear.

She turned to him and gently placed the baby in his arms and he kissed Hope's dewy forehead. The baby reached up and patted his cheek. "Da-da-da."

Eli gazed down at her affectionately. "It never gets old hearing that." He glanced over at Kay. "Holding her always makes me wish for more. Not that I'm saying we should have one right away. I'm sure you want to wait until after the wedding, and it would interfere with your tour schedule." He sighed and snuggled Hope closer. "We're too busy right now I suppose."

"Not too busy for that." She took his free hand and pressed it to her lower abdomen, smiling when his mouth fell open.

He worked his jaw but no sound came out. She solved the problem by kissing him soundly. When she pulled back, she was humbled to see a single tear on his cheek.

Eli pulled back and scrutinized her face. "I am going to be the best father out there. I know you had to do it all by yourself before, but you are *never* going to be alone again. This won't mess with your tour. I can stop working for a while and come with you to take care of the kids. We can make it work. We can do anything together."

Kaylee put a hand on his cheek, overwhelmed by his generosity and loving support. She wasn't worried about whether the album would do well or whether she'd be able to go on tour.

She was surrounded by people who loved her, and that was all that mattered.

Life would go on. It always did. And she'd have her family by her side through it all.

"I have you, don't I?"

"Always." His arms tightened around her, his palm rubbing

possessively over her belly.

"Then that's all I need."

THE END

Author's Note

Each time I release a new Alexander book, I give a special discount price to the fans who have supported the series from the beginning. You can sign up for the notification at my website.

www.MMaloneBooks.com

Also, if you've enjoyed this book, *please* consider leaving a review. Help the authors you love keep prices low by spreading the word. It helps us more than you know. Plus, we love to hear from readers!

THE ALEXANDERS SERIES

AVAILABLE IN PRINT

Book 1 - *One More Day* ~ Jackson + Ridley
(contains Book 0.5 - *Teasing Trent: the prequel)*

Book 2 - *The Things I Do for You* ~ Nick + Raina

Book 3 - *He's the Man* ~ Matt + Penny

Book 4 - *All I Need is You* ~ Eli + Kay
(contains Book 3.5 - *Christmas with The Alexanders)*

FUTURE BOOKS

Book 5 - *Say You Will* ~ Trent + Mara
Book 6 - *Just One Thing* ~ Bennett + Katie

ABOUT THE AUTHOR

NYT & USA TODAY Bestselling author M. Malone lives in the Washington, D.C. metro area with her three favorite guys: her husband and their two sons. She likes dramatic opera music, staid old men wearing suspenders, claw-foot bathtubs and unexpected surprises.

The thing she likes best is getting to make up stuff for a living.

www.MMaloneBooks.com

38193853R00188

Made in the USA
Lexington, KY
26 December 2014